SOJOURNER

Book 2 of
the *Fellowship of the Mystery* trilogy

by Terry L. Craig

SOJOURNER
Published by Wild Flower Press, Inc.
P O Box 2532
Leland, NC 28451
www.wildflowerpress.biz

This book or parts thereof may not be reproduced in any form, stored in a retrieval system, or transmitted in any form by any means—electronic, mechanical, photocopy, recording, or otherwise—without prior written permission of the publisher, except as provided by Copyright laws.

The characters and business entities portrayed in this book are fictitious. Any resemblance to actual people or business entities, of the past or present, is coincidental.

SECOND EDITION

ISBN 13: 978-1-946549-00-6

DEDICATION

To the men who have influenced my life the most:

Bill, whose love, strength, and steadfastness still amaze me

Matt and Dan, who taught me the great joys (and terrors!) of being a mom

My daddy, who taught me the value of a well-told story

Scott, who taught me that I could love other people's children as much as I love my own

My grandpa, who first taught me about the love of God

Frank Cebollero who taught me about integrity—by living it every day

To Michael Tyrrell, who taught me to worship like a child again

And, most of all, Jesus Christ who brought me to life.

ACKNOWLEDGMENTS

Laurels to Matt Craig—your talents helped me in every phase!

I can't thank my sister, Jo Ann, and my mother enough for their tireless efforts in editing all my books.

Many thanks go to Stephanie Bennett for her wisdom, help, and encouragement.

I'm grateful to Jack and Dede Holcomb, who graciously let me stay on their island, Leaf Cay, several times during the writing of this book.

I thank Rebeccah Barker for her friendship and assistance through the years.

ACKNOWLEDGMENTS

PROLOGUE

Although it wasn't safe to travel solo, Jeff Dashe came the last two hundred miles alone, walking silently on a seemingly endless trek. He continued day after day, but not because the military ordered it. His search for Ana drove him ever southward into the hilly terrain of eastern Oklahoma.

Standing on the floor of a brown, stone canyon, he pressed dry, shredded lips together and stared at the first proof of other human life he'd encountered in days. Someone had painted words in olive green paint directly on the face of a large boulder which rested on the right side of the canyon's mouth.

> SOJOURNER'S ROCK
> May all who pass here remember
> they are but sojourners on this earth.
> 1 Peter 1:16-21
> April 29

Beside the words, a huge green hand print, missing the top part of the middle finger, loomed on the surface of the rock. Next to this message, a wooden sign had been staked into the ground. It read:

> ALL PERSONS MUST PASS THROUGH
> QUARANTINE
> BEFORE PROCEEDING SOUTH
> VIOLATORS WILL BE IMPRISONED
> Follow signs to quarantine

Jeff pulled his lower lip into his mouth and tried to resist biting off the dried hunks of skin as he considered the signs. Next, his gaze then swept out over hundreds of inscriptions scrawled on the lower portion of the canyon walls, mostly in green paint–some of them ten feet or more off the ground where people had climbed to make their statements. He looked at one nearby.

> Gabby and Brenda Stevenson of Lincoln,
> Nebraska.
> May 1. Headed for San Angelo

Beside the words were two hand prints—a bigger and a smaller one. Next to this message, another with small, neat lettering said:

> Hal, Barbara, Tom, and Kim Lethgart of Topeka.
> Passed here in April. Lost baby Kelly to a fever.
> Going to Tyler, TX

Underneath the words were four hand prints ranging in size from large to small.

Jeff stepped further into the canyon and realized all these messages had been painted by people wanting to leave a record of their passage south, hoping separated loved ones would see they still lived, and know where to look for them. Some messages were memorials to those who had died. Others, within the space of a few words, communicated volumes of grief, uncertainty, and longing. One said,

> Carly Wilson, 15 years old. May 11th
> Bobby: Mom and Dad are dead.
> I'm going to try to make it to El Paso
> and see if I can find Aunt Dot.
> Please come when you can.

Perhaps, Jeff thought, *Ana passed by this place. Would she have left any sort of message?*

The disasters had come. No matter how much better it got from this time on, the losses from these catastrophes had affected every person living and would be remembered as long as history continued to be recorded. No one would have to ask, "What disasters?"

This story begins a year and a half before Jeff Dashe stood at Sojourner's Rock.

CHAPTER 1

PHILADELPHIA — January 5th

Heather Poole parked her late-model burgundy Buick outside the Attlebury Geriatric Clinic of Philadelphia. She kept the heater on while she made a last-minute addition to her list, hoping no one would accost her for leaving the motor running.

Not wanting to know lurid details about medical procedures, Heather had a tendency to avoid asking questions when she had the chance. This time, however, Heather had a carefully-prepared list of questions and planned to methodically go over each one during her consultation with the doctor.

Today would be her first opportunity to see her father since he'd entered the three-story, brown brick clinic to participate in the experiment. She'd been leery about her father being used as a guinea pig, but after viewing the glowing "documercials" on Regeneration Therapy, Heather, too, held the hope her father could have his vitality restored.

Would he have changed yet? Would he be changed at all? What if he was in the group getting the placebo treatments? *Oh, I hope not. His heart is so set on being one of the pioneers of Regeneration.*

She took comfort in the fact that, even if her father wasn't receiving the actual therapy now, his participation in the clinical trials had secured the promise of the real deal when the government approved Regeneration Therapy.

A picture of her mother in a total-care nursing facility came to mind and she frowned. *Who knows? Maybe, if this works, they could try it on mom.*

No more stalling. She shut off the engine and got out of her car. Walking to the door of the clinic, Heather told herself not to get her hopes too high. It was probably too soon to tell. She slowed her pace, giving the electric door time to respond to her presence.

Once inside, Heather stepped into the lobby and toward the desk at the far end. Questions from her list so preoccupied her, she didn't notice the man walking in her direction.

"Heather," he called to her. "I'm right here."

Her eyes focused on the man. "Dad!" she exclaimed, and hurried to close the remaining distance between them.

They briefly embraced before he led her through a set of french doors into a lovely glass-enclosed courtyard. When they were seated in the dappled shade of indoor trees, she spoke again.

"You look great! How do you feel?"

He laughed. "I feel *wonderful*."

She'd been warned: Even those taking the placebo might feel better for a while, simply because they wanted to feel better. It would probably take a few months to ascertain whether or not any real gains had been made, but she wanted to remain positive.

"Well, whatever you're doing, it's sure put a sparkle in your eye."

He leaned close to her. "More than that, Heather," he said, putting his hands on his chest, "It's putting *life* inside me."

"You think you're getting . . . 'it?'" she whispered.

He closed his eyes and inhaled. "I'm sure of it. I can't tell you how good it feels to not be so . . . old." When he looked at her again, she could see his eyes were moist.

Her own eyes began to well up and she squeezed his hand. "Keep going, Dad. Keep getting better and better."

After their little meeting in the courtyard, Heather left her dad for a few minutes to meet with Dr. Mehndolson in his office. As soon as she felt she had the doctor's attention, she got the list out of her purse.

"Are you monitoring my father's other medications? If he improves, how would you know to reduce or stop it?"

Mehndolson wanted to sound professional, but caring. "We track every single patient every day. We run samples every five days. You needn't worry about that."

She forgot her list for a moment. Although it might be premature, she couldn't help asking, "Just how far can this therapy go? Will his hair revert back to brown? Will he lose his wrinkles or will he just feel a lot younger?"

Mehndolson removed his reading glasses and looked at her. *Why are most people so driven by wishful thinking?* he wondered. *Why can't they wait for facts and then make intelligent decisions?* He cleared his throat. "You must have seen the ads put out by Global-kem and Roller Genetic Labs. The truth is, Ms. Poole, those were advertisements, not documented cases. We don't know 'how far' the therapy will go. That's why we're doing these experiments."

"But weren't tests done over in Europe and Japan?"

"Europe and China," he corrected.

"Whatever. The point is, the experiments were done. Why is it we have to re-do what's already been done? If that stupid President Cole hadn't created this delay, the whole thing would have been over and done with a couple of years ago. Regeneration would have been approved and all these people would be young again."

Thousands of elderly "baby boomers" in the US—who fought aging tooth and nail—had seen ads regarding Regeneration Therapy and inundated doctors with requests for it. While a few scientists said the testing in other countries hadn't met scientific criteria, others accused the US government of being overcautious in restricting the use of a treatment already "proven" elsewhere. Siding with those who wanted more testing, President Cole made quite an issue of the attempt to put approval of the treatment on a "fast track." Regeneration proponents insisted Cole and other politicians were acting as pawns of certain pharmaceutical and cosmetic industries, who made billions from an aging populace. Where was the truth in the midst of all this?

"I'm not a politician," Dr. Mehndolson said, "or a man with a product to sell. I'm a scientist. I don't base my work on the fears or the claims of others. I deal in hard facts. If Regeneration Therapy works, these tests will prove it. If it doesn't, we'll have protected people from a scam."

Heather shifted around in her chair, then looked at her list again. "If my father needs new or different medications, how will we know this?"

Dr. Mehndolson wagged his finger at her in a slightly scolding manner. "Both the literature and the viewing disk we gave you cover all this. We will see he gets the best of care."

"I just want to be sure."

The doctor smiled. "I understand. But remember, it's in everybody's best interest for us to watch our patients very carefully and document every aspect of their care. The eyes of the world will be upon us, and we want to be without reproach."

CHAPTER 2

PHILADELPHIA — January 11th

Zachary Gordon sat in his Philadelphia Arena office, quite amused. Both his telephone and the arena's walkie talkie scanner were currently jacked into his computer. A small band of color across the top of his screen displayed a graph pattern of each voice coming through the speakers and identified the employee to whom it belonged. But Zac ignored both the chitchat between workers in the building and the happy music of a phone line on "hold." While he waited to speak to an actual person on the phone, he accessed an online magazine and started using an art program to put a mustache and glasses on a woman in a deodorant ad.

He stopped to sip the hot mocha-mint whip from his favorite mug. In addition to everything else, the latest news continuously crawled across the bottom of his screen. He briefly scanned the few headlines:

> "Spirit of cooperation plummets as tempers soar over the costs of repairs in the international space station, COSMOS >>>> House Speaker Shane Moffit calls for override of communication bill veto >>>> Millions more may die in the continuing famines of Asia and Africa >>>> E. E. Kressman's 'NEPTUNE' Project in Gulf of Mexico opens for business and is first system in the world to run entirely on Fibertronics >>>> Christian groups pool resources to fund the 'HE is coming soon' campaign >>>> 'Envisionary Faith' teacher Cliff Edison paroled from prison in D.U.I. manslaughter case >>>> "

Zac took his stylus and tapped the last headline on his screen. The article sprung open on his monitor and he began to read it.

> "Envisionary Faith teacher Dr. Cliff Edison was released from prison early this morning and taken

to an undisclosed location after making brief comments to the press. In a high-profile case four years ago, Edison pleaded guilty to D.U.I. manslaughter and leaving the scene of a fatal accident. A pastor, author, and lecturer, Edison was internationally known for motivational teachings which he claimed would guide others to wealth and health. At the time of his arrest, he also admitted to marital infidelity and financial misdeeds. His last confessions led to a federal investigation and forced closure of his ministry. Now claiming to have come through 'godly sorrow to true repentance,' Edison . . ."

A disgusted grunt escaped Zac's mouth before he zipped the article off his screen. He took another sip from his cup and went back to doodling on the deodorant ad. Suddenly, the music coming over his speakers stopped and an actual person came on the phone line.

"Executive Offices, this is Glenna, how may I direct your call?"a woman's soft voice asked.

Zac quickly touched the button reconnecting the earpiece and microphone he wore. "Good morning, Glenna," he said while jotting down her name and the time with the stylus on his computer pad. He watched as what he'd just scrawled appeared on his screen. "This is Zac Gordon in the Events Office," he said, "and I was told to contact the supervisor's office."

"Please hold one moment," he heard before the boring music returned.

His shoulders slumped. He hated being on hold. He kept the headset connection but resumed doodling.

"Mr. Gordon?"

He straightened up. "Yes?"

"Glenna again. Ms. Butterfield would like to meet with you."

"Oh? That would be fine. When?"

"She has an opening in thirty minutes or one at four o'clock." He wanted to get this over with as soon as possible. "I'll take the one in thirty minutes."

"Fine. I'll inform her. See you in thirty minutes, Mr. Gordon."

"Will do." His eyes darted to the spot on the screen where he'd scrawled her name. "Thank you, Glenna. Goodbye." He immediately switched over to the intercom line.

It rang once before his secretary answered.

"Barbara," he said, "could you come in here for a moment?"

"Sure."

He hung up the phone, took out his earpiece, and leaned back in his chair. Within moments, Barbara, a silver-haired woman in a dove-gray business suit entered the office and took a seat in front of his desk. She'd been assigned to him for over a year and they had a good working relationship. He tended to need things in urgent "spurts," but she was a dependable, efficient secretary, who didn't panic when things got in a crunch.

"I just called upstairs," Gordon began, "and the new supervisor wants to see me in thirty minutes. Any idea what it's about?"

She shrugged "Well, you can hope it's nothing more than a 'get acquainted' meeting."

He had become convinced there was nothing about the inner workings of the company that Barbara didn't know. She didn't gossip, but she was a great observer. She could analyze people and events and then just "know" how things would flow out from them.

"Why?" he asked. "You know something?"

"Ms. Annette Glad-Butterfield. With a hyphen," Barbara said, as if she were reading off an imaginary page. "Contrary to the line the company has put out, she isn't here to fill in just because old Donovan kicked the bucket. She was handpicked by the big guys at TIXMAX."

While she spoke, Gordon found a rubber band on his desk and started to play with it. Accustomed to his constant fiddling, Barbara ignored it and continued. "They think she's the greatest thing to come along since liquid connectors. Her last job was at the New Orleans Arena/Complex where she 'streamlined' the operations and took their ink from deep red to black in less than eighteen months."

Mr. Gordon shot the rubber band into the corner. It bounced off the targeted spot on the wall then landed on a pile of at least fifty other rubber bands. He stopped, looked at her, and whistled. "Less than eighteen months?""

"Uh huh. I'll bet what's left of my retirement that if she does well here, they'll eventually send her to all of TIXMAX's arenas and convention centers to make sure they're getting the optimum return for their investments. Word has it she could fire a single mother of three for misuse of paper and walk away humming a happy tune."

Gordon smiled. "Then I guess I'd better pick up those office supplies in the corner before Ms. Annette Glad-with-a-hyphen-Butterfield sees 'em, eh?"

Although he was a bit of a scoundrel, Barbara couldn't bring herself to dislike him. She had studied the boyish face, and the distracted facade. Very good at slight-of-hand illusions, Zac liked practical jokes, and would say or do almost anything to impress a pretty woman. After she'd worked for him a while, she realized he was actually a man of great intelligence, who just didn't want to be an adult on any given day unless he absolutely *had* to be.

Mr. Gordon could sit in a meeting and appear as if he didn't hear a single word, yet later recall entire conversations almost verbatim—often with very amusing accents or voices. He'd goof off for days, and then put together a brilliant plan just hours before a deadline. Even if his methods were a bit unorthodox, she had to admit he got things done. In the final analysis, she had no idea what made Zachary Gordon tick, but she'd be content to leave that mystery to the endless gaggle of females he attracted.

Barbara wanted merely to do her job during the day and go home to her cats and a quiet dinner at night. She wanted to do this for a few more years until her retirement. Thus far, Mr. Gordon had never asked her to lie to anyone, or to fix his sometimes stormy social life. He was kind to her, and, she had to admit in spite of herself, sometimes very amusing.

She looked in the corner and then back at him. A slight smile came to her face. "I'll pick up the rubber bands. You'd better see if you've got a decent tie. If you're gonna store it in your pocket with your planner, don't put it on a till you're ready to work. That one is not only creased, it's got catsup or something on it."

He looked down. "Ha! Right on both counts! You gonna open a detective agency when you retire? I had catsup on my hash browns this morning." He opened a few drawers before producing another tie. "How 'bout this? Got it from the promo guy for the Freedom Party thing that was here last week." He held up a red, white and blue clip-on.

"It'll make a better first impression than catsup."

"Thanks," he said, plucking off the old tie and pushing the new one into place.

A half-hour later, Zac Gordon exited the elevator on the penthouse floor. He found Glenna, an attractive woman with a pile of blond hair on her head, and announced his arrival for his appointment.

"I'm sorry, Mr. Gordon," she said. "But she's running a few minutes late. I tried to call your office, but your secretary said you'd already left. If you'll just have a seat and wait, it shouldn't be long."

"You're new here, aren't you?" he said, flashing his most dazzling smile.

She started to respond but her phone rang.

Zac waited a few moments, but when it appeared she would remain on the phone, he decided to sit down. He'd just found a sports magazine he hadn't read when the door to the supervisor's office opened and a man emerged. Harry Ulrich from Marketing. Ulrich looked like a whipped dog.

Not good, Zac said to himself as he watched poor old Harry skulk to the elevator. At this point, Zac took a few moments to give himself "a good talking to." He knew how prone to silliness or sarcasm he got in stressful situations, and this had all the earmarks of a lynching.

Don't speak unless you're spoken to. Whatever you do, don't try to be clever. You know how you hate yourself when you get clever at the wrong time. Remember, you're a man with a great apartment. A new car. Huge bills . . .

The phone rang again, and Glenna summoned Zac. "You can go in now."

"Thanks," he said, rising and walking to the door.

When he entered the office, a dark-haired woman in a tan suit stood. About five foot six, she had what Zac would refer to as a very "chunky" figure. As he got closer, he tried not to stare. There was a new makeup trend in fashion circles. It was called the "RetroGeisha look"—almost white makeup, lines for eyebrows, and a very small mouth. Multitudes of women had shaved off their eyebrows, stayed out of the sun (for that "naturally pale" look), and, regardless of the actual size of their lips, painted a tiny red mouth, resembling pursed lips, on top of their own. Zac thought it looked ridiculous even on younger women, but seeing it on Ms. Butterfield gave a whole new meaning to the word ridiculous.

Before sitting, he shook her hand. "Zachary Gordon."

She sat down and folded her hands on the desk.

He tried to find something—anything—to look at besides her mouth. *Man! Just look at that mouth! Suppose she knows she looks like a snowman who's been shot with a paintball gun?* He bit his lower lip to keep from smiling. *You're gonna go down in flames if you don't watch it!* His eyes lit on the engraved marble name plate on her desk. It read, "A. Glad-Butterfield." The letters swirled around in Gordon's head. As they re-arranged themselves in dozens of patterns, her voice interrupted his thoughts.

"Of course, in regular conversation you can just call me Ms. Butterfield, but on all documents and, of course, when introducing me, I prefer you use Glad-Butterfield."

"Yes Ma'am," he responded, hoping he looked like the essence of a responsible executive.

She looked at him for a moment before continuing. "Now to get to the reason I asked to speak with you," she began. "As the manager of the Events Office, you are responsible for many things." She stopped speaking and motioned to a small, flat screen on his side of the desk.

He leaned forward and took the 8–by–11 inch piece of thin plexiglass, called a "clip screen," in his hand. "Yes?" he asked.

"Hmmmm," she said, searching for a way to begin. "Let's see. As Event Coordinator, you are responsible for many things. For communication with clients, quality control, maintenance. You are like the traffic manager of a large intersection. You make sure that everyone gets a chance to use the intersection in a timely and efficient manner. You maintain the intersection. You clear out one event, you bring in another. . . . "

He realized his eyes had locked onto her lips again. *Not the mouth, Zac, not the mouth!* The screen he held remained blank, so he forced his gaze to the sweeping motion she made with her hands.

". . . And you, Mr. Gordon, must do this in the most cost-efficient manner possible," she said, folding her hands on top of the desk again.

"Yes ma'am." He chanced a look into her eyes.

"Well, then, let's have a look, shall we?" she said, picking up her stylus and touching her own screen. Her computer sent a signal to the screen Zac held, and she highlighted the portion she wanted him to read with a bright yellow color.

He leaned forward a bit in his chair and scanned through the lines she indicated. "Yes ma'am. That's when the equipment broke down on the day of the hockey game and the ice wasn't happening."

"Do you realize that the cost of this repair was almost twice what it should have been?"

"Yes." He leaned back and smoothed down his tie. "I remember this one well. Our regular company couldn't fix it in time for the game. I had estimates from three other companies. These people," he said, pointing to the screen, "were the most expensive, but the most reliable. I had less than eight hours till game time, and I had to go with the company I knew could make some ice. It's not called *slush* hockey for a reason, you know." He stopped talking and rubbed his right temple. *I can't believe you said that! What did I tell you about getting clever?*

She stiffened in her chair, but then went to other highlighted items. "And what about all these meals on the expense account?"

"Yes, Ms. Butterfield. Like you said, I manage all the events that go in and out of here. Today, I'm clearing out a Princes Di memorabilia show. Tomorrow, the Women of Power group is renting half of the facility. Friday, we have hockey again. Saturday is a sold-out concert." He shrugged, then chanced a glance at the white face. "I have to meet with many of the organizers of these events and, sometimes, I have to smooth ruffled feathers. Eating with the clients is part of it. We may be the most popular arena in Philly, but we can't just assume this will always be so. And the Harvey Center will be open again in another month. We have to shmooze a little now and then." He smiled.

She did not smile back. He fixed his eyes on her desktop as words found a way out of the little red dot on her face. "Well, Mr. Gordon, despite your thoughts on entertaining half of the businessmen in Philadelphia, the cost-effectiveness of your policy has not been proven." She pushed her chair back a few inches from the desk. "You're right. We're the most popular arena in Philly. Let's use this to our advantage. Let's pursue only the cream of the potential clientele. Let the Harvey Center people 'shmooze' the low-budget people." She leaned back slightly before continuing. "It's not only cost-effective, it's the intelligent way to do business. You see what I'm saying?"

Conscious of his need to keep his words at a minimum, Zac shifted around in his seat. "Yes."

"Have you finished your reports for last month yet?"

"No. They're not due until Friday. Would you like them sooner?"

"Friday will do. Then, next week, we'll go over the list of the clients you currently entertain and cut it down to the cream. I can see you need some mentoring in this area."

Up until now, she noticed he'd been a bit too distracted. He'd avoided looking at her much. But now she had his full attention.

"You're kidding," he said.

Obviously she'd gotten through. "No," she said, "I'm not. I will consider it an investment of my time for the benefit of the company." She turned off his clip screen and it became blank once again. "Just be sure your reports are on time and marked to my attention."

Apparently the meeting had ended, so Zac stood. "Right. To Ms. Glad-Butterfield,' he said, making the hyphen in the air with his finger.

"Just one more thing," she said as he turned to leave.

"Yes?"

"I'm the kind of person that cuts to the chase. From what I hear about you, you're a playboy. I'm not impressed with that type, so you'd better plan on working for your money. Got that Mr. Gordon?"

He started to say something and then changed his mind. Instead he just nodded and left the room.

CHAPTER 3

WASHINGTON D. C. Suburb — February 5th

Trina Watson looked in the mirror as she finished putting on her makeup. Should she wear her hair up or down for the day? Did it really matter? Would she even see him today? She got out a brush and quickly pulled it through her light brown hair several times before bundling all of it in the back and putting it in a ponytail.

"Nope," she said after reconsideration, and pulled out the band in her hair, letting it fall back onto her shoulders.

She turned her head from side to side a few times, then drew her hair back into a ponytail. When she looked at her watch, she realized she needed to get out the door and start the long commute to work. She sighed and gave a little shrug to the woman in the mirror before gathering her things and leaving her apartment. Even though she'd spend nearly an hour *en route*, she liked having time on the train to prepare notes, read, or just think.

Once Trina got on the train to D.C. and saw the beautiful morning dawning outside the windows, she decided to sit and relax rather than go through the things in her briefcase. She looked out the window and watched people walking their dogs, jogging, or sitting in cars on their way to work.

She let her head rest against the window pane. . . . Two and a half years ago, she had little hope of working this job. Yet, here she sat . . . commuting to the White House! Almost everything she ever wanted was hers.

Warm sunlight streamed through the window onto her face as she remembered how it all happened. . . . Three years ago, as an assistant press secretary to presidential candidate, Donald Larson Cole, she'd gone to New York with a team of fellow workers to see if they could pick up the pieces from a large setback to the campaign.

Cole had just flown in from Colorado where he'd been released after spending more than two weeks in the quarantine area around Denver. While there, it looked as if his run for the presidency was all but over. He made angry remarks regarding President Todd's handling of disaster relief, and the search for the terrorists believed to have been responsible for the quake. Don told the media that Todd's response seemed bent on fostering paranoia. He also made sharp statements about slanted press coverage. Without a doubt he'd made powerful enemies in the government and the press. Everyone on his staff wondered if the quest for office could go on, considering the damage several news networks sought to inflict on him.

Despite near-fatal blows to the campaign, though, Don's confidence rallied and he emerged from the crisis stronger than ever. Rather than knocking him out of the race for president, the decisions he made following the incidents in Denver propelled him into the White House.

Cole had been a strong, intelligent, moral sort of person as long as she'd known him—in general, a viable candidate for a Presidential run. He had a good political record, was reasonably handsome, and had an excellent grasp of how government should function. He just didn't have that extra "something" needed to connect him with large numbers of voters. But in the days following Denver, he changed.

Peering out the window at passing scenery, Trina's eyes momentarily focused on a church as the train continued to glide down the rails toward Washington. *That was the extra something.*

Her eyes now focused beyond the landscape. She pictured herself arriving at the New York penthouse where the core of campaign leaders had gathered to meet with Don and to watch his first "post Denver quake" interview. That was when she first noticed the difference.

As if it were frozen in time, she recalled it: The whole crew sitting and watching the televised interview together. While Don conveyed his thoughts to viewers, he "connected" with America. When he spoke of his experiences in Denver, his courage, compassion, and intelligence were unmistakable. The trial of what he'd experienced crystallized all his best qualities and strengthened him.

Just when Trina figured nothing could soften jaded American voters, Don allowed himself to be transparent. It was like the shock of seeing the turquoise waters of the

Caribbean when you've spent your whole life near a muddy brown lake.

At a time when "religious" issues could be the kiss-of-death to a campaign, Don revealed that he'd become more spiritual. To Trina's amazement, rather than making him look "wimpy," it added to his appeal. Even she, who hadn't been a very spiritual person in the past, had to admit she'd been touched by his description of a need to relate to God in the midst of deep trials.

So many people she'd known over the years had gotten "religion." Some did it because they were scared the world was coming to an end, others possibly because they needed something to save them. Often, they seemed to turn into loud marshmallows—all noise, no substance . . . saying they "forgave," or that they "loved" people when, actually, they had little power to do anything else.

Don was different. Something, indeed, had happened inside him—something giving him the strength to change, to act, to do. He had the demeanor of a man who could stand toe to toe with an enemy and not back down. When he was gracious, it wasn't because this was his only option.

I suppose it was then that you knew how you felt, she thought as the train clattered along.

From that time on, Trina had to force herself to keep her eyes and her energies harnessed solely on her job. There was a campaign to run and she needed to do what everyone else was doing: plow into her work and ignore everything else.

When election day came however, she knew both a victory and a defeat of sorts. Trina remembered how he'd kindly thanked her for all the work she'd done and said that if she didn't want to stay on as an employee, he'd give her his highest recommendation. Obviously, he'd had some clue about how she felt. She recalled the words he chose, and how he said them. She picked up his unspoken message: Although he valued her work, he was quite willing to release her. As far as he was concerned, the door to a relationship was closed. She managed to hide her devastation for the eternal hour she remained in his presence, then gone back to her hotel room alone.

For weeks, Trina struggled with different emotions and even applied for positions which would take her far away from him. In the end, though, she turned down all offers, realizing she *couldn't* leave. She loved the work she did for Don Cole, and secretly, she still hoped he'd be open to a relationship at a later time.

She'd been serving as an executive assistant to the president, in charge of research and information for two years now. There were few things she liked better than the challenge of digging through tons of data with a short deadline. Sometimes her searches resulted in finding "gems" of hidden information they could use against the opposition. Other times she found "ticking time-bombs" needing to be addressed. Either way, both the search and the find were quite satisfying to her in more ways than one. And, her efforts had paid off. More than once, Trina had been able to deliver information that had been a bargaining chip in negotiations or the key to uncovering hidden motives of adversaries.

A look of satisfaction graced her face for a moment as she thought of a recent checkmate against the Speaker of the House and his cohorts. *Shane Moffit probably wants my head almost as bad as he wants Cole's!* As far as she was concerned, Moffit operated as a puppet of darkness; and any day she could help thwart his enterprises she considered a day well spent.

The train came to a stop at her station. Trina stood and reminded herself, *Almost everything you've ever wanted is yours.*

# # #

A few hours later, in a congressional hearing room, Speaker of the House Shane Moffit squirmed in his chair. The testimonies had been going on forever it seemed, and most of the witnesses were about as interesting as rusty hinges. He tried to look as if he were marking a passage in the written notes he'd been handed.

I hope Vonita orders those special salads for lunch again, he thought. His mind lingered on the creamy salad dressing he liked so much and he hoped she'd remembered to order an extra container of it.

He realized the witness, a gray-haired man who represented one of the technology companies that would be affected by the legislation, had stopped speaking and was searching for a particular statistic.

Moffit looked at the other congressmen at the table, "I think now might be a good time to take a lunch break."

Most of the others seemed to be in agreement.

"It's settled then," he quickly added. "We'll adjourn for lunch and be back at . . ." he looked at his watch, "one forty-five." He smacked his gavel down with an air of finality.

Moffit made his way out of the room and quickly walked to his office, slowing only long enough to wave or shout quick greetings at various friends and acquaintances. As soon as he got through the door to the reception area, he closed it.

"Please tell me," he said, giving his secretary a pleading look, "that you ordered me a salad with extra dressing."

She winced. "Well. No. I didn't know when you'd be back and . . . there's someone on the phone."

The look of frustration on the senator's face was obvious. "Call for a salad with extra dressing now, and bring it into me when it arrives." He pointed to the phone on her desk. "So who's on the line?"

"Yosef."

The pace of his pulse increased as he moved to his office.

He picked up his phone and tried to sound surprised.

"Yosef, it's been ages," he said, picturing the stocky man at the other end of the line–the tailored suit, the gold wristwatch, the huge ring.

"Shane," Yosef said. "So glad I caught you in your office. I hope I didn't call at an inconvenient time."

"No, no," Moffit lied. "Just as long as it's quick. . . . I'm on a lunch break."

"Not a problem. I only wanted a few minutes of your time."

Moffit's blood pressure continued to inch upward. He started to get up and close his office door, but thought better of it. He couldn't afford to look guilty–especially while hearings were in progress. "Not a problem. What do you want?" he said. Certainly Yosef had been around long enough to know what could and could not be said over the phone.

"It's no secret the changes here in Washington are cause for deep concern."

Recent elections had revised the rosters in both houses of congress and shaved the narrow margin Moffit's party held. As usual, lobbyists were scurrying to "educate" those new to office, and it was a stressful time when coalitions (and loyalties) could be realigned.

Moffit didn't respond, so Yosef continued. "Cole will veto your bill today, Shane."

"Which bill? The new communications bill?"

"Yes."

"How do you know this? Has he done it already?" Moffit got up and closed his door, then lowered his voice a notch. "How do you know he's gonna veto it?"

"My sources tell me he will. Perhaps it's part of a strategy to see just how strong you are now."

The congressman's free hand formed into a fist. "I have the support of my constituents."

"Yes, Shane, you do," Yosef responded. "And you're more than just a congressman representing your constituents, aren't you? You're the Speaker of the House . . . but the winds of change might blow everywhere. If just two congressmen decide to switch party affiliation . . . you might be replaced by someone more friendly to Mr. Cole's views."

That would be Lyle Tagger. Moffit bristled at the thought. The man was one of his bitterest enemies in Washington.

"Meanwhile," Yosef continued, "the president has a live interview on Banner Network tomorrow night. I hear he might take some issues to the people."

The speaker growled. "What issues?"

"It's only conjecture, mind you, but I hear his Office of Research and Information has been really busy lately."

A picture of Trina Watson sprang into the congressman's mind. *Oh, how I despise that woman! How I'd like–*

Yosef interrupted his thoughts. "Take the hearings you're conducting today for instance. If you're not careful, a lot can be said about what you choose to support . . . and why. The recommendations you make after these hearings may prove pivotal in gaining a consensus. You'd be wise to clearly define your priorities *now*, a 'preemptive strike,' before others cloud the issue with their own spin. . . . After all, this isn't just about energy enterprises is it? It's about America keeping her technological edge, no?"

CHAPTER 4

Once the door of the room closed, President of the United States, Donald Larson Cole savored the thought of a few moments alone. A quick look confirmed he had at least five minutes before his appointment with Marshall Ellis, a man recently approved for a top-level position at the National Security Agency. Although Don intended to log this next meeting as a briefing, perhaps the most vital communication shared wouldn't be in the documents Ellis carried. Cole wondered how long it had been since their last private conversation.

He leaned back in his chair, recalling his very first impression of Marshall Ellis. Although he now counted the man among the bravest he'd ever known, this had not always been so. He could still remember the jolt of their first encounter, while he was yet a candidate for the presidency and Ellis held a position in the Secret Service.

Utterly exhausted from a long day of campaigning, Don had retired to his Seattle hotel suite for the evening. Assuming he was both safe and alone, he'd stepped out onto the penthouse balcony for some fresh air. He'd only taken a few breaths when someone pressed up behind him, shoved him against the railing, and placed a knife against the middle of his back as a warning not to turn around or call out for help.

The intruder (Ellis) apologized, saying it was the only way he could arrange a "safe," secret meeting. He left no doubt who was totally in command of the situation, yet still referred to the presidential candidate as "sir." At the time, Don figured the man might be a lunatic who had somehow managed to slip past security measures. Having no other options, he listened to the information the intruder presented.

Ellis spoke of two small, yet powerful groups that had secretly formed within the government. His own group was working to prevent the loss of American democracy. The other group wanted to keep President Todd in office, and would stop at nothing to bring about their own agenda–global government, run by a group of elite individuals. If Todd won reelection, the struggle for control might lead to bloodshed.

Although the leaders in Ellis' group believed Don Cole wasn't corrupt, they also believed he was clueless regarding the *real* status of the nation. As an act of "good will," they'd sent Marshall to give Don a video disk, exposing one of Todd's schemes. Prior to election day, they planned to release contents of the disk on the Internet, and hoped it would end Todd's bid to stay in the White House. They also hoped Don's advance viewing of the disk would prepare him for the turmoil (and the opportunity) to come. Having delivered the disk and his message, Ellis disappeared.

Though terribly shaken, Don decided not to call security until he'd viewed the disk. When he did, he saw for himself disturbing evidence of President Sonny Todd's deep corruption, and the potentially lethal consequences awaiting the US as a result of it. Soon, he'd realize the video was merely an introduction to a disturbing reality: Todd was not only a criminal, he was a traitor.

Don exhaled, grateful, once again, he'd won the election without the scandal the video would have brought. Todd did so many unspeakable things before he died, if all of them were told, civil and global war could erupt.

Lost in thought, Don continued to stare in the direction of his intercom. The signal of an incoming message, a small, flashing red light with a short buzzing sound, brought him back to the present.

He leaned forward and touched the light. "Yes?"

"It's time for your one o'clock briefing."

"Send him in," Cole said, before standing. He stretched briefly before the door to his office opened and Marshall Ellis entered. The man stood about five foot ten, had dark blond hair, deep blue eyes, and an athletic appearance. Cole leaned across the desk and shook hands with him.

"Please, take a seat, Marshall." It had been a while since they'd been able to speak freely, so Cole wanted to get to the main reason he'd scheduled the meeting.

"Now you've had some time to dig around where you're at, have you found any new leads on the bombs?"

Ellis shook his head. "Sorry, sir. I don't have anything in the way of new leads right now. I haven't discovered much beyond what we knew already. My only comfort is that Todd's old pals probably know less than we do."

"Well," Don said, "let's recap what we know at this point."

Marshall nodded. "Before Todd could cover himself and have all the weapons loaded back onto planes, two of them disappeared. We picked up the trail again in France, where the devices were put on a ship sailing to New York. Our man, Ross, saw them unloaded there and transferred to arms dealers, who then took them to a storage place. That's the last time we, or the arms dealers, knew where they were.

"When the dealers went off, presumably to finalize a sale, Ross' partner followed them while Ross stayed near the weapons. We identified the partner's body weeks later. Judging by the way he was killed, we figure the dealers did it.

"Of course, the riots broke out the same day the bombs came into town and the storage facility was ripped apart by hundreds of looters. Ross was seriously injured in the free-for-all and left for dead. He never saw who took the devices. Eventually, we discovered all three of the dealers were killed in their car miles from the storage place. They happened to be driving by the park where the riot actually started, at the exact time it started. They probably intended to meet someone in the area but hadn't planned on bedlam breaking loose while they were there. We know they were killed by rioters—we got that much from a security camera across the street.

"Whoever took the bombs from the storage place," Ellis continued, "might have thought he was stealing expensive metal suitcases containing art, or money, or important documents, but once he got the cases open, he'd know what he had. After seeing the labeling, instructions, and radiation warnings, he'd realize these were nuclear bombs.

"So several possibilities exist: The first is that whoever took the cases hid them, then died, or was imprisoned, or deported without passing on the information. If the thief hid them and then died, the bombs may remain undiscovered for years to come. But if he's in prison or outside the US, he could simply be waiting to get access to the devices again.

"Another possibility is that a person or small group has them right now, but is keeping them for a future event. If terrorists have learned anything from recent history, it's that we're listening, so the smart ones stay quiet.

"Meanwhile, we've followed every possible lead while exercising extreme caution to avoid tipping off anyone else that there are two thermonuclear bombs to be had." The look on Ellis' face conveyed frustration he felt over the situation. "Beyond that, we've come up empty. The devices could be lost forever, or appear on the black market tomorrow, or be used without warning."

"And we both know," Cole added, "what would happen if they were detonated. Eventually, testing would show the bombs belonged to the United States." He turned his gaze to the presidential seal on the wall. "Even though we can prove they disappeared during Todd's watch . . ." Don stopped and shook his head before looking directly at Ellis again. He had to believe the weapons would be recovered. "Keep on it and keep me advised."

Ellis straightened in his chair. "Yes, sir. We have agents doing continuous sweeps to see if we can snag anything."

Having finished their covert business, Marshall handed over the official information he'd come to deliver, updating Don on several hot situations developing over the past few days. Among other things, the NSA had intercepted an encrypted message sent from the space station *COSMOS* to Moscow. It referred to continuing unrest among the crew on board the station. Don knew the mounting tensions between the astronauts reflected the turmoil boiling on the planet below, and hoped the upcoming change of space station personnel would serve to cool the situation.

When Ellis left, the president opted to take a very late lunch at his desk. He had one brought in and inquired if Trina Watson was available to talk with him. When she came through the door, he finished crunching some lettuce and swallowed it.

He smiled at her, then pointed to a chair in front of his desk. "Hey stranger! Nice to see you."

"Thanks," she said, before seating herself.

"Want a salad?"

"No. Already had a sandwich."

"Mind if I eat while we talk?"

She shook her head. "Nope."

"So tell me, what's happening over in the offices these days?" He asked before taking another mouthful.

"Well, Miles came in yesterday and said he's getting married next week."

He swallowed. "Whoa. Kind of sudden, isn't it?"

"Yes, but he's had several near-misses with this girl before. We have a pool going as to whether or not he'll actually take the leap this time. . . . And in other news, our computers were down most of the morning while they installed new hardware. It's amazing how much of your memory goes when you have everything stored in your computer . . ."

While she talked, Don watched her. It had been a while since they'd spoken more than a brief "hello" before meetings or in passing, and he remembered once again how much he enjoyed her company.

He wouldn't have been surprised if she'd have taken a job elsewhere. At one point, when he realized she might be developing a crush on him, he almost hoped she would. On election day, while never saying the words exactly, he'd tried to give her a clear message: He'd have no time for anything but work. If he won, the presidency would be enough to occupy all of his waking hours and then some. There wasn't room in his life for the distraction of romantic pursuits, and it was only fair she knew this. Her change of demeanor said she'd received the message.

While he ate, Don listened to her clear voice and watched her long-fingered hands expressively moving while she spoke. He could see her eyes were still as bright as ever. . . . Yes, she could have easily made a life elsewhere. . . . But she'd stayed, and he was glad.

When she'd finished her office "news" report, Don wiped his mouth with his napkin and pushed the salad container away. "Well," he said, "I hope your computer is up and running now, because I need your expert services."

She looked pleased. "Name the topic."

"The space station *COSMOS*. Beginning to end. In layman's terms: What were the original goals, specifications, and projections? Who offered to do what? Have the goals and/or roles of the partnership changed? According to publications in Russia, Europe, and Japan how have their perceptions of us changed as a result of the project. Are we meeting any of the goals we set out to achieve? I need a semi-brief synopsis with important facts listed."

"How soon do you want it?"

"How soon can you put it together?"

She laughed. "I'm trying to recall if you've ever said 'no rush' to me."

He chuckled. "Okay, okay. No rush. But tomorrow would be good."

CHAPTER 5

OKLAHOMA — February 17th

Sara Reisling wiped her mouth with her napkin and exhaled before she leaned back in her seat. "That was great, Mama. Nobody can cook like you. You should let Daddy and Noel have father-daughter weekends more often so you could visit me."

Naomi let her eyes sweep over her daughter's soft features and shiny, dark-blond hair before she replied, "Thanks. But you *still* have to help with the dishes."

Sara scooted back her chair and picked up her plate. "You didn't bring a maid with you?"

The two women went to the kitchen with the dishes and stood at the sink. Just like old times. Naomi would wash and rinse, Sara would dry and put away.

They'd already caught up on all the "news" from home. Who'd moved away, gotten married, had babies, or died. Like it or not, the time to focus on Sara's life had arrived.

Naomi filled the sink. "So. You still like it here? Think you'll stay a long time?"

The weather had been so cold, it was heaven to put her hands in the hot water. Sara smiled as its warmth began to radiate up her arms. "Yes, I really like it. Coming here after all that happened in Denver was such a healing thing for me. I've come to a season of . . ." she paused, searching for the right word, "contentment. I love teaching these kids. I know it doesn't pay well, but I can't think of anywhere else I'd rather be."

"How's that boy, Jack? Have you kept up on what he's doing?"

"He's doin' great. I'm so proud of him. And he's a pretty good artist, too. If we could just do something with his mother, I'd be happy."

"What's she do?"

"Well . . . she may really love him—somewhere deep inside—but she sets such a terrible example for him, and she acts as if he could disappear tomorrow and she wouldn't care. It's really sad."

They were doing the silverware. "You like your church?"

"It's not like home, but, yes. The new pastor's kind of formal. I think it's more because he's nervous though, you know? He's new. I think he's just trying to set his own boundaries, and figure out who's who."

Naomi nodded.

They washed in silence for a while, the familiar ritual as comforting as any conversation. Sara could remember standing on a chair to help when she was little.

"So," Naomi said nonchalantly, "any nice men at the church?"

The dreaded subject had been broached. Nothing could stave it off now that it had been introduced.

"Oh. I haven't checked lately."

"Don't you ever go out?"

"Well, sure I go out. Just not on, you know, 'formal' dates. Several of us will go to dinner or work on a project. Like that."

"I can remember when you were little. Your father said no boy was going to take his little Duchess away." Naomi scrubbed a dish for a moment before continuing. "But now, even *he* would like to see you find someone."

"It's not like being single is a *disease* you know. Like I said, I'm enjoying my life, Mama. Sure, I'd like to find someone special. But I think all the nice ones are taken. What's left are either missing teeth or so stuck on themselves that they don't need anyone to adore them. They adore themselves. . . . And some of the women seem so desperate. I don't ever want to be like that. The available guys we have get chased everywhere but the men's room!"

Sara thought of a man by the name of Brandon Atkins. She'd almost gotten serious about him last year. They'd been seated at the same table for a church dinner and thoroughly enjoyed their first evening together. He was nice looking, well educated. He'd opened a direct marketing health food business and gotten it past the "struggling" stage to the place where he made a good living. Sara had lost weight and was in one of her "thin phases" physically. She enjoyed her job and had the radiance of someone whose heart had been renewed with many blessings.

After they'd known each other a few weeks, Brandon made it clear to Sara he wanted to "settle down." How rare, she'd thought, to find a man willing to make a commitment. Could he be the one God had chosen for her? In addition to the swirl of new found emotions, she'd been pulled closer by fear of the loneliness that might lie ahead if she let Brandon get away.

As their relationship progressed, however, she began to have an increasing sense that she needed to rein in her emotions and take a good look at the road ahead. Other than in the pretend world of dating, she'd had no opportunity to really get to know Brandon. What kind of person was he really? She began to listen carefully to what he said and realized something: While his words conveyed what kind of man he was, they said even more about his future mate.

On many occasions, Brandon expressed his desire for "a Proverbs 31 wife"—the perfect woman. At first, in the swirl of romance, it all sounded so holy, so spiritual, so fulfilling. But as Sara obeyed an inner prompting to really listen, his picture of a "Proverbs 31 wife" began to take shape: This selfless woman would be as loyal as a dog, work like a horse, and look as lovely as a swan at all times. She would be expected to "stay fit," wait on Brandon hand and foot, and become the ultimate "natural" gourmet cook. His wife would make their home an immaculate showplace (on a budget of course) where they could entertain important guests.

But Brandon didn't want his Mrs. to be a mere housewife. No. He wanted her to know she was free to be a success in business—*his* business. Mrs. Atkins would maintain her interest in his business dealings so she could be both an excellent hostess *and* his company's number one worker. She would learn to keep accurate books and adequate inventories. This tireless, beautiful, wonder woman would also attend business seminars and creatively use the insights she learned.

And, eventually, if Brandon ever decided he wanted them, she would bare his children and home school them. In her "spare time," Sara imagined she might be expected to have a happy twinkle in her eye while she simultaneously twirled twenty-one plates on the ends of sticks!

Once the reality of his expectations became clear, she began to think the "joy" of having Brandon for a husband might not compensate for the life he expected her to live once they were married. A life, it seemed, to be lived solely for the benefit and advancement of Brandon Atkins.

To make matters worse, whenever he felt her zeal diminishing, he'd inform Sara that "many" would be glad to take her place and become that "special lady" in his life. After several months of his reminders, she suggested that he go out and find one of those poor, demented women. She wanted to be a mate, not a slave who would be constantly compared to others or threatened with replacement. The couple parted with the standard "we can still be friends" line, then had no more contact.

In no time flat, Cassidy, a perky little brunette who sang in the church choir, did gladly step in to be that special lady. By the end of summer, Cassidy and Brandon were married.

Occasionally, Sara would catch a glimpse of the couple whispering to each other during a church service or walking out to their car holding hands, and she felt a bit sorry for herself. She wondered if perhaps she'd been a bit too quick in sending him away. Then again, maybe he and Cassidy were made for each other, and she would have been miserable with him.

As her mind returned to the present, Sara realized her mother had been watching her and she smiled sheepishly. "Okay. There *was* someone last year." She slowly swirled the suds in the sink with her left hand. "But I didn't think he was the one," she said, scooping up some soap suds and blowing them onto the windowsill, "so I let him move on to better things. Since then, I've kind of lost my zeal to search for a mate."

"Given up?"

"Not entirely. You know my friend Rosa I talk about all the time?"

Naomi nodded.

"If I could have a marriage like hers, I'd take it in a second. You should see the way she and her husband are together. I think their love will last a lifetime." Sara looked at her mother. "Like you and Daddy. They've helped me to hope it's still possible."

Naomi leaned over against her daughter.

Sara tried to reassure her mother. "I'm okay. Really."

"I'm sorry." Naomi patted her hand. "I didn't mean it as a pressure thing. Honest. We would never want you to marry anyone but God's best for you. It's just that as we get older, your dad and I are so grateful for each other. We love you so much, and this world's getting so lonely and so scary. We'd like to think you'd have someone to share your life with. . . . But I'll try not to make such a big deal out of it, okay?"

"Thanks. If the Lord sends someone my way, I hope I don't miss him. But I'm not going to make getting a husband my quest in life." She stopped and thought a moment. "So many other aspects of my life are so good right now. I'm learning to be thankful for what I have every day, not to waste life longing for something I *don't* have. If I ever marry, I want my husband to be someone who's got a kind heart, who'll follow the Lord's leading, who's not pretentious . . . who loves me so much that he'd be willing to risk everything for me. And if it doesn't happen, I want to be content as a single person."

"You're right, Duchess, you're right. Your dad would agree." Naomi pulled the plug and wiped down the area around the sink before changing the subject. "So, your friend Rosa is gonna have another baby. When's she due?"

Sara wiped the last dish and put it away.

"In May. I can hardly wait for you to meet her."

CHAPTER 6

OKLAHOMA — March 2nd

The large, dark-skinned man took the steps to the second floor two at a time, humming to himself. He held the stick of a lime-green sucker in one hand, the handles to a large shopping bag in the other. When he reached his door, he stuck the sucker in his mouth and moved the shopping bag to the other hand so he could rummage in his pocket for his keys. As he unlocked the door, someone inside opened it.

Before he could move, a little girl ran out the door shouting, "Mr. Ricky!" and grabbed both of his legs. He steadied himself, looking down at the child then up to see Rosa, his pregnant wife, standing inside their apartment, smiling.

He grinned at Rosa, and then down at his little, blond assailant. "Well, hello there, Katie."

"Mr. Ricky! My mama's having a baby!" she answered back, still clinging to Ricky's knees. Her smile revealed several missing teeth.

"Really? So is Rosa!"

"Is she havin' hers *today*?" Katie countered.

Ricky eyed his wife's current figure. "Well. Not today, but in a coupla months I think," he said, before putting his keys back in his pocket and setting the bag inside the door. He hoisted the girl into his arms as he entered the apartment, pulling the sucker out of his mouth just long enough to lean over and kiss Rosa.

Thinking she might have heard the sound of their daughter waking from a nap she said, "I'll be right back," and quietly disappeared into another room.

"Well, my mama's havin' ours right now." Katie announced, hoping to keep the conversation focused.

He peered into the bright, blue eyes. "You excited?"

She dramatically nodded her head while her eyes remained fixed on the candy in Ricky's mouth. "Do you have a little brother?" she asked.

He smiled again and spoke as he clenched the sucker between his teeth. "Yeah. Actually, I have four of them. And a little sister, too." He walked into the kitchen and set Katie on the counter.

"Do you like them? Did you have to share?" she asked, eyes fixed on the stick.

Ricky looked serious and nodded, shifting the candy to his cheek. "Oh yes. I had to share a room with all four of my brothers for a while; and until I was ten, I had to share my bed with two of them!"

Katie's eyes got wide.

Ricky nodded, assuring her this was true. "Learning to share takes practice. Like, take now for instance," he said, pulling grape and orange suckers out of his shirt pocket. "I have this other candy and I could just hide it for later—or I could share it. What do you think I should do?"

Knowing most of the adults in her life seemed to share in a conspiracy against sweets and hoping that Ricky might be inclined to break with their tradition, Katie pointed at the grape one and whispered, "Share."

He leaned down and, tearing the plastic wrapper off the purple lollipop, whispered back, "Okay."

Before he could give her the candy, he heard Rosa behind him. "You're gonna ruin her dinner. And she really shouldn't have too much sugar anyway. Her Aunt will be peeling Katie off the ceiling all night if you give her that now."

Ricky kept his back to his wife and got a horrified look on his face. He placed the two new suckers on the counter beside the little girl before taking his own out of his mouth. With a dramatic flair he pulled both of his lips in, put his thumb and index finger together, then pulled an imaginary zipper over his mouth. The official signal for silence had been given. Katie followed suit before Ricky slowly turned to face his accuser. "Guilty as charged, Mrs. Ruiz. What must I do?"

Rosa tried unsuccessfully to keep a straight face. "Well, this is pretty serious, but I suppose if you are really *really* sorry—and you put the candy away for now—we can let it go. This time."

Ricky nodded. "Oh, yeah. I'm really *really* sorry.'"

Soon, he felt a small hand on his back and turned to look at Katie.

"Does this mean I can't have the candy?" she whispered.

He stood sideways and looked from Rosa to Katie several times "Well . . . you *can* have the candy, but not now."

An immediate look of disappointment registered on the girl's face.

He quickly looked back at Rosa "She gonna be here tomorrow?"

"Yep."

He wanted to cushion the letdown. "Tell you what, Katie. I promise you can have it tomorrow after lunch. We'll put it right here in the fridge for you."

"How do I know you won't forget and give it to her?" Katie said, looking over at Rosa. "Or to Angela."

Ricky beamed at her. "*No es un problema!* Not to worry! Here. Stick out your tongue."

Katie complied.

He picked her candy up off the counter and swiped both sides of it on her tongue. "We'll just 'mark' this for you. That way, when Rosa wakes up like a hungry mama bear at 2 a.m. she won't be tempted to eat it."

The little girl caught onto the strategy and she giggled. "I think we missed some."

Rosa shook her head, and looked down.

"*What?*" he asked.

Rosa now zipped her own lips and continued to shake her head.

Ricky swiped the candy on Katie's tongue a couple more times and then got out plastic bags to store the offending objects. "Here. See?" he said, taking them to the refrigerator, "I'm gonna put them right here in the door. Yours is the purple one, mine is green," he stopped and winced for a moment, as if Rosa might throw something at him, "and the orange one is Angela's."

Katie giggled.

"Tomorrow," he continued, "if you eat all your lunch, you can have it. Okay?"

The little girl nodded her head slowly.

"Don't forget and eat mine!" Ricky said. "It's marked, ya know."

The large, toothless grin appeared once more.

He picked Katie up off the counter and hugged her. "Okay?"

She hugged him and he felt her little hand patting him on the back as she said softly, "It's okay, Mr. Ricky. I love you."

He looked at his wife and smiled. Rosa could see that his heart had now been officially and totally melted. They returned to the living room together just as the doorbell sounded.

Rosa looked at the little girl. "Bet that's your aunt! Let's go see!"

Ricky set Katie down and she ran to the door.

"Wait! Wait!" Rosa called after her. "Wait till I see who it is!" After looking through the peephole she allowed Katie to open the door.

The girl's Aunt Carol had come to take her home for the night. There was no "news" yet regarding the long-awaited birth of a baby brother, but, according to reports from Katie's dad, it "could happen any minute now." Carol collected her niece, a small suitcase, and a host of dolls in a bag. She'd bring the girl back tomorrow at ten.

When they were alone, Ricky put his arm around Rosa. "Angela still sleeping?"

Rosa smiled and nodded.

"Then, may I assist you into a seat, my dear?"

She walked over to the king-sized recliner, given to him by teens in his youth group several years ago, in New York. It was one of very few things he considered exclusively his. He went to stand by the piece of furniture as if he were guarding it. "But, that's my chair."

Rosa coolly looked around the room. "Weren't you just discussing something with Katie? What was it now? Sharing?"

"You wanna share my chair? . . . Okay," he finally said, plopping into the seat. "Come on." He helped her to ease onto his lap and groaned before he put both arms around her. "You sure you haven't got twins in there?"

She leaned back in the recliner with him. "Feels like it to me, too! I finally got Katie and Angela down for a nap at three and all I wanted to do was lie down, but wouldn't you know it, your son decided it was time to jump around," Rosa said, rubbing her stomach. "I'm so tired."

"Did my boy do that to you? I'm sorry. I'll sing everybody's favorite songs before we go to bed tonight. Maybe then we'll all rest better."

Rosa closed her eyes and smiled. Tests had shown that their second child would be a son. They'd moved from New York to Oklahoma more than two years ago and started a new life with a new job for Ricky. The couple had survived finding an apartment, the birth of their first child, and—the most traumatic thing—Ricky getting a driver's license. He'd lived in New York City all his life and never owned a vehicle. Being from Miami, Rosa couldn't believe someone could live all the way through their twenties and not own a car or even have a driver's license.

"You mean you've never driven a car?" she'd asked the first time the subject came up.

"I didn't say that. I've driven before," he answered.

"Didn't you just say you'd never had a license?"

"Yeah . . ." He'd looked a bit embarrassed. "But you don't need one to steal cars."

Ricky had been in an inner-city gang as a young man. Many years before she'd met him, he'd actually gone on trial for murder, but eventually was found innocent. While awaiting trial, he'd "gotten saved" after listening to a man who'd come to the jail to talk about Jesus Christ. It changed Ricky's life forever. If it weren't for the scars all over his body from fights, Rosa would never have believed he was capable of the things he said he'd done in the past. She'd heard lots of people talk about being "saved," but Ricky was the first person she'd ever met that was a walking exhibit of God's transforming love.

She shifted slightly to get more comfortable. "I love you," she said, sleepily.

"Oh! I forgot!" he said, scooting over in the huge recliner to slip her off his lap and onto the seat beside him. "You gotta see what I got today."

She'd been so distracted when he first came in, she'd barely noticed it. Now her eyes shot over to the bag beside the door. When he turned it around, she could see the large logo for "BJ's Boots and Western Wear." They'd met "BJ," now one of Ricky's closest friends, at church when they first moved to the area.

An unthinkable thought occurred to her. "You didn't."

"Didn't what?" he asked, opening the bag.

"Buy boots."

"I didn't buy them. BJ gave them to me for helping him put up those fences. And," he said, pulling out a large box and opening it to show her the shiny, new boots, "just look at how wonderful they are!"

The smell of new leather filled the room as she eyed the three-inch heels. Despite his obvious enthusiasm for the footwear she sighed. "Honey . . . perhaps you didn't realize this, but—you're six foot four already. I'll need a ladder to get a goodnight kiss!"

He suddenly pointed to the ceiling, and in his best infomercial-announcer voice said, "But wait! There's more!" He reached into the bag and pulled out a slightly smaller box.

The reality of the situation struck her. "No."

He flashed his best smile. "Yes!"

Her face continued to tighten. "Now Ricky. Did I say anything when you started wearing that cowboy hat? Noooooo."

"You don't like my hat?" he asked, putting his hand on his chest as if he'd been wounded.

She ignored him and continued. "Did I say anything when you started wanting all that spicy Mexican food? Noooo."

"Rosa, you know good and well you like the– "

"Okay, okay I admit I like the food, but honey . . ." Rosa wanted to make another negative remark when she looked into his dark eyes and suddenly became aware this wasn't just about boots. She needed to pay attention. She stopped frowning and softened her voice. "You going to open the box?"

He stepped closer to her as he carefully lifted the lid. "Aren't they pretty?"

She looked at the boots he'd picked for her. Tan in color, they each had a large, silver *concho* on the side, and fringe around the cuff. When she touched them, she realized they were as soft as butter.

He could see she liked them so he pressed his advantage. "I know your feet are a bit swollen, so they might not fit now, but after the baby is born they should . . . and BJ says you can exchange them for any other pair you want."

"You win. They're pretty."

"Yes! And just *look*!" he said, almost leaping back to the bag on the floor and producing two more little boxes.

She looked at the smallest box and couldn't believe it. "You're kidding. They make boots for babies?"

"Of course they do! This is Oklahoma!" He moved toward her once again, opening the larger of the two. Inside were the cutest little boots she'd ever seen—small reproductions of her own, but with soft, moccasin soles.

"Oh Ricky," she said, taking them out of the box. "These are adorable!"

"And look," he said, lifting the lid on the last box. Inside were soft-soled little boots that looked like Ricky's.

"Ohhhhhhh."

"I know. I couldn't help myself," he said, slipping next to her on the recliner and then helping her up onto his lap again. "So, you like 'em?"

"You got me. I have to admit I like them."

He touched his forehead to hers. "But you don't like my hat?"

She thought of the salty sweat stains on it and tried not to make a face. "You want me to like your hat? How come? . . . You wanna become a cowboy in your old age?"

He leaned back and pulled her head over onto his shoulder. "When we were kids, my aunt, Teresa, used to watch me and Greenie. All day, she'd listen to *Tejano* music and we got so we liked it. It spoke of a life so different from the one we knew. We'd dream of escaping the slum and moving to the Southwest where we could ride in trucks or on horses and buy our own land. We wanted to learn to play great music and sing to swarms of lovely *señoritas*–who'd be totally captivated by our machismo." He flexed his arm and a wistful look came to his face. "We actually tried to run away from New York and hitchhike to Texas once. Don't ask me how two Puerto Rican kids were going to survive once we got there, but we were gonna go. Only problem was that we were only, like, nine or ten and had *no* idea which direction to go." He laughed softly as he recalled the end of the incident. "We went the wrong way and ended up on the Canadian border before we were caught and brought back home."

He'd barely mentioned his old friend, Greenie, to Rosa since the man died in his arms during the terrible riots in New York. More than two years had passed since it happened, but Ricky had been unwilling or unable to speak much of his friend. Perhaps some of the sorrow was now being softened by a tie to a childhood dream.

She sat very still for a while before she spoke. "Wouldn't he be happy if he could see you now? You have a hat and boots, a wife, a little cowgirl, and a little buckaroo on the way."

Ricky's whole body seemed to relax. "Yeah. I bet he would. He'd be real happy for me."

CHAPTER 7

PHILADELPHIA — March 2nd

Michael Gordon slid the shoe box back in place. It was five p.m. and his feet hurt. Another employee had called in sick, so he'd been working in the store since eight that morning with only a ten-minute break.

"Hey Mike," called the man from the doorway to the stock room. "Can I leave early today? I need to be someplace."

Michael shook his head. "No. You left early yesterday. You want to keep this job, you keep the hours. You don't like the hours, find another job."

The guy stared at him for a moment and then went back out front. Michael glared back at the empty doorway. *Oh, the joys of management.*

A good number of businesses in this section of Philadelphia had been demolished in the riots two years ago and never rebuilt. The steady migration of people away from the city resulted in the permanent loss of even more businesses, which further depressed the economy in the area. He'd been running this sporting goods store for six months and, even though he didn't like the job, where else could he go?

"Mike! Phone for you!" a man yelled from the front of the store.

Michael walked to the counter in the front of the store, picked up the phone, and spoke into the receiver. "Hoffman's Sporting Goods, Michael Gordon, may I help you?"

"Yeah, Michael. Zac here. You wanted something?"

Michael had called his brother's office at the Philadelphia Arena earlier in the day and left a message. He'd skip any remarks which might reveal his astonishment that Zac actually returned his call. "Hey. I need to talk to you. How 'bout dinner tonight?"

"Where?"

Michael shrugged. "Well, you're the one with the new car. Why don't you pick me up and we'll go someplace?"

"Okay. Seven-thirty good for you?"

"Yeah. See ya," Michael said, before hanging up.

The phone rang again and Michael answered it. "Hoffman's Sporting Goods, how may I help you?"

"Yes," a male voice said, "I'm looking for a Mr. Gordon Michael. Is he there?"

Michael took a breath before responding. "I'm Michael Gordon, will I do?"

"Oh. Sorry. It's just that you have two first names, you know."

Michael had to fight the urge to make a sarcastic remark about the man's great powers of observation. "Yeah. I know that. Did you want to speak with me?"

"Yes. Well, my name is Joe Kaplan and I was hired by the Daily Times Herald to check a reference given to us by Gordon Benjamin. . . . Oh. I suppose that's Benjamin Gordon isn't it?"

"Yes it is. He's my brother. What do you want to know?"

"They're considering him for part-time work in the art department. . ."

Michael answered all the man's questions without lying, relieved that no "health" information had been requested. He knew his brother Benjamin could do anything they would require of him talent-wise, but wasn't sure how long Ben would last health-wise. Michael sighed after he hung up the phone. Although he'd been willing to let Ben move into his apartment, and could pretty much cover the cost of food, they could really use more money. He hoped Ben would get this job and be able to keep it for a while.

When seven-thirty rolled around, Michael let his employee go home and he locked up. Zac eventually pulled up in his new car and honked. Michael hopped in before his brother quickly accelerated toward a favorite restaurant. The small interior of the vehicle had the look of a tightly organized aircraft cockpit, and the pounding sound system gave Michael the sensation that even the air molecules around them were wrestling for space. Each pulse of electric drums and strings crashing out of the surround-sound system assailed his eardrums, sinuses and the bones in his chest. During a pause between songs, Michael reached over and turned the volume down.

The noise of the music still made conversation impossible, but Michael became occupied with thoughts of survival as Zac blazed across lanes and sped through tight spaces. During one pause in the music, Michael thought he heard Zac give a disgusted grunt. Traffic had stopped for the moment, and he followed his brother's gaze to the bumper of the car directly in front of them.

The entire rear of the vehicle was plastered with bumper stickers. One said, "Flash your lights if you love Jesus!" Another said, "In case of rapture, watch out! Driver will disappear!" There were several others, reflecting the latest offering of an advertising campaign of several Christian groups nationwide. These stickers said, "HE is coming soon!" and, "Get right or get LEFT!"

The next song began just as the light turned green and Michael braced himself once again. Zac remained dangerously close to the rear of the bestickered car for more than a mile. Amazingly, the operator of the other vehicle drove as badly as Zac. The two had already drifted through two stop signs and run a red light by the time Zac peeled off into the parking lot for the restaurant. Once the car's engine stopped, Michael started to say something about the death-defying ride but changed his mind. He didn't want to pick a fight over something inconsequential.

Molly, a waitress on duty that evening at *The Glowing Hearth*, saw one of her favorite customers come through the door and smiled.

"Hey, you. How you doin' tonight?" she asked.

"Hungry." Zac answered.

She looked at Zac and the man who'd come in with him. They were both a bit taller than average and slender. Both had the same face. The only distinct difference was that Zac had dark hair and the other guy's was blond.

"You have to be related," she said. "Brothers?"

"Actually," Zac said as Molly led them to a table. "He's my dad."

She laughed and then looked at Michael again. "Looks good for an old codger. You doing that regeneration thing or something?"

"No. I just eat right," Michael responded. He knew he could never match Zac's wit, so he settled for light humor.

"Would you like something from the bar? It's still happy hour."

Michael spoke first. "No. I'll just have an iced tea. No sugar."

Zac had wanted a glass of wine, but silently reconsidered before answering. "I'll have the same."

When the waitress went to fetch the tea, Zac tried to sound casual. "On the wagon now, are we?"

Michael kept looking for a dinner choice. "I can't afford it anymore."

"We talking financially, or otherwise? Don't tell me being the manager of a sporting goods store has actually made you more responsible. Next you'll be buying a house with a 50-year mortgage."

Michael looked over the top of his menu. "Even when I was putting 'em away, I showed up to work sober and managed to get places *on time*. Is my not drinking somehow amusing?"

Zac recognized the need for a change of subject. He looked beyond his brother to the entrance of the restaurant. "Oh, Michael. You should see this one. Suppose she needs to have her coat cleaned?"

Michael sighed. Occasionally, Zac would 'accidentally' spill something on a beautiful woman, then give her his card and offer to pay the cleaning bill if she'd call him with the amount or send the bill to him. More often than not, it resulted in at least one date with the woman. Michael slowly turned and looked. Standing in the doorway, waiting to be seated, stood a woman who looked every bit of 80, but had bright orange hair. He smiled and turned back to Zac. "You chasing ones you can actually catch now?"

They ordered their food and then ate, making small talk about sports during the meal. As dinner drew to a close, Michael knew he needed to begin working toward the reason for their visit. "So, how's the job?"

"Until recently? Pretty good."

"What happened?" Michael asked.

"My new supervisor. Horrible woman. She hates me." Zac took a sip of tea before continuing. "If she had her way, she'd have me gutted and put a nice little candle inside me to light her office at night. Kind of a Zac-o-lantern."

It amused Michael to think of light emanating from Zac's eyes, nose, mouth and ears. "Oh yeah? What'd you do to her?"

"Nothing. Really. She's out to cut costs, and I just happen to annoy her—or at least my 'type' does—so she has it in for me."

"Oh." Michael had finished his food. He knew he would have to say it now or never. "Well, the reason I asked is I think I may need some help from you soon."

Zac knew instantly the word "help" would be interchangeable with the word "money." He looked at his food. "I'm about broke, Mike. What for?"

"Benjamin."

"I thought he . . ."

"It's official, Zac. He's dying." Michael waited for a few moments. His brother said nothing, so he continued. "Look. I may need some help, that's all. He's staying at my apartment, I'm buying the food, but the meds cost more than you can believe. Ben's got a job now," he said, stretching the truth, "but, who knows how long he'll be able to work?"

Zac, rarely at a loss for words, continued to silently cut at the remnants of a steak.

"I know you're still ticked at him for what he did to your apartment—"

Zac suddenly pointed a fork at him and shook it in his face. "Over three thousand bucks, Michael, and after three years, he *still* hasn't given me back a dime of it! He did it just to get even with me. . . . And where are all of his buddies *now?*"

"Most of them are dead now."

The starkness of the remark, and the fact it was probably true, didn't keep Zac from going on. "Ben can stick me for years and you don't care. Then, all he has to do is say he's hurt or needs help and you flock to him like a mother hen."

"That's so easy for you to say." Michael almost spat out the words. "You never needed anybody. Even when we were kids, you could make some funny remark and dad wouldn't hit you. I never noticed you stepping in and being clever when he was beating the stuffings out of Ben and me. As long as you get what you want, everyone else can just go to blazes!"

Zac opened his mouth to say something, but Michael continued. "I'm not minimizing the things he's done, but he's our brother. . . . He's our brother and he's dying." Michael softened his tone for a moment. "You haven't seen how he looks, Zachary. He looks bad."

"Even if I wanted to help you—" Zac began.

Michael quickly cut him off again, getting angrier with each word. "I just wanted you to know what was happening to him and to ask if you'd be willing to help out sometimes. I'm not asking for anything right now. If you don't want to help, then *fine*," he said, throwing his napkin on his plate like a gauntlet.

"Fine!" Zac repeated, throwing his own napkin down as well. "Got any other nifty news before dessert?"

"No."

"Fine then."

"Fine!"

The waitress exited the kitchen and realized both plates had napkins in them, so she approached the table. "Everyone finished? How was the dinner?"

They both looked at her at the same time and said a surly, "*Fine!*"

She'd picked up both of their plates but now stepped back from the table without touching any of the other dishes. She'd never seen Zachary like this before.

He motioned for her to come close again. "I'm sorry. We're just having a 'brother thing' here, okay? Really, dinner was fine. It was great. Thanks."

"Yeah." Michael added.

She quietly cleared off the rest of the dishes and left.

The interruption had given them both a few moments to cool down.

Zac spoke first. "Listen, I know you're . . . I'll see what I can do. As long as I don't have to see him."

Michael knew this would have to do for now. "I'm sorry about the things I said. I was just mad. I knew you'd help. Thanks."

CHAPTER 8

WASHINGTON, D.C. — April 7th

President Don Cole made his way down the hall, past the agent, and into the room where his mother, Eva Cole, sat talking on the phone with a small note pad in her lap. When she saw him, she politely ended her conversation and took off her reading glasses so she could give him her full attention. Although age had turned her auburn hair white, and arthritis had diminished some of her mobility, an air of energy still seemed to hover about the woman.

"Was it a productive meeting?" she asked.

Don sat in the chair nearest to hers. "That remains to be seen. Let's put it this way: A lot of 'frank and open' remarks were exchanged."

"You mean they had a heated argument," she corrected.

"Exactly. But they did agree to more talks next week."

"Good going. You still taking me out to dinner tonight?"

"I believe I've got you in my schedule," he smiled. "You want Italian?"

She shrugged. "That would be good. Garlic is one of the few things I can really taste anymore. Did you invite anyone else?"

He tilted his head and thought a moment. "Well, the Secret Service agents will be coming, but they come whether I invite them or not."

"Don't be smart with your mother. Is anyone else coming?"

"So who is it you wanted me to invite?"

"What about Bob Post? I haven't seen him in ages."

"Since when did you like Bob so much?"

She ignored his question. "James Greer. He and his wife are so nice, what about them?"

Knowing the conversation hadn't reached the desired destination, he decided to play along. "Well, I suppose I could give James a call."

"Or, how about Fred Arnstein."

Bingo! Don thought. *The train has arrived.*

Fred Arnstein was his new appointee for the National Commission on Aging. Of course, Eva, a committed lobbyist for seniors, would want to personally interrogate the man regarding his views on regeneration, official retirement age, and any number of hot topics for those over 60 years of age. Don shook his head and smiled. *There must be a "political gene" in this family.*

"Hmmm," he finally said. "I hadn't given it much thought, but, now you mention it, maybe he *would* like to eat with us. Of course, if he's busy tonight, I might be able to arrange something next time you're here. A quiet dinner for two perhaps? Fred is single, you know. *And the two of you would have so much in common.*"

"Donald Cole, I merely wanted to—"

A short laugh escaped his lips. "I generally have more success making appointments with heads-of-state than getting you to slow down enough to spend time here. I was hoping for a nice, private, mother-son dinner, but if you wanted to make it more of a party. . ."

She looked out a nearby window, then smiled. "Checkmate. I must be losing my touch," she sighed. "I used to be so much better at subtle orchestration."

"Oh. Like making brownies for all the kids in the fifth-grade when I ran for class president? Or getting me to ask out that ugly girl in high school."

"Patty Garfield was *not* ugly."

"Mom. Her teeth stuck out so far she could have eaten an apple through a chain-link fence. Stewart Winters followed us around all evening and, whenever she wasn't looking, he put some of those plastic vampire teeth on and made faces at me. It was the worst date I ever had."

"Stu did that to you? If I'd have known, I would have called his mother."

"Precisely why I didn't tell you."

"What a shame. Patty was such a nice girl, and the two of you had—"

"So much in common," he said in unison with her.

"Well, you did. You probably don't know she ran for a city council position last year."

"You still know what she's doing? How do you keep track of so many people?"

Don heard a knock at the door and got up to answer it. He didn't invite the visitor in. Eva could hear a man speaking quietly from the hallway before Don returned and leaned over to kiss her on the cheek. "I have to go. Something's come up." He started out of the room, then turned and said, "As far as I know, we're still on for dinner. Just you and me. Okay?"

She waved. "See you later."

Within minutes, President Cole and Vice President Cunningham received an emergency briefing regarding the deployment of a new surveillance satellite in space. The satellite had been released into orbit, but then refused to respond to any radio commands. An attempt to fix it resulted in damage. The shuttle crew managed to get the secret device back into the payload bay, but would have to receive further instructions before proceeding. Both the manufacturers of the apparatus and the "payload expert" on board the shuttle doubted it could be repaired with the tools and equipment on hand.

Don listened intently as General Sloan briefed them on the current situation.

". . . and, if we can't fix it within the next 37 hours, we'll hit another snag."

"Snag?" Don asked.

"We need to decide whether leave it up there or to bring it home. If we're bringing it back, we'll have to cancel the rest of the mission. The next stop was supposed to be the space station. They're scheduled to pick up some astronauts—one American, one French, one Russian. Obviously, we can't do it if there's a top secret satellite in the bay of the shuttle. We'd have to find a reason to give the French, the Russians, *and* the press for leaving the station astronauts where they are until the next scheduled mission."

"And when is *that*?"

The vice president answered, "a month from now."

Cole couldn't hide his irritation. "Who decided to combine two missions with such potential for conflict?"

The general straightened in his chair and shot a look at Cunningham before answering, "It wasn't my call, Mr. President. All sorts of compromises are made in order to save money."

Although he wanted to chew somebody out big time, Cole realized it wouldn't help. Reprimands could be passed out when the problem was solved. "We'll need a full briefing with a list of options from agency reps, manufacturer reps, and your people by noon tomorrow."

"Yes sir."

CHAPTER 9

PHILADELPHIA — April 8th

TV news reporter Linda Posner checked the camera. The angle and the lighting had to be perfect. How about the auto focus? Next, she checked her microphone. Everything had to be absolutely flawless.

In keeping with the spring weather, she'd chosen a peach-colored pantsuit with matching shoes–conservative and attractive. In a business market where the "older"generation now dominated, she needed to avoid wearing anything emphasizing her youth. She always chose a look that would appeal to someone like her mother, yet still be attractive enough to hold the attention of men.

On her first "solo" assignment for a local Philadelphia news station, Ms. Posner knew this job would launch her into the spotlight. She'd had a couple of false starts before moving here, but she'd learned some valuable lessons. This job would be "it." As long as another international or local emergency didn't take up her air time tonight, *this* story might be it. If the new India-Pakistan peace accord held, if the Middle East didn't blow up, and the teachers in Philly didn't stage a walkout, she'd be on the six o'clock news.

She smoothed her hair one last time, touched the red record button on her hand-held remote, and looked into the camera.

"Three, two, one . . . Today, I'm standing in front of one of the farms that provide poultry for Chester's Chinese Chicken Shack with . . ." she paused the camera and rolled her eyes.

You're not "with" anybody, dummy! You're even running the camera by yourself!

She took a breath. "Three, two, one. . . Today, I'm standing," she made a sweeping gesture with her hand, "in front of one of the farms that provide poultry for Chester's Chinese Chicken Shack . . ."

She paused the camera again and put her arm down. *What exactly are you DOING here? You're gonna look like some silly game show model that comes out when the guy says, "You've just won a brand new blender!" Keep the hand motions to a minimum. . . Relax!*

She rolled her head around, took a deep breath, and pushed the button. before starting again

"Three, two, one. . . Today, I'm standing in front of a farm that supplies poultry for Chester's Chinese Chicken Shack. In Channel Four's . . ." she paused it and turned her back to the camera.

This is Channel FIVE. You work for Channel Five now! In Philadelphia! Not Cincinnati! Not Dayton!

She went back to the camera and replaced the small disk inside while she spoke to herself out loud. "Let's not hand in something that shows you can't even remember where you work!"

She checked the camera again before she took a compact out of her pocket opened it, and looked in the mirror. Although the "Retro-Geisha" look was in, she knew she'd look positively embalmed with the nearly white makeup it required. She'd opted instead for a pale shade of her own skin tone. When she smiled at her reflection, to her horror, she saw lipstick on one of her front teeth. She quickly rubbed it off with her finger and then checked her hair again.

Within moments, Linda stepped back in front of the camera. "Three, two, one. Today, I'm standing in—oh!"

A sudden gust of wind came up, and the camera teetered on its tripod. She lunged forward to grab it before it fell. As she set it up again, a small section of her hair blew into her face and when she swooped it back, she felt it drag some lipstick across her cheek. She looked at the lock of blond hair, now smudged bright pink on the ends.

Oh, why didn't I use powdered lip tint? Because I wanted that old-fashioned glossy stuff, that makes me look more attractive! Now she hated herself for the choice. She took several deep breaths, knowing she was on the verge of a temperamental outburst. A looming deadline prevented her from having a total tantrum. She had to hurry or she wouldn't have a story to air that evening. Linda soon stood in front of the camera once again, hair combed, makeup fixed.

"Three, two, one." she said, soberly. "This is Linda Posner. I'm standing in front of one of the farms that provides poultry for Chester's Chinese Chicken Chack—!" She stomped her foot but kept going. "Three, two, one. This is Linda Posner. I'm standing in front of one of the farms that provides poultry for Chester's Chinese Shicken Shack— *AAAAAAhhhhhh!* . . . Three, two one. This is Linda Posner. In part one of our story of 'Poison Poultry,' I'm going to show you the horrible conditions on the farm where the—"

A large rooster appeared out of nowhere and began attacking the camera. He flew at it several times, pecking and spurring the lens.

"Stop that! You horrible creature! Shoo!" she yelled, charging at him and waving her arms. When she did this, he turned, and began chasing *her.* She screamed in terror and started running away. During the chase, he got her on the leg. Twice. Soon, the owner of the farm heard her cries for help and ran out to rescue her. He was only momentarily gracious, however. As soon as he found out what she was doing, he demanded that she get off his property or he would call the police.

By the time she got back to the broadcasting location, she had a short clip shot in front of the gate to the farm. She'd been careful to destroy the shots with the falling camera, the twisted-tongue gaffes, and the chicken in hot pursuit of the hysterical news reporter. If she'd accidentally let them fall into the wrong hands, they most certainly would have been aired on a show dedicated to idiot out-takes, and she had no intention of making a national debut in this manner.

Later, from her cubicle, she quickly scanned the local, national, and international headlines on her computer. She read an announcement stating the scheduled docking of the shuttle with the space station *COSMOS* had been canceled due to technical problems with the hatch. There had also been a rollover accident downtown. Big deal. Obviously, there was not much going on today.

"Excellent," she said aloud. Today would be a good day after all.

CHAPTER 10

PHILADELPHIA — April 19th

Michael Gordon finished checking off the inventory of sports equipment that Hoffman's Sporting Goods had received at noon. Everything appeared to be in order and he signed the bottom of the form.

An older woman appeared in the doorway leading to the storefront. "Michael, someone's here for you."

"Thanks. I'll be right there."

Michael put the clipboard on a desk and went out to the front of the store. Even though the man faced the other direction, he recognized the lean frame and the light brown hair of his brother.

"Hey, Ben. Glad you could come down." From the corner of his eye, Michael could see the saleswoman, Mona, gawking at the two of them, figuring out they looked alike, and that Benjamin looked sick. He ignored her and continued speaking to his brother. "You feel like a trip to the arena?"

Ben straightened up. He and older brother Zachary hadn't spoken since, in a fit of rage, he'd trashed Zac's apartment more than three years ago. Michael had sort of smoothed the way by being a go-between recently, but the warring parties still hadn't made direct contact.

"I thought you were gonna get the money from him at lunch." Ben said. "I was just supposed to make the deposit before the bank closed."

"Sorry. One of my people didn't show up here. I couldn't take any time for lunch."

Ben's face reflected the reluctance he felt.

"No time like the present," Michael added.

You knew you'd have to face him eventually, Ben told himself. At first it was easy to avoid Zac because of the angry things said and done. Then, once his life changed, Ben told himself it was better to avoid constant exposure to Zac's hard humor—a painful reminder of their dysfunctional past. But recently, despite a longing to see his oldest brother, he continued to evade the issue due to embarrassment about his own words and actions prior to their estrangement. He closed his eyes. *God, why is apologizing so hard? Why can't I just say, "I'm sorry," without wanting to accuse him of things? Without help, I'll never be able to do it. Please, help me.*

An amused look came to Michael's face. "You're not chicken are you?" Only a year apart in age, they'd often dared each other to new heights of craziness with this very question.

"You calling me chicken?" Ben caught onto the game, giving the standard response one always gave before leaping into the questionable activity.

"Yeah. You proving me wrong?"

"Yeah."

"Here's cab fare," Michael said, putting some money in his brother's hand.

"No. I've got it. I got paid today." Ben put the money back in Michael's shirt pocket.

"Okay. He's in the offices on the north side of the building. If he's not there, his secretary will page him. I hope he's got cash, but if all he's got is a magstrip, take it."

Several customers had entered the store. "Be a brave young man and run along now," Michael said, the smile coming to his lips again.

"Sure, 'Dad,'" Ben replied. Zac, Ben, and sister Jill always responded this way to Michael when he took charge. Even though Zac was the oldest, Michael was the boss—a fact they each resented and appreciated, alternately.

Ben soon found a cab and asked to be taken to the arena. He listened in silence to a radio broadcast as the taxi inched through traffic.

". . . the Senate majority leader acted as spokesperson for the congressional group which called a press conference to express 'deep concern' over possible darkening relations with China. Senator Moffit said he wasn't able to confirm or deny the reports, but was troubled by what appeared to be an aggressive stance taken by China in recent talks with Japan."

The broadcast continued ". . . In other news, White House Press Secretary Bob Post announced President Cole will meet with members of congress this week to ask for an expansion of our military forces. Enlistment incentives and increased pay benefits will be just two of the options the US Commander-in-Chief will be discussing. Another hot topic is likely to be a large expansion of the Army Corps of Engineers which would be used to help repair damaged bridges, decaying roads, and run-down federal buildings across the country . . ."

Ben looked out the window and let his mind drift for a while. It amazed him how so much of the "news" revolved around the assumption of a future. . . . Plans to do this or go in a particular direction. Plans he would most likely never live to see realized.

The cab driver looked at his watch and switched stations on the radio. A woman's voice came through the speakers.

". . . and the topic of the show for several days now has been spirituality. Are all living things endowed with it? Is it a basic element of life? What is spirituality? We want to hear from you so our lines will be open after these messages . . ."

This interested Ben. He wouldn't mind listening to chatter on world religions.

When President Cole first took office, Ben thought the man's main motive in talking about the Bible and other things was to fan the fires of religious bigots. It certainly stirred Ben's hatred for smug Christians with a need to impose their morality on everyone. Then, when he'd suffered his sudden reverse in health, he'd easily imagined how gleeful all of them were at what he and others like him were experiencing. He envisioned how 'vindicated' they felt. How right. He'd even pictured all of them dancing on his grave.

The voice of a caller on the radio talk show intruded on Ben's thoughts.

". . . but, in the final analysis," she said, "all paths lead to God."

Ben leaned his head back and shut his eyes as he considered those words. *All paths lead to God.* In the past couple of years, knowing the fate he faced, he'd truly searched for a way to be at peace with himself . . . and with God.

When he was living as an openly gay man with AIDS, he mostly wanted to vindicate himself against Christians. He wanted to believe they were all hard-hearted idiots, and hating them gave Ben a reason to reject their God.

In the beginning of his illness, in order to stay well, Ben became very "health" conscious and spent a lot of time with others who dedicated much of their lives to the pursuit of fitness. Many of them were devoted to "Eastern" philosophies. Finding physical strength in the foods and practices they advocated, and solace in what he perceived as support of his lifestyle, Ben delved more and more into their teachings.

He learned about "a new spirituality," existing without the "narrow-mindedness and bigotry" he'd seen in "church people" most of his life. Ben heard he could expand his horizons to embrace everything. The names of people like Jesus, Mohammed, and Buddha could *all* be on his list of past "Masters" or "Prophets," but there was no requirement to believe in these men, or even to accept all they had taught. For a while, it gave him such a rush to think he could pass judgment on Jesus and other religious leaders—to personally decide if each one's words or life still had any validity.

Like his friends, Ben took what he considered the "slices" of truth out of each belief and patched them together into a personalized system. He could profess to believe these things in general and limit changes to what suited him. The new spirituality felt so liberating. Life became a giant cafeteria. Take what you want, do what you feel, whatever makes you happy.

But "happy" is such a superficial thing, isn't it? Ben mused. When someone is happy they don't want to look too close, or to poke around too much and pop the bubble.

Being a creative sort of person, however, Ben couldn't live with "happy." Happy meant death to his creativity. His artistic gift made him dig for the deepest corners of things, pulled him to inspect, and compelled him to view life with a hardness that gave him a fresh perspective to depict. In short, it demanded he pop the bubble.

So he started to dig. When he did this, he read about people who were currently considered the latest incarnations of the "Masters." These enlightened, highly evolved people were about to facilitate the birth of a new global society and reveal the world's new "Christ"—a man who, according to many of them, already inhabited a human body somewhere on earth. Why most of these masters and their "Christ" were in hiding was never quite clear, but the quasi-secretness of it all made it more appealing at first.

It made him wonder, *What are the goals of the Masters?* Again Ben searched, and he found their "plan" had been written out in various places for anyone who dared to look: The earth would be returned to its most pristine condition with a reduced human population that had "evolved to its highest" form. On first consideration, this sounded so mystical, lofty, ethereal . . . and so hard to attain. Just the thing for someone wanting to be spiritual (if not happy). If he'd stopped there, he probably could have embraced this sort of life.

However, being Ben, he started looking at others who'd espoused this plan, and discovered something that caused him concern. Despite claiming to work for high-minded goals like embracing all cultures and re-greening the earth, most were totally self-absorbed. While claiming all paths led to God, they treated people who disagreed with them like enemies. And, for all their talk about meditation, auras, chakras, and other super-spiritual things, they were people who were totally obsessed with their own body functions. The difference between what they said and who they were astonished him.

As he contemplated these stark contradictions, Ben learned the Masters had decided the time had come for implementation of the plan, but they needed to nudge it along a bit. There was simply not enough time to let people continue ravaging the planet's resources while they struggled toward enlightenment.

Ben remembered the greasy feeling he got when he read birth control wasn't enough. Now, for the sake of a renewed Earth, sacrifices would have to be endured. "Selective reduction" needed to be implemented. Plagues should be allowed to "run their courses" and disasters allowed to exact their toll. These things, they said, "were Nature's way of realigning the imbalance on earth." And where Mother Earth needed help, people could assist. Homosexuality, abortion, euthanasia, and war, while controversial, could serve the overall plan.

The divergence between the claim to love all people while at the same time wanting the extinction of most of them came into sharp focus. It finally dawned on Ben that it wasn't a matter of "accepting" him and his lifestyle. Rather, his homosexuality aided in preventing even more pesky human inhabitants from spoiling the great global future they envisioned. The fact that so many gays had died and were continuing to die from a terrible disease was just another "sad but necessary" step toward a consummate balance—kind of like a bonus.

In the beginning, he *wanted* to believe all paths were like spokes on a wheel: all headed for the same Center. If this were true, it would mean he could select any path and he wouldn't have to change. But the more he studied these different paths, rather than finding a common center, he saw the world's religions ran in divergent directions. Only in the eyes of someone who held that *nothing* was true could all beliefs be ultimately "the same."

The candor that often descends on someone who is dying forced him to see his beliefs were little more than a crazy quilt of contradictions that brought no lasting warmth to his soul. Ben hadn't found bliss, or health, or even a way to justify himself.

How different might my life have been if I hadn't wasted so much time?

The taxi pulled up in front of the arena, and Ben got out. He located the Events Office and went inside. An older woman at the desk asked if she could help him.

"Zac Gordon, please."

This man's voice seemed familiar to her. Had she talked with him on the phone before? She looked at him for a moment and realized that although he was thin and had lighter brown hair, he looked like Mr. Gordon."

"Are you his brother Michael?"

"No. Michael's our other brother. I'm Ben."

She'd talked to Michael quite a few times on the phone, but wasn't aware another brother even existed. "Oh," she said, and hesitated a moment. "If you'll wait, I'll locate him." She started to dial Zac's number, then remembered her manners and offered her hand. "I'm Barbara. I've talked with Michael before, and your voice sounds quite like his." It wasn't until he clasped her hand that she noticed his sallow skin against her own healthy pink color.

Ben shook her hand without even considering what it might do to him. While he was very careful to never put others at risk, he'd stopped being paranoid about what other people's germs might do to him. He figured, why waste most of his time worrying? He sat down to wait, and then his mouth dropped open as he checked out the office. *Wow. It looks as if Zac might be the only Gordon who'll break with family tradition and actually become a success at something that pays good money.*

The phone rang and Ben could overhear the secretary.

"Yes. Your brother is here. Do you want him to wait? . . . Okay. Okay. If he wants, I'll bring him up." She looked over at Ben after hanging up the phone. "He's in the middle of something up in the control booth for the arena right now. He may be a while but he says you can come up there if you'd like."

Although he felt tired, curiosity made him want to see what the control booth looked like. Besides, Zac would be less likely to react badly if he were in the throes of some other problem and there were people around. "Okay," he replied.

She reached into a desk drawer and produced a clip-on badge which said "VISITOR" in large black letters. "You'll need to wear this. Sorry, it's standard procedure for security."

"No problem," he said, taking the badge and clipping it on the front of his shirt.

"I'll take you to him. Give me just a moment to close down my program."

"Sure."

She quickly exited her current task and locked down her computer terminal. "Just follow me," she said, smiling.

They walked around the perimeter of the main arena and Ben noted everyone wore an I.D. badge of one sort or another. After Barbara used hers in a keyless entry system, they passed through several sets of doors and went up in an elevator which would allow them to get to the control booth.

Once they exited the elevator into a hall, she could see Zac in the distance and she called to him. "Mr. Gordon!" Zac turned and she spoke to him again. "Mr. Gordon. Here he is."

She saw him nod and begin to wave as Ben approached. Once he realized *which* brother, the wave markedly slowed.

Barbara turned to Ben. "You belong to him now. I have to run. Nice meeting you."

"Thanks," he said. "Nice meeting you, too."

She walked back to the elevator as he made his way down the hall.

Someone in the booth was speaking, but Zac couldn't take his eyes off Ben. Three years ago, Ben was strong, handsome, healthy . . . but now he realized Michael was right about Ben wasting away.

Ben checked out Zac as well. He'd been so caught up in his own egocentric pursuits in the past, he hadn't given much thought to what went on in anyone else's life. And, after they'd had their big falling out, he'd avoided thinking of his older brother at *all*. But as Ben approached his brother now, he was struck by something he'd never noticed before. A giant unhappiness living behind Zac's eyes.

"Hey Ben," Zac said, making an effort to sound casual. "I thought Michael was coming." The other men in the booth stopped talking, but Zac didn't offer to introduce anyone. After a few moments of awkward silence, Zac spoke to them.

"Go ahead and take a break. See if you can check with whoever handles the records for mechanical maintenance. Be sure to go over the files with the original specs for the building. There have got to be manuals on this thing somewhere. Maybe we can still figure out a way to get it working." He closed his eyes for a moment and pinched the bridge of his nose. "I'm all tapped out. I have no idea what else to do. Call me if you find anything."

Once the others were out of the booth, Ben spoke. "What's the problem?"

Zac pointed outside the booth to a shadowy mass of machinery near the ceiling of the arena. "Oh, it's that stupid 'lift' thing-a-ma-jig. It's kinda like a crane. It's supposed to enable us to lift and move large objects around inside the arena. We don't use it that often—but wouldn't you know it—I have an 'oldie goldie' rock group from the 80's that needs it for the concert and the stupid thing is broken. This old geezer with a guitar wants to be put down on the stage in a flaming cage tomorrow night but we can't get the lift to budge!" Zac shook his head. "If I have to pay some specialty company to come in here and fix this stupid piece of junk I'll be a Zac-o-lantern for sure."

Ben gave him a strange look.

Zachary noticed it and said, "Oh. Nothing. Arena management doesn't want to pay for a lot of big time repairs, that's all . . . and the thing I was trying to do isn't going to work; so we might as well go back down to my office." Ben watched as Zac used a keyboard to switch off several systems for the arena, then swipe his badge in a slot before turning off the board and monitors in the small enclosure. When they left the booth, Zac made sure the door closed and reset the entry pad before they began walking down the hall. He kept his eyes forward as he spoke.

"I meant to get some cash on my way in this morning, but I was running a little late. I'll have to give you a magstrip."

Now that the reason for his visit had been mentioned, Ben felt embarrassed. A year ago, he'd have been too proud to take any help. All he could say now was, "Sure."

They made their way back down to the office with no further conversation. It wasn't like Zachary to be so quiet and this made things feel even more awkward. They passed through the reception area and Barbara greeted them once again. Ben returned the visitor's badge and Zac ushered him into his own office before returning to speak to Barbara.

"I'm expecting Lenny to get back to me about the problem we're having with the lift. If he calls, put him through to me. If it's anybody else or about anything else, just take a message, okay?"

"Well, you do have a few messages here that might be important," she said.

Zac had turned and walked away from her desk but now stopped just short of his office and sighed. He briefly leaned through the door and spoke to Ben. "I'll be there in just a sec."

Ben felt a dull ache coming on. He sat down and looked around the office. There were posters and ad samples in various places around the room. Being an artist, his interest in the graphics was more than casual. His eyes eventually lit on the renderings for an upcoming auto show on his brother's desk.

When Zachary entered the room he moved swiftly to his chair and dropped into it. He rotated around to sign on at his terminal and get into his financial program. Noticing Ben had fixed on the auto show drawings, he quickly seized the opportunity to break the uncomfortable silence.

"Like 'em?"

Ben shrugged, then after a few moments said, "Actually, they're kinda blah."

Zac hadn't been too thrilled with them, either. "Think so?"

"Well, they're just so . . . bland. They have no style . . . no appeal. I mean, just look at this." Without thinking, Ben stood up and grabbed a pen off the desk. "Look at this background color. Talk about lifeless. And the car is too small." He started to mark on the poster, then realized what he was doing. He stopped and looked at Zac. "May I?"

Zachary looked into his brother's eyes and noticed the whites were pale orange. "Yeah. Go ahead."

"Are you guys doing this advertising or someone else?"

"Actually, it's a cooperative thing. Go ahead."

"Okay," Ben said, starting to make bold lines across the poster. "The car needs to be sized up, rotated about an eighth of a turn, and moved forward. Put your 'Auto Show' headline along the side. Like this. And this is an electric car, right? Then the whole thing should have an electric feel to it. Sharp lines. And definitely change the background to black or bright blue."

As Ben spoke, Zac realized how much he'd missed his high-strung but talented sibling. In a rare moment of total honesty, he admitted to himself the real reason for their split had been one of his own practical jokes. The prank went too far and ended with his enraged brother nearly demolishing his apartment. Instead of the old, familiar anger, regret now crept into Zac's soul. Seeing Ben in this state made their long-standing grudge seem so . . . dumb. He looked down at the drawing.

"Can I show these changes to the people who did the original?" Zac asked.

"Sure. Why not?"

"If you were free-lancing this, how much would you have charged for it?"

Ben started to say something, then stopped and looked a little embarrassed. "Rounded off? Three thousand bucks. . . . I'd have used it to pay you back. I'm sorry I wrecked your apartment, Zac."

Zac looked down at his desk. Although he found the simple apology satisfying, he suddenly remembered something their brother Michael recently said. Ben, of all things, had "found Jesus." He'd even renounced being a homosexual! His apology could quickly turn into a testimonial of some sort–like the disgusting, sappy words of that awful Cliff Edison, the television preacher who'd just gotten out on parole and was speaking of how Jesus had changed him while he was in prison. Christians were nothing more than desperate, humorless, intellectually bankrupt losers who had nothing better to do than try to prove it. No, he decided, we're not going to go there.

"Of course," Zac said, quickly, "you know how it is when you're on a project and someone else comes along and changes your idea. The lovely lady who did these will definitely need some consoling when I show the improvements to her boss and he likes your work better than hers. I'll probably have to take her to dinner."

Ben shook his head and smiled. "That's my Zac."

"Tell you what, Ben, maybe I can get you some jobs with them in the future if you're interested."

"Okay. Great."

Zac got out a small slip of plastic with a magnetic strip on it, placed it in the printer slot and then started typing. "How do you want this magstrip made out?"

If the bank closed before Ben got there and he had to deposit the strip in a machine, he'd only be able to get out a certain amount of money against it until tomorrow. Even though they needed food and Ben needed medicine, this would have to do. "Make it out to me. I'll stick it in the night teller if I don't get to the bank before it closes."

"No problem," Zac said. He filled out the information and printed it out before handing the strip to his brother. "That enough?"

Ben took it but didn't look at the amount. "Sure. I mean, you don't have to give us . . . me . . . anything. Thanks."

Zac wanted to breathe a sigh of relief when his phone rang. He pushed a button activating the microphone and speakers on his computer. "Zac Gordon."

"Yeah," the voice coming through the speakers said. "This is Lenny. I found one of the manuals to the lift."

Ben stood to leave and waved. "I need to get going. Thanks."

"Just a sec, Lenny," Zac said before pushing the hold button and looking at Ben again. "No problem, man. Keep in touch."

Ben nodded and left the office.

Zachary returned to his conversation with Lenny. "Okay. Get Ron and come over to my office. We have to get this fixed tonight."

As soon as the phone conversation was over, he went back to his financial program. He'd have to make a transfer from his credit account to his debit account to cover the magstrip he'd given to Ben.

He looked over the figures and he knew the time had come to give himself another little talk. *Better not mess anything up any time soon, boy. You're in over your eyebrows now, so you'd better head for shore and swim fast.*

He was interrupted when Barbara entered the office with a package. "This just arrived for you," she said, setting it on his desk, then seating herself. "What's wrong with your brother?"

Zac looked at her for a moment. He could've said "cancer" or named one of several other deadly things and, technically, he would have been making a truthful statement. But Barbara wasn't the judgmental type so he decided to tell her the simple truth. "He's one of the original people who got that 'miracle cure' for AIDS and now he's one of the few survivors. He's got Multiple Return AIDS."

Outside the arena, Ben got into the taxi for the ride to a teller machine, glad to encounter silence. His heart was broken for his brothers, his sister, his parents. *How lost they all are! God, I'm so very sorry I've paid so little attention to anyone but me. I know it's late, Lord, but I'm willing to do whatever You ask. Help me to make a difference for them.*

CHAPTER 11

Vice President Lawrence Cunningham stood just outside the small briefing room at the White House. His left foot, feeling like it had been squeezed into a shoe one size too small, told him he should have gotten up and walked around on the flight. However, before he could go home and remove his footwear, he'd need to talk to the president about his trip.

On the day they were elected, Don Cole and Lawrence Cunningham agreed to make the time for frequent, face-to-face meetings to help them stay in stride with one another. The small, secured room the vice president prepared to enter was used specifically for these candid talks; and its well appointed, comfortably lit space had a friendly feel. Through the open door he could see President Cole, already seated, in one of the two chairs which faced each other at the center of a hand-loomed rug. Cole had taken off his coat and tie and was reading something in a folder. Even after all that had happened in the past two years, Don still looked strong, confident. The strands of silver hair at his temples were the only indication he'd aged since becoming president.

Don had called during Lawrence's flight back to the US to request the meeting. Lawrence stuck his head into the room and lightly tapped on the open door, asking, "Am I too late?"

President Cole shook his head. "Oh, no. We should talk. You up to it?"

The desire to share his success made him forget his fatigue. "I'm fine."

Cole motioned to the other chair in the room. "Then c'mon in and sit down. You want anything? Hungry?"

After closing the door, Cunningham studied the president for a second. Although Don looked pensive, he didn't appear stressed. Lawrence hoped this might be a good sign, and that perhaps Cole had asked for this meeting merely because he wanted to hear about the trip. "No. I had a nice dinner on the plane, thanks."

As soon as they were comfortable, the vice president shared his insights regarding the summit in Central America, describing which leaders had been difficult, what ideas were the most popular, and why. Many of the subtleties he'd picked up on and used to formulate strategies would be shared only in this room. As he came to the end of his narration, he had a great sense of satisfaction.

"Overall, I would classify the summit a success. There was finally agreement in the wording we were so concerned about—you know, regarding value exchange. We struck some good bargains with Guatemala and Mexico on the . . ."

Don watched him as he spoke. Even after a long day, Lawrence still sat with perfect posture, every hair on his head remained in place, his buffed nails shone, and there wasn't a speck of lint on the suit tailored to maximize his small frame. He remained the embodiment of an ivy-league graduate with degrees in business and government. Formal to the bone, he hated the shortened version of his name, and never responded if someone called him Larry.

Despite being high-strung and a bit obsessed about his personal cleanliness, he did, however, have keen abilities in trade and finance. In fact, his business connections and skills were what led the party to nominate him for vice president. While differences in ideology and personal style were major barriers to the two men in the beginning, each had made efforts to ignore the other's idiosyncrasies and appreciate the other one's strengths.

"The crown jewel, really," Lawrence concluded, "was the percentage point concession we got in exchange for some modifications in the restrictions. Mr. Fernandez really became an ally on this. Even with his support, we didn't reach a consensus till late this afternoon—but it's a solid part of the agreement now. I'll try to have a copy of the whole thing on your desk by tomorrow afternoon."

"Great. I can't tell you how grateful I am to have you negotiating for us."

Lawrence sensed sincere praise and smiled. "Thanks. It's what I do best."

Although the topic seemed to have closed, Don made no effort to get up or to indicate the meeting was over. Obviously the president wanted to tell him something.

He asked the dreaded question. "Anything happen I should know about?"

"Several things, actually."

Already, he could feel himself beginning to perspire. Though Don appeared calm, Lawrence had learned from experience that this wasn't always an indicator of fair weather in the White House. He could only hope the "things" Cole wanted to share would be manageable situations, like another sudden increase in wheat prices or a bill stalled in committee. Then again, a US airbase might have just blown up.

Because three serious attempts had been made on Don's life in the past few months, they were both aware that Lawrence might suddenly become the one in charge. Despite the fact that details of military and terrorist actions made the vice president nervous, Cole wanted to be sure the second-in-command had a constant grasp of things. In reality, doing this taught Lawrence only one thing: Regardless of how capable he'd thought he would be as president in the past, exposure to the gory details of life and death situations had led him to one conclusion: He didn't want Don's job.

The president looked at his watch. "I see it's late, but I'll be busy in the morning, so I'd like to give you an update on several items." He pointed to a wet bar at the end of the room. "I had your special water brought in, if you'd like some."

Lawrence shook his head. "No, thank you. Go ahead."

"Well, *my* morning started with a reality check. I met with the Joint Chiefs, and the new assessments are in. Even with the recent realignments, we still haven't plugged the drain on troop strength and weapons reserves. The main hemorrhages, of course, are our commitments to the Alliance. Bottom line is that we're still vulnerable should a national emergency arise."

Larry considered the figures that had crossed his desk in recent weeks. "Well, there's certainly no money for another increase in military personnel."

"I know. But that's just the front bumper. The rest of the bus is still coming. After that, I had a meeting with the Space Agency guys. Remember the backup systems for the space station the Agency threw so much money at five years ago?"

Lawrence nodded.

"I realize they did it because they figured the foreign hardware might not be provided on time or might fail. But I guess that's the rub as well, isn't it? The French, the Russians, and the Japanese all got in a twist because our agency assumed they couldn't come through with quality on time."

Lawrence frowned. "Well, in some cases, that was true, wasn't it?"

"That's our take on it, but the facts haven't changed feelings in the matter. Remember the last shuttle mission—you know, the one we had to waylay so it could bring back our damaged spy satellite?"

Lawrence remembered how Don had him send shock waves through the "old boy" network at the Space Agency once the shuttle returned home. He nodded.

"We not only had to bring back the satellite," Don continued, "but some Russian and French equipment couldn't be delivered—because we had a satellite we couldn't let their astronauts see in our cargo bay. Well, since the Russian and French parts couldn't be delivered, we used ours. And now it's coming back to bite us. You were briefed on the loss of the experimental probe yesterday, weren't you?"

"Yes," the vice president said. He'd inquired about the monetary loss to the US when he first heard about the incident and seen it was substantial. "You think the loss of the probe was due to *our* equipment? Are you saying you think the others will try to hold us liable?"

"Who knows? This project is such a runaway catastrophe." Don rolled his eyes. "The average guy on the street pictures some wistful television series about space. You know, the nations of Earth coming together technologically, bringing world peace, ending poverty, conquering space, or at least defending us against a future threat from giant space insects."

Lawrence finished Don's thoughts. "What we have, though, are billions of dollars in parts and personnel floating around in space—half of which are already stretched to the max or don't fit together."

"Exactly." The president looked at his watch again. "I'm just trying to give this to you in some semblance of order."

Lawrence's stomach tightened as he saw Don trying to formulate his next statements. How bad was this news? His eyes followed Don's gaze to a bronze sculpture of an eagle on a bookshelf. He held is breath and waited.

"Late this morning, I had a meeting with Bryce," Cole finally said, referring to the Secretary of State, Gavin Bryce. "He told me the Russians were ready to lodge formal complaints, saying we're 'sabotaging' their technical efforts in the space station." Don exhaled heavily. "Then the plot thickened. I just got a call thirty minutes ago, saying that one of our astronauts–Trevor King–and one of the Russian astronauts got in an altercation up there tonight. They had to be separated and confined to their respective quarters. I'm hoping the parties will cool off while we decide what should be done. Both of them would have come home on the changed shuttle mission; but they're stuck there right now. Too bad we can't call the cops and have them picked up. Who knows what the Russians will make of this? As head of the Space Agency, you need be the point man on the investigation. Put together a team if you need to."

"Have you spoken to anyone representing Russia yet?"

"Not directly. I figure we'll exchange some words shortly. Our astronauts maintain it was just a shoving match, but we can't afford to let this escalate."

Lawrence was secretly relieved. *This isn't so bad. We've worked out bigger misunderstandings with the Russians before. And he's right, it's good for me to know all these things. I'm learning to get a handle on situations with violent potential.*

Before the vice president could relish his new-found confidence, Don leaned forward and spoke quietly. "But that's not all, Lawrence. Late this afternoon I got the most recent update on China. Hard intelligence confirms several new pieces of technological weaponry are up and at least some of it is functional. It's a clone of our Echelon II system, with full pulse capability. While none of it is over us at the moment, it's all in orbit and could be positioned over Japan in less than three minutes, and over us in less than half an hour." Cole ran his fingers across the stubble on his chin and looked directly at the vice president as he carefully considered his next words.

Lawrence felt his stomach tightening again. "That's not everything is it?"

"No."

Lawrence now felt certain the worst piece of news had been saved for last. "Maybe I'll have that drink of water after all." He stood up, strode to the small refrigerator, retrieved the bottle, then walked back and sat down before he opened the cap and took a big slug of it—as if it were whiskey and it would brace him for anything else Don might say. "Shoot."

"At seven forty-five this evening, I had a meeting with representatives of China. They are *demanding* the US withdraw from current 'negotiations' with Japan." Don inhaled slowly then spoke again. "You and I both know that if we tuck our tails and run, Japan may go down. Just for a moment we'll forget the satellites, the missiles, the aircraft, the ships, the troops and all that. Even if it were a bloodless thing. . . ."

Lawrence screwed the cap back onto his water bottle as he completed Don's sentence. ". . . if Japan folds, the economic crisis will flatten us." He already felt as if he'd been struck and flattened. As panic rose, he started speaking again, more to himself than to Don. "But it's not as simple as that, is it? Only God knows if we could survive a conflict with them."

"I know it's a lot to absorb all at once. Your plane was in the air when it started unfolding so I decided to wait until you got here to tell you. We're gonna have to work on a response. I'll be meeting with members of congress and our advisors within the hour. Consultations will continue tomorrow, so you'll have to take up some of the slack in my schedule. We want things to appear as normal as possible while we work on what to do."

The vice president looked as it he'd frozen to the chair. Don tried to offer reassurance to him. "These are serious situations to be sure, Lawrence, but I'm sure we can emerge on the other side. I know we'll be led to the right decisions."

A few minutes later, the ashen-faced vice president left the White House.

CHAPTER 12

PHILADELPHIA — April 27th

Zac Gordon tried not to squirm while his supervisor, Ms. A. Glad-Butterfield, gave him yet another lecture from her vast storehouse of wisdom. Not staring at the tiny, red lips painted on top of her regular-sized mouth had become easier, but Zac still had trouble finding a way to appear attentive while not actually looking at the woman. Dozens of things about her begged for cruel jokes. She'd dyed her hair too dark, she wore clothes too small for her ample size, and she sat in her giant, leather chair like the queen of some large country. Even if she wasn't his boss, he'd despise her.

". . . so, by eliminating these maintenance positions you saved," Ms. Butterfield continued. "Eighteen thousand, four hundred, fifty-seven dollars!"

He tried not to look disgusted. *Those weren't positions we eliminated, they were people.*

She had long fingernails, so she used an inverted pen to touch the numbers on the keyboard. He watched her happily punching out the figures and thought, *You know, thinking of her as a bloated snowman is just too friendly a picture. She'd be more true-to-life if she were green and had a large wart on her chin.*

She continued speaking. ". . . and by following my simple suggestions, just look at the costs we've cut out of your budget! And at virtually no loss to you."

Oh yeah? YOU didn't have to fire the two guys we let go last month. One of them is so old, he probably won't be able to get a job anyplace else. If I didn't need this job so bad . . . Zac cleared his throat before speaking. "I'm not so sure that cutting personnel was prudent, Ms. Butterfield. We were working with a virtual skeleton crew as it was. There are only so many tasks the rest of us can absorb. We're going to see a dramatic loss of efficiency if we encounter any unexpected problems."

"If and when that time comes, we'll re-evaluate," she said coldly.

The pause before she went on to the next topic allowed Zac to realize how late it had gotten. He could almost hear the seconds ticking away. He had a ten o'clock appointment, and the final figures for it weren't done yet. He chided himself for waiting so long to finish the necessary update. He'd been out late every night this week and hadn't exactly been operating at peak performance. *It's a good thing I can work under pressure.*

"Just two more items to note." Ms. A. Glad-Butterfield said, "Your 'Exchange Event' idea seems to be working out to be profitable for the Arena. I must admit I had some doubts at first."

I had to fight you tooth and nail, he thought.

"But," she said wistfully, "I don't suppose anyone is right one hundred percent of the time."

A picture of a newspaper slamming to the pavement zoomed into Zac's thoughts. The headline on the paper read *"THE END OF THE WORLD IS NEAR!!! Thousands jump to their deaths after the 'infallible' Ms. A. Glad-Butterfield admits error!"* He had to force himself to concentrate on her words.

". . . I just didn't think a flea market type thing was suited to the image we wanted for our facilities."

"But," Zac countered, "I believe it's been profitable both monetarily and in boosting our image. Exchange Events prove that we have a heart for the people of the city, not just business. It's an 'image' that will bring us business for years to come."

"Yes. That's my last point," she said, looking at her agenda. "I know we haven't seen eye to eye on a number of things, but I think you've learned a thing or two in these past months. Congratulations are in order. Is everything on track for the conference?"

He coughed. "Yes. I've got everything under control so far. I'll be meeting with their representative later today. And I've got an appointment for another event," he said, casually looking at his watch, "in just a matter of minutes actually. So, if we're through here . . ."

"By all means. Good luck."

Once back in his office, Zac's fingers flew around the keyboard on his computer. In addition to his presentation of the current preparations for the annual World Conference on Spirituality, another proposal needed to be ready. If he hurried, he could have duplicate copies printed out just as their man arrived.

Hard times made it difficult to keep something as large as the arena busy. They currently had two dependable money-makers. One of them was sporting events—which were sometimes the only diversion people had from their desperate lives. The other was a chaotic phenomenon known as an "Exchange Event" which was sponsored by a consolidated group of businesspeople. These weekly happenings involved renting a booth, table, or "floater badge" (for those, who wanted to work their way through the crowds) to anyone who had something to market. Virtually anything could be bought, sold, or traded at the Exchange. It was a combination open market/pawn-shop/temp-worker/talent show *event*.

The biggest boost to the arena, however, would be the upcoming World Conference on Spirituality. In the wake of riots three years ago, organizers for the conference considered moving it to another city, but Zac worked beside city leaders and hotel owners to convince them Philadelphia would be up and running for the event. Being a part of this successful effort made him some influential friends in the business community, and helped to secure his job. But Zac reminded himself daily not to take his current favorable position for granted. Ms. A. Glad-Butterfield could turn on him any moment and give his job to one of the multitudes of people applying for it every week.

He glanced at his watch again and sped up his pace. A representative for a medical convention would be arriving any minute. While he made last-minute changes, his secretary, Barbara, busied herself in the outer office printing agendas for appointments later in the day. She looked up when she heard someone enter the room. A lovely woman with strawberry blond hair stood before her.

"Hello, I'm Judy Olsen," the woman said in a pleasant voice. "Dr. Doyle couldn't make it this morning. I'm his assistant and I'm here to keep the appointment with Mr. Gordon."

"Let me just call in and tell him you've arrived," Barbara said, punching in the number for Zac's office. "Mr. Gordon? Dr. Doyle couldn't make it this morning, but his assistant, Ms. Olsen, is here to keep his appointment."

"*What?*" Zac, said. "He's not here?"

Ms. Olsen watched Barbara, who said serenely, "That's right."

Zac drummed his fingers on his desk. "Isn't that just what I need?" he said, more to himself than to Barbara. "Okay. See if there's room to move my next appointment if necessary. I may have to backtrack and explain half of this to her."

"Yes," Barbara replied.

"And tell her I'd rather be getting orthopedic surgery on both my feet than doing this, would ya?"

Barbara couldn't help smiling. She knew as soon as Zac saw this woman he'd be on his best behavior. *I wouldn't be at all surprised if he found a way to schedule a "dinner meeting" with this one,* she mused.

"Certainly, Mr. Gordon. I'll tell Ms. Olsen," she said, and hung up before looking at the woman again. "If you'll take a seat, he'll be ready momentarily."

Back in his office, as Gordon hung up the line he said, "Mizzz Olsen," and jotted it down on his computer pad. Within a minute the necessary changes had been made to the contract and highlighted. He straightened his tie and put on a coat while he continued to hope the absence of Dr. Doyle wouldn't tie up a lot of extra time. He'd be running behind on a number of projects today.

On the other hand, the assistant *was* a woman. Gordon smoothed his hair, threw a mint in the air, and caught it in his mouth before buzzing Barbara and telling her to send Ms. Olsen in. He rose from his chair and buttoned his coat while he moved to the door.

CHAPTER 13

WASHINGTON D.C. — April 27th

President of the United States, Donald Larson Cole, sat quietly at his desk in the Oval Office. A wistful look came to his face before he opened the top drawer to his left and pulled out a small dark-blue, velvet pouch. Years of being carried about from place to place in Don's briefcase had taken their toll on the little bag. Constant chafing had worn off the blue fuzz and now it had a leather-like appearance.

Don carefully opened the drawstring and poured the contents of the bag into the palm of his hand. The shiny medal attached to a ribbon had been awarded to his father in Vietnam when Don was a toddler. A sense of longing briefly settled on him. How he missed his father. Joseph Cole had been a man of such wisdom before Alzheimer's had stolen his mind and then his life.

Don set the medal in the center of the blotter on his desk and just looked at it for a while. *Was Dad ever sorry he'd fought and suffered injuries for something that ended so badly? Was he ever sorry he'd participated in a war that became so unpopular? Was he angry at the lack of gratitude for his sacrifice?*

If so, he'd never said it to Don.

What would he have thought of all the conflicts the country is facing now?

Don slowly shook his head as he considered the tenuous positions he'd face today. Tensions between China and Japan continued to mount. Ambassador to China, Joseph Tarrance, remained at the ready, and it was hoped negotiations could be resumed. When the Chinese delegation walked out of the talks a week ago they said they wouldn't return unless their "rights" in the region were recognized.

As pressures continued to rise, additional Alliance forces, including American soldiers, were sent to the area to help protect Japan's interests. These forces faced real threats—not only from China, but from nationalistic factions in Japan. But if Japan's government toppled, a domino effect would send a shockwave around the world. With the American economy barely treading water, the loss of Japan in the world market would be devastating.

An even more ominous problem loomed: For decades, the US and other nations happily consumed inexpensive goods from Chinese forced labor. Americans looked the other way while the government of China crushed opposition within its own borders, stole weapons technology, and built a formidable military machine. Now, security advisors and the Joint Chiefs warned Don, it might be too late to stand against them should the Chinese opt to expand their boundaries.

The president eyed the stack of folders on his desk, each one describing the tensions, factors, and possible outcomes for different conflicts around the world. Any one of them could be a flashpoint for global conflict.

In Indonesia, a ghastly civil war, unlikely to be won by either side, continued. International forces had suffered large losses in efforts to protect civilians from the continuing slaughter.

The face-off between India and Pakistan continued. US soldiers, sent by former President Todd, had been deployed in the region for quite some time in a contingent of Alliance forces that occupied the border between the countries. Despite this, ground troops from the warring sides still managed to engage each other in sporadic fighting. Only a month ago, the Alliance intervened mere hours before a nuclear launch. Don feared it was only a matter of time before one side or the other pushed the button. Was it time to remove our troops while we still could? Hadn't one of Don's complaints about Todd been that he'd sent too much of America's military out to participate in too many foreign police actions?

He rubbed his eyes. If we pull out, will it remove the last restraints against all out war?

In addition to this, the Middle East continued to simmer. The situation had been complex for generations, but an added complication now existed. Shortly before he lost the election, former President Todd allowed and "informal liaison" to engage in talks with Middle East factions. That liaison, had all but promised that the US would abandon previous agreements in the region in favor of a "more equitable" settlement ensuring the rights of "the majority" population in the area. Now the situation threatened to heat up again, and the leaders who had received these assurances warned of violence on a whole new scale if America didn't follow up on her offers. Meanwhile, Russia threatened action if the US didn't back off.

Diplomatic relations between all of the old "superpower" countries had reached an alarming low before Don took office. Despite his efforts, things hadn't improved.

Don picked up his father's medal and put it away before spreading his hands on his desk and bowing his head. *God, is there anything worth the lives of our young people? If we do nothing, won't more people die and multitudes live under terrible oppression? Todd sold us out on so many levels. . . . Show me what to do, Lord.*

The tone sounded and the light on his intercom flashed.

"Yes," he said, touching the light.

"The Secretary of State and the Secretary of Defense have arrived with the Joint Chiefs."

"I'll be there momentarily."

"Yes, sir."

At the meeting, Don learned more about the loss of fifty-seven American soldiers who had been killed during the previous twenty-four hours. Fifteen were killed at sea outside Japanese waters in a training accident. Twenty-one had perished in an ambush of a small village in Indonesia. Four were lost in crossfire on the India Pakistan border. Seventeen had been killed within the past hour in a plane crash involving the transport of troops to Puerto Rico.

At one point, Don looked around the room. "I can't decide which is worse . . . the fact that twenty-five have given their lives in actual fighting or that thirty-two probably died due to incompetence and/or deteriorating equipment. Billions of dollars have been spent on high-tech gadgets that are nearly impossible to maintain now the companies that made them have folded and formed new conglomerates. The new conglomerates claim to have no responsibility for the gadgets, but will be happy to sign contracts to make new, improved gadgets.

"We've already made commitments to seek simple, functional, and repairable military hardware. The problem is the lag time. While we wait on improvements, lives depend on current equipment. Ladies and gentlemen, this must be remedied as soon as possible."

As the meeting ended, all agreed American troops should stay where they'd been placed while a technical problem was resolved. An old Executive Order allowing a large number of US troops to be deployed under Alliance Force command remained in effect. It was decided the language of the Order could be taken to mean those troops would be at the *total* discretion of the Commander of the *Alliance* Force. Cole would soon have the order amended or revoked to ensure all US forces remained under the ultimate control of their Commander-in-Chief, the President of the United States.

By the end of the day, an envoy had been dispatched to the Middle East and a message sent to Moscow reiterating America's position: The solutions offered by Todd's informal liaison were neither proper nor binding. In the future, all offers would be made by a formal representative of the United States who had legitimate authority to negotiate binding agreements which didn't violate long-standing commitments in the region. Don could only await their responses.

CHAPTER 14

PHILADELPHIA — April 27th

In the Events Office of the Philadelphia Arena, Judy Olsen smiled and shook Zac's hand as she spoke. "Nice to meet you, Mr. Gordon. Dr. Doyle had to be out of town this morning. Sorry for the inconvenience. I should be pretty up to speed with things though."

Zac realized he was staring at her and that he hadn't let go of her hand. Not only did she look amazingly like someone he'd known years ago, Ms. Olsen was probably about the same age she would have been. He released her hand and moved back to his seat behind the desk. "No problem. I have the details he requested listed here."

"'Zac' Gordon . . . as in Zachariah?" she asked.

"Zachary, actually."

She squinted for a second. "Well, one would be a derivative of the other. Let's see . . . the entomology of names is one of my favorite things. I used to know what that name meant." She seated herself and then shrugged. "Oh well. Can't think of it now."

"May I have my secretary get you anything? Herbal tea? A muffin?" he asked, wanting to change the subject.

Ms. Olsen smiled. "No thanks."

She placed her briefcase on her lap, and his eyes were drawn to her delicate hands. He picked up the clip screen and passed it across the desk to her.

"This is the document with all the figures and the changes Dr. Doyle wanted," he said. "You may want to take a few minutes to go over it first, then we can cover any questions you might have. We'll make whatever changes you need and then we'll both initial them."

"Great. Thanks." She took the screen and began scanning the document.

Zac allowed himself to glance at her again while she read. Yes. The beautiful skin. The same hair. The eyes were slightly different, though.

Momentarily a younger face, filled with radiance and beauty, flashed into his mind as if it were yesterday. He remembered her looking up from a book and smiling at him.

"Mr. Gordon?. . . Mr. Gordon?"

Zachary focused. Judy Olsen was speaking to him.

"Oh. I'm sorry, I've had so much to think of this week," he said while he rubbed two fingers on his forehead, "I've got a bit of a headache, and I guess I wasn't paying attention. Yes? You were saying?"

"On paragraph seventeen. Will you make a mark there, and we'll go back to it?"

Although the meeting lasted less than the scheduled hour, Zac felt increasingly ill and struggled to remain businesslike. "Well," he finally said, grateful it was coming to a close, "you came so well prepared, I can't seem to think of any other details that need to be covered."

"Great," she said sweetly, before returning his clip screen. "You can send the contract to Dr. Doyle's office. He'll call tomorrow if he has any other questions."

Zac rose to his feet, they exchanged goodbyes and she moved to the door. Just as she opened it, she turned. "The Lord remembers."

"What?" Zac asked.

"I remember what your name means. Zachary means, 'the Lord remembers.' Did you know that?"

Zac's countenance seemed to darken. "Yes, I knew that," he responded.

She realized this might have been what made him act so odd throughout the whole meeting and she was sorry that her attempt to be friendly had ended so badly.

"Hope your headache gets better," she said before leaving his office.

As soon as she closed the door, Zac threw himself into preparations for his next appointment, actually glad he was running behind on preparations. At least he'd have no time to think.

When the workday ended, he decided not to stay and work late. He'd promised himself that very morning he would go straight home after work and get a decent night's sleep.

Once he got home, though, he couldn't rest. After a small snack, he turned on the TV. He watched an old sci-fi movie, then browsed through other programs with his new remote control, a high-tech gadget he'd recently purchased that took voice commands and operated several systems in his apartment.

After scanning the guide for fifteen minutes, he realized there wasn't a thing he wanted to watch on television. He decided to listen to music while he played a game on his computer, and spoke to his remote as he moved to his desk. "Television off. Activate sound system two. Activate 'favorite songs.' Volume up." He sat the remote next to his screen and called up the game he wanted to play. Still, something lingered at the edge of his thoughts. Something he wanted to keep at bay.

He started the game with a great amount of intensity, but soon relaxed. Within minutes, his mind drifted back to the first time he'd ever seen Stephanie Neilson.

There he was. Once again, a new kid in a new school, sitting alone at lunch. Stephanie and a bunch of girls made their entrance to the cafeteria, laughing and talking as if they were the only ones in the room. After a few minutes though, she noticed him and came to his table.

"You're the new kid, aren't you?"

Zac at sixteen, a junior, still hadn't hit his "growth spurt." He looked up from his hamburger and after the jolt of seeing her, he said, "That depends. I could tell you who I am, but if you're not with the CIA, I might have to shoot ya' afterwards."

Stephanie, also sixteen, had the confidence he only pretended to have. She smiled and said, "Hi. I'm Stephanie Neilson."

Zac had learned early in life that humor was a great tension-breaker and he quickly thought of a silly remark to make her laugh. She sat down and he kept her laughing for the remainder of the lunch period. When the bell rang, she'd said goodbye and rushed off to class.

It turned out that Stephanie was in two of his afternoon classes: computer science and algebra. As the weeks went on, he found himself being a bigger clown in the classes he shared with her than in any of the others. Even though it sometimes landed him in hot water, it was all worth it if only to hear Stephanie laugh. After she found out that, despite his comedy routines, Zac was a virtual genius, she sought his help with homework.

He'd been more than happy to tutor her. It was a way to spend more time with Steph at her house, a peaceful sanctuary from the stormy life he knew at his own. If her parents noticed he was a bit too boisterous, they didn't show it. Her father, an elder in a local church, seemed to genuinely like Zac. Her mother always hugged him and welcomed him when he came in. Although a bit embarrassed by their affection, he secretly craved it. This had been the only time in his life he felt he belonged someplace.

Several times a week he tried to help Steph understand math and computers—two things which seemed entirely foreign to her. With Zac's help, however, she passed both subjects, and by the end of the school year, she considered him one of her closest friends. Zac, on the other hand, had fallen desperately in love.

During this time Zachary started attending Stephanie's church. At first, he did it only because Steph went there. Although his own family had gone to church for a few short bursts when he was smaller, he'd never *willingly* gone to church before. Looking back, he'd say the services at Stephanie's church were stiff and formal; but back then, the sweetness and the life he felt in the Neilson's home made it all seem softer, and his love for Stephanie made him desire to lead a life that would be pleasing to her. Eventually, church began to mean more to him than just a means of capturing her heart, but this had been his secret. He stashed the Bible the church gave him in the attic for fear of being ridiculed by his father and younger siblings, who gave him a hard time about going to church.

Near the end of his junior year, Zac prayed to receive Jesus as his savior and got baptized. After that, he didn't mind the teasing so much. A whole other life had opened for him. He'd sometimes spend hours holed up in the attic—the only place he could be alone—memorizing scriptures. During those times he'd fantasize about becoming a famous preacher. Of course, in his dreams, Steph would be right there with him, looking at him with admiration and love.

The harsh reality of life, however, threatened to dash Zac's dreams. His father, Harold Gordon, was an alcoholic who had dragged the family around the country as he went from job to job. Each time Mr. Gordon became unemployed, there'd be a season of intense anger, followed by remorse, a vow to make a fresh start, a move, a short spate of soberness, and a new job. But as bills for a family of six, and problems of day to day life got to him, the drinking binges would begin again.

As summer came that year, Zac recognized the downward end of the cycle had started. It was only a matter of time before his dad was jobless again. In an uncharacteristically responsible maneuver, Zac took a job working six days a week in a car wash to bring extra cash to the family. This time, he wanted to be sure they had enough income to stay in one place awhile. Stephanie went to visit cousins for the summer, and Zac wanted to still be around when she returned.

When summer vacation finally drew to a close, Zac had grown more than half a foot taller, and was working overtime to be able to buy himself some "cool" clothes. In August, the long awaited reunion with Steph took place and she saw him with new eyes. Her funny friend had become a young man— and she began to love him as much as he loved her. They started to dream of a future together.

Just after Thanksgiving, she invited him for a special weekend "retreat" given for church teens. Stephanie was only *part* of the reason he wanted to go. Without the sanctuary of the Neilson's home that summer, he'd had to endure more time at home, which was once again a war zone. He'd often stayed awake nights reading Psalms. The man who wrote most of them—David—seemed to have had a pretty stormy life, too. When Zac read the words, it was as if someone was reaching across thousands of years, encouraging him to go on. He believed it was God. When Steph asked him to go to the retreat, he felt drawn there by more than his affection for her. Something inside was calling him.

Almost against his will, Zac now recalled a specific moment during the retreat. The speaker for the event had spent two days talking to them about what serving God would mean. As the man spoke, Zac's heart bounced around like a basketball. Every word seemed to be addressed directly to him. When he'd read the scriptures for each session, he felt the words were almost jumping off the page and speaking to him. On the final night, the speaker asked all of them to bow their heads. He asked if anyone felt called to be an evangelist or a pastor.

As he sat there, Zac would've sworn he'd heard a voice say, "That's you, Zac, stand up."

Before he thought about it, he stood. The next thing he knew, he'd gone up to the front of the church and everyone began praying for him.

The phone in his apartment rang and jolted Zac to the present, causing him to bump his remote control onto the floor. He quickly picked it up.

"Music pause. Incoming caller identification."

A computer-generated female voice came through the apartment's speaker system and said, "Current incoming call from . . . Hoffman's Sporting Goods. To activate answering service, say 'record' or let the line ring. To reject call, say 'reject.' To forward call. . ."

Zac picked up the phone receiver. "Yeah."

"It's me, Michael."

"What do you need, Mike?"

"I wanted to tell you I had to put Ben in the hospital this afternoon. He's got pneumonia again."

"Oh?"

"You want to go visit him with me?"

Zac couldn't bear to see Ben lying on a bed in the hospital. Not today. He cleared his throat. "Uhhh. No. I think I'm coming down with something and I probably shouldn't go near him."

He could feel Michael's condemnation oozing through the long silence on the line. Despite the guilt he felt, a compromise was the best Zac could do. He cleared his throat again. "Well, tell me what room he's in and I'll try to give him a call later."

Michael's spoke quietly. "City Hospital. Room 815."

"Maybe in a day or so, if I'm feeling better, I'll drop by. . . . In case my call doesn't reach him, send him my best, will ya?"

"Sure. Talk to you later."

Zac hung up and sank back into his chair.

A picture unfolded in his mind. Stephanie, thin and pale in her hospital bed, wearing a pink hat to cover the loss of her beautiful hair.

Zac had talked one of her girlfriends into a special visit with Steph to cheer her up. They went to her room with costumes and props. Zac sat in a wheelchair with a big red nose and a rainbow wig that had huge patches shaved off. Their mutual friend, Valerie, had dressed as a nurse and they'd put several helium balloons on an IV pole. Just before they entered Stephanie's room, Zac inhaled an extra balloon of helium.

Steph smiled weakly as they careened to the side of her bed with Zac complaining in a voice octaves higher than usual, "Oh!!! Slow down!!! My head is about to spin right off!"

"Well, okay," Valerie replied in a cruel tone, "but you simply must eat your lunch today." She then whipped out a covered tray and plopped it on Zac's lap.

Steph, who sometimes felt as if she were being tortured instead of cured, let out a small giggle.

"What is it?" Zac asked in a tremulous tone.

"Robert, our cook, prepares only the best in this hospital!" Nurse Valerie said. Then, taking off the cover to the tray, she exclaimed, "Viola! Chicken RRRRO-BERRRR!" with her best french accent.

On the tray lay a fake, plucked chicken—complete with head and feet. Zac eyed it with suspicion. "Chicken Rrro-berrr, eh?"

"You simply must eat it!" Nurse Valerie demanded.

"Okay," he said. He gnawed on the mid-section of the bird before throwing it back on the tray. "Oi! This chicken tastes like rubber!"

Valerie put her hands on her hips. "Maybe he said Chicken *RRRRRub*-berrrr."

Stephanie laughed.

"And, look! There's hair on my food!" Zac yelled. He picked up a long clump of black hair. "It *couldn't* be mine," he declared, while holding it up to his forehead by a hairy spot on the rainbow wig.

Valerie was no longer able to maintain character. She laughed as hard as Steph.

When Zac pulled the lock of hair away from his face, his clown nose fell off and landed on the tray next to the chicken. Always able to improvise, he snatched it up and cried loudly, "Oh no! I knew I'd loose my hair, but no one said *anything* about my *nose* falling off!"

Both girls became hysterical and Zac was in his glory.

Later, when Valerie left, Zac got a regular chair and sat near the bed. After a moment, he reached up and tried to gently straighten her hat which had slipped to one side of her head. Fearing at first that he might remove the hat, she grabbed it and held on.

"I was just fixing it," he said, quickly pulling his hand away. Then, he leaned over and put his face close to Stephanie's.

"It'll grow back," he said softly.

"Sometimes," she confided, "I'm afraid it won't."

"That's okay," he said in a lighter tone, "then I'll just shave my head. We'll be the only bald couple in the ministry."

She smiled and squeezed his hand.

He kissed her cheek. "Just get well for me . . ."

Zac suddenly stopped the daydream and looked around his apartment. "I gotta get out of here," he said aloud.

He hurriedly put his shoes on, then donned a sweater as he left his apartment. Once outside, he decided not to drive anywhere. He needed to walk. He kept a brisk pace for several blocks while he formulated a plan for the evening.

I could go to one of my favorite restaurants. . . yes, I could go to Marcianos and have dinner. I could give that new girl at the office, Julie, a call and ask her to join me there. He rounded a corner and stopped.

Maybe I should call her now.

As he paused, it started to rain. The first few drops quickly turned into a deluge and he ducked into a nearby bus stop for cover.

In recent years, goods and services previously rendered by the government were being shared by corporations. In exchange for being able to advertise or profit in some way from the enterprises, private businesses helped with such tasks as delivering mail, providing water, replacing aging sewer and natural gas lines. Every day it seemed somebody thought of a new way to "co-op" with the government. Bus stops were yet another example.

As soon as Zac stepped into the bus stop, he was quickly enveloped in a herd of other pedestrians hoping to escape the rain. The enclosure with benches along three walls, stood about 10 feet high. The reason for the added height was to enable those inside the bus stop to view the top portion of the walls.

In days gone by, passengers could read or ignore the advertisements posted in the stop as they waited for a bus. Now it wasn't printed matter vying for attention, it was television—complete with sound. The top of each wall was a screen where products or ideas could be shown. Where would it end?

To his dismay, Zac soon realized this particular bus stop had apparently been rented by some church group. A live signal, broadcast to who knows how many bus stops, gave short Bible teachings and offered prayer. When Zac entered the enclosure, the man on the screens closed a Bible and said, "I know that some of you out there today are burdened. But God cares about everything that concerns you. Can I pray for you?"

Zac rolled his eyes. *Oh great, just when I thought it couldn't get any worse.*

All the walls in the enclosure carried the image of the man who spoke. Zac soon noticed the guy was concentrating so hard it looked as if someone had one of his toes in a vice.

Rain pounded louder on the roof of the bus stop, but the sound-sensitive system turned up the volume as the man on the screens began to pray. "Lord, there are people out there today who are tired and discouraged. But You are our Comforter. You are an ever-present help in time of trouble. Open their eyes, Lord, to see the help You are sending their way. . . . There are so many people whose hearts are broken. But You said in Your word that You were a man of sorrows and well acquainted with grief. . . that a broken and contrite heart You would not despise. You understand our pain."

A welcome distraction came as a bus arrived and a brief exchange of people took place before the bus departed. Zac tried to move closer to the opening, thinking he could possibly make a dash for home, but he ended up being jammed in a corner, tighter than before. Like it or not, he became a captive audience.

The man on the screens said, "The Lord is telling me there's a girl out there who's looking for a job. . . but He says to seek Him first. You're looking in the wrong direction."

Right! I bet there's only a million girls looking for a job today! As if God talks to anybody. What a joke.

The man on the screen continued, ". . . and there's a guy watching me right now. You're saying to yourself this is all a joke, that He doesn't speak anymore. . . ."

Zac froze while listening to the words.

"But God knows that you didn't always think serving Him was a joke. He called to you a long time ago. You heard Him. You pledged yourself. . . . And He wants me to remind you. . . 'the Lord remembers.'"

Suddenly the bus stop seemed to have no more air. Zac had to escape. He pushed with all his might through the tangled mass of wet coats, arms, umbrellas, and packages. Finally, he popped out through the opening into an unrelenting downpour.

As he ran down the sidewalk toward his apartment building, a piece of a conversation he'd had with Steph's dad in a hospital chapel replayed in his head.

"But, Mr. Neilson, why can't God just heal her?" he'd asked.

"Miracles passed away with the apostles, son."

"That can't be true! Why would He stop doing miracles?"

Mr. Neilson's face filled with pain. "Well, son, once we got the Bible, that was all that we needed to keep the church running."

"How stupid!" Zac had said in a rage. "Why would He have bothered to write down all that stuff about miracles and tell people how to use His gifts if He wasn't going to do it anymore?"

The older man put an arm around him. "Oh, God, how I wish you were right, Zac. But the truth is . . . His ways are higher than our ways."

Zac yanked away and pointed to the cross hanging on the wall of the chapel. "What would be the point of praying or anything else if God wasn't going to do anything?"

"True prayer asks for God's will, not our own, son."

"And God's will is just for everyone to die? No! I won't serve a God who does nothing!" He ran from the chapel to Steph's room with hot tears streaming down his face. The room was darkened and her eyes were closed. He leaned down next to her.

"I won't serve Him without you, Stephanie. I won't serve a God who doesn't heal, or speak, or care."

Her eyes remained closed, but she'd put her hand on the back of his head. "He's a good God, Zac. You'll see."

The scene in his mind ended, and Zac stopped running. He looked up into the pouring rain, and spoke aloud. "I thought we had a deal. I wasn't going to bother You anymore, and You weren't going to bother me."

He realized as he finished the sentence that people who had gathered under store awnings along the sidewalk were staring at him as if he were fresh out of a sanitarium. He stopped talking and walked. There was no point in hurrying home. His clothes were soaked already.

As he moved along, he began thinking, *It was all just a scam. I only imagined He called me because I wanted her to love me. Life is a pain or it's a joke.*

He entered the lobby of his apartment building and heard the security guard speaking to a man and a woman with a small boy. All of the family members were shabbily dressed and the boy coughed repeatedly.

"No," the guard said, "you'll have to move along. You can't stay in here."

Zac went to the elevator and pushed the "up" button.

"But can't you see it's pouring out there?" the man pleaded. "My boy is sick. We were going to catch a bus, but it's just raining too hard to get there."

The boy leaned against his mother's leg. She picked him up and spoke lovingly to him. "It's okay, Joey. We'll be home soon."

"I can call you a cab," the guard said. "But that's the best I can do. If a resident asks about you being in here and you're not someone's guest, I could lose my job."

The man spoke softly, "All I've got is money for the boy's medicine and for the bus. Listen, I'll go outside, but couldn't you just let my wife and the boy sit here for a few minutes till the rain slows down?"

"Sorry. It might rain all night. You have to—"

Zac stepped up to the group. He looked at the stranger and said the first name that came to his mind. "John! Is that you?" He pumped the confused man's hand, then moved to the woman and gave her and the boy a little hug. "Edna! You've lost some weight, haven't you? And this couldn't be baby Joey, could it? Boy, how time flies!"

The man and woman looked stunned.

"It's *me*! Zac!" he said, trying to give them a cue.

"Oh!" the man said, catching on. "Zac . . . how are you?"

Zachary looked at the security guard. "I know these people. This is John, that's Edna, and this is little Joey. If anyone asks, they're my guests."

The security guard knew a lie when he heard one, but as long as Zachary Gordon wanted to take responsibility for them, why should he care? "Sure, whatever," he said, turning and walking away.

"So . . ." Zac said, wringing out the bottom of his sweater, "what brings you all the way here?"

"We had to bring Joey to the doctor. None of the docs near our place will take him without us being in the Program." The man leaned forward and whispered. "Thanks. All we need to do is stay here till the rain lets up enough to get down around the corner. Then, there'll be plenty of places we can wait without causing a problem."

Zac asked them to wait in the lobby for a few minutes while he changed clothes, then he drove them to a pharmacy in his car. While "Edna" got the prescription, Zac entertained her husband and the little boy in the car with slight-of-hand tricks. Soon, the child had his medicine and fell asleep in his father's arms as Zac drove the family home. The father carefully cradled his son while getting out of the vehicle.

"Hey," Zac called to the woman as she exited the car.

She leaned back in and Zac pressed the last of his cash into her hand.

"Here. Buy yourselves a good dinner."

Her eyes brimmed with tears. "Thank God. He must have timed all this so we'd cross your path. May He richly bless you."

Zac didn't bother to correct her. She meant well. "Yeah. Take care."

He went home and went to bed. The last thing that went through his mind before he fell asleep were Stephanie's words to him that day in the hospital.

"Don't look at this like God doesn't care, Zac. Maybe I'm done."

"No! That can't be true! There's still lots for you to do. . . . Look at me, Steph. There's too much for you to do here. You can't leave me."

She closed her eyes. "I had a dream today, Zac. I was home and it was the most wonderful place. And there were so many people there. And more people kept coming. A lot of them thanked me for inviting them, and encouraging them. But I couldn't remember doing those things. I hadn't even seen them before. I said to them, 'But I don't remember inviting you, I don't even remember seeing you before.' I was confused. The man next to me seemed to understand, so I asked him, 'Why do these people think I invited them here?' He said, 'In a way, you *did*.' The man pointed to someone who had just entered the room and said, 'Because you invited him, so that he could invite all of them.'

"I looked . . . and it was you, Zac. It was you. Maybe my whole purpose was to invite you."

CHAPTER 15

OKLAHOMA — MAY 5th

While he waited at the red light, Brandon Atkins leaned sideways and quickly glanced at his hair in the rear view mirror. How satisfying to see the new, all-natural hair gel he marketed could hold a style even on a windy day. He loved having quality products to sell. The light turned green, so he straightened to a driving position and pushed the accelerator. Wanting to catch the latest headlines before they reached their destination, he turned up the radio. He listened to a report on the latest negotiations in the newest Middle East crisis.

". . . and Envoy Tracy Stoltz has flown to the Middle East to represent the US in this latest round of talks. Meanwhile, an unnamed source said refusal by the US to honor commitments made during secret, informal talks with the Todd administration have caused the impasse. Sources tell UIG a deadline for current negotiations looms on Wednesday, with tensions growing beyond the scope of the current conflict. In a statement issued today, Russian leaders continued to demand the US stop expanding their own interests in the region and allow neutral parties to bring a settlement in the crisis."

"There's always *something* going on over there, isn't there?" Brandon said aloud during a pause in the reporting.

The radio announcer continued. "The State Department announced that Ambassador Albert Tarrance will once again take part in talks aimed at easing tensions between China and Japan."

Brandon's ears perked up. He'd made a handsome living by being sensitive to marketing trends and this could influence sales. These days, survival supplies had become very marketable.

"In other news, doctors in Baltimore and other cities along the Chesapeake Bay and the Susquehanna River continue to report cases of a new flesh-eating bacteria. The United Nations Biological Control Task Force has been dispatched to the area with representatives of the U. S. Office of Disease Control to ascertain the source of this new bacteria, and possible means of eradication without further endangering the environment. Meanwhile, seven people have been infected with the bacteria, one has died. This is Aaron Ellison reporting on UIG radio, we'll return after these messages."

Brandon turned down the radio. "Perhaps," he said, putting both hands on the steering wheel, "we should think about selling some of that new virus-blocking, multi-spectrum antibacterial shampoo and body lotion." He glanced at his wife, Cassidy, sitting in the passenger seat. Her eyes stayed locked on the road, her posture rigid, and her arms were folded, but he didn't notice. What he noticed was that her hair spray wasn't as good as his gel. They could talk about sales later. "You're hair needs a little help, pumpkin," he said, trying to keep a critical tone out of his voice.

She didn't look at him. "Oh! I guess I can't do anything right! I let your breakfast get cold, I shorted your delivery this morning, and now my hair is a mess! I thought your obvious relief that I'm not pregnant would carry you through the whole week!" She burst into tears and he pulled to the side of the road.

He took a nicely ironed hankie out of his pocket and offered it to her. "Oh, Cassy. Please don't cry. You wouldn't want to show up at school with your makeup all smudged from crying, would you?" She sobbed uncontrollably while he continued talking. "I know you didn't mean to ruin breakfast or mix up my order."

He tried to smooth the frizzy clump of hair at the back of her head and realized it would have to be wet before it would flatten out. But he'd have to try to forget her hair for the moment. The subject of children had come up again.

"We have each other right now, honey," he said, petting the wiry tuft of hair. "*You're* enough for me. . . . Aren't *I* enough for you?"

She wiped her eyes and looked at him. Although she desperately wanted a baby, she knew if she'd been expecting one, it could have been a serious blow to their already shaky relationship. "Brandon, please forgive me. I don't know what's wrong with me. I'm just not myself."

"I know you're just in a slump, honey. Now just blow that cute little nose and we'll get back on the road."

She complied; and within minutes they were in the parking lot of the elementary school where Cassidy worked as a music teacher. Tonight there would be a fund-raising "community dinner" in the school's cafeteria.

He looked around at all the cars and smiled. "It looks like a good turnout. And some of these are newer cars too. Could mean money."

She looked out the passenger window. "I sure hope so. We really need some repairs. The school will be rubble before the county gets around to paying for renovations. The only new music we've gotten in ages is what I bought last year. And it would be nice if the school had some sporting equipment."

"It's too bad there's no big corporations around here to co-op with," her husband responded. "It just doesn't pay to live in little towns anymore."

Her head whipped around. "You want to *move*? Brandon, I can't leave my mom! She doesn't have anyone but me."

"Whoa! Back it up, Cassy! I didn't say anything about moving. I just mentioned the fact there are no big companies around here, that's all. As long as we can make good money there's no reason to leave. We just need to be sure we take advantage of the opportunities we get here."

"Oh."

Once they'd exited the vehicle he tried to sound casual. "Do you have any of the provisions on hand?" His car was always properly stocked, but they'd decided to take her car at the last minute.

She nodded. She'd personally loaded several hefty boxes of supplies into the trunk that morning.

"Good girl!" He said, giving her a kiss on top of her head as they walked toward the school. "See? You've got more on the ball than you think. If I get a few sales going, could you put the orders together out here?"

"I . . . I'm sure I can."

He opened the door of the gymnasium for her, and then leaned over to whisper in her ear when they got inside. "Sweetheart?"

She'd been really angry a few minutes ago, but at the soft tone and endearing name, she warmed up. "Yes?"

He kept his mouth close to her ear and whispered. "Your hair's a little messy in back. Maybe you'd want to fix it before anyone saw you."

Without a word she spun around and walked to the faculty ladies' room. She shoved the door as hard as she could, and the sound of it smacking against the tiled wall resounded around the room before she realized other women were inside.

"Oops!" she said, trying to look surprised. Then, in a lilting southern accent, she quickly added, "I guess I don't know my own strength!"

Her heart sank when she realized the two women standing in front of the mirror were Brandon's former girlfriend, Sara, and a woman named Rosalinda Ruiz. They'd been talking when Cassidy came in. Sara taught at the school and all of them attended the same church, so Cassidy acknowledged them. "Hey, Sara. Hi, Rosalinda." She quickly pulled out a compact to cover her red nose and upper lip. *As if my day hasn't been bad enough already! She would have to be here and see me like this.*

Sara and Rosa returned her greeting before continuing their own conversation. Cassy got out a brush to fix her hair while she listened.

Sara noticed something new. "Oh, Rosa, what a pretty cross! You just get it?"

Rosalinda blushed as her hand went up to touch the little pendant around her neck. "Actually, he gave it to me a couple of months ago."

Sara knew from the response there must be a story behind the gift. "What was the occasion?"

Cassidy casually brushed her hair then washed her hands as they continued.

"It was the anniversary of when I fell in love with him. Literally."

"Don't tell me," Sara said quickly. "You tripped and fell on him."

"No. It's worse than that actually."

"Tell me!"

Rosa smiled. "Some other time."

"Excuse me," Cassidy interrupted. "I need some paper towels and the dispenser over here is out. Would you mind?"

The two friends simultaneously stepped back from the dispenser near them and stopped talking.

Cassidy grabbed a few towels and dried her hands, while smiling her perkiest smile and eying the two of them in the mirror. She looked at Rosalinda's pretty maternity outfit which displayed a large, perfectly round tummy.

Rosa felt the growing tension in the air. Wanting to break it, she decided to say something about the jeweled pin Cassy wore. "That pin is lovely."

"Why, thank you. My Brandon gave it to me." Cassidy said, turning to face the two women. She allowed herself another glimpse of Rosalinda's stomach in full blossom. Next, she reached out to the small, gold cross around Rosa's neck and picked it up as if to inspect it. "Of course, I'm so petite, I probably should wear teeny things like this." She let go of the cross and put her hand on her own pin. "I know this is too big and showy, but Brandon always wants me to have the biggest and best. You probably know how it is, when your husband is so wonderful to you, and you wouldn't hurt his feelings for the world!" Cassy finally allowed herself to look directly at her rival and continued. "You could wear something like this pin, Sara. In fact, it would probably look better on you. You're just so much bigger boned than I."

Sara's eyes seemed to pop open wider for a second.

Cassy could see her little barb had found its mark. "Don't you worry, though. You've got such a pretty face," she said, smiling. "You take off a few pounds again, honey, and you'll catch a man before you know it!"

Silence hung in the air.

Cassidy nervously looked at her watch. "Oh! Goodness! I need to get in there before the thing starts!" She collected her purse and headed for the door. "See you!" she called over her shoulder.

When the door closed, Sara and Rosalinda stood in stunned silence.

Finally, Rosalinda asked, "What did you do to *her*?"

Sara looked around to be sure they were alone. "Brandon and I dated for a while before I called it quits. Shortly after that, he found Cassidy, and they got married almost instantly. He's probably got her convinced that I'm dying to get him back if she doesn't stay on her toes."

"You're not *serious*, are you? A Christian man wouldn't do that, would he?"

"Weren't you just here for the lovely conversation we had with his wife?"

Rosalinda reflected on some of the spiteful and selfish things she herself had done for years while thinking herself a Christian. Obviously, it was possible to be religious and rotten at the same time. Her offense at Cassidy's hurtful remarks softened somewhat at this realization.

Later in the evening, during the dinner, Cassy occasionally glanced over to the table where Sara sat. The woman looked a bit somber even when the others were laughing. Each time Cassy looked at Sara, she felt worse.

She recalled the shocked look on Sara's face when she just as much as called her fat. *How could I have been so mean to her? I WANTED to hurt her feelings.* Yet the moment the words had come out of her mouth Cassy wanted to take them back. She closed her eyes. *Why couldn't I just have shut up? Why am I so jealous of her? And now I'm jealous of her friend! What's wrong with me, Lord? I used to be a nice person. Being with other people was such a joy to me. . . . Now I dread going anywhere . . . I can't seem to get a grip. I'm so sorry. . .*

Brandon watched as his wife looked repeatedly at Sara. Normally this would please him, but tonight, Cassy was already out of control. He slipped an arm around her and she looked over at him.

"You're still my kitten, aren't you?" he said in a whisper.

You see that? she chided herself. *There's no reason to be jealous.* The look on her face softened and she whispered back. "Forever."

After the dinner, people started slowly filtering out of the building while others lingered and talked. Brandon's eyes scanned the room for possible sales. He saw Enrique Ruiz, a man he knew from church, standing with his wife about twenty feet away. Recently, he'd become increasingly aware of the respect Ruiz had in several local spheres of influence.

He looked around for Cassidy and realized she'd slipped away somewhere. He frowned and tapped his fingers on the back of the chair in front of him. Perhaps she'd gone to touch-up her makeup again.

In the back of the cafeteria, Cassidy stood behind Sara and waited for a chance to say something. Despite the near-panic she felt, she resisted the urge to run away.

Sara remained unaware of Cassy's presence until she finished talking to an elderly lady and backed up a couple of steps, bumping into Cassidy.

"Oh! . . . I'm sorry," Sara said. She assumed Cassidy had been trying to get by, so moved out of her way.

No one else was within earshot of them so Cassy found the courage to speak. "No. *I'm* sorry . . . I mean . . ." her knees shook and her heart trembled as she spoke, "I'm . . ." she took a breath and tried to continue, "I said some mean things to you and your friend." She swallowed. If she didn't do it quickly, she wouldn't get it all out. Her words began pouring out in rapid succession. "I *knew* I was being ugly and I don't know why, I mean, I guess I'm just jealous of the two of you and I know I must have hurt you and I'm so sorry!" She took a deep breath.

Sara needed to process what was said for a moment. She sighed then embraced Cassidy. During the last hour, she'd seen some unresolved things in her own heart. She'd had to admit to herself that sometimes, when she saw Brandon and Cassidy walking hand in hand, she'd felt somewhat jealous as well. "I'm sorry, too," Sara said. "Can we start over?"

Blowing her nose on a napkin from a nearby table, Cassy nodded. "Could we?"

"Yes. Let's do that."

Five minutes later, Cassidy found her way back to her husband. She looked happy, so he decided not to scold her for disappearing.

He gave her a little squeeze. "Let's go talk to a few people. Just follow my lead, okay?"

Mr. Ruiz still stood a few feet away, so Brandon stepped over to him and stuck out his hand. "Your name is Enrique Ruiz isn't it? I've seen you at church."

Ruiz took his hand and shook it. "Yeah. But call me Ricky. Your name is . . . Brandon?"

"Yes! Brandon Atkins. And this is my wife, Cassidy."

Ricky tuned to Rosa. "Rosa? Have you met Brandon before?"

She forced herself to smile at him. "No. I don't believe we've ever formally met." She shook his hand.

"And this is my wife, Cassidy." Brandon said, moving sideways and pulling her forward a bit.

"We've met." Cassy said, somewhat embarrassed.

Looking up at Ruiz, Brandon suddenly felt unusually awkward. He leaned toward his wife and whispered. "Sweetheart? Do you have any 'introductory baskets' in your car?"

"Yes. I do." Cassidy responded

"Why don't you run and get one?" he asked, smiling.

"Okay, honey."

Cassy walked toward the doors and Brandon spoke to Ricky and Rosa. "I hear you came here from New York."

They nodded.

Brandon looked at Ricky and continued. "I also heard you were one of the leaders of the youth group in Daniel Ingram's church. That church is famous."

"It was a great experience." Ricky said.

Brandon turned to Rosa. "And I see you're expecting again! Haven't figured out what causes that, eh? Well, congratulations. Cassy can hardly wait to start a family." He reached into his jacket and retrieved a card. "If you should need a bigger place to live, I'm a realtor and I'd be happy to help you out."

Ricky took the card and stuck it in his shirt pocket. "Thanks."

"Any plans to help with the youth group here at our church?"

Ricky shrugged. "We're pretty busy being a family right now. And, I work full time out at Henderson's Youth Ranch, so I get plenty of interaction with teens."

"Maybe," Brandon said, "it's time to do something new then? You know, I just have this feeling . . . we might be able to work together on a few things. I'd sure like to have you over to dinner sometime this week. Think you'd be able to come?"

The couple looked at each other then back at Brandon. "Sure," Ricky responded.

"Great! We just need to pick the date. Cassy should be back in just a second, and I'll check our schedule. . . . She went out to get you guys something." He waited for them to look appropriately puzzled before going on. "I represent a great line of Christian nutritional, hygienic, and cosmetic provisions—"

"Really?" Ricky said before a huge smile appeared on his face.

Rosa knew that particular smile all too well. Usually, it meant he could see right through somebody . . . and it usually signaled an oncoming truth.

"I didn't know that 'provisions' could become Christians," Ricky said.

Brandon winked and pointed a finger at Ricky. "Got me there, pardner. What I meant was, these are provisions made to the highest standards by a Christian family in Montana."

Cassy returned with a basket laden with small packets.

"That's really kind of you," Ricky said as Cassidy handed him the basket, "but Rosa can tell you I'm not much into expensive specialty foods."

Brandon held his hands up. "Hey! These are free samples. And I think they're so good they sell themselves. Just take 'em home and give 'em a try. No obligation." He leaned forward a bit, as if he were sharing a confidence. "Never hurts to have emergency stores on hand. And, don't forget, Christ could come back soon. Don't we owe it to Him to be in peak condition so we can get as much of His work done as possible?" He straightened up and shook Ricky's hand. "Even if you decide you don't like the products, I'd appreciate your honest input."

Ricky smiled again. "Sure. I'll let ya' know."

CHAPTER 16

PHILADELPHIA — May 10th

"I understand that he can't come out for visits, but, as long as my daughter shows no sign of illness, couldn't she visit him here? She really misses him."

Dr. Mehndolson tightly squeezed the pencil in his hands with his thumbs braced at the center, ready to snap it in half. He'd had a number of visits with Heather Poole since the start of the experiments at the Attlebury Clinic of Philadelphia. The guidelines had been given to her several times since her father, Ethan Poole, had been accepted as a test patient in a study on Regeneration Therapy. But, it seemed no matter how many times Ms. Poole heard the ground rules, she always had to come in and try to push for something not permitted. She'd sit there with a list of stupid questions—all of which had been covered in the material she'd been given, if she'd ever bother to go over it. Then she'd want to change something that *couldn't* be changed. As if, just for her, they'd trash the entire process. And if something went wrong, she'd be the first one to sue the clinic.

Dr. Mehndolson forced himself to let go of the pencil and flexed his hands several times. Hadn't he gotten into research because he didn't like to deal with people?

He looked at Ms. Poole and shook his head. "Sorry. This is a critical phase in the tests. All participants must be kept away from outsiders. We can't risk ruining all this work."

She opened her mouth but he didn't let her speak.

"Children," he said quickly, "are notorious carriers of so many illnesses. We must insist on computer or voice communication only between your daughter and your father. You understand, don't you?"

"Well, I want to see him."

Dr. Mehndolson sighed. "You can't see him either."

"I insist."

"You can insist all you want, Ms. Poole. You aren't your father's guardian. He signed himself into the program and unless he wants out of the program, he can't see you."

"Not even through a window?"

"You don't have video on your computer or your phone?"

"It's just not the same as seeing him in person." Her chin quivered as if she were about to cry. "You know my mother is in an institution and this is just so . . . scary."

His left hand slowly grasped the pencil again. He knew that as soon as she left his office she'd be down at the office of the clinic director, complaining again. She could well have an impact on his future employment offers with the clinic.

"Well," he finally offered, "we do have an observation room with a window in it and a speaker system. I can have him taken there—if you promise it will be our little secret."

A concession. She smiled as she tucked her list into her purse. "Oh, that would be so nice of you, Dr. Mehndolson."

He said a hasty goodbye and left the room to make the arrangements. However, when he spoke to the nurse in charge of Mr. Poole, she hinted she had a few concerns about the man.

Dr. Mehndolson felt his stomach tying up in knots. "What do you mean?"

"Well, maybe it's not for me to say. And he's so much better. Physically."

For as long as Mehndolson could remember, the pursuit of truth, at any cost, had been his obsession. "You're with him more than anyone else," he finally said. "I'd really like to hear your observations."

She looked down and lowered her voice. "Well, Dr. Ron hates it when he thinks we're analyzing his cases."

"I'll handle Dr. Ron. Just tell me."

"It's just that . . . it's not *real* noticeable, but Mr. Poole seems to be deteriorating mentally."

"Give me an example."

"He was always the first one up in here. He was always joking . . . always sure of what he liked or didn't like . . . breakfast for instance: He'd let us know in no uncertain terms if we gave him prunes or expected him to eat oatmeal . . . But now he seems like he's getting . . . passive. Like he doesn't know the difference. Or, like he doesn't care. And he stares at things now . . . kinda like he's . . . blank."

"He could just be depressed," Dr. Mehndolson quickly offered, but inwardly he knew his worst fears could be springing to life. *And wouldn't you know it would be HER father who's going sour. A picture of Heather Poole in a courtroom popped into his mind. And wouldn't it have to be a patient you share with Dr. Ron—a man who would sell his soul for a grant or a research job that paid sufficiently.*

"Is Mr. Poole the only one?" the doctor inquired.

"It's really not for me to say." The nurse looked around nervously. "I hope you won't tell anyone I said anything. I need this job, Dr. Mehndolson."

"Don't worry. I'll not tell a soul." He bit his lip while he thought a moment. "In fact, we can trade favors. I need you to take Mr. Poole down to observation room three."

"You want to see for yourself?"

"Yes." It wasn't a lie. He would stay in the room with Mr. Poole and watch the interaction between father and daughter. If she appeared to have any concerns, he'd have the old man perform some physical feat to impress her and redirect her thoughts. He didn't want her creating pandemonium over what might be a temporary problem.

When the visit was over, the doctor pulled out all charts and files on Mr. Poole and several others. He'd spend the night pouring over them. Even though Mr. Poole acted differently, his daughter hadn't seemed to notice it. The excitement over her little victory with obtaining the visit must have colored her perception of how things actually went.

But, in truth, there was a slackness about Mr. Poole's countenance that concerned Dr. Mehndolson. The nurse was right. Although many physical indicators of the old man's health—muscle tone, balance, stamina—were improving daily, there were also times when he seemed . . . zoned out.

Within two days of the father/daughter visit, Mehndolson covered hundreds of pages of data regarding his patients (Mr. Poole and ten others) who were receiving the actual Regeneration Therapy. In the following week, he examined all of the patients at the clinic who were getting the therapy. Of the forty test subjects actually on the treatment, all showed at least some physical improvement. While this, in and of itself, would have been encouraging, his other findings were sobering. Eight patients seemed to be operating at normal mental capacity, twelve exhibited small signs of diminished mental capacity, and twenty of the patients showed measurable deterioration. Unfortunately, Mr. Poole was part of the last group.

When Dr. Mehndolson met with the other doctors for their weekly progress report, he shared his findings. Dr. Ron, of course, had noted a few things as well, but wanted to assign them to other sources. He said perhaps the patients' other medications needed to be reduced.

Mehndolson didn't buy it. "Thirty-two out of forty have the same symptoms and you think it's their meds? They're not all taking the same meds, so how could that be the common factor?"

Dr. Fortner, the clinic director got up from his chair. "Perhaps," he said slowly, "this is just a temporary anomaly. I think we have to keep cool heads and stay the course of the trials. Meanwhile, I'll contact the tech rep for Global-kem and Roller Genetic Labs. I'm sure if this is a real problem, they would have encountered something like it before."

"It's not in their literature. I checked." Dr. Mehndolson said. "Although, yesterday, I did manage to lay hold of two articles describing these same symptoms. The doctors who wrote them were later discredited by Global and Roller, but, given what we're seeing here, perhaps we should take them more seriously."

"Let's not be hasty," Dr. Fortner said. "Dr. Ron and I will see that their reps are notified as soon as possible and we'll give them a chance to review what we're doing."

Mehndolson realized things had switched from "the team" to "Dr. Ron and I." He was about to be cut out of the flow. "Fine. But you may have a problem if families try to communicate with these patients."

CHAPTER 17

OKLAHOMA — May 14th

Rosa Ruiz sat up in bed. The clock on the night stand said 1:00 a.m. She couldn't wait any longer. She simply must have something to eat. Not the health bars, protein sticks, or any of the veggie gel packs Brandon Atkins had given them in that sample basket of health food. And not marinated cucumbers with onions, either. She had to have some of Ricky's cereal. Of course, after all the remarks she'd made in the past about his choice of breakfast food, she knew this must be a covert operation. If she could just slip out of bed without waking him, she'd be home free.

As gracefully as any woman who's nine months pregnant could, she pushed herself off the mattress and softly crept to the door. After entering the living room, she slowly eased the door closed. He'd never know.

"Oh yeah," she whispered Ricky's favorite expression to herself just the way he would—like it was one word.

She scuffed across the carpet to the kitchen, snapped on the light, and went directly to the cupboard containing the contraband. Ricky had been very understanding of her craving for the exotic foods of her youth, like mangoes, but she knew this was another matter altogether.

"Oh yeah," she said again, standing on tiptoe and grabbing the box.

"And just what, may I ask," Ricky's voice suddenly echoed around the kitchen, "do you think you're doing with my *CHOCO BOOMS*?"

She jumped and almost dropped the box.

"I'm sorry," he said with a show of milky-white teeth. "Did I scare you?"

She knew she'd been caught in the act. She sat the box on the counter and cradled her stomach. "I just wanted a little something to eat."

"Hmmmmm," he said. "I see. But surely you weren't going to eat my *CHOCO BOOMS*, were you?"

She had no defense. She rubbed her tummy and nodded.

He gazed directly at her. "I think this sharing thing has gone too far."

The conversation had taken an unanticipated turn. She'd expected a lecture on the contents of the box itself, not whether Ricky would be willing to share it. "What do you mean?"

He moved closer, put a hand on his hip and spoke in a higher pitch, trying to imitate her voice. "Did I say anything when you started wanting to sit in what you used to call my 'big ugly chair?' Nooooo."

She smiled up at him.

"Did I say anything," he said, pulling on her sleeve, "when you started using my T-shirts for maternity nighties? Noooooo."

"Well, they're big, stretchy, and soft. And comfortable."

He looked at the current state of the shirt, then spoke in his regular voice. "I think you've about 'stretchied' them out, Rosa. And now you want to eat my *CHOCO BOOMS*—a cereal you wouldn't even hold in your mouth when we first married. In fact, if I remember correctly, you even refused to buy them at first."

Her chin slumped to her chest. She had not escaped.

She remembered the first time she tasted a spoonful of his cereal. She spat them out and said, "Oh! They're fizzy!" He'd laughed and told her it was because this was "a man's" cereal. Most women, he ventured, needed something "more feminny," like *VANILLA DREAM PUFFS* or, maybe, for more active women like her, *FRUITY BOINGERS*—a "kid's cereal"—would do.

"And they make these sexist remarks in their advertising?" she'd asked.

"Of course they can't. They use code words and subliminal messages."

"'Code words and subliminal messages,'" She'd repeated. "Well, like, give me some proof," she said.

He beamed at her. "Okay! Just think, now, Rosa. . . . Here." He'd made her sit in a chair, close her eyes, and relax. "Now just listen to the words. . . ." He cleared his throat. "Ready? Keep your eyes closed. Okay? Now, ask yourself with each name: Masculine or feminine?" After a brief silence, his voice suddenly thundered, "*CHOCO BOOOOMS!*"

When her eyes snapped wide open, he'd said, "Masculine or feminine?"

"If you put it that way, masculine, I suppose."

"Oh yeah! Now you're thinking. Okay, okay. Next name. Close your eyes."

She'd complied and then just sat for a few moments of silence before this I've-just-taken-tranquillizers-and-had-a-warm-bubble-bath voice said, "*Vanillaaahhhh Drrrreeeeaam Puffssss . . .* masculine or feminine?"

"You sure you don't secretly work for the cereal company? Or in advertising?"

The debates over this—and whether or not these cereals could actually qualify as *food*—were never settled to either Ricky or Rosa's satisfaction.

But now she'd been cornered with the object of all her lectures in her very own hands. Somehow she had gotten to like *CHOCO BOOMS*. And worse, against her will it seemed, now she craved them. She looked at her husband. "I know it's wrong. But I just have to have them." She plunged her hand in the box and pulled out a handful.

"I thought the boxes were getting light awful quick," Ricky said. Then he watched her put some of the cereal in her mouth. "Wow. Don't you want some milk with those?"

"No," she said, with a full mouth.

"So you just want 'A MaximumMeltdown Of Choc-o-licity That Will Detonate On Your Taste Buds' do ya?"

She swallowed. "Huh?"

"If you were the discriminating shopper you want me to be," Ricky said, taking the box then reaching in for a handful, "you'd read the labels the way you should, and you'd see all of this pertinent information is right here on the front." He held the box so she could see his very words, tastefully surrounded by lightning bolts, on a mushroom-cloud background, just below the giant, glowing name, "*CHOCO BOOMS!*"

Ricky put a handful of the cereal in his mouth and started chewing. Then he began shaking his head and muttering something as he moved to the refrigerator. She couldn't understand him. He quickly got out the milk and drank some right from the carton. "Oh. Rosa," he said, wiping off his mouth. "Even I can't eat 'em dry. You sure you don't want to put 'em in a bowl and have some milk with them?"

Rosa put more in her mouth and chewed. After swallowing, she said, "I'm sure."

Partly in admiration, he watched her eat another handful. When she said she'd had enough they headed back to bed. As he turned out the kitchen light, he said, "You'd better have that baby before you start craving nails or something."

They had both grown accustomed to Rosa's middle-of-the-night snack times, and soon they snuggled back together and fell asleep. Until five-fifteen.

The little lamp on the night stand came on. The small-watt bulb, that gave no useful light at all in other circumstances, now seemed almost like daylight to Ricky. He squinted and tried to cover his eyes with the back of his hand. "What's wrong, Rosa? I knew you shouldn't have eaten those CHOCO BOOMS like that. Feeling sick?"

"No. I think it's time, Ricky."

"It's still dark out . . . how could it be time to—" Suddenly he realized what she meant and sat up.

"Now? You sure?"

Rosa nodded. "The pains are about twenty minutes apart."

Ricky put a hand up in the air. "Oh yeah!" he said, before he leaned toward her. "You okay?" he asked in an excited whisper.

She nodded.

He quickly got up. While he dressed, she had another contraction.

"Oh, oh, *oh!*" she cried out, grabbing her back.

He reached around her and instinctively began to pray. "Oh, Father, here we are. We're excited . . . and a little scared. Help us tonight, surround us with Your love and protection. Help Rosa to get through this without any complications. Help our little boy along the way. We acknowledge he has come from You, Lord, and You have lent him to us. We thank You, even now for health and strength for him. I pray for every hand that will touch Rosa and our son tonight. May each one be Your hand extended. Guard us from all harm, whether hidden or open. Grant us peace, Lord, as we bring this little one out into the world. In Jesus' name, amen."

Rosa relaxed as the pain subsided and she put her arms around Ricky's neck. "Yes, Lord. Thank You for life and health. Thank You for all the sweet things You have given to us already. We can't wait to hold him in our arms. We love You, Lord. Thank You."

Soon, their friend Sara arrived to watch their daughter, Angela, and the couple zoomed down the road to the hospital, arriving in plenty of time. Four and a half hours later, Daniel Tomás Ruiz came into the world. As the midwife handed the child to him, Ricky looked into the eyes of his son. The baby had stopped wailing and looked right into his father's eyes.

"Thank you, Jesus," Ricky said softly. With one finger, he gently brushed tears off his son's face then touched the little hand. Tiny fingers wrapped around his fingertip and it made him feel weak all over. *Oh Lord, who could ever imagine how awesome and marvelous this is. . . . How is it that someone so small could make me feel so powerless?*

"Look, Rosa. Our little Daniel," he said, placing him in his mother's arms. The little hand still clung tenaciously to his finger.

Soaked with sweat and exhausted, Rosa cradled her baby. The sight of him brought some color back to her face. "Hello there, little Daniel," she said softly. "We've been waiting for you."

CHAPTER 18

CAMP DAVID — June 29th

Joshua Thornton sat at the dining room table of the Camp David house amusing his friend, Don Cole, with tales of a recent trip in a New York subway. Josh and Don had met three years ago, before Don was elected president, when they'd served as volunteers together. The work they'd done, digging people out of the rubble after the Denver quake, had been dirty and dangerous but during that time, a lasting friendship formed.

Earlier in the day, Josh flew down from New York and then was transported to Camp David to spend a couple of days with Don. The main reason he'd wanted to come was to share a message he believed to be of great importance.

It had been several months since they'd had a long conversation and they both looked forward to spending some time together. When their late dinner was over, they were in no hurry to move to another room so they lingered at the table. Josh scrunched the last few crumbs of a cheesecake crust onto the back of his fork and ate them. Don adjusted the position of the chair next to him and put his feet upon it.

"How are Carol and the kids?" Don asked.

"Mostly well. Elijah brought home a cold from school and gave it to all of us, but everybody's about over it now. Carol seems to be the last one in the recovery line. And, before I forget, I have to tell you Amy is *still* soaring over the gifts you sent for her birthday. Her friends think they're 'entirely enormous,' which, in our language, means they're way cool."

Don was pleased. "It's not every day a girl turns seventeen, and she's the closest thing I have to a niece. When I went to Japan a few months ago, I saw them and thought of her. . . . How's Paul?"

Josh chuckled. "He's totally recovered from the loss of the election for class president. He really took your advice to heart and he's already got a plan together for next year."

Don made a signal with his hands like a referee declaring a score. "I may get a politician out of the family yet!"

The small talk continued while a woman came in and cleared the last utensils from the table. Once they were alone again, Josh cleared his throat.

"Don, I wanted to come down here because I have a word for you from the Lord."

The president's eyebrows shot up.

Josh continued. "I wanted to have the time, not only to give you the word, but to have some exchange with you about it. . . . I mean, I know you have people trying to give you advice all the time, and everybody thinks the wisdom they share should be taken. But I want you to remember I've never tried to use our friendship like a tool to get things from you or from others. I've never lied to you—even when saying nice things would have been much easier. And, even now, I want you to measure what I say tonight by the highest standard. The biggest difference between what I'm about to give you and the words of, say some psychic for instance, is that these words should glorify the Lord and not me or you. They should encourage you in well doing, make you want to turn away from any sin, and cause you to seek the Lord. If you don't feel what I say meets this standard, discard it. I'm serious."

Don took his feet off the chair and sat upright. "Okay. So what is it?"

Josh paused and closed his eyes. "Last week, I had a vision. In this vision, I could see you standing before a great, stone wall which extended out of sight in either direction. As you walked along it, you could see the wall was damaged in many places. There were places where some of the stones had fallen out. In some places significant cracks had developed, and in other spots the roots of trees were undermining it and pushing it out of alignment. At one point, you climbed to the top of the wall. When you looked out to the horizon you saw a huge, dark, tidal wave rolling toward you, and you knew, in its current condition, the wall wouldn't sustain the force of the wave's impact."

As he listened, Don felt a small shudder run through him.

Josh kept speaking. "You quickly set about repairing the wall. Different men came and went—some giving advice or moving at your direction, others attempting to further damage the wall. Two men were even trying to blow up the wall with these little, round bomb things . . ."

Cole knew instantly what the "little bombs" were. They were the missing Enhanced Radiation Weapons. He couldn't help but interrupt. "What happened with these two men?"

Josh stopped and thought a moment. Obviously, something here had struck a cord in Don. "They were discovered and stopped."

Don nodded, then seemed to relax slightly. "Go ahead."

"You accepted the good help you got, and fought off those who were trying to destroy the wall. All the while, even though you couldn't see it from where you worked, there was an increasing sense of the immense wave approaching.

"Still, you labored on. Some of the stones that had fallen out were still usable, so you placed them back in the wall. One large stone was crumbling, so you decided not to use it. You located several cracks in the wall. A few of them went from top to bottom, and you spent time repairing them. You cut the roots of trees which threatened to topple the wall and tried to reinforce weakened spots. It was a seemingly endless task on a barricade that stretched on and on. Eventually, you came to an opening where a gate once stood in the wall. Someone had removed the gate so the gateway stood empty.

As you stood there, you heard the roar of the oncoming wave and looked through the opening to see it only yards away. Almost in a panic, you looked back at all the fortifications you'd made and wondered if they would be enough to hold back the crushing, dark water about to smash against the wall. Then, you stepped into the opening where the gate had been, spread out your arms and legs to press against the frame and braced yourself.

"Next, I saw everything like I was above the whole scene. The water pounded into the wall with unbelievable force. Although much of it was held back, the wave was higher than the wall, so some of it still came over the top and rushed into the land beyond.

"And then, the ground inside the wall shook and began to rise. The debris from the flood rolled away as the ground became a mountain. . . . And that was all I saw."

Josh pulled a folded paper out of his pocket and lightly tossed it over to his friend. "I wrote all this down, but I wanted to say it to you as well. I wanted to tell you the vision, and then its interpretation."

Don remained riveted in his seat. "Okay. Go ahead."

"Remember, years ago, when you came to my house after the riots and we talked about you becoming president? You wondered how much you might accomplish when you got into office. Remember how you were hoping that if God called you to be president, maybe He'd use you to turn things around?"

Don nodded, a somber look on his face. He'd hoped for so much and had worked every day to "turn things around," but recently, he'd gotten discouraged by what seemed to be an endless number of significant problems. He'd had to fight a constant sense that he was on the Titanic, bailing it out with a bucket.

Josh spoke again. "Back then I told you that there are certain things that we can change, but that there are other things, events fixed by God, that will happen *regardless* of our efforts. You remember this conversation?"

"Yes," Don said with a sinking feeling.

"Well, in this vision, the wall is a barrier that was set in place as a protection for this country, but it had fallen into disrepair. People did not design this wall, God did. Many have participated in building and maintaining it at His will. The condition of the wall was something that could be changed by what people chose to do. In years gone by, many people chose to do nothing. They could have sought God, they could have prayed, they could have done things to make a difference—but they didn't. That's why the wall in this vision was in such disrepair.

"The dark wave in the vision was something that wouldn't be taken away—a fixed event. The wall could significantly slow its progress, but the wave would come whether the wall was ready or not.

"The stones in the wall represented actual people. Some, for whatever reason, were out of their place. Some fell, others were removed. As you walked along the wall you inspected the stones that had come out, and if they were useable, you put them back in place. There are people all around who possibly failed in the past, or they got pulled out of place, but God's given you the ability to see if they are sound now, and able to be used again.

"In one case, you looked at a rather large stone and saw it was crumbling. Even though it left a big hole where it came out of the wall, you realized re-installing it was a bad idea. You used several sturdy, smaller stones instead. . . . Someone who's been in service before will be offered as a large, convenient choice in a place of great need, but if you see signs of decay around this person, go with your discernment and choose several reliable people who'll work as a team instead.

"In the vision, men came. Some offered advice or help, others tried to damage, or even blow up the wall. All of these represent people with great influence behind them, but the bottom line is that the influence behind them is either God or the enemy. Look at their works and you'll know who sent them. Don't compromise with destructive people just because they're powerful. Send them packing. The wave is coming. Your job is that wall. Keep acknowledging the Lord in all of your ways and He will guide you. He will send people to help you. You are not alone in this work.

"There were trees whose roots were undermining the wall. These are old traditions that have been at work for a long time. Your job isn't cutting down the trees, but restoring the wall. You are to cut any root that's growing under the wall, then make repairs and go on.

"There were cracks in the wall—spots where stones have remained in place, but have parted ways and no longer want to fit together. Your job, when you find one of these cracks, is to put the mortar back in there, to get these stones–the people–back into a cohesive unit, so that the integrity of the wall is restored. Ask the Lord, and He will continue to use you to bring factions together, to help people see they must function together.

"There were places in the wall where you found reinforcement was needed. . . . You know, some people just need others alongside them so they'll be able to stand. Where you can send more help, do it.

"The gate, of course, is the place you are meant to occupy. You will fill the breach so it won't be like an open floodgate.

"Remember, the wall did not stop the wave, but kept it from bringing total destruction. And afterward, a mountain arose–like a sleeping giant, shaken and awakened. God will yet bring true faith to this nation—His people will rise up and shake off the debris of this world, and they will live to His glory.

"The Lord is saying that, in the past, you've seen the wave coming. He's saying you've gone about your work with a sense it was coming. Now, you feel more urgency, but God says don't panic or get distracted. Keep at it. Do what is in your hand to do. If something is out of your control—trust it to God. If something would take you away from the wall, don't pursue it. Be faithful with what's in your sphere each day. And when you get to the place where the wave is upon us, take your place and pray. The Bible says, do all you can to stand . . . then stand."

Every hair on Don's body stood up. Inside him rose the certainty that the Lord had spoken.

Josh continued. "You know, Don, some people waste their whole lives waiting for a 'big thing' to happen to them. They sit and wait for that big thing to come, not knowing it's being faithful in what's at hand that will get them to—and through— the 'big thing.'

"The work-out you've engaged in as you do those everyday things will give you the strength to be victorious. Because making choices for Him is a habit, you won't need to worry you'll fail when the big thing hits. . . . God is acknowledging your faithfulness with what has been placed in your hand. Keep doing it. Don't think all is lost when you see the darkness coming . . . know that your labors will hold— each repair in that seemingly endless task is worth something and will add to the integrity of the whole work.

"And, He wants you to know when you get to that time, when it's closing in, He has arranged it so you will be in the right place. You'll see your place in that wall and you'll occupy it. The wave will come, and some of it will even spill over the top of the wall, but because the wall was repaired, and you took your place, the outcome will be different. Know what you are doing is making a difference. . . . You were born for such a time as this, look to God and you will not fail."

Don felt as if a huge burden had been lifted off him and he bowed his head. "Oh God . . . thank You."

CHAPTER 19

PHILADELPHIA — August 15th

Dr. Timothy Mehndolson waited while the security guard searched through the last of his personal belongings. The director of the Attlebury Clinic wanted to be certain Mehndolson didn't take copies of any data with him. He'd been fired from the Regeneration Therapy project, and the clinic had given him until the end of the day to clean out his office and turn in his key.

They didn't seem to remember he had a photographic memory. There was nothing about the clinical trials, the patients, or the volumes of material he'd read during the course of the experiment that he couldn't recall at will.

The security guard folded the top of the box once again and said, "Okay. You can take it."

"Thank you," he mumbled before hefting up the box and leaving the room. On his way out of the building, he stopped by the director's office. "Is Dr. Fortner available?"

"Yes," the receptionist said, "He's expecting you. Go right in."

Mehndolson shifted the box to his left arm and opened the door to Dr. Fortner's office. The director, continuing to work at his computer/prompter, said, "Oh. Tim. Take a seat. I'll be right with you. . . . There never seems to be an end to these stupid forms." After making a few entries, he electronically book-marked the spot where he'd stopped, then quit the program and turned to face Mehndolson. "I see you're ready to go," he said, motioning to the box.

"Yes. I didn't have much in the office to start with. Do I give the key to you or leave it at the desk outside?"

"Out there with Donna is fine."

Mehndolson continued sitting, holding the small trinkets gathered over the course of two years at the clinic, and staring at the little man behind the desk.

Dr. Fortner became increasingly uncomfortable. "Listen," he offered, "I'm sorry things ended the way they did."

"Really?" Mehndolson sounded truly surprised. "So being a puppet for those big corporations is something you don't want to do, but have to? Gee, it must be awful for you."

"I know you're angry, Tim, but things aren't always just black and white. You want to live in a world where everything is clearly defined, and, most of the time, that's simply not the case. Not everyone shares your ideals, you know."

"Oh. I see. Having an aversion to turning old people into broccoli is an 'ideal' now, is it? Just when was it that money started to mean more to you than the truth . . . or human beings?"

Dr. Fortner's little mustache twitched. "It's so easy for you to judge everything and everybody." He took a breath and tried to calm himself. "Even if you're right about Regeneration Therapy," he said quietly, "this could be just the first step to perfecting the technique and making it a fountain of youth. Of course, you wouldn't think this was our motive. No one has pure motives except you. What you refuse to see is the larger view here, Tim. Do you know how many elderly people there are? How the resources to keep them going are dwindling every day? Somebody has to do something. Somebody has to make the hard choices. Besides, no one is really asking us to make those choices. We're just running a scientific experiment. It's not up to us to like or dislike the results. We just report them."

Mehndolson remained unmoved. "And you think the big boys at Roller and Global-kem are ever gonna let you report these results to anyone? You think any of this is going to stop them? Get serious."

"We were contracted to run clinical trials and to give the results to the manufacturer. If we were doing taste tests here, you wouldn't debate the morality of keeping the data confidential."

"If the food we were testing caused massive brain damage, I sure would."

Dr. Mehndolson had been told by a nurse that families of the patients who were adversely affected were being brought in, one at a time, and informed that—at least for their loved one—something had not panned out well. Whether or not they were told the truth regarding the probable cause of the damage, the nurse didn't know.

Mehndolson spoke calmly and clearly. "If this 'therapy' can't stand in the cold light of day, with everyone at least having some idea what they're getting into, then it shouldn't be allowed on the market. They shouldn't even be allowed to test it on people till they work out the more serious problems."

"Well, I've duly noted your viewpoint."

Mehndolson stood, shifted the box around to a more comfortable position. "I'll give the key to Donna."

"Just keep in mind, Dr. Mehndolson," the director said, "that the courts have issued a gag order regarding all aspects of the clinical trials on Regeneration Therapy. You are not allowed to discuss your work here, the patients, or any material you may have read with anyone. This isn't an idle threat. I'm positive they'll prosecute."

CHAPTER 20

OKLAHOMA — August 16th

Ricky Ruiz hurried down the road in the ranch's late-model car. Only awake for twenty minutes, and due at work in less time than it would take to get there, he knew the day was not going well. He'd been up much of the night, taking turns with Rosa, rocking Daniel—who, for the past week, seemed to prefer sleeping during the day and crying most of the night.

Ruiz drove with one hand, occasionally glancing down as he fiddled with the buttons on the car radio. A male voice came over the speakers and he quickly pushed the volume-up button as he listened.

". . .while talks with China are continuing. Meanwhile, the situation on the India Pakistan border, according to General Gilbert Thrumbolt, looks bleak. The general, speaking before a Senate committee yesterday, said a call-up of reserve soldiers may be necessary as the scope of the conflict widens and more US troops may be needed to help contain the fighting.

"On a positive note, city officials and organizers from around the world say most of the preparations are nearly complete in the Philadelphia area for the World Convention on Spirituality to be held in six weeks. The three-day conference will bring a much needed financial boost to the city of brotherly love. It is the sixth such meeting in recent years and will be a global summit for people of all faiths who wish to unite for a better world."

Ricky jolted when he looked in the rear-view mirror and saw a trooper right behind him with lights flashing. His eyes shot down to the speedometer. He was doing twelve miles an hour over the posted limit. He took his foot off the gas and pulled to the side of the road. After he'd brought the car to a stop, Ricky reached around to get into his back pocket for his wallet.

"Please keep both hands where I can see 'em," the approaching officer said with a nasal Oklahoma twang.

Ricky instantly put both hands back on the steering wheel.

"Exit the vehicle please. Slowly."

"Sure," he said, and slowly lumbered out of his car. When he came to his full height, he was a head taller than the officer.

"May I have your driver's license?"

Ricky reached into his pocket, pulled out his wallet, retrieved his license, then offered it to the trooper whose name tag said "TATE."

The policeman read the name on the license aloud. "Enrique Tomás Ruiz." After inspecting it further, he looked up. "Mr. Ruiz, did you know that the chip in your tag isn't broadcasting? Do you have proof of registration?"

Ricky leaned into the vehicle and retrieved the yellow card from the console. "Here. This isn't my car. It belongs to Henderson's Youth Ranch and I get the use of it. I'm on their insurance and everything. I don't know why the chip isn't sending out a signal."

"Do you know the posted limit on this road?" the officer inquired.

"Yes, I do."

"Do you know how fast you were going?"

"About twelve miles an hour faster than I should have been going." Before Ricky saw the cop, several other cars had blown by him as if he were standing still. Offering this information would not alter the fact that he'd been the one who'd been caught speeding. "I don't have any excuse. I was trying to get to work on time and I guess I just didn't pay attention until I saw your lights." He hoped his honesty would bring a little mercy into the situation.

The trooper pulled the license through a slot in a hand-held computer which would scan it. Then he repeated the motion with the registration card while he watched the screen. "You work at that ranch do ya?"

"Yeah."

"Doin' what?"

"Activities Director."

The officer grunted. "I'll need to post all this in your record and print it up. Just get back into your car and wait."

Ricky eased back into the seat and closed the door. He wanted to kick himself. Now he'd be late and have the added bonus of a ticket. His very first ticket. He sat and waited for several minutes while Officer Tate accessed his records and posted changes. Eventually, the trooper returned with two slips of paper. One was a ticket for speeding, the other was a warning for not having a functional chip in the auto tag.

Ricky endured a brief lecture about road safety in silence.

As the officer turned to walk to his patrol car he said, "Slow down, and get that tag checked. Have a good day, sir."

Before he pulled back onto the road, Ricky reached up and moved the rear view mirror to look at himself for a moment before saying a loud, "DOINK!" It was a word made popular in a comic strip. The main character in the series, a little man named Mr. Boogle, constantly ran into things, or fell on things, or tripped over things that were easily seen by everyone but Mr. Boogle. Each time he struck something, a little "doink!" was written above him. It became a national fad. Saying it became like the opposite of *eureka!* "Doink" became the ultimate expression of, "what an idiot!"

By the time he got to the ranch and parked, he was twenty-five minutes late. Chapel would have started by now. He went directly to the small room in the administration building where the staff gathered every morning. He opened the door slightly and peeked in. He could hear his friend, Chuck, praying aloud. Ricky quietly crept into the room and sat down near the door. His heart sank when Myra Ballardi, the office secretary, looked up at him and then bowed her head again.

". . . as we continue to seek Your will for China we depend upon Your mercy. . . ." Chuck concluded.

"And, Lord," Myra began when Chuck paused for breath, "we ask that You would forgive *some* of us who find it easy to compromise every day. Forgive some of us who just don't know how to serve You in the proper way. Forgive some of us who think they are so spiritual yet won't take the opportunity to spend time in Your presence. Help them to become real Christians who can set an example . . . and give the rest of us the grace to deal with it."

A momentary pause came, but no one moved. No one was foolish enough to think it was over.

When Ricky first came to the ranch, he'd rejoiced at the prospect of beginning each workday with "corporate prayer." He'd always wanted to work someplace where the employees would pray together, so chapel each morning seemed like a great idea. But it wasn't long before the reality of the situation struck him. In the past, Ricky hadn't spent required prayer time with someone who had a personal agenda every day. Clothing her words in religious terms and addressing them to God, Myra indulged in endless repetitions and accusations.

At the first opportunity, she would launch into a whole litany of items she wanted others to review. Once she'd finished her list of regular items, she'd move on to public correction of anything falling short of her strict, personal code of behavior. Names were never mentioned, of course, but each "somebody," or "one of us" became acutely aware of it when they erred. Ricky, in particular, seemed to garner a lot of Myra's attention.

Now, as he sat there, the object of another roast, something occurred to Ricky. Something he'd not thought possible had happened. He'd begun to dread chapel time.

Finally, it ended and he had to get to work. He left the room and started toward his office.

Chuck Talbot, a resident teacher at the ranch, jogged a few steps to catch up. "Some of us were pretty late this morning," he observed.

Ricky groaned. "Oh yeah. And some of us are real sorry, too."

Chuck smiled and put a hand on his friend's shoulder as he leaned closer. "You're in obvious need of help, son. Her Holiness may have to devote more time to your behavior tomorrow."

Ricky started to say something, then stopped and cleared his throat. "Any problems reported last night?"

"Yep. Guess who needed stitches in a broken right hand and then said he 'couldn't remember' how it happened?"

Ricky instantly knew. A fifteen-year-old boy had been admitted to the ranch just days ago. "Shawn?"

"You got it."

"Where did it happen?"

"This is where it gets intriguing. When Nigel made his rounds at three this morning, he found Shawn washing blood off his hand in a third-floor bathroom. I had a good look around after I got him back from the infirmary and what I found wasn't on the third floor but the second floor."

Ricky looked surprised. "Second floor?

"Yeah. Two nice new holes in the wall by the utility closet. One of the holes is about the size of someone's fist, the other one's quite a bit larger."

For security purposes, cameras observed the third floors, exits, and stairwells of the dorms. Ricky was puzzled. "And you have nothing on tape?"

"The whole system in our building went down last night. It's up again this morning, but that won't help us now."

"You think Jason might have been part of this?" Ricky asked.

"My thoughts exactly. What better way for Shawn to prove himself than by beating Jason? He'd have heard some talk and figured Jason as the one to beat. The fact that it happened on Jason's floor was like confirmation to me, but I checked on Jason just after it happened. He was in his bed and he didn't have any black eyes, or fat lips, or cuts I could see." Chuck shook his head and shrugged. "I know Shawn did it somehow, but there's no evidence he got off the third floor. I'm requesting we have an extra man at night in my dorm till we figure this out."

Ricky nodded. "We're really gonna have to watch this one."

"No kidding. By the way, Henderson wants to see you as soon as you're settled. Probably about Shawn. He's called for an emergency evaluation this afternoon." Chuck looked at his watch. "I've got a class now. I'll talk to you later."

"Yeah. Later."

From the moment he'd laid eyes on Shawn, Ricky knew there would be a struggle ahead. He had no direct information, but the distinct feeling this young man had done something *very* bad. Maybe killed someone. Whatever Shawn had done, nothing about his demeanor showed remorse or fear of punishment. Ricky's internal caution lights flashed as soon as he saw the kid.

He unlocked his office door and went inside, leaving the door open. A quick look at the calendar on his desk confirmed the day. Thursday. He wouldn't have any classes until after lunch.

"Got a minute?" Mr. Henderson said from the open doorway. A skinny man in his early sixties, nearly everything about Paul Henderson's crooked body confirmed a hard life. His badly pockmarked skin showed the thickness of heavy drug use in his youth. He had tattoos everywhere but his face and he walked with a slight limp. Despite his battered appearance, his eyes often shone with joy, and when he smiled, so many creases materialized that his whole face smiled. This morning, however, there was no smile.

Ricky remained standing. "Sure. I was just about to head over to your office. Wanna talk here or there?"

The older man entered and closed the door. Both men sat, and Henderson got right to the point. "Anybody talk to you yet about last night?"

"Yeah. Chuck told me."

"Well, we need some answers and we need 'em quick. I know this seems like a small incident, and I don't want to overreact, but I have a bad feeling about it. I don't want to break a confidence, but I'll risk telling you that I went out on a limb for this kid, Shawn. Now I'm afraid he could become a serious problem for the ranch if the situation isn't attended to. I'm asking Chuck, Vinnie, and you to investigate the whole deal. If we need to change security procedures, we'll do it. If we need to remove Shawn Thatcher from the Ranch. . ."

Ricky closed his eyes.

"I know, Ricky, I know. I feel the same way. I don't want to lose even one boy. But if he's not ours to work with, we'd better find out and do something about it."

Although Henderson and Ricky both believed no one should be considered "too bad" to be saved, they also knew some boys would refuse to be helped. Both men had the sinking feeling Shawn might be one of those they wouldn't reach.

"You're right." Ricky finally said. "This is either God's appointment for him or the enemy trying to harm the ranch in some way. I'll go right over to building five and look around."

Henderson rose to his feet. "Thanks. We'll all meet in my office after school's out." He started for the door, then turned. "Oh. With all this I almost forgot to tell you. Tomorrow after lunch that recruiter for the Zenith Corps is coming."

Ricky's heart sank. "You couldn't stall 'em any longer?"

Mr. Henderson shrugged. "They threatened to appeal for another investigation of our tax status if I refused. I couldn't afford to get everything frozen in an audit right now. It's as simple as that. But after the Corps holds their little rally, we'll show them off the property and have our own little assemblies to discuss it with the boys."

Shortly after the turn of the millennium, in an attempt to deal with a large number of young people who were increasingly out of control, politicians enacted a series of laws. Under certain circumstances, by order of a court or with permission from the legal guardians, a boy or girl aged 12 or older could be placed in a pre-military program known as the Zenith Corps. Children over the age of 16 could enlist in the program.

Ricky sighed. "It's too bad things have gotten so desperate.

Henderson shook his head. "Twenty years ago, unless you met all sorts of criteria, the military wouldn't take you."

Ricky picked up a pencil and drew on a notepad. "Ever think that might still be the case?"

"You mean that they're recruiting criminals so that they can exploit their . . . 'talents?' Yes. It's occurred to me. But I gotta admit Zenith's spin on it must sound good to all those frustrated parents, and the people in the justice system, who are overwhelmed at this point. They're relieved of all responsibility, and can walk away from what was going to be a long-term problem. And then, there's the bonus money."

The Zenith Corps would pay lump sum "bonuses" to those who signed over children to the corps. The money could serve as "repayment" to guardians for past civil judgments against them, or it could be collected by the justice system. Then, the boy or girl would work off this sum of money during their term of service. Zenith declared it was a "positive solution which made the guilty—not parents or the system— pay for their deeds." Both voluntary enlistment and the court order to serve were considered binding contracts. Some child advocates became alarmed. Wasn't this like slavery? At the very least, it was indentured servanthood. While people at the highest levels of the Cole administration promised to "look into" the allegations, everyone figured the president had bigger fish to fry.

Ricky shook his head. "So many families can barely scrape by anymore. It's got to be a temptation to get the money."

The old man rose, walked to the door, and opened it. "God help us. See what you can find over in the dorm."

Within a few minutes, Ricky stood in building five, the dorm where Chuck Talbot, Shawn, and Jason resided. The third floor of every dorm was basically a "lockdown" for new boys and for those who committed serious infractions on the ranch. The higher security of this floor allowed the staff to evaluate newcomers or isolate trouble makers. Once a student was deemed no longer apt to run away, or a danger to other students, he would be allowed on the second floor—moderate security—and eventually, with good behavior, to the ground floor which had only light security. A boy could be returned to the third floor three times; but after his fourth serious infraction, he would be expelled from the ranch.

After looking around the building, Ricky figured Chuck must be right. As impossible as it seemed, Shawn Thatcher might have actually passed beyond locked doors, escaped from the third floor and returned without being seen. If so, they'd have to find out how he did it before something more serious occurred. The last stop in Ricky's search for clues would be the room of the most feared boy in the dorm: Jason McAllister. Just as a formality, Ricky knocked on the door of the second-floor bedroom before entering. Jason and his roommate would be in class so there was time to look around.

The boys would be on full alert now so he doubted there would be any contraband in the room, unless they hadn't found a way to ditch it. He checked their mattresses first and found no evidence of re-sewn seams. He looked for objects which might be taped under drawers or tied to the stopper in the drain of the sink. Nothing. As he checked to see if the air vent in the room remained welded in place, he sensed someone else's presence. He looked over at the doorway and saw Jason eying him with disgust. Sixteen years old and the product of multiple foster homes, the boy had learned the best way to protect himself was to intimidate others. Everything about the posture of his muscular, 5- foot 10- inch body said he wanted to fight. Of course, on a ranch filled with other delinquents, he'd had to go a notch meaner in order to keep the other residents at bay.

"Just a snap inspection," Ricky said, matter-of-factly. "So far, you're clean. Whatcha doing here? Don't you have class?"

"Forgot my book," Jason replied, walking over and snatching one out of a stack.

"Oh. So that kid, uh, what does everyone call him? Squeaky? He didn't come and tell you he saw me up here?"

Jason remained silent.

Ricky continued, "Of course, if I had a lookout, I'd want him to be less obvious, you know?"

Jason turned to leave.

"Since you're here and all," Ricky said quickly, "why don't we have a talk?"

The boy stopped but kept his back to Ruiz. "I'll be late to class," he said.

"No problem." Ricky pulled a small notepad from his shirt pocket. "I'll just make myself a little note here to run by your—what class is it?"

"Geometry." Jason turned around. Did he hate Ruiz more than Geometry? It was a toss-up.

Ricky smiled. "Right. Mr. Keene. I'll just run by Mr. Keene's class when we're done and tell him I detained you."

Jason shifted the book from one hand to the other; then, out of habit, flipped his stringy brown hair out of his eyes. As he did so, an involuntary jerk went through him, as if he'd hurt himself or done something he hadn't meant to do.

Ricky pretended not to notice. "I just need to ask you a few questions."

Jason frowned. "I didn't do nothin' Mr. Ruiz. Mr. Talbot already talked to me."

"Okay. But why don't you just help me clarify a few things."

Ricky casually pulled a chair out from the desk, straddled it like a horse, and sat down as he folded his arms across its back. It became obvious no one would be leaving until an interview had taken place.

The boy made no attempt to hide his irritation as he sat on the end of his bed. "How come you're not asking anybody else around here? What makes you think I had anything to do with it? He's on the third floor, Mr. Ruiz. I was here in my room all night. Bobby can tell you that," he said, pointing to his roommate's bed. "And why are you always after me anyway?" When he finished the question, he looked over at the doorway and then broke a cocky, they'll-never-make-me-squeal kind of smile.

Ricky turned to follow the young man's gaze and saw a group of boys who'd gathered in the hall to watch and listen.

He smiled and gave them a little wave before addressing them in a cheerful voice.

"Did all of you come up here to check on that pack of cigarettes hidden in the empty soap box on the back of the top shelf of the utility closet?" The remark seemed to register with a couple of the boys, and, in his peripheral vision, Ricky could see Jason's whole countenance fall. "Sorry," Ruiz continued in the same upbeat tone. "They're all down the toilet now. Or were you guys just bored? No classes? Need extra chores?"

The boys scattered and Ruiz looked at Jason again. Visible through long strands of oily hair, Ruiz could see bright red skin on the boy's right ear.

"What were we talking about anyway?" Ricky asked. "Oh yeah. You just got back down to the second floor last week. You like it up there on the third floor? You wanna go back? I'm telling you, if you start going after that Shawn kid you're back where you started."

With studied casualness, Jason said, "Like I need to worry about him."

Ricky let his focus drift from Jason to the mini-blinds in the window behind the boy's left shoulder. He kept staring at them as if something there had captured his attention. "Fine. Because . . . if Shawn somehow got off . . . the third floor and sneaked up on you, it wouldn't be entirely your fault . . . this time . . . you know? But if you. . ."

Jason couldn't stand it any longer. He shifted around to look at the window. "What are you lookin' at?"

"See that bottom casing on the mini-blinds?" Ricky asked, sticking out his hand to point at it. Perfectly timed with Jason's turn, he let his knuckles brush up against the right side of the boy's head.

The boy jumped to his feet and clapped a hand on his ear. He started to cry out but quickly stopped and put his hand down. His jaw flexed repeatedly as he struggled to compose himself.

"Sorry." Ricky said. "You moved in front of my hand. So what's wrong with your head?"

"Nothing. I'm fine, Mr. Ruiz. You want anything else?"

"Can I have a look at your head?"

"Do I have a choice?"

"No. Not really. I need to be sure you're not badly hurt."

Jason realized it was futile to resist. "Whatever."

Ricky took him over by the window and opened the blinds further for better light. "Move your hair out of the way."

The young man pulled dirty hair over the top of his head. The skin wasn't broken, but a red and blue swollen area engulfed his right ear and ended at the back of his skull. When Ricky lightly pressed a spot behind the ear Jason straightened up and inhaled loudly.

"You have a bad headache?"

"Not until you smacked me."

"You injured anyplace else?"

"No."

"What happened? Someone use your head to knock a hole in a wall maybe?"

The boy stared defiantly ahead. "I don't remember."

"I see. Amnesia could be a symptom of a serious injury. I think we need to go to the infirmary."

"I've been hurt worse."

"I have no doubt of that," Ricky said. "But you still need to have this looked at. I'll speak with Mr. Keene later." He glanced at the doorway to make sure they were still alone. "Meanwhile, stay away from Shawn."

A sneer came to Jason's lips. "I'm not scared of him. If he wants to try to cut—" he stopped talking.

"Cut rank?" Ricky said, using the popular term for humiliating someone superior in strength or power in order to undermine them. "You think I don't know how this works? If he wants to take over, he's gotta start cutting your rank. When are you going to wise up and stop playing these dumb games? Don't you ever get tired of looking over your shoulder night and day? Of having to be tough all the time?"

No reply came.

Ricky wanted to be very clear. "You can waste a very short life living like this if you want to, but I'm telling you, Jason, all your victories and all your highs will be temporary. You'll never know lasting satisfaction. Know what else? There will never be a day of rest. When ranking is what matters, there is no rest. Every minute of every day, you'll know down inside that, eventually there'll be someone bigger than you, smarter than you." Ricky leaned forward. "Or able to lay a better trap than you." He saw a glint of recognition in Jason's eyes. "And it will be all over."

Ricky pointed to the door. "Out there in the world, once someone really cuts rank on ya, you're less than a dog. Even if you retaliate, everyone remembers you were cut. You were vulnerable. Then they remember the things you did to them, and it makes all of them think about cuttin' your rank. The only way to win, Jason, is to drop out of the game."

The boy gave him a hard stare. "I remember now. I slipped and hit my head in the shower. That's how it happened."

Ricky's heart sank. Obviously, he hadn't connected on any level with Jason other than to possibly awaken a greater need to prevail over Shawn.

"Okay," Ricky sighed, "I'll walk you over to the infirmary."

By the time he drove home that evening, he felt tired and discouraged. He barely touched his dinner, and then retreated to his favorite chair while Rosa put Angela Rose and Daniel to bed. When she came back to the living room, she found her husband leaning back in his chair, staring at the ceiling.

"You not feeling well?" she asked.

"I'm okay."

"You didn't like the dinner?"

"Dinner was good."

"Something is definitely wrong. You're exhausted. I'll stay up with Daniel tonight."

"No," he quickly answered. "We'll take turns. You're tired, too."

As long as she'd known him, Ricky had always been a joyful person, often singing or humming one tune or another. But over the past few weeks he'd gradually become quiet. Tonight, he seemed almost sullen.

She tried to consider other possible causes. Since they'd moved from New York, they'd been on a very tight budget. If at all possible, she wanted to stay home with her children, so the couple looked for alternatives. They rented a tiny apartment and purchased only necessities. Rosa babysat for other people's children and Ricky sometimes worked on Saturdays for extra money. As a side-benefit, Henderson let the Ruiz's use a car from the ranch as long as they paid for fuel. Even so, their budget strained at its seams.

After another few minutes of silence, Rosa could bear it no longer. "Ooooookay," she said, sitting on the arm of the chair and pulling his chin around. "It's time to talk, Señor

Ruiz. If this is about the ticket, we have a little money saved up. Don't be so hard on yourself. Just look at all the money I threw away before we were married."

He sat there for a moment, looking at her. "That's not it."

"Then, what's wrong?" she asked.

He looked around the room. "So much is happening."

"Tell me," she softly pleaded.

"Well, for one thing, there's the problem with the boys," he said, tapping his fingers on the other arm of the chair. "After I talked to Jason this morning, I had this terrible feeling inside all day. I'm sure he has every intention of beating up that new boy." He glanced at Rosa. "All of the kids are important to me, but Jason . . ."

She tried to comfort him. "If anyone has ever demonstrated how God can make someone's life good, Ricky, it's you. Jason will see. That all?"

He shook his head. "Henderson told me he couldn't keep the Zenith Corps away any longer. They're coming tomorrow with a recruiter." He frowned. "Why can't they leave our boys alone?"

Rosa knew what a sore subject this was with him. She leaned over to peer into his eyes. "We can pray, can't we?"

"Which brings me to the embarrassing part," he said.

"Embarrassing part?"

"Yeah." He started tapping on the arm of the chair again. "There I was, flying down that road this morning because I didn't want Myra to toast me in front of everybody for being late. . . . Well, I got a ticket, I was late, *and* I got toasted. And just as I was gettin' cooked nice and crispy, I realized something else. It's gotten so I hate going to chapel. I hate sitting there for Myra's daily prayer/lectures about whoever has fallen from her good graces."

Rosa looked shocked.

He saw the look. "Yeah." He exhaled loudly. "I know . . . all evening, I've been thinking of that scripture where Paul says: 'be careful when you think you stand, lest you fall . . .' Oh, Rosa, I need, more than ever, to be listening to God and I've let myself get pulled off track." He reached over and grasped her hand before closing his eyes. "Lord, I want to run to You. You rescued me, Father. I want to show it every day, yet somehow I've gotten caught up in living to please people and not You. How stupid of me! Help me to set it right, Lord. I want to reflect Your love. I want to bless others, not hate them or curse them."

Rosa prayed silently. She'd never known anyone with a purer heart than Ricky. She only hoped she could learn to be as honest about her own shortcomings.

CHAPTER 21

PHILADELPHIA — August 16th

Bragjesh Advani and Sven Borgeson sat opposite one another at the large table, preparing for a late-evening board meeting. Even though the men were poles apart in many ways, they had a common cause for which they'd both labored. The two had co-chaired the organizing committee for the World Conference on Spirituality for nearly two years. Sven, a blond, blue-eyed Swede had a generally happy, gregarious personality. Bragjesh had dark eyes and skin and, while Oxford educated, still retained much of his Indian culture and tended to be more pensive.

The Conference would take place in less than six weeks and the enormous demands of implementing all the final details were taking a toll on most of the committee. Bragjesh, in particular, found the need for lengthy stays in America increasingly trying.

When Sven and many of the Europeans on the committee spearheaded the original drive to hold the conference in the United States, it hadn't been Bragjesh's first choice. It wasn't even his second choice. The US was such a hard place for the movement, really.

Then, after all the riots, Bragjesh took the opportunity to suggest they move the conference elsewhere. But Sven felt certain the problem would work in their favor. So many large cities were desperate for tourism dollars, the committee could get bargain prices. Philadelphia—the city of brotherly love—became so cooperative, shouldn't that be seen as a fore-shadowing of something good?

Even now, Bragjesh shook his head thinking of America's current condition. Maybe, if they'd have had the conference here thirty years ago . . . or even ten, it would have been easier. America had been ripe during those seasons and never fully brought to harvest. Increasingly, however, a current had begun to flow against the movement. Trying to accomplish things here now turned into one problem after another. He told Sven they were like salmon swimming upstream.

Sven merely smiled and said, "Isn't that what ensures the strongest salmon survive?"

The final straw, to Bragjesh, came when he heard UN headquarters would be moved out of America. "Don't you see?" he said to Sven. "The UN leaving is just another sign that things are going to the dogs in this country. Things have changed—especially in the last couple of years, and I don't mean for the better. Don't you see? The international community is washing its hands of America. We would have been better off to have the conference in Brussels, as I suggested."

"Ahhhhh . . . My dear friend," Sven chided. "You're still angry President Cole refused to give us an official welcome for the opening ceremonies . . . Don't you see? This is fantastic! These things will prove our point. Even when politics, diplomacy, and other ways of man fail, we will succeed! So many things are in place for the last, great Transition, how could you not see how strategic this is?"

"What I see is that this is a mistake," Bragjesh said. "We should have washed our hands of this country two years ago and settled for a smaller conference elsewhere. Take note of my words."

A small chime notified them the secretary had a message. Sven reached for the flashing light on his screen and touched it. "Yes?"

A woman's soft, accented voice came back through the speaker. "Mr. Gordon from the Philadelphia Arena is here with the final draft documents."

"Send him in, please."

The door to the room opened and Zac Gordon, dressed in a dark blue suit, entered the room. He shook hands with both men and seated himself.

"I wanted to bring the final plan down personally," he said, "so we could dialog face to face if there were any unsettled issues."

"Really?" Sven said, exposing gleaming teeth in the middle of a perfectly trimmed blond beard. He shot a glance at Bragjesh before saying, "How accommodating of you. I was just saying how I'd found the people of Philadelphia to be so helpful."

Contrary to the friendly words, Zac had the distinct impression he'd come at a bad moment. "Of course, you don't have to look over it right now," he said, taking the small disk out of his pocket and handing it to Sven. "But I thought I'd make myself available in case you had any further questions or needs."

Sven popped the disk into a slot in his processor and his screen lit up with text. He scanned the document for the highlighted changes before looking at Mr. Gordon again. "This all appears to be satisfactory, but we'll need to look it over in more depth with the others. Is that all right with you?"

"Yes. I just wanted to be sure you had it all in hand before the transfer of funds on Monday."

"Thank you. I'm sure we'll be getting back to you first thing tomorrow."

Zac rose from his chair to leave.

Bragjesh spoke for the first time. "There is something, though. A point of interest—not related to the services you are providing."

"Yes?"

"Would you agree that America is ready for broad social change?"

Gordon was at a loss. What did this guy want, anyway? Certain things did need to change in America, yet there was something about the man's question that made Zac want to say, no. He quickly reminded himself, though, that this could be the most important business transaction of his life. He smiled at the man from India. "What kind of change do you mean?"

"A willingness to embrace a broader spectrum in life. A true willingness to love those of other cultures."

Zac wanted very badly to say, *Yeah. Some people don't love everybody. I just hate people like that.* Instead, he shrugged. "I'm afraid, Mr. Advani, that you've caught me out of my depth. I'm not a very spiritual person, so my viewpoint wouldn't be of much value on such a question."

"Never the less," Bragjesh pressed, "would you say the heart of the average man or woman here is ready to receive change? Do they want to embrace a deeper life?"

Sven added, "Surely you must have a few thoughts on the matter. We'd be interested in hearing what they are."

Zac looked at the two men, certain it would be to his benefit to at least sound receptive to their general view. Yet, part of him was rising up to resist—as if he'd been challenged. "This side of death, who can truly know what is in the heart of a man, or what he might do?"

Sven, laughed. "Cleverly spoken, Mr. Gordon. We will all have to walk out our destinies, trusting the unseen, eh?"

Zac knew he was dancing with trouble. He wanted to say, *I trust nothing*, but decided to just excuse himself and head home. As long as they paid to use the arena these people could hold any views they wished.

CHAPTER 22

OKLAHOMA — August 17th

After a good night's sleep, Enrique Ruiz awoke early. He watched the muted light of sunrise come through the curtains and highlight objects in the room. He slipped from the bed and quickly dressed, lingering only a moment to look at his wife, Rosa, before he quietly left the room.

Yesterday, he'd had such a rotten day, but today would be different. He could feel it already. Releasing his problems often became so easy once he allowed himself to be honest about them. He opened the curtains to the living room window and looked out on the glowing horizon.

Father, I'm so sorry I stopped being grateful to You lately. I've let worries about the world and circumstances at work weigh me down, but I'm glad I can start again. Thank You for a new day. Thank You for my love, my Rosa. Thank You for my little ones. God, You give me so much. . .

He placed a hand on the window sill and bowed his head, overwhelmed with a sense of awe. He left a silent place in his thoughts, just listening, soaking in the joy rising in his heart before continuing his inward prayer.

Thank You for the opportunity to tell those boys they can be set free. Even now, as I'm thinking of him, please Lord, help Jason. Only You know all of the terrible things that have been done to him. Only You can rescue him from the cage in his mind. I commit him to Your care today, and ask that You begin to loose him from the thoughts, attitudes, and intentions of his heart that the enemy is using to lead him to his death. I place him in Your care and ask for Your mercy, Lord. . . . And as for Shawn . . . give me the wisdom to know what to do, what to say. What can I pray for him? May all the plans and snares the enemy intends to use in him be overtaken. Father, I know no one is beyond Your ability to save. I'm asking for his life, Lord . . . and if we're not the ones who can show him the way, I ask You send him where he belongs . . .

Rosa opened the door to the living room just a crack and peered out. She saw Ricky, leaning against the windowsill and closed the door again. It wasn't time for breakfast yet, so she would give him another few minutes alone.

Soon, she heard the bedroom door open and looked up to see him peeking around it. A large grin lit his face. "Hi! Look who's up?" he said, opening the door wider.

In his arms he held a chubby twelve-week-old Daniel Tomás. Ricky bounced into the room with the baby before holding him up in the air, then bringing the infant's face close to his several times. He laughed as Daniel rewarded him with a gummy grin.

Rosa took the baby. "Good morning, sunshine! You want some breakfast?"

"You talking to me or to him?" Ricky asked.

"Yes."

"No breakfast for me," he said, looking over a few dollars and putting them back in his pocket. "I've got some extra time today, and I have a little money, so I think I'll stop and pick up some things to take to work."

"Things. Like donut things?"

He straightened. "Who me? My wife has declared she'll perish if she doesn't lose those 'last' ten pounds. Would I buy donuts?"

"Yes."

He cocked his head to one side. "You want me to save you one?"

She sighed loudly before saying a quiet, "No."

"Ohhhhh. That was so pathetic, Rosa. The sigh at the beginning was particularly pitiful. The angels are probably weeping, even now."

She wanted very badly to look sternly at him but couldn't help laughing at herself. "It was good, wasn't it? I'll expect an Oscar on the shelf tonight."

Ricky kissed mother and child. "Promise me. If he does anything new today, you'll take a picture?"

"Yes sir."

Less than an hour later, Ricky entered the administration building of the Henderson Youth Ranch with a box of fresh pastries. He grabbed one and left the open box on the counter of the employee's little kitchen. When he exited, he saw Myra sitting at her desk reading a Bible.

"Hey, Myra," he said in a cheerful voice. "There's donuts and danish in the kitchen if you want any."

She looked up and her eyes narrowed slightly. "No, thank you."

"If you change your mind, they're in there," he said, before turning and striding down the hall, humming a little tune.

When it came time for chapel, Ricky's good mood even withstood Myra's continued toasting. This time, instead of being angry, he felt sorry for her. Obviously, a good portion of her life had been overshadowed by things she felt she wasn't allowed to do . . . and who could live like that? No wonder she was cranky.

Myra opened her eyes several times while she prayed. The serene look on Mr. Ruiz' face angered her even more. She asked herself, *how could they have hired such a senseless man?*

After chapel, Ricky asked Chuck about the dorm.

"How'd it go last night? Any incidents?"

Chuck shook his head. "Not a thing to report. I figure it will stay that way for a while. They know we're watching 'em."

Ricky agreed, but both men knew it wasn't over.

A full schedule made the morning pass quickly. After lunch, Capt. Foster of the Zenith Corps would be presenting information about enlistment to the boys. When the Captain finished, the owner of the ranch, Mr. Henderson, would send the boys to their individual dorms for discussions with the staff about what they'd heard.

As the time for the assembly arrived, Ricky stood in the back of the gym. He wanted to be able to see the whole room.

Shawn Thatcher strutted into the gym and smiled with satisfaction as some foot-stomping echoed around the room. A number of boys were sounding for him.

"Hey now," Ricky said in a slightly raised voice, "none of that."

Sounding was the latest extension of gang culture to take its place alongside graffiti, signs, and colors. Sounding was intended to both intimidate and declare personal territory. Every gang leader, hard case, or wanna-be had a sound. Whenever he/she roamed home turf, acknowledgment took the form of a tune, a shout, or a noise—distinctively his or hers—sounded by representatives or those who, through admiration or intimidation, thought they should pay this audible tribute. If it were a tune, a whole neighborhood might resound with stereos playing it when a gang leader moved about. Sounding served as both a recognition to the honored one, and a warning to foes. If two leaders came into the same place, only the one perceived to be the stronger was allowed "sound." If both groups sounded, violence generally settled the matter.

While the practice was forbidden on the ranch, the stomping noise coming to Ricky's ears said Shawn had won some points over the past twenty-four hours. Some of the boys were declaring him the winner of whatever contest had taken place—by giving him sound.

Ricky refocused his attention on the stage where the man representing the Zenith Corps prepared to address the assembly. Capt. Foster, a man with a youthful appearance, brought two other guest speakers with him. One of them, a lovely girl named Gail, about twenty years old, had "graduated" from the Zenith Corps, and had opted to serve in the Army for an additional two years. The other, a seventeen-year-old boy named Mark, had been in the Zenith Corps for a year. Both Gail and Mark appeared in prime physical condition and carried themselves with confidence.

Foster stood at the podium and addressed the assembly first.

"I'm really glad to be here today and I hope, after my presentation, I can get to know some of you personally.

"Several years ago, the Zenith Corps was started in order to take young men and young women who, without intervention, might be deprived of a productive and successful future. At the time, many youth were destined to spend their valuable potential spinning into dead ends. Some had begun lives of crime. Some were dropouts. Most of them were doomed to fail in life . . . until the Corps came into the picture.

"Today, the Zenith Corps is where the military looks to find specialists, where corporations look to fill those entry-level positions, and where many tech schools look for new trainees. Why? Because we offer the 'total program' that can change lives and give young men and women the edge they didn't have before.

"In a few minutes, Gail and Mark here will speak of their own experiences. After they've spoken, we'll entertain questions from all of you. At the close of the assembly, the three of us will be at the table by the door to pass out information and enlistment forms or to answer any further questions you might have."

Ricky looked around the room at the audience. Captain Foster was speaking, but most of the eyes in the room had focused on Gail. Noticing this, Foster made sure to stress all Zenith facilities were "coed."

In about fifteen minutes, the captain described the Zenith Corps plan. The program had two levels to accommodate boys from the ranch: The first was for fourteen and fifteen-year-olds. The second was for people of sixteen and seventeen years. Foster elaborated for the throng of eager listeners.

"Both levels stress total fitness—body and soul—specifically tailored to the needs of the age group," Foster said. "In short, we teach you how to maximize your life." He looked out and surveyed his audience. "But this program isn't for everyone. If you're satisfied with a dead-end life, you won't want the opportunities we offer. If you're happy being a scrawny little nobody, our martial arts training would be wasted on you. If you like being an acne-covered blimp, our strict dietary program is not for you. If you don't mind being powerless, you won't want to unlock the raw potential that's dormant in you right now. If you don't want to change, stay right where you are . . . because the Zenith program is about transformation. We turn failures into self-realized success stories."

Ricky realized every secret desire these boys had was being offered to them in a way that would appeal to their rebellious natures. Foster was definitely good at what he did.

Gail spoke next. When one of the boys in the audience loudly made a rude offer, she looked directly at him and coolly replied, "I've been liberated by the Zenith Corps. I am free to say yes to anyone I choose . . . I choose men of strength, of intelligence, and power . . . men who are successful. Needless to say, I wouldn't say yes to someone like you—and with a black belt in Karate I'll never have to." She smiled with satisfaction as most of the boys in the gym looked at the humiliated taunter and echos of "Doink!" reverberated around the room.

The next speaker, Mark, made an equally vivid impression with his story of being "the one in class everyone picked on," a dropout, and druggie before the Zenith Corps "unleashed" his potential. He ended with, "I went home last month for my first visit . . . I control my own destiny now. Nobody 'doinks' at me anymore."

The way the boy said the words made Ricky's blood run cold.

When the presentation ended, Capt. Foster reminded the boys they could speak with him or with Gail and Mark over at the information table. Ricky watched more than twenty boys swarm over the table and an even larger crowd form off to the side, around Gail who smiled as she passed out information forms and applications. Several more boys hovered in the vicinity undecidedly. One young man, moving through groups of boys milling about the room, caught Ricky's attention. Jason McAllister casually walked to the table, picked up several different papers and left.

Fifteen minutes later, in the large recreation room of building five, Ricky and Chuck had gathered the boys from all three floors. Similar meetings were going on in the other two dorms at the Ranch. Without being assigned places, it seemed the boys living on the first floor sat mostly toward the front of the room, the second floor boys sat in the middle, and the boys from the third floor occupied the back.

Waiting until the room became quiet, Ricky spoke first.

"I gotta say, if I were one of you guys, what Capt. Foster offered would sound pretty good. I think what he said, in a nutshell, was if you sign up for the Corps you'll become desirable. Wasn't that it? Desirable to the military, big corporations, women . . ."

"Everybody except Hal Neusbaum!" a boy in the back yelled through cupped hands, referring to the boy who'd been humiliated by Gail.

Laughter momentarily filled the room followed by a chorus of boys saying, "Doink!"

"Hey!" another boy shouted, "No sounding! Everyone knows that's Hal's sound!"

Another roar of hysteria went through the boys followed by more doinks.

Ricky raised his hands for silence. "Okay, that's enough. Let's get back to the subject here. The people at Zenith have had their time to state what they want you to believe. Now it's time to give it some thought." Ricky looked around the room.

"Zenith wants you to think their program is the ticket to the life of your dreams. But is it as easy as they want you to believe?" The room became still and he tried to make eye contact with the boys. "Is it really so easy?"

"You're always selling that Christian junk. What gives you the right to put those Corps people down?" a hostile voice in the back said.

Ricky knew who asked the question. He recognized the voice. He looked right at the boy before answering. "First of all, Jason, I don't recall ever 'selling' my faith. It isn't for sale. Secondly, I don't believe I put them down."

The atmosphere tightened when the young man stood to his feet with his fists clenched. All eyes focused on him. Was Jason stupid enough to challenge Mr. Ruiz to a fight?

Ricky continued. "So, let me see if I have this right. You say I have no right to express what I think, but you can say any insulting thing you want? That about it?"

Jason gave no response.

Ricky crossed his arms and spoke calmly. "Go ahead. This isn't a test. I'm not going to have you electrocuted for giving your opinion. . . . You're relatively new, but," he said, looking at the other young men in the room, "can anyone say Mr. Talbot or I have kept you from voicing an opinion?"

"No, Mr. Ruiz," several boys in the front answered.

Jason glared at them in disgust. *Goody-goody little choir boys.*

Ruiz spoke again. "We let Capt. Foster have his say. Now I'll let you have a go at it. I only ask one thing: Make your point without using profanity. You can do that, can't you?"

Jason's words shot out like daggers. "I'm sayin' it's all the same. It's all like jail. And jail is where all you Christian hypocrites belong—like that evangelist guy. What does it matter if we're here or with Zenith? At least we could get something out of Zenith."

"Oh yeah?" Ricky asked. "Like what would you get?"

Jason thought for a moment. "Like power to escape."

Ricky gave him a questioning look. "Don't kid yourself Jason. If you enlist, they own you. If you change your mind or screw up, they won't send you back here or to the justice system. They have their own detention camps. Labor camps. You'll work off what you owe—what they've paid for you—one way or another. I believe Capt. Foster neglected to mention that little fact. Here's the difference: While you're here, you are in our custody, but you're not our property. We don't believe anyone has the right to own another person. No government agency pays us to keep you, and we don't pay anybody to keep you." Ricky's voice softened and he looked around the room. "As far as we're concerned, each of you was created in the image and likeness of God, and the only one who has a right to all you are and all you have is God." His words took some of the tension out of the room.

"And there's another difference between this ranch and the Corps: We don't believe there's some sort of power hidden in you somewhere. We don't believe you have some secret force we can unlock to make you rich, successful, or famous. You were made with gifts and talents God can bless in you, but power only flows through you. It's not your power.

"Listen, guys," Ricky continued, "just about any 'program' will work to some extent if you believe in it and are willing to discipline yourself. You can take body building here on the ranch. You can have a vegetarian diet here on the ranch . . . we just won't make you do it."

He stopped a moment and thought before continuing. "I know most of you guys. Which one of you wouldn't want to be free to start over? Which one of you, way down inside, wouldn't be willing to give up the dream Capt. Foster talked about just to have a regular life with some real joy in it? Some real friends? Maybe even one special woman to share it with?"

"Right," Jason interrupted. "Like the pathetic thing who's *your* shackle?" He'd never seen Ricky's wife, but just assumed she had to be stupid, homely, or both. What other kind of woman would settle for Mr. Ruiz?

Another challenge had been thrown out. All heads turned from Jason to Ricky.

Ricky looked at him, then smiled.

How Jason hated that smile. *What would I give to knock it off his face?*

The smile faded before Ruiz spoke. "This isn't about me, Jason, it's about you and how you're gonna end up spending your life. If you think memorizing rules, or eating certain foods, or training your muscles will empower you—enable you to control your life—you're sadly mistaken."

Ricky looked around the room once more. "I'll tell you the truth. Giving your life to God won't suddenly make all your problems go away. But if you let this decision turn into a relationship with Him, He can bring you through each thing that put you here at this ranch . . . each thing that holds you like a prisoner in your own heart. Every one of you is a unique person with unique talents . . . and unique problems. The One who made you is the only One who can work all these things to your good.

"Anyone sixteen or older in this room has the option to join the Corps and leave the ranch. But I beg you to think about it. It's a decision you'll be stuck with for a long time."

CHAPTER 23

WASHINGTON, D.C. — September 4th

President Don Cole, wearing a charcoal suit and a dark red tie, walked down the corridor to the meeting, considering what the real agenda of the meeting "regarding the China issue" might be. He had no doubt E.E. Kressman's emissary had come to make a deal of some sort.

Cole remembered his first, and only, meeting with Kressman, owner of the largest news network on the planet, while still a candidate for the presidency. In the midst of large-scale rioting, Kressman had dispatched a helicopter to fly Don to a huge complex not far from New York City. The man sat behind an immense desk in a plush office, then invited him to dine in the most opulent setting imaginable.

Every moment of that evening had been carefully orchestrated to make Don feel like a beggar dropped into a regal palace. The media mogul, considered by all parties to be "a key player" in negotiating an end to the riots, offered to deal him into the game. In fact, Kressman as much as said he could give Cole the office of President of the United States. Don made it clear, however, that he intended only to work for America's best interest. Since then, Don had neither sought nor received any communication from the corporate CEO . . . but the country hadn't been in such a crisis until now, had it?

Don slowed his pace and looked at the aide walking beside him. "Mark, do you know if anyone has canceled my nine o'clock?"

"Yes," Mark said, consulting a small screen in his hand. "We've cleared your schedule till ten."

"Thanks. Be sure no one disturbs us unless it's urgent," the president said, before an agent stationed by a door opened it.

Mark would not be attending the meeting, so he stopped short of the threshold. "Yes, sir. Buzz me if you need anything."

Cole stepped into the small conference room and the door closed behind him. John Klost and Admiral Fleming rose from their seats.

"Good morning, Mr. President," the Admiral said.

"Good morning, Mr. President," Mr. Klost offered as well. "Thank you for agreeing to meet at such short notice."

Don shook Klost's hand and realized how much the man resembled his employer. He had the same slender frame that made him seem taller than his average height, salt-and-pepper hair, the same prominent cheek and jawbones. Even his voice, soft yet commanding, was reminiscent of E. E. Kressman—and it put Don on alert.

Last night, Don received word that Kressman wanted to transmit information of a secret, urgent nature regarding China through John Klost. Don accepted the meeting, but it would not take place in the Oval Office, and it would not be the one-on-one encounter requested.

As the three men seated themselves at a small table, Don noted Klost's almost-white suit. It was typical of the "East meets West" styles worn by most of Kressman's inner circle. The coat reached half-way to the man's knees, and his tie-less, saffron-colored shirt had a notched-out Nehru collar. A small gold pin with three interlocking triangles graced his lapel. Cole and Admiral Fleming sat on one side of the table, Kressman's messenger on the other.

"Time is of the essence for all of us," Klost said, "so I'll get right to the point."

Don was more than willing to get right to it. "I was told you have some information regarding China."

"Actually, we have information and an offer."

"And what are they?" Fleming, chief advisor for the region, asked.

Klost had an air of stillness about him. He seemed more like a statue of a man in a chair. Only his eyes and his lips moved as he spoke. "Dealing with China, as we all know, is an extremely complex issue. It's so unfortunate that Ambassador Tarrance passed away at such a crucial time in the negotiations. He had such a wealth of wisdom regarding Asia. We can see how you might feel hard pressed in this situation."

In recent weeks, talks with China had once again hit a major snag. To make matters worse, the US Ambassador to China, Joseph Tarrance, had died of a massive heart attack just two days ago. He'd been a patient negotiator in an excruciatingly slow process.

So what did Kressman have to do with all this? "You have information which might be useful?" Don asked.

"Yes," Klost said, slowly lifting an arm to look at his watch. "Less than twenty-four hours ago, a high-ranking official in China contacted Mr. Kressman to say the negotiations might be allowed to continue, with Kressman as a temporary broker."

Don leaned back in his seat and appeared to be thinking for a moment before he responded. "And why, with so much at stake, would I want to send a businessman to negotiate for us? Mr. Kressman isn't even a US citizen."

"Think of it as more of a means around a temporary impasse. Obviously, you'd want to reestablish official negotiations as soon as possible. But for now, the Chinese find dealing with Mr. Kressman palatable, and he's willing to help. It's a role he's successfully assumed in the past, as you know. He not only has favor with the Chinese, but with the European community and the UN, whom you've increasingly alienated. America may have placed itself in the middle of this situation but, frankly, her influence is crumbling. Although Mr. Kressman realizes you and he may not see all things in the same light, he is in a position to help you . . . in more ways than one."

"What sort of ways would those be?"

"I will be direct. Our news organization, UIG, is one of the few 'outside news' bureaus still allowed in mainland China. We have connections you don't have. Let's face it, although the NSA has an enormous capacity for gathering information, they aren't omnipotent or omniscient. They can't know everything or be everywhere. We have access to information which might prove useful in the days to come. In addition, coverage of this situation is continually being broadcast around the world. It certainly would help if America were portrayed in the best possible light internationally, wouldn't it?"

The president looked unmoved. Obviously he was not as unsure of himself as he'd seemed to Kressman two years ago. Since Cole didn't respond, Klost took his case to the next level.

"The US is now in violation of many United Nations' directives—especially those regarding land and water. Your government signed agreements on these matters over a decade ago which are still binding. More than reprimands and fines may be imposed if large strides to comply aren't made soon."

Don knew it was a possibility. During the last part of the twentieth century, agreements were quietly signed, stating the United States would comply with all "resolutions passed by the UN." Former President Todd merely restarted work on neglected "zones" projects. The controversial action of cordoning off large tracts of land and many waterways for "zero population zones," was merely a partial fulfillment of the larger Biosphere Plan passed by the UN years before Todd got into office. Much of America's sovereignty had been signed away during yet *another* former president's watch.

"If you continue to lose favor in the international community," Klost said, looking at Cole and Fleming, "certain countries may succeed in rallying support for international enforcement. China and Russia aren't exactly responsible environmental citizens—or even friends—but they may decide to cooperate at the UN and use your lack of compliance on these issues against you."

This was the truth. The announcement that the UN headquarters would be moved to Europe was just the latest stab at the country's prestige. While many Americans had a "good riddance" attitude about it, Cole knew it would result in a further loss of influence. Many in the UN were looking for any excuse to further humiliate the US—a country whose armed forces had acted as policemen in their countries in years past.

If the United States didn't continue expanding and maintaining environmental projects, the UN could threaten intervention. Arguing that America was a "sovereign nation" would be irrelevant. Weren't Bosnia, Afghanistan, Iraq, Indonesia, India, Pakistan and dozens of other countries sovereign nations? Had this stopped Alliance or United Nations troops from entering these countries and forcing them to comply with international directives? Even now, the US itself was participating in several such police actions. Intervention in the US was possible . . . but not likely.

Don snapped open a bottle of water, poured it in a nearby glass and took a sip. "At some distant point in the future," he finally said, "when the 'global family' is getting along better, they might consider ganging up on us. But, right now, despite UIG's continuing ad campaigns—which would lead people to believe we are a giant pollution factory—we have more square miles of green space per capita than any other country in the world. We've also made good strides towards better air and water. And, candidly, I think most of the other nations have more pressing problems at the moment."

But Klost had come prepared to debate. "There are economic issues to be considered as well. After World War II, the US accounted for about forty percent of the gross world product, but now only accounts for fifteen percent. You have less than five percent of the world's population and only slightly more than six percent of the world's landmass."

Kressman's emissary turned his unblinking stare on Admiral Fleming to make a special point. "Your military commitments haven't diminished in proportion to your economic status. What makes you think you can go on like this? The days when America could bully her way through an issue are about over. Right now, this country has neither the unity nor the strength to meet a serious challenge."

He turned his gaze to the president once again. "China, on the other hand, has nearly twenty-five percent of the world's population and the world's largest economy. If you don't realign yourself more closely with more of the global community, you may find yourself overwhelmed on every side. You and I both know former President Todd had a very poor sense of timing when it came to picking his battles. I hope you're not about to make the same mistake."

The man's employer had sent him with quite an ultimatum. Kressman wanted movement on global and environmental issues as well as a dominant role in negotiating with China. No one could accuse the guy of thinking small.

Don changed the course of the conversation. "So which Chinese official approached Kressman?"

"None other than Guangsheng himself. We are prepared to offer proof of this, should you be favorable toward the offer."

Don looked down at his glass of water and ran his index finger around the rim. He wondered, *What did Kressman threaten the Chinese with?*

"Obviously, this is something I would have to take under advisement," Cole said before looking up. "But I won't mislead you. Unless we feel it would be in the best interest of this country and those we've been asked to represent, the offer won't be accepted."

"Several past administrations," Klost said in an urgent, confidential tone, "have depended upon Mr. Kressman in times of need."

Don's finger stopped moving around the glass. "You mean, it's a tradition. Kind of like a tree, planted by one of my predecessors. One that has grown over the years and extended its influence far beyond what a new tree could . . ."

"Exactly. And, while Mr. Kressman is helping set things up for talks to resume, you could be in the process of bringing in a replacement for Ambassador Tarrance. I'm sure you've heard many suggestions; however, with so much hanging in the balance, we felt that former Ambassador Echols would be the best choice."

Don looked at Admiral Fleming and then back at Klost. Was there no end to this man's *chutzpah*? "And, I'm sure you came prepared to present a good case for this choice."

"Aside from the fact that he has a tremendous amount of experience in the region, Echols is an intelligent man who would be able to get up to speed quickly in the situation. He has many contacts in the area who would be valuable as well."

E. E. Kressman being just one of them, Don thought.

Within an hour of his meeting with John Klost, Don received an intelligence report that a Chinese submarine had been parked two hundred miles off the California coastline for several hours but now was moving away. Had it been intended as a message that they were ready to strike at any time? Or, was it evidence something had changed and they were now backing off?

As Don and his advisors pondered all the possible angles to this new situation, a plan started formulating in his mind. Regardless of demands made on him, his main objective was to protect America, and, in his heart, he still believed it was in her long-term interest to remain firm against Chinese threats.

Until tonight, former Ambassador Derek Echols would have been the obvious (and most qualified) choice for the newly vacated ambassador's post to China. Until tonight. Now, President Cole wanted to personally see all the files regarding Derek Echols. He also wanted the list of other possible candidates expanded to include people who might have limited expertise in some necessary arenas, but were superbly qualified in military, diplomatic, or intelligence fields.

Before leaving his desk that evening, he drafted a directive, forbidding the use of employees of the Universal Information Group as informants or operatives without prior authorization. Any association between covert operatives and UIG personnel would have to be disclosed.

CHAPTER 24

PHILADELPHIA — September 9th

One of Philadelphia's Channel Five News reporters, Linda Posner, waited outside the office of the producer. She didn't want to open the glass door until he invited her in.

Mr. Baumgardener stood at the windows to his office looking out at the buildings, which seemed so much cleaner from a distance. He'd unbuttoned his long-sleeved blue shirt at the collar and rolled up his cuffs, exposing incredibly hairy forearms. He continued listening to the phone headset he wore, but turned to get a pen off his desk and noticed Linda outside his door. He beckoned her with one hand while he covered his microphone with the other. "Come in, come in. Take a seat. I'll be right with you," he said quickly.

She entered the room and sat down, realizing the room still smelled the same way it had the last time she'd been there. Like popcorn. Baumgardener dropped into his chair and turned back to the windows while continuing his conversation with someone at the federal courthouse. "Yeah. Uh huh. . . . Well, if you can get us the background before five, we'll air it."

He'd slouched down in his chair now and, with his elbow on the armrest, he ran a pudgy finger around and around on the bald spot at the back of his head. Whenever she saw him do this, Linda imagined he was searching for a stray hair. She tried to listen to what he was saying.

"It's been a slow day. No . . . his wife's background. What made her live with a man like that, you know, that sort of thing . . . Okay. Yeah . . . five o'clock. Bye."

He turned to his desk and activated another call. "Yeah. It's me. Baumgardener. Take it all down one notch and see if we can get a better lead before air time . . . yeah . . ."

He stood and moved back to his spot by the windows, then shifted his weight from one foot to the other while he gazed at the view and continued his phone conversation. In his fifties, and paunchy, there was nothing about him that made her want to watch him for any length of time, so Linda decided to look around his office instead. She'd been here before, but now she'd take the time to admire the many awards which were randomly scattered around the room. She'd reached over to pick one up, from a shelf nearby when he hung up the phone.

"Got that one for my reports from Kosovo," he said. He sat down again, ready to give her his full attention.

"Really? What about that one," she said, pointing to a larger award.

"Indonesia. Four years ago."

"You were there?"

"Yeah."

"Gosh. When I see things like this I realize I've got so much to learn." The remark was somewhat sincere. He really had accomplished quite a few things. But there was something she wanted to know more than anything else: How did someone who had been at his professional peak end up running the news in Philly? He'd been an anchor and a foreign correspondent for Universal Information Group. How did he end up here? Obviously, he'd fallen from grace somehow.

"I'm an alcoholic," he said.

"What?"

"You were wondering what I'm doing here. Short version: I got lost at the bottom of a bottle and my work got, shall we say, less than professional. I've been dry for three and a half years now, and, actually I think I like this job. Plenty of variety, just enough stress to make it interesting."

"You could always start a second career as a mind reader," she responded.

"Intuition, deductive reasoning, and the wisdom to know when to tell the story are what make a great reporter. Which brings me to why I asked to see you. I've liked your work recently and I've given another look at that three-part piece on 'Poison Poultry' you did a while back. I have to say it was pretty good. We had two other reporters turn down the opportunity to do that story. You were smart enough to see the potential. Would you like another one?"

She tried to look calm. "Certainly."

"You know, everyone eventually did stories on President Cole's inauguration speech. But when he first made it, the press was so stunned it took us all several hours to get up to speed on it. I mean, he'd sort of played his 'I'm spiritual' card after the Denver quake, but that was sort of generic, and it struck a chord in a lot of people."

Normally Baumgardener liked a no-nonsense-cut-to-the-chase type of conversation. For some unknown reason, though, he'd decided to get introspective on her. He stopped talking and started rocking back and forth in his swivel chair, staring out the window again.

She held her breath. He hadn't asked her a question, so she remained silent.

He finally turned back to her. "No one ever figured Cole would go so far with his inauguration speech. Who'd have guessed he'd use it to make such a passionate plea for old time religion?. . . And I think a bigger surprise was some of the support he got at first." Baumgardener stopped rocking and looked at Linda "Were you surprised?"

"Shocked is more like it," she said. Her toes had curled up inside her shoes. *And NOW . . . you wanted to say . . . what?*

"But, I guess, after the Denver quake, and then riots, lots of people were just more rattled than we realized. At first, a lot of people might have been scared enough to think they needed to go back . . . back to the 'thou shalts' and 'thou shalt nots.' The religious right sure has tried to use it. And now we have to look at all those annoying 'HE is coming!' and, 'Get right or get left!' commercials. Have you seen 'em?"

Linda thought about the ads tracking across her internet screen that very morning. "Yes" she groaned.

Baumgardener nodded. "Personally, I'd like to go through a whole week without hearing that some event is another 'sign' of an 'imminent return.' Someone washed my coffee mug last night. Think it's a sign?"

A nervous chortle popped out of her mouth.

Baumgardener continued. "My instincts tell me America wants to find spirituality—even I have come to believe there's a Higher Power—but what people want might be a different kind of spirituality than Cole and conservative Christians envisioned. The chord Cole originally struck in people—perhaps the one he misinterpreted—was that people want to find God, but in a new way." He leaned forward and gave her a questioning look.

Linda's mind finally leaped ahead to the destination. *A story on the World Conference on Spirituality!* She followed his cue. "You know, I've wondered that, too."

"As you know," he finally said, "the World Conference on Spirituality is going to happen right here in Philly in less than three weeks, and I figure we can do a double-play on it. First, we can punch up our ratings with some local stories before the national media show up."

Her boss now leaned back in his chair and stretched out his arms with his fingers and thumbs at angles, forming a pretend TV screen before he continued. "I'm seeing interviews with people in the diners, hotel workers, etc. What do they think of the conference? Will it benefit Philly? The second part of the double play is a sort of informal poll: Is spirituality important to the locals? If the interviews play out well, and the Chinese don't steal the show by blowing the Japanese to kingdom come, we'll take the best parts of the interviews and sew them together with a shot at air-time on UIG when they get here to cover the conference. I still have friends at the network. Think you want to try it?"

She wanted to strike a balance between the thrill she felt and professionalism. "Mr. Baumgardener, how can I thank you for the opportunity? I'll do my very best."

CHAPTER 25

OKLAHOMA — September 10th

Ricky Ruiz cleared off his desk, glad to be getting away for the day. He and a teacher from the ranch, Chuck Talbot, planned to take a load of supplies up to a remote area where most of the boys from the ranch would be treated to a camping trip. Ricky's friend, Bart Jackson, was going to let the ranch use his remote property for the event. Mr. Jackson, who insisted that everyone call him "BJ," would meet Ricky and Chuck Talbot at the campsite at 10:00 a.m. this morning to help them finish preparations around the small cabin to be used for storing supplies.

Ruiz looked up when he heard a knock at his open door.

"Ready to fly?" Chuck said, entering the room.

"Just give me one second," he answered, trying to find the proper spot to stash several papers. "You get the keys already?"

"Not yet. I figured we'd face that peril together."

Ricky went to a file cabinet with one last document.

"Sure is time for a break from routine," Chuck observed.

Something had shaken all the residents at the facility: The Zenith Corps, a "pre-military" program, had obtained ten boys from the ranch. After requesting more information, only two of the boys liked the offers the Corps made and signed their own contracts to be inducted. When the other eight boys didn't respond positively to their offers, Zenith "followed up" by accessing the boys records, then approaching their families or the courts to sign over custody. All eight of the youths had been signed over in exchange for the "bonus"cash settlements and a release from future liability.

"No kidding." Ricky responded. "Zenith's trying to empty the ranch. Did you hear the latest? Now four of the boys who were recommended 'by a friend' have heard Zenith is talking to their families." He shook his head. "This might be our last opportunity for quality one-on-one with a lot of them."

According to Henderson's lawyers, appeals could continue to move forward, but, so far, the courts were giving custody to Zenith. Sadly, the process might take so long, those inducted could well serve their entire contract before a final ruling.

Ricky exhaled. "Maybe we're all about to be called to a greater level of faith."

He closed the file cabinet before he and Talbot exited the office together, walking down the long hall toward the front desk.

"Henderson said we could take one of the boys and let him help with some of the grunt work," Chuck said. "Who should be our victim?"

"How about Jason MacAllister?" Ricky asked in a low voice. He knew he was pushing it.

Jason and Shawn Thatcher had been involved in yet another altercation. Despite his smaller size, Shawn had managed to get the better of Jason again. Ricky felt certain Shawn enlisted the help of others in this most recent attack, but couldn't prove it. Meanwhile, Jason, had to know he was in the process of losing his status—getting his rank cut—big time.

"Are you *kidding*?" Chuck said in a hushed voice. "He and Shawn are just getting out of lockdown."

"Yeah. I know," Ricky said. "But, obviously, standard operating procedures aren't working for Jason. Maybe he needs a day away from here to think. Besides, the physical activity might help him let off some steam before he gets back to the dorm tonight. I talked to Paul and he said it's still possible for Jason to come to the camp out, depending on his behavior the rest of the week."

Ricky knew the great potential for trouble now Shawn and Jason were being released from lockdown. He wanted to do what he could to keep the warring boys apart—before Jason lost his last chance to stay on the ranch. If he got in trouble again, he'd be returned to the juvenile justice system and do jail time. Jason knew this . . . and so did Shawn, who had the luxury of two more sessions in the "penalty box" before he'd get kicked off the ranch.

Chuck saw the somber look on Ricky's face. "Jason means a lot to you, doesn't he?"

"I was just like him once. I was so full of anger. I know God can set him free, but I'm hoping he won't have to go as far as I did for it to happen. If I could just connect with him somehow."

Chuck considered it for a moment. Each of them identified with a particular kid now and then and had a special desire to see that kid succeed. "Okay. He can be our grunt worker for the day."

Ricky smiled. "Thanks."

They'd walked down the hall and stopped at a door. Chuck opened it and they stepped into the reception area. At a desk nearby sat the secretary, Myra. She would make sure all was in order before they departed the ranch.

"Good morning!" Ricky said.

She looked up from her desk and took off her reading glasses. "Yes?" she said, ignoring his greeting. Everything about Ricky Ruiz irritated her: The way he prayed, the way he seemed to think God "led" him to do this or that, the way he hummed little tunes all the time, and, mostly, the way he talked about "grace." How this vexed her. As if someone could just walk right up to a Holy God and talk to Him the way you would talk to a person! As if *holiness* wasn't the essence of a walk with God! And, Mr. Ruiz seemed totally unaware of the importance of order in religious life.

In short, Ricky pushed every button Myra had. Worse yet, his attitude appeared to be contagious. Some of the teachers and even Mr. Henderson seemed to be affected by his foolish behavior. What kind of example was this for boys who were on their way to Hell?

Often, she'd tried subtly hinting about Ricky's shortcomings at prayer time, but, obviously he was dense. Everything she said seemed to go right over his head. At times, she didn't know why she bothered trying to set them all straight, but reminded herself each person had a cross to bear. Maybe hers was to keep Mr. Ruiz from dragging the whole ranch to ruin.

"Mr. Talbot and I," Ricky tried to sound friendly, "are about to take the ranch van out to the campsite. We need the keys and the paperwork to pick up the supplies."

"Are you and Mr. Talbot both going?" she asked, opening a drawer. "Who is driving?" If Mr. Ruiz wanted to drive she thought she might have to bring up the matter of a ticket he'd gotten a few weeks ago. She'd found out about it when she went to settle a problem with the tag on the car.

"Mr. Talbot can drive." Ricky answered.

She got out the keys and handed them to Chuck.

Ricky cleared his throat and signaled Chuck to press in on the other issue.

"And we'll need a pass for one of the students," Chuck said.

She raised an eyebrow.

"Mr. Henderson okayed it already," he quickly added.

She got out a slip of paper and a pen. "I don't know why I wasn't informed. This involves work for me, you know. We can't function with a constant flow of last-minute changes to things. What's the boy's name?"

Ricky looked at Chuck who coughed and responded, "Jason McAllister."

She set her pen down. "He's in lockdown."

"Well, uh," Chuck looked at his watch, "technically, he's out. I mean, he's supposed to be out this morning."

She looked at both of the men. "And you're going to reward this ani—" she corrected herself, "his animal behavior with an outing?"

"He's out of lockdown. He's finished his punishment," Ricky replied quietly. "And doesn't the Word say it's God's kindness that leads people to repentance?" After he said this, Ricky suddenly remembered Jason had called Myra a number of very bad names as he left the office for his last detention. "And, I recall," he added quickly, "a request you had in prayer last week, Myra, about God helping us to find His way to reach these lost young men. That was food for thought, Myra. And I was thinking just this morning, didn't Jesus say we should bless those who curse us, and go a second mile for people, even when they don't deserve it?"

He thought he noticed her neck muscles twitching, but she didn't say another word. She signed the slip, then gave them the keys and the requisition forms.

They swung by building five and managed to catch up with Jason just as he returned to a second-floor room.

Chuck greeted him first. "Hey Jason!"

The boy looked up at the two men and dropped his duffle bag before asking, "What do ya' want?"

"I'm fine, thanks," Chuck said. "And you?"

"What do you want? I just got here, so whatever happened, I didn't do it."

"You got us all wrong," Ricky said. "You're gonna get sprung for the day. We're taking you on a trip up to the campsite with us."

Jason thought it must be some kind of joke. "What for?"

"We're taking some supplies out and covering a few last minute details for the camp out."

"Camp out," Jason echoed. From the time the event was first discussed, he figured he'd never be considered as a candidate for the trip. He'd not allowed himself to think of it much since then.

"You know. A camp out." Chuck said the words slowly. "Tents, campfires, trees—that sorta stuff."

"Gee, Mr. Talbot, thanks for the info," Jason said, sarcastically. "I wouldn't have known if you hadn't explained it to me."

"Let's not get off to a bad start here," Ricky interrupted. "It's a great day to be outdoors and we're wasting time."

Much to Jason's surprise, Ricky and Chuck actually did take him on their jaunt out to the campsite. After they got there, however, he realized they expected him to do quite a bit of the labor.

"Oh. *Now* I get it," he said to Ruiz, "you only brought me so you could make me do all the work . . . I won't even get to come to this thing and you're making me do all the work for it. I know how this gig works. If I were getting paid, you'd keep the money, too. I bet you're gettin' a real hoot outta this."

Obviously the accusations came from sad experience. Ricky ignored them. "No one said you couldn't come. It's kinda up to you."

"Right," the boy said, putting the last large sack of flour on a shelf in the cabin. *You're just waiting,* he thought, *for me to do something you can get me for . . . but you'll be sure all this is done first.*

"Jason, believe it or not, we don't have it in for you. We're trying to help you."

"Right, Mr. Ruiz," Jason said, while thinking, *Always dogging me, takin' my cigarettes, searching my stuff.*

Ricky's friend, BJ leaned into the door of the cabin. "Hey. Y'all 'bout finished in here?"

"Yeah." Ricky replied before looking over at Jason. "C'mon, let's see what needs to be done outside."

Jason muttered something to himself.

"You say something, Jason?" BJ asked.

"Nothin'," was the hostile reply.

When they got outside, Chuck Talbot said he realized he'd have to make another trip to town to pick up a few more items and drove off. BJ noted a lot more ground would have to be cleared. He got out an old, gas-powered push mower and showed Ricky and Jason how to use it.

"You try it first, Jason." Ricky said.

The boy gave Ruiz a hard stare. "Right."

BJ called Ricky into the cabin for a moment so he could show him how to light the stove. After that, they talked for a while before BJ got some metal cups out of a cupboard.

"Want a drink of water?" the older man asked.

"Yeah. And I'll take one out to Jason and have my turn with the mower."

"He sure is a scrappy kid," BJ observed.

"Oh yeah. He's got a chip on his shoulder the size of Texas. And, until recently, he was the toughest kid in the dorm."

"Tougher kid move in?"

"Oh yeah. The other kid's name is Shawn, and I think 'colder' is a better word for him. Jason's real angry, but in his heart, I think he knows right from wrong. Shawn is like . . . cold steel. And he really knows how to get to people. He's baited Jason into the penalty box for the final time. Next deal, Jason's outta here."

"I suppose you've tried talking to him," BJ said.

"I've tried everything I can think of. So far, he's not letting anybody in."

"Keep tryin'."

"Yeah," Ricky said, picking up his cup of water and another one for Jason. By the time he got outside, the boy had worked up quite a sweat. Ricky assumed Jason's red face was from the sun and the heat.

Just look at him, Jason thought, *walking around as if he was the boss of the whole world. I'm getting blisters and he's enjoying every moment of it.* He was pushing the mower uphill and getting angrier by the moment. *If he gives me that stupid smile . . .*

Ricky, holding the two cups in his hands, stepped toward the boy when the mower stalled out in a thicket. He smiled. "Looks like you're stuck," he began.

Jason heaved on the pull cord with all his might several times but the mower wouldn't start. In frustration, he tipped the machine over and started swearing.

Ricky realized how angry Jason had gotten and tried to calm him down. "That's okay. It's my turn any—"

The young man flew at Ricky. "Stop laughing at me!" he shrieked.

The water in both of the cups sloshed out as Ricky quickly dodged out of the way.

BJ exited the cabin and saw Jason going at Ricky. "Whoa there! What's goin' on?" he said, trotting closer. Jason took a few swings at Ricky, missing every time, his fury growing with each missed punch.

Ricky's eyes were flashing as he kept bouncing out of Jason's reach. Despite his large size, he was quite graceful. "Really mad, eh? Wanna hit me?"

"I hate you!" Jason said, lunging at him again.

"Oh yeah? Why's that?" Ruiz asked.

BJ started to get between them.

"No! Stay out of it BJ." Ricky said.

"I knew it!" Jason said. "You *want* me to hit you. You've just been waiting for me to do it so you can finally get rid of me!"

"Is that what you think? No matter what happens, Jason," Ricky said, tossing the cups to the ground, "this won't be what gets you off the ranch." He kept his eyes on the boy as he called to his friend, "BJ? Just stay back."

"What?" the old man said loudly. "You can't fight with him!"

"We're not fighting. We're having a lively discussion." Ricky said, then spread his hands in an open gesture. "I won't turn you in, Jason. And I wasn't making fun of you. This can end right here. Just talk to me. What is it you think I've done to you?"

Jason rushed forward. In a flurry of swings, he got Ricky on the mouth. Ruiz stepped back and danced out of reach while he ran his tongue between his teeth and a bleeding lip.

"You're always following me," Jason said, "always picking on me . . . always talking to Henderson about me. Well, this time, I'm gonna make it worthwhile. I'm not getting shipped off till I knock that stupid smile off your face."

Ricky deflected a punch in such a way that Jason ended up hitting himself just above the right eyebrow. The boy spewed out every foul name he could think of and threw himself at Ruiz again, managing to connect with two more good blows. One caught Ricky in the chest and the other in the left eye.

When Jason tried to kick him, he swiveled to the side to avoid it, then pointed at the boy. "No kicking. I've let you swing at me, but there'll be no kicking."

Jason swung a few more times and then tried to kick him again. Ricky grabbed his foot and sent him onto his rear. "I said no kicking."

The young man jumped to his feet and rushed at him. Ricky managed to deflect or dodge most of the punches while Jason continued to hurl insults about his intelligence, his skin color, his size, his race, and his faith.

"I'm not fighting you." Ricky said again.

Jason managed to get a couple more hits in but began to tire. When Ricky noticed the boy might be running out of strength he spoke again. "I hope you're getting this out of your system!"

"I hate you!" he said again, getting a good sock into Ricky's mid-section.

Ricky had to catch his breath. "No you don't."

"Yes! I . . . do!" he said, grazing Ricky's shoulder with a deflected blow.

Ricky pushed him back. "I'm not your enemy, Jason. Satan is."

The boy made a growling noise and charged again. Ricky stepped aside at the last second and Jason went face first onto the ground. He rolled over quickly, thinking Ricky would be ready to finish him off now.

Ricky stood at a distance. "I'm not fighting you, Jason, and you still aren't winning. Shawn's beaten you, too. Not because he's better in a fight, but because he knows how to make you crazy. He's goading you to do stupid things you'll get punished for. You're letting him decide your fate like you don't have a choice in the matter. Don't you see? Satan is using Shawn to get you to do things that could lead to your destruction. The devil wants you to think you have no other options . . . that nobody is on your side, that you have to stand up to everyone no matter what . . . that you *have* to go the way he's directing you. He wants you to think it's inevitable you'll die in prison or in an alley someplace. That's a lie. You still have choices, Jason."

The young man was totally spent. Covered with sweat, grass clippings, and dirt, he was too tired to get up. When Ricky stepped closer, Jason scooted back and wiped his face on his sleeve. "Give me just a second. I'll get up and we'll finish this."

"No," Ricky said. "It's finished now." He waited a moment before slowly sitting down to face the boy, then looked up at his friend. "BJ? All this talk has made me thirsty. Could we have that cup of water now?"

BJ knew this was his cue to back off for a few minutes. He sized up the situation. Jason looked too drained to mount another attack.

He picked up the cups Ricky had tossed down and retreated to the cabin, but watched through the window to be sure nothing happened.

Ricky and the boy talked quietly.

"You know," Ricky said, "there was a guy in the Bible who was just like you."

The boy laid back on the grass and let out a sarcastic laugh. "And he went to Hell, right?"

"No. His name was David and the Lord loved him very much. But there were times when David made really stupid mistakes. One time, when he felt like he was being chased by his own people, he went and hid with his enemies. He decided these people would want to kill him, too, so he acted real crazy. He drooled all over himself and everything . . . he figured if they were scared of him they'd leave him alone."

Jason looked up at the sky. "Did it work?"

"For a while. And he did bad things, too. He even contracted a murder."

Jason looked over at him.

"Those things," Ricky continued, "didn't stop God from loving him, but, while he was doing them, they stopped David from hearing God. Only when he recognized his mistakes and turned around did he find comfort from the Lord and have victory in his life . . . I made a lot of really bad mistakes Jason. Like David—and like you—I felt like I was in a corner. I had to be tougher than anyone else. I'd do whatever it took . . . and in my heart I had no hope of ever leaving that lifestyle . . . I had no hope of living beyond my youth."

BJ continued watching through the window as Ricky talked to the boy. At one point, Ricky lifted up his left hand— presumably to show Jason where a bullet had taken off half of his middle finger. Jason nodded a few times while Ricky talked, and turned his head away once. Eventually, Ricky looked over at the cabin and saw BJ in the window. He motioned for his friend to come out. They all had a drink of water before Ricky sent Jason into the cabin to wash up.

"Well?" BJ said with hushed anticipation. "What did he say?"

"Not much . . . but I know he was listening. He almost started to cry at one point, before he managed to get a hold of himself." Ricky stopped talking for a moment to feel around in his mouth with a couple of fingers, then spit out some blood. "You know, I think one of my teeth is loose. That kid can really hit," he said, then grinned. "But God has a plan going here, I just know it, BJ!"

Even after they'd washed, both of them still looked roughed up. Jason's clothes were covered with dirt, his knuckles were swollen, and he had a small cut in his eyebrow. Ricky had a swollen eye and a fat lip, but for the first time that he could remember, Jason smiled at him.

"You look pretty bad, you know?" the boy said.

BJ had to agree. "You'd better put some ice on your face when you get home."

When Chuck showed up and saw Ricky, at first he thought there'd been some sort of accident. "What happened to you?"

"Huh?" Ricky asked.

"What hap—"

Ricky walked by him and started unloading the van. "If you don't ask, I won't have to *not* tell you."

"Oh," Chuck said. Of course, when he saw Jason, he knew what had happened.

Jason fell asleep in the van on the way back to the ranch.

Chuck kept his eyes on the road. "You think he got rid of any steam?"

"Oh yeah," Ricky said, rubbing his ribs. He was sore, but his heart was singing. He could hardly wait to tell Rosa. For the first time, he had real hope Jason might make it.

It was past five o'clock when they reached the ranch. They dropped Jason off at the dorm before parking the van, and Chuck said he'd take the keys by the office so Ricky could start for home.

When Ricky got to the apartment, he could see Rosa in the baby's room. As soon as she heard him enter the apartment, she began to slowly back out of the nursery then closed the door without a sound. Before she could turn around, he covered her eyes and backed her up a few more paces.

"Before you see me," he said quietly, "I want you to know that it looks a lot worse than it really is."

She turned around, "*What* looks . . . Oh! Ricky!" she said, then lowered her voice. "What happened to you?"

Even though it hurt, he grinned from ear to ear. "The best thing, *mi amor*."

"What's that?" she said in a loud whisper and touched his lip.

"Ouch! Jason hit me."

"Oh, no!"

"But it was *good*."

"How could this be good?" She touched the area under his left eye.

"Ouch! It's a guy thing, Rosa. He just needed to do it. So I let him. BJ made sure it didn't get out of hand."

Since she looked as if he was speaking a language she didn't comprehend, he decided perhaps he'd leave out the gory details and get right to the good part. "I let him realize I wasn't trying to get him. For the first time, Rosa, I think he's willing to let his guard down," Ricky said, with a spark of delight in his eyes. "I'm sure this is a breakthrough. As long as he doesn't tangle with Shawn this weekend—please, Lord— Jason will be allowed to come to the camp out."

She put her arms around him and hugged him.

"*Aye*," he groaned.

"I thought you said it looked a lot worse than it really was." She let go and held onto his arms.

He winced. He'd used his arms to deflect most of the punches.

"You're really hurt!" she said.

"Well, there's no broken bones or anything."

"Tell me the whole thing."

"I'll tell you about it while we eat. I'm starved. What are we eating?"

Her stance stiffened a little. "Don't you remember?"

Ricky got a sinking feeling. He hated questions like this and, *Do you think I look fat in this dress?* But, try as hard as he might, he couldn't remember whatever it was she wanted him to recall. He decided honesty was the best policy. "Sorry. I don't remember."

"We're going to the county fair. You wanted to go, remember? Last week you said you'd take me. Sara is coming over to watch the babies."

"Oh . . . yeah." There wasn't an ounce of enthusiasm in his voice.

Two years ago, the "old" Rosa would have had a tantrum over this. A year ago, she would have said "Never mind," then pouted, and given him the cold shoulder for the evening. But now? She looked at him. He looked awful and it was obvious he hurt all over. She realized God was giving her an opportunity to be gracious.

"That's okay," she said, finding what appeared to be an undamaged spot on his cheek and giving him a little peck. "I'll see what's in the fridge."

When she headed for the kitchen, Ricky noticed she was wearing the boots he'd gotten for her.

"No way," he said. "I wouldn't miss taking you and those boots out for anything. Let me grab a hot shower and we're on our way."

After the shower he felt better and he was happy he'd decided to go. He turned off the radio in the car. The day's bad news would go unheard and he would enjoy his wife's company. Hungry for adult companionship and thrilled to be getting out for the evening, Rosa chattered all the way there.

Once they got to the fair, they spent a couple of hours touring the different exhibits and sampling the food. Rosa wanted to watch things, like barrel racing, that involved good horsemanship, but she refused to stay for the shows with dangerous stunts.

While they walked, Rosa noticed kids in their early teens, but few people who looked like they might be in their late teens or twenties. Probably due to the military actions overseas, Ricky told her. It was a sad reminder that things were not going well in the world.

They walked by a few booths before they got to the stage in the center of the fairgrounds. A band played twangy western music and, amused, they stopped to listen. An older couple on the stage sang a comic duet about the differences between men and women.

Ricky looked at Rosa. Once again, he was filled with the knowledge he'd been given so much. *Oh, Lord, he thought, I am so blessed. I want to be grateful for every day, every moment. Thank you. . . . Thank you. . . . THANK YOU!* He became so filled with joy, he couldn't restrain it. He took Rosa's hand and twirled her around while the music played. It was like the first time he ever saw her. . . . She'd been celebrating with her friend, Edwina, laughing and spinning around in a little "victory dance." He'd loved her from that very moment. Now, he pulled her close, and they moved together for a few steps before the music stopped.

He pushed back his hat and looked down at her as he put on his best Oklahoma accent. "How'd I git a purty little filly like yew anyways?"

She burst out laughing. "What a smooth talker! And I didn't know you could dance, either. Is there any limit to what you know?"

"Oh yeah. Cars." He made a flat line with his hand. "I know almost nothing about fixing cars."

"Me neither. But I like riding in them."

They'd had a wonderful evening but it was getting late.

"Well," he said, "there's no time like the present for a car ride, *señora*. Shall we go?"

CHAPTER 26

PHILADELPHIA — September 28th

A horde of people mingled around the grand buffet table in the penthouse suite. Excitement buzzed through all who'd gathered to celebrate what would surely be a hallmark event: The World Conference on Spirituality.

When Edith Todd entered the room, everyone stopped and focused on her. The widow of former President Sonny Todd had only recently stepped back into public life—and she looked radiant. She scanned the room and smiled. What a comfort to be surrounded by so many supporters.

When Sonny died so unexpectedly she'd been taken by surprise. After the shock of his passing wore off, she'd slipped into a deep depression. If the truth were known, it wasn't so much that she missed him as the guilt she felt. The day he died, they weren't even on speaking terms.

It took her a year to work through the issues Sonny's death brought into focus, and another year to re-dig the wells of her own spirituality. Then, a series of events swept her into places she'd never imagined she'd go. Her circle of friends suddenly widened to include some of the most powerful spiritual leaders in the world.

Last month, while attending seminars in Vancouver, Canada, Edith received a revelation that secured her place among world visionaries. This revelation resulted in an invitation to appear at the World Conference on Spirituality. Tomorrow she would share what she'd received with the world, and hoped it would help to birth the New Age so many had hoped to see.

Now, as Edith Todd returned the gaze of so many gathered in the hotel suite, she felt their strength. They, in turn, could sense the stories about her were true. Like the sun, Edith's rising star would soon burst into the world.

"Tony," she said, when she saw her dear friend, Tony Benson. "How good of you to come." Opening her arms and looking around the room once more, she said, "How wonderful all of you have come."

Spontaneous applause and congratulations arose.

For the next thirty minutes, she mingled among old friends and new, but when the crowd around her thinned a little, Tony Benson made his way to her side. He'd been part of Edith's "secret" spiritual life in the past, but in recent months—since his return from the Himalayas—more people knew about his influence in her life.

The night was a total high for Tony. After years of disappointment and delay, the door had finally opened. It appeared they all might be on the threshold of a great spiritual event. Though it would come with great shaking, he knew the result would change mankind.

"We're all so proud of you, Edith," he said. "Our thoughts and energies are with you. Tonight we celebrate your victory. Tomorrow, *Earth's* victory."

"Quiet!" someone said, excitedly. "It's on! It's on!"

They all turned to look at the big screen television at one end of the room. The image of a man everyone knew filled the screen. The face of E.E. Kressman came into sharp focus.

Only recently had Edith and others been told the man was a "fellow believer." While the information had come through "credible" sources, it came to them privately. Each of them understood Mr. Kressman wanted confidentiality on the subject. He owned the Universal Information Group as well as many other multi-national businesses, and needed to keep a "neutral" image. Edith comprehended all too well what the poor man must have to endure.

To everyone's amazement, however, word went out to event organizers earlier in the day that Kressman himself would make comments, to be aired on UIG, regarding the conference!

As a hush fell in the room, he spoke with his familiar accent. He had a soft, pleasant voice and they all listened very intently for its message.

"While it is not my habit to make so public an appearance, I thought I should take just a few moments of your time to speak with you." The camera shot became tighter, filling the screen with his head and shoulders.

"Anyone who has kept abreast of news in recent weeks would be aware of the potentially grave situations taking place on the international scene. Now, more than ever, humanity must work together to overcome all barriers, in order to secure a future for us all. While we are gratified tensions between China and her neighbors have eased, we also know from thousands of years of recorded history that diplomacy and the signing of treaties—although they may be a beginning—won't assure lasting harmony in the world.

"We believe it is no coincidence that during a time of so much global tension, a conference of great significance is about to take place in the United States. It is the World Conference on Spirituality. The people attending this conference have come from around the world to partake in this summit of universal importance. The delegates are not ambassadors or diplomats of governments, yet their highest goal is to bring forth global reconciliation.

"Throughout history, there have been a few enlightened ones who would have guided humanity but were rejected for their message of sharing, justice, and peace. And, now, although darkness has once again threatened our very existence, a light is dawning. Can humanity finally be ready to receive the next step?

"I'm asking all of you listening to this broadcast to give thought to the serious situations around the world. Situations which cry out for better answers. Situations which call for more than 'paper' solutions. Perhaps the solution is finally coming to us.

"The World Conference on Spirituality can be a new launch point for man's wisdom. I'm asking all of you to tune in, to listen to the wisdom which will spring forth at this conference, and think of the significant strides to be achieved if all will connect for peace.

"As many of you may of heard just moments ago on UIG, announcement of a diplomatic accord with China is immanent."

Expressions of gratitude and sighs of relief went around the hotel suite. An end to the threat of war with China would, indeed, be a most auspicious omen for the Conference! Those in the room quickly quieted themselves to hear more.

"We can settle," Kressman continued, "for yet another temporary solution made by a few men, or, we can unite our positive energies and make it just the beginning of a new era. With the momentum of this conference, we can call forth a dawn of true understanding and bring an end to the hopeless negativity of those who criticize and divide. Unified, we can build without limit, and achieve the vision of world peace.

"I thank you. . ."

All of the people in the hotel suite embraced one another. Some cried. A huge momentum was gathering . . . Dare they hope the time had come?

WASHINGTON, D.C.

Miles away, in the White House, President Cole and several of his staff watched the news. They'd heard UIG was about to leak information regarding the accord with China, and, sure enough, quoting "unnamed, high-ranking sources in China," they'd broken the story. Although he hadn't expected to see Mr. Kressman, President Cole wasn't entirely surprised. The man was determined to plant himself in the middle of world affairs.

The general public didn't know anything about Kressman's offer to be a secret negotiator, or that Cole had denied him the position, but the media mogul, apparently, wasn't going to settle for any sort of back seat. If he couldn't further his agendas privately, he'd seek to advance them in another court–public opinion.

"I just hate it when UIG gets the jump on us," the press secretary grumbled. "And, exactly *what* was Kressman trying to say? That some conference in Philadelphia is going to bring world peace?"

Don thought about the tense time following his refusal to permit Kressman to negotiate. Several roadblocks suddenly developed between the White House and Japan as well as with China. Intense lobbying, opposing virtually all of Don's decisions, took place in Congress and with America's allies.

But Cole hadn't blinked. Armed with a certainty he was doing what would ultimately work, he kept at it every day. He made calls, researched his choices well, and maintained open lines of communications with everyone involved in the process.

Though irritated at Kressman for claiming the agreement signed in the Far East wasn't enough before the details were even out, he also had a certain amount of satisfaction in success without compromising with the would-be world leader.

"Let him crow all he wants about his 'energies,'" Cole replied. "Eventually we'll see what's of lasting value and what isn't."

PHILADELPHIA, PA

At the Philadelphia Arena, Events Manager Zac Gordon got ready to leave his office. His date for the evening, Sharrise, had arrived an hour earlier and they'd eaten a catered dinner.

This had been one of Zac's worst weeks on the job, but the logistical nightmare known as the World Conference of Spirituality would finally begin tomorrow.

This day had been filled with one tense moment after another. Former First Lady, Edith Todd, was a last-minute addition to the line-up of speakers, so now her personal security force would be crawling all over the place and making demands. This meant he'd have to spend even more of his conference budget on security. Even so, his supervisor, Ms. A. Glad-Butterfield, remained unyielding regarding expenditures. He'd have to "get creative," and "make do" with his remaining conference funds. He'd been forced to cut back more workers.

Tonight, he'd stay at the arena until the night shift came on duty. These workers would be making final preparations for the first general session tomorrow and Zac's only remaining "official" task for the evening was to give last-minute instructions to them.

Then, he'd take his date on a tour of the Arena and impress her with his executiveness. Having spent all the time he cared to with the event's coordinators, Zac passed up the opportunity to hobnob with them at a party in a nearby hotel. He'd managed to keep them happy, but personally found some of them kind of spooky. It wasn't an obvious thing. Most of them looked pretty normal, but a weird intensity hovered about many of them. It made him uncomfortable.

He watched his date for a few moments. There certainly wasn't a weird intensity about this lovely little thing.

He'd actually only met Sharrise in a restaurant the day before. His "spill maneuver"worked perfectly. She was a good sport about her splattered dress, and even agreed to a date after knowing him scarcely more than a few minutes.

She's about as deep as a teaspoon, he thought with satisfaction. Nearly everything he said or did created the same response—a silly little laugh that, under normal circumstances, would have really annoyed him. But tonight, after getting so tired and so stressed-out, he felt a bit giddy himself. At one point during their private dinner party, they'd both started laughing and couldn't stop for ten minutes.

Now, the time had come to rally the evening shift workers. Zac straightened his tie. "How do I look?"

Sharrise, for the first time in over an hour, got a serious look on her face. She studied him for a moment. "You know what I think?" she asked, soberly.

"I haven't got a clue. What?"

She suddenly burst out laughing again. "You look . . . like a monkey!"

He laughed as well. He couldn't help himself. It took him another minute to get back his composure. He sighed and wiped a tear out of his eye. "I can't remember the last time I laughed so much. . . . Okay now. I've got to go talk to the crew. You can come with me, but you have to stop laughing."

This caused them both to laugh hysterically for another three minutes before they got underway.

Soon, they stood in a huge kitchen where much of the catering for the entertainment suites in the Arena would be done. Zac juggled oranges for Sharrie's amusement, until the shift rolled over. All ten managers from the previous shift asked if they could speak to him about some concerns before going home.

"Sure," Zac said, eying the unhappy bunch.

They looked grim. All the tension, and worry of pulling off such a large event showed on them. Once they started talking, Zac realized the main gripe was about Ms. A. Glad-Butterfield. She'd been in at the beginning of their shift to berate them over small delays, despite the very limited staffing. They were tired, angry, and fed up with the relentless demands of Ms. Butterfield.

Zachary, as well, felt he'd had enough of the huge workload, the problems, and Ms. A. Glad-Butterfield. But he was too tired to get angry. He looked at Sharrise and laughed.

This was the only encouragement she needed. Everyone else in the room gazed at the giddy couple.

"What's with you guys?" Zac finally said to the managers. "You look like you're going to your own funerals! Lighten up!" He glanced around the room and saw a table loaded with hors d'oeuvres, fruits, veggies, and tofu wedges. He walked to the other side of the table and faced the assembled crew. A bowl of powdered mix and a large sifter sat on the table to his left.

"Today, class . . ." he said in a falsetto voice.

They stared wide-eyed at him.

". . .we're going to learn how to flame broil a manager," he said, donning an apron with a flourish. "First, we must make sure we are ready," he continued, in the same high pitch. Then he took the sifter out of the bowl and smudged the nearly-white powder all over his hands and face. Finally, with dramatic flair, he grabbed a small pastry, squeezed its bright red filling out onto a plate, and used his pinky finger to put a dot of it on the center of his mouth.

When he did this, the whole crew started laughing.

"There!" he shouted the silly voice. "Am I beautiful yet? No matter. It's time to cook that pesky little fellow!"

"Who are you supposed to be?" Sharrise asked loudly.

The others in the room roared when Zac put his hands on his hips and said, "Who am I? Who am I? . . . I'm Mizzz A. Glob-o-butterfat, with a hyphen, thank you!"

It was going so well. Zac was in his glory. Hysterical laughter filled the room . . . but suddenly, it stopped. A look of dread came over all of them as their eyes went from Zac to someone just behind him.

Even before he'd turned around, a sinking feeling invaded the pit of his stomach. When he did, he wasn't surprised to see Ms. Butterfield herself standing there.

# # #

Miles away, Zac's brother Benjamin sat in the apartment he shared with their other brother, Michael. Ben had seated himself in a wingback chair. Maybe, if he didn't move, the throbbing pain assaulting muscle, bone, and brain, would ease somewhat. Years ago, his body would have taken up most of the chair. *Now,* he thought, looking down at all the empty folds of clothing and the new hole he'd had to punch in his belt that morning, *two of me would fit here.*

He'd just come home from work, and needed to rest for a while, so he leaned back and closed his eyes. After working only three hours, the pain in his body made him feel as if he'd been slowly and methodically staple-gunned to a wall.

It had been twelve years since he'd first been diagnosed as HIV positive, seven since he'd developed full-blown AIDS. Six years ago, when asked to be part of the test group for a new treatment, Ben figured it would be his moment in history. He went into the program knowing the risks and willing to stop all other medications. At the very least, he figured, if he died he'd probably go quickly; and maybe what scientists learned in the experiment could be used as a guide to a cure in the future.

Over a period of time, to his great delight, he and about one forth of the others treated with the therapy were thought to have recovered from the virus. Although scientists tried to moderate their excitement with a "wait and see" attitude, many hailed it as one of the great miracles of the twenty-first century.

Thousands of people applied for the treatment, only hundreds were chosen. Even if only one-fourth were "cured," many were desperate to try.

The first year passed, and he enjoyed a healthy life. The second year passed, and Ben's group remained free of the virus. By the end of the third year, even he began to think it might truly be the miracle he'd hoped for.

In fourth year after the treatment, though, Ben and many of the other test patients noticed frightening symptoms—unexplained swelling, infections, and fevers. When the winter flu season came around, nearly half of those thought to have been cured, died. Among patients who hadn't known full "recovery" from taking the experimental treatment, the flu death rate rose to eighty percent.

Tests confirmed they had a new strain of the HIV virus. It had the combined characteristics of several other forms of the virus and it was ravaging virtually every system in their bodies. Resistant to all of the previous therapies, it was dubbed "MR—AIDS," for Multiple-Return Acquired Immune Deficiency Syndrome.

Would everyone who took the treatment suffer the same fate? What about all the blood taken from Ben and the others when they were "well?" Much of it had been used to make serums for victims in Africa—where desperation and poverty overruled the need to wait for long-term results. What would happen to those who'd taken the serums?

Ben survived the fourth year, and the fifth, with the aid of many herbs and drugs. But lately, he'd had several serious bouts with illnesses and his body had run out of fight.

It's finally catching up with me, he thought.

His anguish, when he first realized the disease had returned, was that his "moment" had been lost. The one thing of value he'd hoped to help give the world—a cure—had vanished like visions of cool water in hot desert sands. When he first realized this, he wanted to die. What was the point in waiting around for the inevitable, painful end? If he hadn't been so afraid of dying back then, he might have found an easy solution.

Peace now flooded his soul as he recalled it once again: A year and a half ago, instead of taking his life, he'd decided to give it to the Lord. While his body would soon perish, his soul had already grasped eternal life.

And now, he had only one thing he wanted to accomplish with the days he had left. He wanted to communicate to his family and friends the only thing of value he'd ever found: Jesus.

Ben sighed as he thought of several recent unsuccessful attempts at "witnessing" to his brother Michael. *Why is it so hard to share my heart with the people I love?*

He turned on the television. Perhaps if he just sat here and rested for a few moments, he'd have the strength to go to the kitchen and get something to eat.

NEW YORK, NY

Jeff Lutz and Sharon Webb, co-anchors of the evening segment for Universal Information Group (UIG), prepared for live reports from the Philadelphia Arena. In the days to come, the network planned extensive coverage of the World Conference on Spirituality. UIG executives had already opted to air a segment of a story done by Linda Posner of local affiliate station, Channel Five. Her story covered

Philadelphia's preparations for the event, and the general outlook of the city's people.

Libby Steinberg, in charge of convention coverage, planned several positive segments about the convention, which would air in the coming days. UIG had taken some raps about prior coverage of religious and political events, and Ms. Steinberg, for one, hoped to demonstrate the essence of "fair, upbeat" reporting for this conference.

She remained well aware of the fact that the Banner Network, now a real contender in the media market, had managed in recent years to expand by calling into question UIG's objectivity—especially with regard to "conservative," and religious issues. A serious chink had been poked in the armor of the Universal Information Group. It could not be allowed to grow into a gaping hole.

For the World Conference on Spirituality, orders came from the highest levels: UIG would have the most comprehensive coverage. The owner of the network himself made clear his desire to demonstrate (to America in particular) UIG's ability to be objective and open on the subject of spirituality. Reporters were told there would be a minimum of commentary regarding the convention. The network would "tell" the story through interviews and coverage of activities in the arena.

On the New York set for UIG, co-anchors Jeff Lutz and Sharon Webb, watched for their cue.

A man behind the camera counted down with his fingers. Three, two, one, and pointed to Sharon.

"Good evening. I'm Sharon Webb," she said.

"And I'm Jeff Lutz," her co-anchor continued, "with the top stories on UIG tonight." He turned slightly as a switch in cameras gave viewers a tighter shot of his head. "Topping our news tonight are two reports on the international scene. One of the stories is confirmation of a UIG exclusive. Sources in the State Department are confirming our earlier reports: A tentative agreement has been reached in talks between China and Japan. We are being told that, within the hour, a news conference will be held to discuss the new accord. Again, we've just heard from sources at the State Department, a news conference will be held within the hour to announce an agreement between China and Japan. UIG will be there when it happens. Sharon?"

Sharon Webb looked into the lens of camera two, as she ad-libbed, "Yes, Jeff, that's good news indeed." Her eyes now focused on the words appearing on the teleprompter. "Our other international story topping the news tonight is about the World Conference on Spirituality, which will begin in Philadelphia tomorrow. Cathy Beecham is live at the Philadelphia Arena with our story."

The scene switched to Cathy.

"Good evening, Sharon. I'm here in Philadelphia," she said as the camera pulled back to give a view of the arena behind her. "And we are getting ready to cover the World Conference on Spirituality. This will be a gathering of Hindus, Buddhists, Christians, Muslim, Jews, and those of many other faiths from around the world," Cathy said, preparing to introduce a short news clip. "In a press conference this morning one of the conference organizers, Sven Borgesen had this to say:"

The clip showed a fair skinned, middle-aged man with a blond beard speaking to the assembled press. "I can state unequivocally," he said, with a Swedish accent, "that we, the organizers of the World Conference on Spirituality are thrilled with the overwhelming response we have received. Despite boycotts by a few fundamentalist groups, we have representatives from all religions. This will be the culmination of years of exchanges between men and women, spiritual leaders from all faiths, whose deepest desire is to bring all people into greater spiritual awareness.

"Apparently, it's an idea whose time has come. We will be representing the combined spiritual force of the vast majority of people in the world, and we are hoping our united energies will begin the release of a new era of oneness."

The clip from the conference ended, and Cathy Beecham's face appeared on the screen once again as she continued her report.

"In the next few days, we will be covering the convention live and interviewing all sorts of people here. We'll talk to convention goers, some of the speakers, and average people on the street outside.

"As we all know, many other international events, such as those involving trade, have become targets of illegal and sometimes violent protests. However, both the organizers and the police in Philadelphia say they're prepared, but they expect only sporadic, peaceful dissent during the World Conference on Spirituality.

"So far, planners say preparations are on schedule. Hotels in the Philadelphia area are packed, planes coming into the airport are loaded, and the tourism board here is elated to see spiritual leaders from around the globe converging on the city for the three-day event. I am told there will be translation for sixty-six languages available for this colossal 'UN of Faith' which has been in the planning stages for several years. We've been informed that as many as sixty thousand delegates may be present for 'general sessions' at the convention.

"Organizers of the event have called for a ban on any sort of 'distractions' from the goal of unity and peace once participants are inside the arena. No one will be allowed to carry signs, flags, banners, or posters into the arena—so no individual 'causes' will be touted. Also on the list of forbidden items is anything that could be used as a weapon. Given the tight security, we'll just have to wait and see if the convention can stay on schedule.

"Until tomorrow, this is Cathy Beecham, reporting live from the Philadelphia Arena. Back to you Jeff and Sharon."

Jeff Lutz looked directly at camera one. "Thank you for that report Cathy. We will be looking forward to hearing from you in the coming days."

# # #

As Benjamin Gordon sat in his room in watching the UIG reports, he didn't know how he'd muster the strength to get up in the morning and go to the arena to get more money from Zac. Michael couldn't take any more time off from work, so Ben had been elected again. Even without the conference, going there would be a challenge for him.

He closed his eyes. *The day is coming, probably soon, when you won't be able to get out any more. And you know Zac won't come to the hospital. He can't cope with it for some reason.* The faintest imprint of a memory flickered for a moment: A girl Zac had loved in high school. A pretty girl with strawberry blond hair.

That's right, he recalled, nodding slightly. *She got very sick . . . and she died just before Zac moved away from home. Oh, Lord, Ben silently prayed. So much sorrow in our family.*

I probably won't be here to see it all work out. But You've given me time to understand them, and pray for them. I know You'll do it somehow. I'm not scared of dying anymore. I'm almost looking forward to coming Home, now. But, please, just give me the opportunity to talk to them one more time, okay?

CHAPTER 27

PHILADELPHIA — September 29th

"This is Cathy Beecham reporting for UIG in Philadelphia," said the young woman facing the camera. In the steady wind, her close-cropped, black hair fluttered like bird feathers around her face. "Today we will be giving live reports from the opening ceremonies of the World Conference on Spirituality. Several hours remain before the event begins, and already thousands of people have flocked to the streets outside the arena. While many of those gathered are delegates waiting for the doors to open, others have come to watch, meditate, or pray. Some have come to protest."

Cathy continued to speak while the camera's focus zoomed in on particular people in the crowd. "As you can see, there is an entire range of sentiment represented here. Many carry messages of general support for the conference, like, 'Many Ways to God,' or 'A Unified World Will Know Peace,' or 'Unity in Diversity!' Some express opinions that aren't exactly mainstream. I don't know if the camera can catch it or not, but further down the street we have one guy who came to make a statement!" The camera lens zoomed in on a man with a large signboard which said in large letters, "THERE IS ONLY ONE LORD! IF YOU WON'T RELATE, HE'LL CREMATE!"

"And can you get that one over there?" Cathy asked the cameraman. She watched the monitor as he focused on one woman in particular. "Yes. That's the one."

The female protestor, wearing a space alien costume, held a large sign which read: "THIS SHOULD HAVE BEEN AN INTERPLANETARY CONFERENCE!"

The camera panned back for a wider shot and Cathy Beecham's amused face appeared on screen once again. "All in all, though, I'd say the majority of those who've gathered here want to show their support of, and unity with, those inside the arena. . ."

# # #

While the crowds outside continued to increase and the media coverage expanded, inside the Philadelphia Arena, Zac Gordon and others were doing a last "walk through" of the facility. The coordinator for each team on the event staff used a two-way radio to report last-minute details.

Despite the babel from the radio in his ear and the harried movements of employees nearby, Zac calmly walked through the wide expanse in front of a dining area, taking in every detail. He stopped. *Something's missing. What is it?* Several seconds elapsed before he realized what was wrong and smiled. *There are no hot dogs, cinnamon rolls, or popcorn being cooked in here today!* All the familiar smells were gone, and the scents which greeted him now were curry, cumin, scented oils, aromatic spices, and incense. Having solved the mystery, Zac resumed his inspection.

After the unfortunate miss-hap in the arena's kitchen the night before, Ms. A. Glad-Butterfield spent only a few moments alone with him. She informed him that he *would* be in her office at exactly nine o'clock on the first regular business morning (Monday) following the conference. She left little doubt that his stellar impersonation of her in front of other workers would be his "swan song" at the arena. Zac, always his most productive under stress, was determined to make his last work at the arena his best.

Because a former First Lady, Edith Todd, would be giving the opening address for the event, he'd already attended a short briefing with her security force early in the morning and made some last-minute changes. These alterations would result in a twenty-minute delay in the master schedule and the need to pay overtime to some workers—two things which would most likely be unacceptable to Ms. Butterfield.

Oh well, he thought. *What's she gonna do? Fire me?*

"Fearless Leader, Fearless Leader this is Oliver at the front doors. We're ready to open them at your command."

Zac had a small wireless "ear bud" in his left ear for listening, and a pin on his lapel served as a wireless microphone. He took a slow, deep breath and keyed the switch on his belt before saying, "This is Fearless Leader to all bases. Is everyone ready?"

He listened as each base called in, one at a time, to report their final status. "This is One, check. . . . Two, Check. . . ."

Each of fourteen bases called in "check," meaning all of them were ready.

"Okay," Gordon said, "this is Fearless Leader, we have a go. Repeat, we have a go—open the floodgates!" He stood on the mezzanine above the lobby as he watched the sea of humanity pour through the doors, filter through security points, then cascade into the main lobby.

His radio suddenly crackled to life with a call about seating for the handicapped in the main hall. He looked at his watch and grinned. *Well, it worked for a whole minute and a half.* He headed for the main hall and went to the special seating section. As soon as he had the problem solved, he took time to check with each of the coordinators. Everything was running pretty close to plan. *Actually,* he thought, *it doesn't get much better than this.*

# # #

Blocks away, Benjamin Gordon occupied the passenger seat of a car being driven by his friend Lyza. Seeing him sitting almost motionless in his seat, Lyza now regretted offering to take him to the arena. Why was he so urgent about going? Why had she listened?

She thought of when they'd first met almost two years ago when they both started attending the same meetings. They kept encountering each other and gradually found they had quite a bit in common. Both were struggling commercial artists, both had come from larger families, both were homosexuals, and both were seeking God. Eventually, they had two more things in common: they made commitments to Jesus and they abandoned their former lifestyles.

Who'd have thought the two of us would be so different now, she reflected.

The greatest of ironies was they'd both found "coming out" as Christians had a bigger backlash than any revelation they'd announced before. Many family members figured they were trying "one more weird thing," and some former friends considered them traitors of the worst kind. During this time, they'd shared thoughts and struggles, praying for each other as a deep friendship formed.

At a stop light, Lyza studied him again, noting his labored breathing. "You sure you should be doing this?" she asked.

He remained still, but his voice sounded surprisingly bright. "I'm fine. Just conserving my energy, that's all."

Because they'd become so close, she understood what it cost Ben to come to terms with his diminished capacity. He'd had to abandon his pride and accept help from people—more and more on a daily basis now. But he'd refused to let this boil his life down to nothing more than an unending feast of sorrows. As long as he had any strength remaining, he wanted to spend it for the Lord. "After all," he'd said, "I've wasted so much time. I want to make good use of what I've got left. Doesn't God deserve that much from me?" The words echoed in her head as she chanced another glimpse at the frail man next to her. Despite what anyone else might think, he was very brave.

The roads leading to the arena were gorged with cars and trucks pushing in the same direction. Police stood everywhere, often stopping traffic to let hordes of walking protestors or supporters continue their trek toward the arena.

Ben hadn't planned on such a long commute and realized his medication for pain and fever would wear out before he got back home. He chided himself for not bringing some of it along. The familiar stinging sensation inside his lips, under his tongue and on the roof of his mouth told him the infection in his throat had spread.

Lyza finally pulled up to the large iron gate Ben indicated, and stopped. They rolled down their windows as two men in light brown security uniforms approached then split up, moving to either side of the vehicle. Ben spoke to the burly guard who stood by his window.

"I'm here to see Zac Gordon. He's the Event Coordinator at the arena and he's expecting me. You can call him at extension five three two or you can contact him on your radio."

"What's your name?" the guard asked, a beefy finger on his microphone key.

"Ben Gordon."

The man waited for a break in the radio chatter, then spoke into his microphone. "Mr. Gordon, this is security at the back gate."

Zac's voice came right back. "This is Gordon, security. What do you need?"

"There's a Ben Gordon here to see you."

Inside the main hall, Zac heard the guard's last radio transmission. With all the changes taking place during the night and this morning, he'd totally forgotten about Ben. He briefly pinched the bridge of his nose and rubbed in small circles as he mentally re-arranged his plans. "Yes," he said. "Issue him a visitor's pass and let him in the West doors. I'll meet him there in a few minutes."

"Will do," the guard answered, then looked at Ben again. "Okay, you can get out, and I'll have someone walk you in."

"But where will I park my car?" Lyza asked.

She watched the guard crouch down until his face appeared in Ben's window. He pushed his hat back a bit and looked past Ben at her. "This car? You can't park this car in here. All those trucks you see," he said, pointing to the delivery vehicles inside the fence, "had to be on a master list *yesterday*. If you don't have a reserve ticket for one of the regular lots, or haven't made other arrangements for your car, you're not gonna find a parking space for miles around here. You're just going to have to drop him off."

Lyza looked at Ben. He'd sat up and seemed more alert now but she could tell he felt ill. "How would you get home?" she asked.

Ben could see her struggling with the idea of letting him go on alone. There was no time to explain again how he knew he had to do this. "I'm sure I'll be able to get a cab or something. I'll be fine."

A brief smile lit his face, and the last remains of the handsome man he'd once been seemed to shine at her. It was something warm, yet it made her hurt inside. Half of her feared to let him out of her sight. The other half wanted to run as far as she could to get from the approaching loss of something so precious. She squeezed the steering wheel tighter. *Being an iron-clad empress of ice was so much easier.*

"You're right," she said, wanting very much to sound casual. "There will probably be lots of empty cabs leaving out front. Call me when you're home."

Within minutes, Ben sat in an office inside the freight entrance of the arena. Although entering this way allowed him to bypass the lines with thousands of convention participants, he wouldn't be able to gain access any further into this part of the building without an escort. After waiting for a visitor's pass and then the long walk inside, he was grateful for another spate of rest before Zac arrived.

He sat looking out the large windows facing the area where people were scrambling about in an effort to finish unloading trucks and depart. A familiar face caught his attention. As a man in the dark green overalls worn by arena service workers approached, Ben squinted to see if this could actually be someone he'd known years ago. Soon he felt certain it was Jimmy Hearst.

Years ago he'd known Jimmy was also HIV positive, and that he hadn't taken the "cure." Although he'd aged a bit since the last time Ben had seen him, his muscular form said he remained in good shape.

Jimmy walked past the large windows of the office, then came through the open door and looked right at Ben without recognizing him. It was a common occurrence these days.

"Hey Jimmy."

Jimmy moved the clipboard from his right hand to the crook of his left elbow, and held it against his chest, then stood there with a questioning look on his face. Obviously he'd need further assistance.

"It's Ben Gordon," Ben said.

Jimmy openly gawked for another moment before speaking. "Whoa. Ben! Haven't seen you in ages. When you dropped out of the scene—how long ago?—I just figured you were a goner."

They'd had some friends in common years ago, but had never been chummy. *Why didn't I just leave it alone? Ben thought while the man blundered on.*

"I mean, you know how it is, gone usually means gone." Jimmy said, moving his hand in a flat line.

The remark, while true, still left Ben speechless.

They heard a burst of laughter just outside the door and both of them looked as Zac and another worker entered the room. Relieved to see his brother, Ben smiled before slowly rising from his chair.

"Been waiting long?" Zac asked.

"No. I just got here a couple of minutes ago," Ben answered.

Jimmy made hasty retreat back out to the trucks in the bay.

Zac glanced at his watch. It was ten seventeen. "Let's swing by my office," he said, "and I'll give you the magstrip. Sorry I couldn't bring it by your place, but I've been almost living here for days. I probably won't have any free time till Monday."

"No bother," Ben said.

Zac looked at his watch again. "Look, if you'd like to wait here, I could just send my secretary down with it."

While money was the excuse for the visit, right now Ben didn't care about it. He knew this wasn't a good time, but he wanted to talk with his brother. He'd tried on several occasions to plan dinners or other meetings where he and Zac could discuss things, but Zac always managed to cancel at the last minute in favor of a hot date or because he needed to work late at the office. Ben knew time was running out. He'd probably be back in the hospital later today, maybe tomorrow if he held out.

These might be the last moments I have with Zac for a while, he thought. Against his will, a picture flashed through his head. He could see the shock on Jimmy's face and hear the comment about the presumption that he was already dead. *Maybe this is your last chance to talk to Zac EVER . . . Wait! he quickly warned himself. Don't go there! Don't let the 'woe is me' thing start. You know how it spirals out of control. This isn't about me, it's about Zac. I can do this! I can do all things through Christ who strengthens me. Lord, I believe You want me here . . . work through me to do my part.*

"If it's okay," Ben said. "I'd like to go with you."

"Okay."

The two brothers started trudging down halls reserved for people with badges. Zac slowed his pace considerably so Ben could keep up, noting it was now ten twenty-six. Edith Todd would be arriving in twenty-four minutes. The main event would start in thirty-four minutes.

To Ben, it seemed as if they were moving along at quite a clip. He could only speak in short bursts. "You know," he said, "I've been thinking of you . . . a lot lately, Zac. I've really wanted to talk to you. We haven't done that since . . . well, since before the thing . . . with your apartment. A lot has happened and I—"

Zac heard someone calling on his radio, so he stopped walking and interrupted his brother. "Just a second, Ben. This is Mr. Gordon," he answered into his microphone, "What do you need?" He stood there for a few seconds, listening to a conversation Ben couldn't hear, then responded again. "Don't put them there, try the C-7 section. Okay. Get back to me." He looked at his watch, then back at Ben before he started walking again. "Sorry. You were saying?"

"I was saying I just wanted to be able . . . to spend some time with you, Zac. There are things—"

Zac stopped walking. "This is Fearless Leader."

Ben realized the radio conversation must be on again—either that or Zac was having some really strange delusions.

"Listen to me, Amber," Zac said. "I'm sure there's room in—Am . . . Am . . . *Amber*! Mission Control to Spaceship Ammmmber! Hey, come down out of orbit, would ya?" He said with a laugh. "They're in room in A-5. . . . Yes, I'm certain. I'm right below it and I'll meet you there in sixty seconds." He looked back at Ben again. "Man, I'm sorry. I have to meet this woman for just one sec. She's so zinged up today security could probably use her as a stun gun!"

"No problem," Ben answered. He thought about how much he'd like to get some water on a handkerchief to put on his face and possibly get something cool for his mouth and throat. His fever reducer was definitely wearing off. "Is there a water fountain nearby?"

"Yeah. There's a break room just up here. Second door on the left. Tell you what, Ben," Zac said, striding to the door and opening it, "there are some tables and chairs as well as some vending machines and water fountain. Just hang out in here and I'll be right back. I promise, this will only take a moment."

"Sure," Ben said with resignation. *This isn't going to work,* he thought. *Lord, I was so sure You wanted me here, I'm sorry if I misunderstood.*

Fifteen minutes later, Zac had quashed yet another minor emergency and realized he didn't have the time to walk around with his brother. He quickly got a magstrip from his office (made out for twice the normal amount) then asked Barbara to run it down to Ben and escort him to a taxi. She could tell him Zac would definitely do dinner with him next week sometime.

# # #

Just as Barbara left Zac's office, Ben was standing very still in a large supply closet down the hall from the break room where his brother had left him. The man he'd recognized in the shipping office, Jimmy, now held him at knife-point. A short, muscular man with light brown hair stood with his back to them and peered through the crack of the slightly open door. After a quick survey he eased it shut.

Minutes earlier, Jimmy and this man, both wearing ID tags and green arena overalls had come into the break room where Ben waited for Zac. It was then Ben noticed the tag clipped on the pocket of Jimmy's overalls said, "Anthony Anderson." Next, he remembered how Jimmy suddenly moved his clipboard to cover the tag when they'd been in the freight office . . . and that he'd acted nervous.

When Jimmy realized Ben had seen the phony name tag, he turned away and said something to his companion. The two men watched Ben in a mirrored wall while they exchanged additional muffled comments.

The man with Jimmy had whispered. "Even if you think he's probably okay, we can't leave him here."

"Just look at him, Charlie," Jimmy whispered back. "I'm telling you he's one of those M.R.—AIDS guys. If anyone should be on our side, he should."

"That may be so but, we still can't leave him here. You'll have to put him someplace till we're gone." Charlie eyed Ben's reflection for a moment. "Too bad we didn't have him around when we were filling the containers."

Jimmy suppressed a laugh. "Yeah."

Even though he couldn't hear them, it didn't take a gigantic leap of intellect for Ben to figure the pair was up to no good and that he'd become the glue in the gearbox. The next thing he knew, they both showed him they had knives in their pockets and escorted him to the small room they now occupied. They briefly appeared on a screen in the security office, but since they weren't running, or doing anything overtly suspicious, no one noticed them.

Charlie moved away from the door and pointed at Ben. "Sit down. On the floor."

Ben slowly complied, leaning his back against the far wall of the room. Charlie motioned for Jimmy to come closer, then whispered something to him. Jimmy's eyes bounced around in their sockets for a moment while he struggled to think. Finally, he nodded and whispered something back.

Straining, Ben could barely make out the next words they spoke. "Take him there. Stay there till it's time to meet us at the truck," Charlie said.

"All I was supposed to do after this was drive the truck."

Charlie shrugged. "Sure, Jimmy. But you're the one who wanted to prove you could handle more responsibility."

A look of resolve came to Jimmy's face. "I'll do it."

# # #

Zac heard someone addressing him over the radio.

"Mr. Gordon, this is security."

"Yes," he responded. Doubtless, it was an update on the status of the former First Lady, Edith Todd.

The man in security gave the pre-arranged message. "All the chairs are in place."

"Excellent," Zac said. She'd arrived safely in the building. He couldn't help thinking, *Good as it gets,* as he reached a balcony overlooking the lobby. The area below had filled with people wearing all sorts of costumes for a grand entrance during the opening ceremonies. They had trumpets, drums, and multicolored streamers. The people wearing dancing slippers were warming up in preparation to perform. Others, dressed in elegant choir robes, quietly hummed their singing parts.

Who paid for all this? Zac wondered. The entire production had been lavish and this was no exception. *But yours is not to question why . . . just to take the money for the gig.*

Zac looked at his watch. It was time to get up in the control booth. Not that he wanted to watch the festivities, but he needed to be someplace where he had an overview of as many activities as possible. He wanted this to be seamless.

Soon, he'd entered the small enclosure and stood next to Wes, the lead engineer for the control booth. Wes would assist the technicians who had been supplied by the sponsors of the event—two women who would synchronize the lighting and sound production for the opening ceremony.

# # #

Charlie stood in front of the arena elevators for Section A. He'd gone to the men's room, shed his green overalls, and emerged wearing matching navy-blue pants and shirt with Philadelphia Arena's logo and the words "EVENT STAFF" printed on the front and back in bright yellow. He had an I.D. badge on a plastic chain around his neck which bore his picture and a phony name. Before he could swipe the badge to gain access to the elevator, the doors opened. A petite, silver-haired woman with a similar badge exited holding an envelope in her hand.

Charlie entered the elevator and allowed the doors to close before selecting his desired floor. By now, he figured, Jimmy had already taken their prisoner to another location in the building.

# # #

During his two months working at the arena, Jimmy discovered the room adjacent to the freight bay was used only at night to process all the paper, plastic, and metals placed in trash cans throughout the facility during an event. For now, the room would be a perfect place to keep Benjamin Gordon.

Ben clutched the railing and looked at the pile of shredded metal just below them. Soon, he'd lack the strength to remain standing. "Are you going to kill me?" he finally asked.

Jimmy seemed startled by the question. "Nah," he finally said. "We just have to make sure you don't talk to anyone until we're done."

"Done doing what?"

Jimmy couldn't resist telling. "We're just gonna give them a sample of what millions of us face all the time."

"And what's that, Jimmy?"

"You of all people should know."

It suddenly came to Ben. "AIDS? You want to give them a sample of *AIDS*?" He began to panic. "What do you mean? How?"

"We're going to spray the virus on them. Then they can all wonder if they got it. *They* can see how it is to be treated like some unimportant little statistic. You of all people should appreciate the humor of it."

Ben felt dizzy at the thought. He squinted to focus on Jimmy. "You're joking, right? You wouldn't really. . ."

Jimmy smiled broadly. "Yes we would!"

"You can't do this. Not to anyone. It's murder."

Now Jimmy got angry. "You know," he said, pointing his knife in the direction of the main hall, "if most of the people in that convention had their way, you'd have been dead a long time ago."

Ben didn't respond.

"At least," Jimmy observed, "you'll have the satisfaction of knowing some of them will probably go, too."

"So you'd really kill them to make your point?"

Jimmy seemed to draw strength from the remark. He straightened up and said, "It's only fair. They want to let all of us croak, don't they? What do they call it? Selective reduction?"

Ben let go of the railing and put his hands up. "Wait, Jimmy. Think about what you're saying. You're saying they have no right to live. Isn't that why you hate them? For deciding who has value?" He could feel himself burning up. When he tried to swallow, it was if a thousand acid-laced thorns were stabbing every square inch of his tongue, mouth and throat. His infection was raging out of control, but he had to continue. "Please, think about what you're doing, Jimmy." Every word caused spikes of pain. "All life has value. Your life. Their lives . . . my life. I'm telling you, I've finally gotten so I understand how much God loves people, Jimmy. It's not too late. I'm begging you. Don't do this terrible thing."

"There is no God," Jimmy hissed.

Ben's voice remained soft, but unrelenting. "Yes there is and He's set me free . . . His name is Je–"

Jimmy moved forward in a threatening manner. "Shut up! Shut up or I'll make you sorry!"

Ben realized talking was a waste of time. Zac and thousands of others were in that arena. He started walking toward the door.

Jimmy stepped in front of Ben and flashed the knife around. "Stop! Don't make me hurt you."

Even if Jimmy already had AIDS, every exposure to other strains of it presented new risks of infection. "What?" Ben said. "And get my nasty blood all over you? I don't think so." He started moving forward again.

"How stupid are you? I said stop and I meant it!" Jimmy gave him a big shove. In his desperation, he pushed Ben with much greater force than required. Ben reeled a few steps and flipped over the railing into the pile of shredded metal below. Jagged shards and sharp corners cut into him, but he didn't have the strength to escape from their treacherous grasp.

Horrified, Jimmy ran from the room and locked the door.

Ben's last particle of physical strength ebbed away. He couldn't even make a sound. All he could do was pray in his mind.

Father . . . please don't hold this against Jimmy. And, please, spare my Zac. I know I can't make deals, but You know I'd give anything for You to save him . . . You've given me such a heart for him . . . there has to be a reason for it. Please, God, let him live. . . . Help him find his way.

# # #

In the arena control booth, Zac Gordon watched expert hands make fine adjustments to the sound and lighting panels, then observed the result in the arena below. The music reached a crescendo. A storm of bright lights flashed on men and women leaping from the stage into the area just in front of the first row of seats. Each of them held a wand attached to an immense ribbon, wielded like a giant slash of silk lightning, as the dancers plunged into a foaming sea of bright costumes below.

A worker on Zac's radio spoke of a glitch involving a "dignitary" in the seating directly in front of the podium.

"No problem," he answered. "I'll be there in a sec." But, just as he opened the door, he heard his secretary's voice come over the radio.

"Fearless Leader, Fearless Leader, this is Silver Fox." Although she used the playful names Zac invented, she sounded tense.

He closed the door to the booth and stood in the hallway behind it. "This is Fearless. What do you need?"

Barbara stood in the break room where she was supposed to find Ben. She carefully considered what she would say. Ben shouldn't have been left unattended in this part of the building.

"I just need some direction," she finally said, acutely aware the radios were being monitored throughout the arena. "I . . . can't find the thing you sent me for. Any ideas?"

Zac's voice instantly cracked back through her earpiece. "Are you in the break room, section A, basement level?"

"Yes, I am, and I don't know where else to look."

Zac thought a moment while the two women who had done the lighting exited the booth with an arena escort and walked past him.

# # #

Today of all days, Zac scolded himself. *If Butterfat sees Ben walking around without an escort . . .* A picture of Ben struggling to get out of the chair in the freight office went through his mind. *What if he's gotten really sick someplace?*

"No problem, Silver Fox." he radioed back. "I'll be right there." There was still the seating problem in the main hall. "Tino?" he said, while striding toward the elevator.

A man's voice answered. "Yes?"

"Handle the seating thing without me. Just apologize to everyone and give whoever's losing the seat some sort of perk, okay?"

# # #

At center stage in the main hall of the arena, Ira Goldman, a leader in the New Innovation Judaism Movement, prepared to address the assembly. The remarks he'd laboriously assembled over the past two months, would have to wait. He'd been forced to yield his time slot to someone else. Instead of getting a prime speaking spot for the convention, he'd only be introducing his replacement.

Sure, he said to himself while he waited for the audience to become quiet, *you'll get to deliver your speech tomorrow— to a mere fraction of the television audience. They decided someone of importance in American politics should be seen here. President Cole wouldn't even acknowledge them, so they got HER.*

When informed of the change last night, Ira had threatened to leave the conference altogether. He'd only been persuaded to stay when he received pleas from Sven Borgeson, one of the directors of the organizing committee.

Sven recognized Ira's years of effort for the movement and apologized for the change. It had to be made if they wanted the convention to receive optimum coverage in America. Wouldn't Ira, who had such "remarkable insight" and such "bold vision for the future" consider the greater good? The loss of his "intelligent voice" would be a tragedy.

Finally, Ira agreed to stay when they gave him the opportunity to have a few opening remarks and the honor of introducing his replacement. But he had no intention of forgetting the offense. *When they're trying to get the movement into the next phase, they'll need me.*

"My name is Ira Goldman and I bid welcome to our honored guests," he said, when the arena became quiet. He remembered to speak slowly so that the translators had time to transmit his every word.

"I bid welcome to the sons and daughters of our beloved Mother Earth. I bid welcome to all who have come in peace. Most of all," Ira said, with a sweeping motion of his hand toward the cameras. "I bid welcome to those who are looking upon our assembly with curiosity and hope."

# # #

The other members of the group taking part in the protest were already assembled when Charlie arrived. He meant to tell Stan, the group's leader, about the problem he and Jimmy had encountered in the break room, but someone approached him as soon as he got in the door.

"You'll never guess what," the man said in a hushed voice. "I overheard some employees talking. President Todd's widow is about to go on!"

Charlie didn't know how to respond. Was this a good thing or a bad thing? He tried not to commit himself to any sort of reaction until he could hear what Stan thought. He looked at Stan and asked, "We're still going through with the plan, though, right?"

"Why not?" Stan responded quickly. He'd overheard the same thing earlier and knew it was inevitable they'd find out. Although all of them spoke of getting away after the protest and living like heroes-in-hiding, they'd also declared they were ready to die or go to prison for the cause.

Stan knew the enhanced security would greatly increase the risk of getting caught, but he looked at them and smiled confidently. "Look, we've planned this carefully. Everything is in place already, and all of you should be outside the building by the time it goes down. That woman's presence will get us even more press coverage. We couldn't have asked for a better turn of events." He reached over and switched off the lights so their eyes would be ready for the dimly lit areas around the control booth.

Charlie decided to keep the news about Jimmy and the temporary hostage a secret. Hopefully, Jimmy had already tied up the scrawny fellow and stashed him where he wouldn't be discovered until they were long gone. So what if the guy could identify them? All the members of the group would eventually be identified, but this didn't matter. Once they were out of the state they'd be hidden by others who supported the cause.

Stan, the group leader, sat near the door, relishing the sense of control he had, the sense of power. He'd been brought up in a home where the very things being promoted at this convention were taught. He'd been raised with the idea that certain individuals came to Earth as teachers to raise the consciousness of humanity.

Now, the reality of this day was almost more than he imagined. He'd be the teacher and he would give the world an unforgettable lesson. People would learn life could take sudden, unwanted turns, much the same way his own had.

As his eyes slowly adjusted to the darkness, he took a breath and considered it. What would the press say about his life? Would they focus on the fact he was rich?

In an increasingly health-conscious world, Stan's medical lab business made him a wealthy man. Catering to the wealthy clients of holistic practitioners, he couldn't deposit their money fast enough. He had everything. Who would have figured his wife could hide such a secret from him? Until the day after she delivered their son, Stan had no idea she'd already passed the HIV virus to him and their child.

Her death came so quickly after the revelation of her illness, he had no time to work out all of his emotions. But his precious son, Ethan, was another story. Even though Stan responded well to conventional treatments, Ethan didn't. No matter what doctors tried, the boy continued to fade. When he died, his father couldn't be consoled.

A few months later, Stan overheard two family members talking. His Aunt commented to his sister that "Stan's bad karma" must have caught up with him. When he heard it, something inside him snapped.

Almost everyone, it seemed, had an excuse to look the other way while millions suffered and died of AIDS. Whether they wrote it off to karma, bad living, or judgment from God, people figured most AIDS patients got what they deserved.

Stan became obsessed with letting the world know how it felt to be the object of such calloused indifference. Then, he read a newspaper article about the selection of Philadelphia, his own city, for the World Conference on Spirituality. Before he finished reading the article, he realized he had the money, the equipment, and the expertise to make something extraordinary happen at this international event. With a small group of extreme activists to help him, he could become the teacher of a great lesson.

The sound of applause in the arena below reminded Stan the time had nearly come. He cracked the door and looked down the hall. Only one man remained in the booth. Fantastic.

From down below, the voice of Ira Goldman resonated throughout the main hall.

# # #

"Today," Ira said, "I come, not as a religious person . . . not as a citizen of a country . . . not even as a man . . . but I present myself to you as a child of Earth . . . a soul who has shared a common burden with so many of you for the renewal of our planet and the rebirthing of all people. . . . "

Ira listened as rounds of cheers seemed to accumulate and swell, starting with those who understood English, the momentum growing as his remarks were interpreted to the rest of the audience.

"This morning," he continued, "I have the distinct honor of introducing you to a speaker who is not listed on your programs. She has graciously come to us today and is here, I am certain, by divine appointment. This woman, familiar to us all, has endured hardship for the sake of our common cause."

Goldman slowly stretched his hand toward the left of the stage, "Brothers and sisters, will all of you rise and welcome, the former first Lady of the United States, Edith Todd. . . "

# # #

All of the protestors had sharp knives created out of a carbon composite material, making them invisible to most detection devices. Stan unsheathed his before he and Charlie walked down the hall to the arena control booth. Stan walked in front, Charlie slightly behind. The man in the booth, busy adjusting sound equipment, barely heard them enter the small enclosure.

Charlie quickly placed a hand over the man's mouth and a knife to his neck, while Stan pushed the button to turn off the booth's microphone.

Stan spoke in a clear, low voice. "Put both of your hands on the arms of your chair."

The startled man quickly complied, his eyes wide with terror. Stan rolled the chair back from the control panel, then put down his knife and pulled a pouch out of his pocket. In the pouch were pre-cut pieces of tape, wrapped around a flat piece of plastic. He pulled one piece off and taped the man's mouth shut. Next, he pulled several large tie-wraps out of the pouch and bound the man's hands to the chair, his feet together.

"I have no desire to hurt you, Wes . . ." Stan said, looking at the man's I.D., "but we're serious about getting a few moments with the audience. You do want to cooperate, don't you, Wes?"

Wes nodded.

"We just want to give a little demonstration here, and then, if you've been a good boy, you can still go home unharmed . . . got that?"

Wes nodded again.

"Okay," Stan said to Charlie, "Go. And be sure the door locks."

Charlie backed out of the control booth and closed the door. He made sure it locked and Stan gave him the thumbs up signal. There was little danger anyone would hear any noises they might make. It was a sound-proof booth. Should someone pass by, as long as Stan kept Wes' back to the door, no one would think anything was amiss. Stan had an EVENT STAFF outfit on and a functional tag. Who would know he didn't belong in the booth?

"Now." Stan said, "I want to use the lift and I'm pretty sure I know how, but perhaps you can help me. I'd hate to drop something heavy on unsuspecting people in the audience. Wouldn't that be a tragedy?"

He yanked the tape off Wes' mouth.

"Yes, it would." Wes said, in a shaky voice.

# # #

At the sound of her introduction, Edith Todd let go of the hand of her old friend and spiritual mentor, Tony Benson. She walked from behind the curtain to the center of the stage, then waved to the audience, waiting for the applause to stop before she spoke. She stood there, amazed at her own lack of stage fright. She'd been in seclusion for so long, yet this seemed . . . easy. It was as if she had stepped from a cocoon into a great expanse. The old Edith wasn't standing there, but a transformed individual who radiated energy to the waiting world.

# # #

On the basement level, Zac Gordon came out of the men's restroom. His secretary knew from the look on his face he hadn't found his brother inside.

He changed the frequency on his radio and keyed his microphone. "Security, this is Zac Gordon."

"Yes Mr. Gordon, this is Gannet in security."

"Yeah, Paul," Zac said, "can you have two guards report to the West elevator, basement level?"

"Give 'em three minutes, Mr. Gordon."

Barbara put a hand on Zac's arm. "You want to go back up to the Main Hall? I can meet them and get them searching."

Again, Zac recalled Ben slowly getting out of the chair, then struggling to keep up with him . . . he inwardly swore at himself before he looked at Barbara once again. "No. I'll stay here. I have my radio. I can hear what's going on. If everybody does their job, they don't need me."

# # #

Edith Todd let her gaze sweep across the entire arena before she started speaking, sure the assembled energies were feeding her. She opened her mouth and heard herself speaking.

"I come today having spent time under the dark cloud of oppression and secrecy. Like many of you, I found the road to this meeting to be a long and difficult one . . . a journey filled with sorrows and persecutions . . . where those of a narrow way sought to block the exodus of so many of us to a higher plane. But tonight, I stand as one who's been liberated, and I offer an official welcome to all of you from this country!"

After a short delay the applause grew.

"As we know, and many watching from around the world will discover . . . there are millions of us who have seen the glorious future that can come if we will only unite and believe . . . believe that the paths to this future are varied, wide, and wonderful."

"I come here today with a mandate. That mandate is to embolden all of you to implement the plan established before the ages. As the power of the plan spreads into every sphere of influence, it will bring a new age of peace.

"I come today to ask each of you to return to your homes with determination to open the gates of your cities, your regions, and your nations to the plan. It's a simple plan. Simple yet profound. Simple yet hard. Simple yet universal . . . an idea whose time has come.

"One people, one belief, one world . . . respecting the life-force abiding within air, sea, soil, and every creature . . . holding as precious every corner of this little oasis in the galaxy which we call Earth.

"This plan involves no longer yielding to zealous nationalistic interests which parade as patriotism, or to the greed of unscrupulous businesses who are poisoning our Mother Earth, or to fanatical 'fundamental' religions claiming they are the only way to God. . . . It calls for us to be empowered beyond the tiny bounds of small men's minds.

"We are no longer content to live with borders or boundaries of nationality, race, religion or gender. Right now, at this very moment in time, we purpose to begin the move towards true global wholeness.

"We have gathered here hoping to be filled with the positive, focused forces of each other and of the Masters . . . and to move from this place empowered as One. We will save this planet from darkness . . ."

From behind the curtain her friend, Tony Benson, continued to have an odd feeling. Instead of elation for Edith, or even a thrill that her message was going worldwide, an ominous sensation steadily grew. He tried to focus its source but could only conclude it was all around them. He'd experienced a sense of dread before, when channeling certain spirits, but this had more of a tangible threat attached to it. What was it? He rationalized, the forces were in flux weren't they? Possibly this could account for the disturbance he felt. He'd been taught there was no real good or evil . . . only the shifting of forces for different purposes. Fear was irrational. He would lean on this knowledge and press beyond the temporary anomaly.

Edith continued to speak. "In the coming days we will renew ourselves and open the portals for the energies who have been waiting for this very time to come and fill this country and the world.

"On August 19th of this year, during a time of deep meditation, I received a vision– a promise, really. A promise to all who seek the fulfillment of the ages: Your time has come!"

Once the translation was complete, the response from the audience grew to a roar. Edith, stood there, drinking in the power of it for a few seconds before resuming.

"In this vision, I was caught up in the sky and I soared above the clouds, going higher and higher. I saw an exquisite angel of light, and he pointed at the sun. As I looked, the brightness of the sun called to me and drew me further out into space, hovering over the earth, outside of time. I looked down and I could see sparks of light flashing briefly throughout the ages, in India, China, the Middle East, Europe, and many other places around the world. Each time, the spark would shoot out smaller sparks, which remained after the larger one had passed.

"Then the voice of the sun talked to me. He said, 'Behold, it comes!' Next, I saw the energies of those smaller sparks reuniting under the returning Masters. Their lights grew, and burst up toward the outer shell of our atmosphere, then expanded, and merged, encircling the globe.

"The voice spoke again, saying, 'Behold, it comes quickly!' I saw a war between darkness and light in the atmosphere while the energies of the Masters washed over the whole earth.

"After this, the sun drew near to the earth and filled it with the Presence, the great incarnation, and I heard the voice saying, 'Behold the time is short!'"

"I remained in a trance for two days following this vision. During this same time, two others, one in England and one in Nepal, received the same revelation . . . We believe this constitutes a confirmation. Brothers and sisters, we are on the eve of the expansion of enlightenment!"

Sounds of elation filled the arena. Edith closed her eyes and focused on her center, many seeing what she was doing on the large wall screens, followed her example, and a hush fell on those assembled. After nearly a minute of silence, she opened her eyes and spoke.

"This is a moment of power, brothers and sisters. Let us unite and magnify it . . . I want to recite the words of The Universal Invocation. Rise and let the words flow through and around you. . . . As you hear the words, I invite all of you" she said, with a sweeping gesture of her arms, "to empty yourselves, then open yourselves fully. Embrace the light, draw it into your innermost selves, then let it expand outward into the atmosphere."

Everyone stood to their feet and Edith read the words.

"From the essence of Light within the Mind of God
Let enlightenment stream forth into our minds
Let Light expand on Earth
"From the apex of love in the Heart of God
Let love come forth into the hearts of all people
May the next Christ, our Sun, be revealed on Earth
"From the centeredness where God's Will is known
Let that plan guide the small will of man—
The Plan which the Masters know and facilitate

"From those who are called to the highest
reasoning
Let the plan of Love and Enlightenment expand
And may it push through the gate where darkness
dwells
"Let our Enlightenment, Love, and Energy restore
The Plan on Earth."

# # #

In the control booth, Stan had turned on the speakers so they both could hear Edith Todd's words.

"Let me ask you, Wes," Stan said in an almost friendly tone. "You ever heard such a rambling bunch of drivel before?"

Wes, consumed with a desire to live, hadn't exactly been listening to what was going on outside the booth. Did his captor want a 'no'? He shook his head no.

"Well, that's not the half of it," Stan said. "But I think it's about show time . . ."

They heard a tap on the glass behind them. Stan placed a hand on Wes' shoulder to keep him from turning around, then looked to see who it was. Charlie stood outside the door to the booth, again giving him the thumbs up signal. This meant all the lights on the remote units were green— waiting for a signal. Stan saluted and waved before Charlie disappeared into the darkness. Stan could do the rest by himself. Charlie and the others would only remain a few more seconds to be certain the remote devices worked properly. If any sort of malfunction occurred, they were prepared to put Charlie in the cage so he could do the job manually—something that would almost certainly draw unwanted attention and shorten, or possibly end, their demonstration prematurely.

Stan pulled a device out of his pocket and turned it on, then slowly twisted a knob on the device half-way around. He could just imagine his special concoction beginning to spray into the air, the glittery substance mixed with it being the most ingenious part of all. Charlie appeared again and gave him another thumbs up. All was well.

Stan took a few seconds to savor his euphoria. *It's almost done.*

He went back to his hostage. "Okie dokie, Wes. I want to move the lift out over the center of the arena very, very slowly" he said, putting his hands on the controls. "Like this? This one is for forward movement?"

Wes didn't know what to do. Would resisting or giving mis-directions be a good idea? As long as they were just going to protest, wasn't it better to play along and let the cops deal with these men later? "Yes," he finally answered. "But it needs a real light touch, so be careful."

The lift, carrying the canisters, inched along its track toward the center of the ceiling in virtual silence, unnoticed below. Wes watched, tied helplessly to his chair, as the dark shadow moved slowly away from the booth, then stopped.

On an impulse, Stan let go of the controls, and got another piece of tape to put on Wes' mouth. He saw the frightened look in Wes' eyes grow. "It's for your own good," he said. "I mean, after all, you *have* been cooperative."

Stan knew security forces might target the booth once it became clear this was the center of the protest. If sharpshooters could see the tape on Wes' mouth, they'd know he wasn't doing the talking and they might not shoot him.

Down below, in the main hall of the arena, the multitudes were listening to Edith. Most had been completely absorbed in her words, but some began to notice a fine, sparkling mist softly falling around the room. A gentle, golden snowfall.

Edith stopped in mid-sentence when she noticed it. A glimmering cloud descending through the lights onto her and the others. She looked down at her hands, which rested on the podium. Little flecks of gold were reflecting off her skin. She looked around and realized there were gold particles everywhere—on the podium, the tele-prompters, the bullet-proof shield, the floor, and beyond. Part of her wanted to be delighted at this seemingly supernatural happening.

Sounds of awe came out of the audience as people began to look at themselves and others. Then, just as Stan planned, almost as if they were all given the same command, curiosity caused everyone to look up, most with their mouths wide open, straining to see the source of the shimmering phenomenon.

Stan suddenly twisted the knob on his sending unit. The valves on the canisters responded and went from spraying a light mist to a full down burst. He listened for the sounds of those below as they responded to the liquid striking their upturned faces.

He knew Charlie and the others would have fled the scene as soon as the mist began. Soon emergency response forces, police, and arena security would be trying to seal off the building and get to the booth. Stan hoped his men had successfully blocked the stairwell door and jammed the elevator controls when they departed. He knelt down and cut the tie-wrap holding Wes' right arm to the chair.

"Listen Wes. There's only one more thing you must do. You have to make sure the people down there keep hearing what I am saying. As long as I can still hear the feed coming back to me in my earphone, I won't do a thing to you. You must make sure no one cuts off my transmission. Got that?"

Wes nodded.

Stan sat on the floor next to his captive, keyed his microphone into the main system and spoke in a calm voice.

"What you have just experienced, ladies and gentlemen, was not, I repeat, not, a mystic event. What was it then? A reality check! I sure hope the TV cameras and translators are getting this!

"You see, while all of you are in here 'bonding' for world oneness, tens of thousands of actual human beings are dying. Not that you cared. Most of you have sat and watched for decades while *millions* of people died of AIDS. You outwardly spoke of what a 'tragedy' it was, and how awful it was that other religious groups shunned us or political groups slowly choked off our funding. . . . But secretly, you thought it was actually a good thing.

"Years ago, you decided enough of your precious world's resources had been wasted on us. You had better things to spend the time, effort, and money on. You used your influence with governments and large pharmaceutical companies to block creation and distribution of generic drugs to treat us. You reasoned with those in power to spend their money on things which were more important, more 'green friendly'

"Do you think our brains are too far gone to figure out you have no room for sick people in your perfect-bodied, vegetarian little world? Well, it's high time everyone else realized you have an agenda. It's not just for the exclusion of someone of differing belief and status . . . it's for the extinction of all who don't fit into your 'plan.'

"Already, unless someone with AIDS is rich, the only thing you'll help them do is 'die with dignity.' What is our crime? Why are we so expendable? Let's just be honest, shall we? It's because most of those who are infected live in third-world countries where you and the news media could care less about what happens. The poor victims in Africa, the Caribbean, and Latin countries aren't internet consumers or corporate leaders. They're just expendable users of Mother Earth the press will make sure aren't missed! The sooner our karma catches up to us, the better, eh?"

Stan saw the flash of a door down the hall being blown open and knew any moment they could be rushing down the hall to the booth. It was time for the punch line. "Well, we, the victims of HIV and AIDS just wanted to let you know how much we think about you. We wanted you to know we accept you. In fact, we want to feel 'one' with you. We want you to feel like you're our brothers and sisters. Welcome! Welcome to the fold! Most of you have just gotten a dose of several strains of HIV in the face!"

He imagined he could hear some of the people below shrieking and he smiled. "Don't panic. Obviously, this was your destiny, your karma. Accept that in your centeredness, then die well, won't you?. . . Meanwhile, do have a nice day."

CHAPTER 28

REGENT HOSPITAL, PHILADELPHIA

He became distantly aware of sounds. And he knew he was hot. Very hot. The fever howled from every cell in his body. Was someone speaking to him? Yes. They were tapping on his chest. Why couldn't he just rest? The voice sounded persistent. Urgent.

"Mr. Gordon. Benjamin. Can you hear me? . . . Answer me Mr. Gordon."

A light in the eyes.

"What," he finally said.

"Mr. Gordon, you're at the Regent Hospital in the emergency unit. We need your help, Mr. Gordon. Talk to me."

"What?"

"What medications are you taking?"

Ben only groaned. Even his thoughts were moving slowly. *I'm too hot . . . too tired. I've gotta rest up.* The hand was tapping on his chest again.

"What meds are you taking, Mr. Gordon? Your brother says you take lots, but he doesn't know what they are."

"Mike knows."

The voice kept pressing. "Who's Mike? Is Mike your doctor?"

"No. Brother."

"Your brother says he doesn't know."

"Other . . . brother."

He began to disconnect. He knew he was burning up, but the sensation was becoming more distant. It got harder to hold on to important thoughts. *By now, my brain must look like . . . what would it look like? . . . a poached oyster. . . . Wait. I must conserve my strength. . . . I must speak to Zac.*

Outside the trauma unit stood Zachary Gordon. The doors flew open as a nurse rushed out. He heard someone inside say, "This one's collapsed, get another line in," while another voice called, "Where are the cold packs? I need them now."

Zac turned as he heard the sound of rapid footsteps coming in his direction. Half of the SWAT team and some of the federal agents who had accompanied them to the hospital remained in the waiting area with Zac. Several of them now trained weapons in the direction of the hall door.

Beyond the door, Zac saw two men in uniform moving rapidly toward the waiting room. When they parted, he saw an anguished looking Michael behind them.

Zac rushed to him. "Michael! I'm so glad you're here. They need to know what meds Ben takes," Zac said before grabbing the arm of a woman entering the trauma room. "He knows what medications our brother takes."

Michael gave the nurse all vital information then looked through the doors as she entered the trauma unit where they worked on Ben. Everyone in the room was garbed head to foot to protect themselves from Ben's blood. Michael could hear two or three people giving orders at the same time in the rush of frantic activity.

When he turned around, he saw Zac had been taken to a chair in the corner where two men in business suits interrogated him. *What happened?* What was going on? What were all these people with large weapons doing here? All the police told him when they whisked him out of his store was that his brothers were on the way to the hospital and he must come immediately.

One of the doctors emerged and stood in the room. Zac jumped up from between the men in suits and brushed by uniformed officers to join Michael. The plainclothesmen rose and stood behind the throng.

"I'm Doctor Franz," the man said. "Are you his brothers?"

"Yes," Michael responded.

"Your brother is a very sick man. We have him stabilized at this point, but he'll have to be put in intensive care. Once they've moved him, you may see him for a few minutes." Dr. Franz took a deep breath. Next would come the part of the job he really hated. "I feel a need to be honest with you here. He might have a day. Days at most."

# # #

Ben woke again. Hours had passed.

Man, do I feel rotten, he thought. Worse than last time. *This really hurts. . . . Oh yeah*, he thought, remembering the pile of metal. *No wonder.*

A nurse nearby saw his eyelids flutter. "You awake Mr. Gordon? Can you open your eyes Benjamin?"

He opened them and tried to focus on the woman beside the bed. At least it sounded like a woman. The person standing there wore a hooded, baggy blue outfit. She had a visor over her face, making it hard to see her eyes past his own reflection in the plastic.

Funny how I never get used to seeing them dressed like this.

"So there you are!" she said in a perky voice.

He grunted and thought. *Oh, God, not a perky person. I don't think I can take a perky person right now. I feel so bad. Can't someone feel sorry for me, even if it's only for five minutes?*

"Would you like some ice?" She chirped.

He nodded. *Ah, yes, ice. Melting in my mouth. Maybe I could forgive her for being perky.*

"Your brothers were here earlier. You were out of it when we brought you up here, so you probably don't remember that part, do you?" She decided not to tell him that federal agents took the dark-haired one away in hand restraints.

Ben could barely talk. "Where's the man from the ER?"

"Which man?"

"The one . . . who held on."

She realized he must be disoriented. "I'll check."

Ben drifted back to sleep before she left the room. When he opened his eyes again, another three hours had passed. He became aware someone was touching him. He looked to his right and saw a man standing beside the bed. The man's gloved hand rested on his arm. He looked into the eyes of the man.

"It's you." he said, barely above a whisper.

"You remember me?"

"Yes." Ben said. At one point in the ER, when he feared he was slipping away, he felt someone take hold of his hand. It wasn't like the other hands which were urgently pushing and poking. This hand simply held on. And there was wonderful peace in this hand. The peace flowed up Ben's arm and into his whole body.

"I'm Matthew North," the man said, quietly. "I'm a chaplain here at the hospital."

# # #

Outside Regent Hospital, a large number of reporters hoped to get some prime-time exposure with a story about the man being held in the intensive care unit. So far, they knew only that the injured man had been found during a search for perpetrators of a potentially deadly "protest" at the Philadelphia Arena. He'd been rushed to the hospital with a large contingent of armed guards. Obviously something was up.

Millions of viewers would want to know all the details. What was his name? What connection did he have with the protest? How had he gotten injured? Was it a suicide attempt or had he been downed by law enforcement officers? Another protestor had committed suicide in the control booth before he could be captured.

The protest had taken place two hours ago during live, world-wide television coverage, and several accomplices remained at large. It was a breaking story.

# # #

Federal agents, now descending *en masse* upon the Philadelphia Arena and Regent Hospital, hadn't been able to interview the man they'd identified as Benjamin Gordon, but they already had three pieces of evidence to link him to the crime. First, review of security video taken prior to the incident showed him moving around in a secured area in the arena with two other men who were suspects in the case. Second, Gordon's brother, Zachary, worked at the arena and left the main hall just minutes before the canisters containing the virus were sprayed on the crowd. Third, Benjamin Gordon had AIDS.

# # #

"This is Cathy Beecham reporting live for UIG outside the Philadelphia Arena," the woman said into the microphone. "It's been seven hours since the protest and we continue to stay on the scene, covering this dramatic story as it unfolds."

The camera shot pulled back from Cathy so she filled only a small portion on the left of the shot. Night had fallen, so the only objects to be seen were hundreds of flashing red, blue, and yellow lights on the armada of emergency and police vehicles behind huge police barricades, blocking all access within several blocks of the arena.

"As you can see behind me, myriads of law enforcement, Haz-Mat, and emergency crews of other kinds are still inside the arena where a group of protestors managed to spray some sort of liquid on more than a thousand people attending the World Conference on Spirituality. A man who is presumed to be the leader of the protestors claimed the substance sprayed from canisters near the ceiling of the arena contained, and I quote, 'several strains of HIV' virus.

"I think we have an aerial shot available, so let's see if we can go to it."

A view from a helicopter flying at low altitude near the arena showed the parking areas and streets surrounding the building all pulsing with flashing lights.

Cathy continued, saying, "I'd like to take you to a recording of what UIG captured at the scene just after the protest ended. Our brave crew kept going to bring all of you the scenes of chaos that erupted in the arena. . . ."

In the short clip, viewers could see the pandemonium as men and women tried to run from their seats and exit the main hall. There were shouts and screams when people who hadn't been sprayed ran from those who had. The picture jostled, and then went blank before Ms. Beecham appeared on screen again.

"As you could see in this shot, our cameraperson, Debbie Lockman, was trampled in the stampede to get out of the main hall of the arena. She suffered a broken arm and collar bone and had to be transported with many others to a local hospital where she is receiving treatment.

"At our last count the casualty list was as follows: Ten people are dead—one of an heart attack, nine from fatal injuries sustained when they were trampled. Sixty-three people remain in local hospitals with various injuries.

"But the biggest story right now is that more than one thousand people, including former First Lady Edith Todd, and our own reporter, Jody Vaughn, who were sprayed with this substance but suffered no other injuries were held at the arena until just an hour ago. In a phone report given forty-five minutes ago, Jody told us once they received treatment, they were shuttled by chartered buses and taken to a hangar at a nearby military base where they are being issued fresh clothing. At this point agents are still searching the building, and all the vehicles parked outside, for any bombs or other devices which may still be active.

"And, in another breaking story—which is possibly related to this one—this afternoon, the FBI arrested two men in a raid on an apartment building in New York City. Witnesses at the scene say two metal suitcases were removed from the apartment and placed in a special truck as the men were taken into custody. There have been no further releases from the FBI regarding these arrests, so we don't know if the two men were part of this plot or if the cases contained more of the virus. Bert Shotman will have more for you on this at the top of the hour when we try to sequence the day's news for you.

"Meanwhile, back here in Philly, I've been told special teams from the Office of Disease Control and the Terrorism Task Force have been flown in and are working with others at what is now being classified as a crime scene. They are taking samples of the liquid in the canisters and doing what they can to treat those sprayed with this substance. We are told by a local specialist that treatment would include infusion of large doses of the new enzyme therapy. In addition to all this, once the search for dangerous devices is over, experts will try to determine what needs to be done to decontaminate the building itself and make it safe for the general public again.

"There has been no word yet on the status of the conference at this point. Law enforcement officials have told us privately that the conference, for all intents and purposes, is over. We're still waiting for confirmation of this from either the management of the Philadelphia Arena or conference organizers."

Cathy stopped and covered her ear with her left hand. "I'm just receiving word there have already been arrests and more are to come in this horrible act of terrorism." Ms. Beecham stopped speaking for a moment as she listened to her earpiece. "And I'm getting confirmation the Event Coordinator for the Philadelphia Arena has been taken into custody. Obviously, we'll get more about this to you as soon as possible.

"Already, strong words of criticism are beginning to pour into the United Nations, the White House, and the news media regarding what could already be termed an international incident. The White House itself has already issued a statement condemning the protest, along with Attorney General Gregg Siden's promise for a full investigation."

Cathy Beecham looked off to her right. "What's amazing is, despite all that's going on, hundreds of supporters and some protestors remain on the streets approaching the Philadelphia Arena."

The camera panned a crowd of people who had gathered within the halo of lights for the camera. Cathy approached several people and spoke to them. She moved close to one woman.

"Do you have any connection with the conference?" Cathy asked.

"No," the woman said, wiping away a tear. "I just came down to express my sympathy and support for those poor people."

"You're speaking of the people who got sprayed?"

"Of course."

Cathy moved on down to a man who stood with his arms outstretched toward the arena. "And why are you here tonight, sir?"

The man's eyes had been closed, but now he opened them and allowed his arms to relax at his sides. "I'm here with many others. We've come just to be a presence here. We want to send our positive energies to those inside the arena. What a terrible tragedy this is. . . . All these wonderful souls came to bring people together in unity and peace, and some group of twisted people has to go and do something like this. It just shows you how much darkness there still is out there and how much harder we're all going to have to work to overcome it." The man extended a hand in the direction of the arena as Cathy moved on down through those who had gathered nearby.

Another man stood with a poster that read, "Repent! Jesus IS COMING!"

Cathy approached him to ask, "And why are you here this evening, sir?"

The man spoke with utmost earnestness. "Because God told me to come. I've been carrying this poster around outside the arena since yesterday. Yesterday, people thought this was a big joke," he said, indicating his poster, "but this convention was a great wickedness, it was an affront to God! These people are going to be reaping what they have sowed if they don't repent! They need to turn away from this perversion and seek Jesus, the only Savior. The Bible says God is not willing that any should perish, but that people have to repent to live. I'm not rejoicing that anyone got hurt, but I'm saying if they don't get right with God, they're going to be left here when He comes—and they'll face His wrath."

Professionalism required that Cathy not display emotions. She had to resist giving the camera a look that said, *Is this guy nuts or what?* She simply moved away from him. The man moved parallel with her for a few feet as he said loudly, "Turn away while you can! Turn away while you can!"

He could still be heard in the background as she tried to wrap up her report.

"We have to go to a commercial break, but once again, we are continuing our live coverage outside the Philadelphia Arena. Remember, emergency hotlines have been set up and you will see them being displayed continuously at the bottom of your screen."

# # #

Someone turned the television's volume down as Cathy Beecham finished her report. Conference planner Bragjesh Advani sat there, seething. He turned to Sven and the others, his eyes fairly ablaze with anger. "Isn't this what I said? Did you see that man! How dare he say those things about us and the conference! Why did you insist we come to this country to be disgraced in such a manner?" He now looked at Sven in particular. "I told you what a mistake it was!"

Bragjesh, other conference organizers, and dignitaries were preparing to finish interviews with FBI agents, then be released. They'd been given the opportunity to take showers and don fresh clothing after being assessed and treated. While waiting in a military briefing room, they'd been allowed to watch television.

Obviously, it had been too much for Bragjesh. Two officers by the door prepared to intervene if he became violent.

"You see?" he continued. "This country is not ready! It will *never* be ready. I hope they *stay* in their darkness and pass into oblivion!"

Sven put an arm around his old friend and spoke quietly. "Perhaps you were right . . . We'll try to sort it all out soon. But, for now, we will have to pull ourselves together and be able to face the cameras when we leave here."

# # #

At the White House, President Don Cole switched off the television. In the past twenty minutes, he and Lawrence Cunningham had watched "summary" coverage on all the major networks.

Lawrence looked at Don. "You know how bad this looks, don't you? I can already hear what is going to be said at the UN about this next week."

Don nodded then allowed his gaze to sweep around the small briefing room where they'd talked through so many problems during their time in office. "I know we'll take a hit over it." He looked at the vice president again. "We might as well pack it in for the night. Unless there's a major break in the case, we won't have our next reports until tomorrow anyway."

Lawrence kept moving his hands, as if he were washing them. "I wonder what the chances are that there was really any live virus in those containers. I didn't think the virus would live long outside a host."

"That's what I thought . . . but apparently new freezing techniques and suspension fluids, developed so labs could use samples longer, have extended the viability of many viruses."

"What is going to happen with those people? What about Edith Todd? Any word on her yet?"

"I talked to Bill just before you came in. He says she's shaken up, of course, but at least she didn't get injured in the melee of those who were trying to escape. She was up on the stage, so her exit was away from theirs. Even if tests show that the liquid had live virus in it, they all got immediate treatment. We'll just have to wait now and see what happens with them."

"Gives me the shivers just to think of it." the vice president said, shuddering.

"I imagine a lot of people are feeling pretty scared right now." Don bit his lip and looked at the shiny tabletop beside his chair. While he thought, he made a pattern on its surface with his finger, then added, "There are just too many desperate people out there, Lawrence."

An hour later, when he was alone, the president tried to piece together his disjointed day. He'd only been up for half an hour before he'd received a report stating that agents had possibly located the missing Enhanced Radiation Weapons in an apartment building in New York.

Marshal Ellis' hunch had been right, and agents had eventually picked up a small lead about a man they believed might have the bombs. This man and an accomplice had just gotten out of prison and were possibly preparing to sell the weapons. Intelligence indicated the bombs might have been placed in the apartment of the criminal's sister just after the riots, nearly three years ago. The FBI planned on raiding the building.

After leaving orders to be informed if the FBI located the devices, Don went into a meeting with the "team of three," the negotiators who'd had the breakthrough in talks with China regarding Japan and the waters between the two countries. Although possible problems still lurked in the future, a large step had been made in defusing tensions in the area.

If he'd had a few moments to rejoice over this victory, he would have. But before he his meeting with the team had wrapped up, he got the first reports of the protest at the Philadelphia Arena. As information on the protest began to come in, he received word the Enhanced Radiation Weapons had been retrieved.

He went up to his quarters and tried to decompress for a few moments before going to bed. He told himself there was nothing else he could do tonight regarding the protest in Philadelphia. He would continue to pray, and as the investigation unfolded, it would all get sorted out. He willed his muscles to relax and reminded himself there was much to be grateful for. The China thing was on the mend. He'd successfully gotten two federal agencies to cooperate and find the ERW's. The bombs were safely stored away for the first time in three years. So why the feeling of disquiet? There was something . . . something he couldn't quite grasp at the moment. Eventually, Don fell asleep.

He awoke hours later. What was wrong? Was the phone ringing? No. He wanted to roll over and reach for the light beside his bed but couldn't work up the strength. The air around him felt so heavy it seemed to resist movement.

Lying there in the dark, he felt so alone, overwhelmed . . . and, strangely, he also had the thought that he should "escape" back into sleep . . . it was as if he was being held down and anesthetized. He slowly closed his eyes.

Then it was as if a hand was on his chest, shaking him. *No! Wake up and pray!*

He managed to get out of bed and make his way to the living room. Standing there, he still felt as if he'd been swallowed up in darkness. "Lord, what am I doing?" he asked aloud. "And why do I feel like things are so . . . hopeless?" His words were slow and leaden. He could almost picture them dropping down onto the carpet around his feet. The ominous, crushing sensation enveloped him further. He closed his eyes.

Oh God . . . the enemy has been stirred up and he has come. I know he is here and he wants to stop me from going on . . . he wants to conquer me. Help me.

A scripture verse came to mind: *The Lord is my Light and my salvation; whom shall I fear? The Lord is the strength of my life; of whom shall I be afraid?. . . Though an host should encamp against me, my heart shall not fear; though war should rise against me, in this will I be confident.*

Don got face down on the floor and started to pray inwardly again. *Lord, I trust You alone. I take my eyes off everything else—good or bad—and I choose to look at You. . . . I am president, but you are Lord, and You have put me in this place. You are the King and the Ruler of my life. You are my Guide and my Shield. You have said that You are for me. No matter what it looks like, You're here with me. . . . Help me now, Lord, for without You, I will fail.*

I read that someday I'll face You and all my works will be tested with fire. All the things I did without You will burn like hay and turn to ashes. Only those things I did with You will endure the fire and remain like precious metal and jewels. God, I want what I do to remain after the fire. I don't want to look at a pile of ashes and realize it's too late to change. Please, show me the way.

The smothering stillness around him grew. In response, he forced his mind to recall all he knew about God. Doing this, he'd learned, was a way to increase awareness of the Lord's presence in the midst of oppression. When believers praised the Lord out loud, He "inhabited" their words, putting darkness to flight.

As an act of will, Don locked his attention on the Lord. As God's attributes and works came to mind, he began to acknowledge them and give thanks aloud.

"Lord, I thank You, that You are everywhere. You are my light."

The words sounded flat, rehearsed. He pushed aside the thought this was an exercise in futility, and commanded himself to continue.

"I'm so grateful I don't have to know everything, because You already do. You are the Creator of the whole universe, even of realms I cannot see. You are the Author of life itself. There really is no god like You, nor one that can do the works You alone can do.

"You are the King of Glory and the Lord of Hosts . . . You have said You will never leave or forsake me. *Nothing*, seen or unseen, can separate me from Your love."

A little thread of light came to Don's soul as he continued to voice his praise.

"I thank You because You are full of mercy. You are the fountain of all grace. Oh, God, how Wonderful You are. You are not willing that any should perish, You are the way-making God."

His very words cut through the weighted shroud of darkness and brought life to the dead air around him. In addition, faith began to rise up from deep within him and fill every particle of his being as he continued.

"I rejoice that *Your* power is unlimited, *Your* greatness is endless. I'm so grateful You saved me, and that You hear my prayers. I worship You as the God of all flesh, the Almighty God, Jehovah . . . I boast of Your majesty . . . I give honor and praise to You as the Most High, my Father, my Comforter . . . my Friend."

The sense of foreboding had fled away and now he became inundated by the knowledge that he was filled and surrounded by his Maker. He was entirely visible, his every thought and motive laid bare, yet he was still loved. A tremendous sense of awe overtook him.

Oh, God, he prayed inwardly, *We tell ourselves we are "good" but, truly, You are the only one who is good.*

Words came to him. Slowly at first. Like thoughts filtering through to his mind.

"Then how will you stand . . . in the gate . . . and seek Me for this nation?"

Only by Jesus, Lord. The Lamb of God who takes away my sins. By His blood, I come to reason with You for America. I cannot save this country from what is coming. Only You can.

"But many here no longer choose Me . . . and the sins of this nation are so great. . . . I hear the cries of the destitute, the lost, the oppressed . . . the blood of the innocent ones cries out to me for judgment. Why do you come to Me and ask Me to turn back the justice so many are due?"

Don could hardly breathe. *Because it's what You want. It's what You've always wanted. I've learned You want mercy to triumph over judgment. You are longsuffering. You are willing give more time so more can be saved. You look for someone to stand in the place of judgment and to call upon You to extend Your mercy for yet another season. Here I am. I'm asking for mercy.*

"Stand up on your feet."

"Yes, Lord," Don said, getting up.

"Didn't I warn you this would be a hard place? To whom much is given much is required. Didn't I warn you that it would cost you everything? Will you be able to stand in that place?"

Don spread out his hands. *Yes, Lord. Here I am. As long as You give me the strength, I will stand.*

"And so you shall. Be not afraid. Though fiery trials will come, My provision will spring up among the people. . . . This nation shall not be destroyed. My faithful ones will shine like the stars . . . and many more will come into My kingdom."

CHAPTER 29

PHILADELPHIA — September 30th

Inside the intensive care unit of Philadelphia's Regent Hospital, Chaplain Matthew North sat beside Benjamin Gordon. The chaplain's shift was over, but he didn't want to leave. He'd checked on Benjamin throughout the night. The man's condition continued to be critical. An infection smoldered deep inside him, and the numerous cuts on his body were beginning to turn sour as well. The latest enzyme treatments were being pumped into his veins, but doctors held out little hope they'd work.

Each time Matthew came to stand by the bed, Benjamin opened his eyes and said, "Please, pray I can hold on. I'm not done yet."

From the moment they rolled Mr. Gordon into the ER, Matt felt compelled to stay close to him. The staff at the hospital pretty much let the chaplain go wherever he wished. He worked well with patient's families, did not engage in hospital politics, and knew when to get out of the way.

Even now, he felt an urgent need to stay with Ben. Matt phoned his housekeeper to inform her of his decision to stay at the hospital; then, he spoke to both of his children. When his daughter, Rachel, came on the line he asked her, "Do you remember what we talked about the other day when you came home from the hospital?"

"Yes, Dad," she'd answered. "Taking things back from the devil."

"This is one of those times, Rachel. One of those times when God's asking me to stay here for someone who needs help right now."

"Is it the guy from the arena?"

"I can't tell you."

This was his way of saying yes without saying it. She understood. "Okay, Dad," she said. "We'll pray, too."

Now seated at Benjamin's bedside, Matt felt strength in knowing his children were praying for him. He reached up and took hold of Ben's hand. Death might be inevitable, but not yet. He would not let go. After a few minutes, Ben awoke again.

"You."

Matthew stood and leaned close to him. "Yes. It's me. I'm praying for you Ben."

"Thank you . . . I can feel it . . . Where are my brothers?"

A nurse came through the door. "Chaplain North? Addison wants to see you."

Matt kept his eyes on Ben for a moment. The man drifted off again.

"Tell Mr. Addison I'll be there momentarily."

# # #

In the diner across from the hospital, TV reporter for Philadelphia's channel five, Linda Posner, sipped her lemon herbal tea and thought about how she could squeeze the last of a large sandwich into her small purse.

Rumors concerning the man taken from the arena continued to make rounds among the press pool. One story said he was a victim of the terrorists. Another one stated he'd been tortured by them. Yet another spin said he'd been tortured by the feds! The world wanted details.

Media coverage had gotten so huge that the administrator of the hospital agreed to hold press conferences every four hours. All he'd done so far was confirm the hospital had a patient, and that the patient remained alive. Big deal. He used most of his time in front of the microphones telling reporters to remain outside the hospital, away from the emergency entrance. Despite this, the large number of news crews continued to clog traffic to and from the facility.

Linda played with a lock of her shoulder-length blond hair for a moment before inspecting it for split ends. She knew if she couldn't find a way to get closer, her time here would be wasted. But how could she get closer? One of her colleagues had already been arrested for dressing in hospital blues and trying to sneak in, so *that* idea was out.

The phone in her purse rang. She quickly located the device and answered it.

"Hello."

"Linda. This is Baumgardner," her boss said. "We got a news release from conference organizers saying they'll want to meet with the press later today."

She glanced around to see if anyone could overhear her before answering. "I'll bet. That guy reduced their 'oneness for all mankind' thing to ashes in a matter of thirty seconds. They'll have to smooth this over somehow. You want footage of it?"

"Yes. As soon as we find out the location I'll let you know."

"Okay," she said casually.

"'Bye," Baumgardner said before she heard him hang up.

She took the last gulp of her tea before the phone rang again.

"Hello?"

"It's me again," Baumgardner said.

"Yes?"

"We just got word Thad Seager is on his way from the airport to the hospital."

She looked around again. A reporter from channel seven had taken a seat behind her so she got up and walked toward the restroom. "You mean the activist?"

"Yeah."

The man was totally obnoxious. A great story might be in the making. People either loved him or hated him. "Wonderful," she said, "but he's such a camera hog, I'm sure the other crews will be informed soon if they don't know already."

"Probably. But who knows? Maybe you can make this more than a photo op for him."

The unspoken message here? She had permission to go for the juggler on this one.

"Who knows?" she said with a smile.

"'Bye." he said before hanging up.

# # #

Chaplain Matthew North seated himself in the office of hospital administrator Gabe Addison. Until now North hadn't realized just how tired he was.

"Coffee?" Addison offered with his hand reaching for the handle of a pot nearby. The aging administrator was tall, slim, and had a whiny voice that scratched Matthew's nerves. It seemed worse on days, like today, when Addison was nervous.

"No thanks. I have to get some sleep soon. It would keep me awake."

"How's your daughter's leg?"

"Fine. Doctors say she's so active she probably won't need a lot of therapy."

"Good, good." Addison took a sip of coffee and glanced out the window at the growing collection of media trucks with relay dishes. "I hear," he finally said, "you've spent quite a bit of time with Mr. Gordon."

Matt shrugged. "He hasn't been conscious for most of it, but yes."

"Well, Matthew, I don't have to tell you what a spot we're in because of him."

"I've heard."

"What a nightmare this is. If we shut out the media altogether, they'll say we're hiding something. If we let any of them get hold of information not approved by the feds or his family, we could be liable. If these press people keep clogging up the parking lot and all the entrances, and so much as one patient suffers for it, we'll be sued for that," he said, his voice becoming almost shrill. "If his group or others gather outside to demonstrate or show support, the police may bill us for the personnel needed to handle it. And if any of the people outside found out about the *confinement* . . . well, my job just wouldn't be worth having. "

"I understand."

Even though Ben posed little threat in his current state, he was still under arrest. Federal agents, who would be guarding Ben around the clock, wanted to be sure he couldn't get out of bed and pose a threat to anyone. Doctors nixed the use of restraints because his skin was severely damaged from cuts already. The solution? To construct a confinement structure, resembling a large cage, around the bed. Once inside its locked door, medical personnel or visitors could move around the bed unhindered.

When the man's brother, Michael Gordon, first saw it, he'd raised quite a ruckus over it. He had to be taken to another room and calmed down before they could convince him that, as bad as it looked, it was more humane for Ben.

Although still upset about it, he'd stopped asking for its removal when he realized Ben was too "out-of-it" to notice.

But Addison's right. Matt thought. *If the press managed to get a single picture of Benjamin Gordon in that thing, there might be a big deal over it.*

"I don't mean to sound cruel," Addison said, "but I hope he's out of here soon—one way or the other. His family wants this handled as quietly as possible, and that suits me fine. This is a quality health facility, not a circus. I'm just sorry we're the closest hospital to the arena," he said, referring to the law dictating emergency patients had to be admitted at the nearest hospital.

Too tired for an extended conversation, Matt asked, "So why did you want to talk to me?"

"I've just been informed Thad Seager is on his way here to demand an audience with me and with Ben Gordon. We can't make it seem as if we're preventing Gordon from getting help or Seager will cry foul to the media. He'll probably find some way to slap us with lawsuits or have gay rights or AIDS demonstrators lining the streets for weeks!"

Matthew thought of the many times the illustrious Thad Seager had managed to drop into the news like a bomb. He would suddenly appear on the scene, defending "the oppressed" wherever they were. Obviously, Seager considered himself the lone champion of human rights on the planet. Those who didn't cooperate could prepare for an ugly, public battle. Even if the facts didn't support Mr. Seager, he could still stir up enough negative sentiment to make his enemies absolutely miserable.

Exhaustion would not allow Matt to follow Addison's line of thinking. He needed a bigger hint. "And you want me to . . . what?"

"I want you to stay in the office here for the meeting. You've been with Gordon. You can testify—as one with a sacred responsibility—that Mr. Gordon has not asked to talk with anyone. The doctors can say he's not able—but I need you to say he's not willing. You can say you've been by his side and you've observed his needs are being met . . . that you're 'there' for him. And that he's getting the best of care."

Matthew looked a little pained.

"I'm not asking you to divulge any requests or confessions. I only want you to say you're there to hear them should they be expressed."

The intercom on Addison's desk buzzed. He activated it. "Yes?"

"Mr. Seager has arrived with a number of people. They've stopped to speak to reporters outside."

Addison groaned. "Just what I need." He paused a moment before speaking again. "Frieda?"

"Yes?"

"When Mr. Seager gets here, his 'entourage' will have to wait in your office. I'll not have a public debate with the man."

In the end, Seager got a concession. His personal assistant (a man large enough to be a body guard) was allowed to attend the meeting. In the past, Seager maintained, he'd often been the "victim" of "misunderstandings" and wanted to bring another person in to serve as a witness.

Once they were seated in the administrator's office, Seager eyed Addison, quickly sizing him up, before speaking in his famous slow, southern drawl. "Thank you for seeing me. I know you must be a busy man."

"Not a problem." Addison said. "What can I do for you?"

"I'd like an opportunity to speak to the patient in the ICU," Seager said.

Chaplain North noticed the man's presence seemed to be filling the entire room—and sucking the air out of Addison.

"I'm sorry, it's not possible," Addison responded. "Mr. Gordon . . ." As soon as the words were out of his mouth, he realized his mistake. Until that moment, no one other than federal agents and a few hospital staff knew Benjamin's name. This was a grievous mistake (one that would have gotten a lesser employee fired), but the glint in Seager's eye said it was too late to gloss over. The only thing Addison could do was continue. "The man is drifting in and out of consciousness. Neither he nor his family have expressed any desire to speak with you. Even if they had, such a request would have to go through the FBI or the Terrorism Task Force investigating the case. In addition, the hospital has rules about all patients, especially those in the ICU."

Matthew could see Seager, having obtained the choicest of morsels—the patient's name—wasn't about to quit.

Seager inspected a manicured fingernail for a moment before speaking. "Perhaps you're unaware of the fact that I'm a practicing attorney. Doubtless, Mr. Gordon will need one," Seager said. "Have his rights to have one present been honored?"

Addison said nothing.

Seager looked satisfied. "I'll speak to the family. Perhaps they just don't realize how important it is to challenge government encroachment on personal freedoms. Could be a landmark case. It would be a shame to let the opportunity fade. You may not have considered it, but if I were allowed to represent Mr. Gordon, much of the burden for speaking to the press would be removed from the hospital. I could coordinate statements from doctors, Mr. Gordon, and his family, and give regular conferences to the media for all of you." A master of intimidation, Seager had zoned in on the administrator.

Addison didn't want to provoke Seager, but had to please the hospital board, who wanted this to be quick and quiet. "I want you to understand. *Our* interest is in tending to the patient's medical needs. If the man has other needs," Addison said, now pointing in Matt's direction, "Chaplain North, who's been at his side constantly, will tend to them for now."

Seager wouldn't be put off so easily. He leaned forward and spoke again, his voice conveying an iron fist while the southern-gent accent clothed it in a velvet glove. "This is a big story. People want to know about this man."

Matthew spoke for the first time. "You may be right, Mr. Seager, but right now he's in grave condition. Even when he's conscious, he can barely put words together."

Seager had ignored Matthew until this point, but now turned to focus on the chaplain. With one sweep, he'd taken in a mental snapshot to work from. The chaplain was small and balding and his clothes appeared to be of a better-than-moderate price range. He was middle-aged, wore no wedding ring, and the toes of his shoes were scuffed. But, most importantly, although obviously tired, he wasn't intimidated.

The civil rights activist switched gears. "You know, Chaplain North," he said in a friendlier tone, "I also have a degree in Divinity . . . and I've found people so seldom appreciate the long hours people like us give to their work. I'm sure you have your hands full every single day. But think of the ordeal this man is enduring without aid of legal counsel.

Even if he participated in this protest, his rights must be maintained . . . and I'm the man who'll see it gets done. . . . Freedom is at stake and I can't let this slide."

Matthew spoke quietly. "Personally, Mr. Seager, I'm having trouble believing Mr. Gordon was involved in any protest. He's too sick to have participated if you ask me, and I don't think he'll live long enough to stand trial. He's one man with one soul and he's gravely ill. He doesn't need to spend his last hours as a hostage in your circus."

"I find your stance disappointing."

The chaplain did not move. "When he dies, you can make it as big a deal as you want. I couldn't stop you."

The meeting ended, and a "disappointed" Seager departed after lodging a formal request that Ben be informed he was ready and waiting to work on his behalf.

As soon as Seager left the office, Addison turned to Matthew and said, "You shouldn't have antagonized him."

# # #

By the time he exited the building, Seager had already formulated a plan. He'd see if there were any video tapes of Gordon being pulled out of the arena and carted off to the hospital, or at least an official time-line showing how long they let him lay there, injured, before they did anything. If nothing else he might be able to show these things to the man's family in excruciating detail and convince them to enter into a lawsuit against the arena, the police, and the security company handling the facility. Gordon had probably been left on the cold arena floor for a while before they packed him into an ambulance. This could be a building block for public demonstrations against unconstitutional treatment of suspects. Perhaps he could also tap into sentiment about unfair treatment of those with AIDS.

# # #

Back inside the hospital, Matthew North crawled into a bed at the hospital where he hoped he could sleep for a few hours. He made a request to be notified if Ben asked for him or if any of the family arrived.

Before he fell asleep, he thought about the day's events.

Lord, he prayed silently, *so many people want something from Benjamin Gordon. Father, I'm asking You to cancel any agenda that doesn't line up with Your plan for him. If any of these people would do him harm, please keep them away. If moving him would harm him, please block them from doing it. I'm asking for mercy, Lord. I get the sense he belongs to You. You've said You've carved us in the palms of your hands. Close Your protecting hand around this man and help him finish anything You desire him to do.*

# # #

Outside the hospital, Thad Seager agreed to an interview. He unbuttoned his jacket and put one hand in his pocket as he faced the cameras.

"I've spoken at length with the hospital administrator and even the chaplain. For now, it's wise to postpone any visit with Mr. Gordon until the man's condition has improved."

Dozens of voices shouted in unison: "His name is Mr. Gordon?" Then, chaos broke out. A barrage of questions about Mr. Gordon flew in Seager's direction.

He raised his hands for quiet, then spoke soberly. "I'm not at liberty to disclose any other information concerning Mr. Gordon at this time, but I hope to meet with his family at the first available opportunity. I promise I will notify you if there are any further developments."

Linda hadn't gotten Seager's attention to ask a question. She'd have to be content with the same tidbit he'd thrown to everyone else. She quickly filed a report giving the new information, then retreated back to the diner across the street to think.

She'd heard a rumor the producers for UIG had gotten in big-time trouble for airing the demonstration as it happened. The network's owner, E. E. Kressman had gone on the air just the day before to endorse the Conference, so the accusations of the protestors against those putting on the event—even if they weren't true—might make him look bad.

Of course, she agreed with the UIG producers. News was news. The other stations aired it, so why not?

She ordered another cup of tea and thought, *I have to find some way to get this story.*

CHAPTER 30

It was a couple minutes after two in the afternoon. Lyza Brewer leaned forward and took Ben's hand. Even through her glove, she could feel his clammy skin. His wounds were covered, so there wasn't any danger, but hospital staff insisted she put on gloves before she'd be allowed in the enclosure with him. She took off one of them and touched his hand again. "Are you cold?"

"Maybe, a little," he said.

Lyza pulled an extra blanket over his arms and up to his chin. Looking at him all covered up like this, she could imagine he was recuperating at home. As long as she kept her eyes on Ben and the bed, it all seemed so normal. Normal and comforting somehow, like he was going to get better. Like she could just breeze into the next room and fix him a cup of his favorite soup.

Ben felt another surge of energy and, although he kept his eyes closed, he spoke.

"I want you to have the large folder with my big drawings in it. You don't have to keep them all, but keep at least one, won't you?"

His words forced reality into the space between them. She couldn't just go fix him some soup. He wasn't going to recover. He was drifting away from her.

She looked at the metal confinement structure surrounding them and realized even this could not hold Ben here. Although he'd rallied somewhat, doctors weren't holding out any hope of survival beyond a week or so. He had no desire for food, and nourishment would not be supplied to him through other means. His ravaged body couldn't last much longer.

Now he opened his eyes to gaze at Lyza as she sat in a chair with her chin resting on the bed rail, her sad brown eyes watching him. Her naturally blond hair had a sort of wiry texture. Only about an inch long when he'd first met her, now it flowed down past her jaw line and it reminded him of a lion's mane. He slowly brought his hand out of the covers and stroked it one time. How lion-like she was. Bold, powerful.

"I've always loved your hair," he said. "I hope . . . when you find your husband, that he loves it, too."

Lyza wanted so very much not to cry, but all the strength of will she possessed couldn't make her eyes stop stinging, and when she blinked, giant tears shot out and dropped onto his blanket.

"See that?" he said in an almost dreamy voice, closing his eyes again. "Lyza Brewer can cry. . . . It's a good thing Lyza. Don't ever be stingy with your tears again. They're not a sign of weakness, they're washing hard things out of your heart."

She grabbed some tissues from the stand beside the bed and blew her nose with a loud honking sound.

"Work on dainty nose blowing, though, okay?"

She gave a short laugh and clasped his hand again.

"Oh Ben. Whatever will I do . . ." She couldn't finish the question.

"Promise me you'll pray for my family." A hint of a smile brightened his face. "Zac alone could keep you busy until the next century."

"I promise."

# # #

Several floors down from Ben's room, a meeting regarding his status continued. Hospital officials and federal agents had been wrangling for two days about where he could be moved, and when.

Hospital Administrator Gabe Addison felt he'd been squeezed from all sides in this no-win situation. But now he had an opportunity to squirt out of the deadlock. "Mr. Gordon's condition has improved," he said. "I need to know when you'll want to move him. There's an open bed in the lockup section at City Hospital, and we could arrange for transport this afternoon."

"I'm afraid it's not going to happen today," said Special Agent Hayzel, who was in charge of Ben's case. Actually, Hayzel could have dropped the charges hours ago, but after spending time with Ben, and then talking to the hospital Chaplain, he'd hesitated. Normally, he didn't allow himself to get personally involved in cases, but something about Ben Gordon just wouldn't let him go.

As soon as they dropped the criminal investigation, the protection Ben currently had would also be dropped. With no federal agency to interfere, Regent Hospital officials would be free to make arrangements to have him moved. His family could only afford a transfer to his home or to the hospice ward at City Hospital, where people without money could not be turned away.

Of course, given the recent public insanity over the case, the whole apartment complex where Ben had lived with his brother would be completely invaded by the media if Ben was there. The other alternative—the hospice ward at City Hospital—while somewhat safer, was overrun with destitute, dying people. AIDS was so cost-intensive it managed to break the wallets of most of its victims and their families, so the ward was filled with its victims . . . stacked on bunk beds, stripped of privacy, kept sedated until they passed on. Hayzel thought it horrible anyone should have to die like this. Even worse, an underpaid employee, or another patient's family, would certainly take pictures of Ben. The photos would be snapped up by the press in no time flat. Didn't this poor man, who'd mistakenly become the center of such a frenzy, deserve a break?

The stories and opinions surrounding the protest at the Philadelphia Arena had gone to wild extremes. Some news groups had embellished the few known facts and made harsh editorial statements. In response, several gay rights groups clamored for equal air time to disavow any encouragement of or participation in "this deplorable act."

Agent Hayzel's gaze drifted outside the window of the hospital administrator's office to a billboard half a block away. It said "*HE is coming soon . . . get right, or get left!*"

It reminded Hayzel of how one network, when they found out Ben was a Christian, reported a radical, "fundamentalist Christian" group was suspected of being responsible for the protest. Ira Goldman, a speaker for the World Conference on Spirituality, had immediately given an angry interview (aired on several networks) referring to right-wing conspiracies and "mindless monotheists."

A frustrated Agent Hayzel could make no official comment to set the record straight. His eyes moved from the billboard to all the news media trucks gathered on the street outside the hospital and he made a decision. *Later today,* he decided, *the agency will have an information leak. The media will find out the case against Ben is "about" to be dropped. We'll keep Gordon here while I stall the paperwork long enough for the press to abandon the story. Maybe this will allow him to just go home with his brother and die quietly in his own bed.*

Hayzel looked at the hospital administrator. "There are several technicalities we need to work out before we can talk about transporting Mr. Gordon. I'll let you know."

Addison clenched his jaw. These government types were all alike. Everything by the book. They didn't care what all this did to anybody else. . .

# # #

At 3:14 p.m., civil rights advocate Thad Seager eyed his airline ticket for a Seattle flight due to take off in five hours. He'd been blocked at virtually every level here in Philadelphia and would be glad to move on to better prospects.

Seager placed his ticket with the rest of the things from his pockets and went to the sink to shave. As he watched himself in the mirror, he tried to shake the notion he'd lost his touch somehow. He couldn't remember the last time he felt so frustrated. If it were possible, he'd almost think there'd been some giant conspiracy to make sure he failed . . . or some large, invisible hand that snuffed out every fire he'd tried to ignite.

It all began with that little fellow, the chaplain at the hospital. What was his name? North. The administrator would've been soft clay in his hands if North hadn't been there. But the chaplain looked him right in the eye and said no—a rare occurrence. Usually, people were too intimidated by his commanding presence to just say no.

From there, it had all gone downhill. AIDS advocates feared to march because they didn't want to possibly be identified with the group responsible for the protest, and see their financial support dry up. Several church denominations who had helped Thad in the past turned him down for the same reason. And, once homosexual groups found out Ben was a Christian who renounced the gay lifestyle, they'd have nothing to do with the case. Mr. Gordon's parents wanted to remain silent on the issue, and his two brothers told Thad exactly where he could stick his big plans.

He thought of the hospital chaplain again and a mental snapshot of the scuffed toes on the shoes came to focus in his mind. Seager had seen shoes with scuffs like this before . . . his grandfather's shoes. And his mother's. Footwear with toes worn out long before the rest of the shoe . . . from all the time spent kneeling.

Seager searched his own eyes in the mirror. Was he really fighting for truth and justice anymore? Was he running away from a good fight or from himself? Perhaps soon he'd have to stop and give some serious consideration to these questions.

He applied shaving gel to his face, thinking how very glad he'd be to leave Philadelphia.

# # #

At 5:57 p.m., former First Lady Edith Todd stood in the living room of her hotel suite with her dear friend and spiritual mentor, Tony Benson. She sank into an overstuffed floral print chair, he took another one directly facing hers. The room was elegantly appointed in soothing off-white tones. Beautiful bouquets, sent to Edith in the past day, vied for attention from large, crystal vases.

The surroundings and the flowers had done little to calm or distract Edith, however. In fact, she felt as if she'd been plucked out of a beautiful dream and thrown into a hideous nightmare. One minute, she felt immensely empowered as she addressed the world and poured out incredible energy; the next, she became the unplugged victim of a horrible act.

How could all this have happened? How could it have happened to *her*?

"I know you have many questions," Tony said in a soothing voice, "but trying to settle them with your natural mind won't work. Remember, you were the one who chose who you'd be in this lifetime and which body you would inhabit. You need to remember what lessons you wanted to learn. You'll have to reach into—"

She shook her head. "That's not helping me, Tony. I'm just not getting *any* comfort from your words." She'd already had enough of other people's well-intentioned theories. What she wanted was to find the real cause of her misery. "Didn't you say you had a bad feeling before this all happened to me? What if Ira Goldman is right and those awful Christians did this to us to try and defeat the plan? Have you seen those disgusting ads they placed all around the city? They're desperate to prove they're 'right,' but the only thing surpassing their supreme gall is their lack of intelligence!"

Tony frowned. "Don't do this, Edith. Investigations prove the guy who planned the whole thing had nothing to do with Christians . . . and I just heard on the radio, when I was on the way over here, the government is about to drop the case against the guy in the hospital. Please, don't get like Ira and some of the others. They're hard and bitter and they want to paint stereotypes of everyone who disagrees with them. We don't want to be like them, do we?"

He leaned forward and clasped her hand. "Listen to me. Although we've evolved to a higher level than the majority of Christians, I actually believe I've met a few I would consider equals." Tony's mind flashed to one encounter in particular he'd had on an airplane years ago. The man in the seat next to him had eyes alive with light as he spoke of Jesus as his God and encouraged Tony to seek the ultimate Truth. Tony didn't know if he'd ever sensed such a melodious energy emanating from another human being. When the man put a hand on him to pray, Tony felt a tremendous warmth shoot through his body. . . . No. He couldn't discount Christians entirely, or say they were all going the wrong direction. He'd experienced evidence to the contrary.

He wanted to reason with Edith. "Consider this, Edith. You said that in your vision war broke out in the atmosphere. Have you ever considered this may be the beginning of its fulfillment? Darkness is trying to intimidate you—fight back! Let's meditate on your immune system and energize it. Let's visualize the solution. You were the one declaring to the world we were on the verge of a new reality, weren't you? Wonderful things may be at hand. The Transition may be right on the doorstep! The transformation of the whole earth is going to take place! Don't be irritated with those ads—think of them as evidence that even Christians sense something is about to happen! Stretch out and grab it!"

He could tell Edith didn't want to see what he was saying yet, but what rebuttal did she have? He'd challenged her to act on what she professed to believe.

"Yes," she finally said. "Let's visualize it together."

He could sense her dark emotions. It would take a lot of energy to force them away, but he'd try.

# # #

At 8:17 p.m. Michael and Zac Gordon stood outside Ben's room at Regent Hospital. An agent unfamiliar with either of them stood guard at the door.

Michael, now accustomed to procedures, approached the man. "We're here to see Ben Gordon, please."

"Are you on the list?" the agent asked, getting out the newly-revised roster. There was no end of people who wanted to see Ben Gordon.

"Yes, we're on the list. We're his brothers," Michael responded, pulling an ID out of his pocket.

The officer had been ordered to carefully check everyone who wanted access to the room, no matter how they were dressed or who they said they were. "What's your name?" he said, taking the ID, then comparing it with the owner first, then the list.

"Michael Gordon."

The agent checked the list. "Uhhhh. I don't see your name here."

"Check again. Michael Gordon."

He scanned it once more. "Sorry, sir, you're not on this list."

Michael sighed. "Try Gordon Michael."

The lawman searched again. "Well, there is a Gordon Michael here," he said, inspecting the ID again, "but that's not your name, now, is it?"

Michael thought, someday, this would happen to him just one more time and he'd go ballistic. All he needed now was for this idiot to make the observation that he had "two first names, you know." Even now, he felt as if he might lose control. "My name is Michael Gordon, his name" he said, pointing to his brother, "is Zachary Gordon. It's a common mistake people make."

The guard put a finger on the key to his radio. "I'll have to check on this."

"*Doink!*" Michael said in a raised voice. "Michael *Gordon,* Zachary *Gordon, Ben Gordon,* get it? Did you have to eat lots of stuff with lead in it before you were allowed to work for the government?"

Zac nudged his brother back a bit and calmly spoke to the policeman. "Sorry. Perhaps you can understand we're a bit stressed out. Go ahead and check. We'll wait."

Minutes later the agent received approval for the visitors. Only one person at a time could visit, so Zac, wanting to delay the inevitable as long as possible, told Michael he could go first. The a nurse watched Michael put on gloves before she opened the door to the room, then let him inside the enclosure with Ben.

Michael sat and waited for a while inside the cage in the dimly lit room. He could see how Ben had lost all perception of night or day behind the thick drapes and soft-pink neon lights which gave the room a sense of constant, quiet twilight.

"Mikey?" Only Ben and their sister, Jill, dared to call him this.

"Yes, I'm here."

"I was just praying for you and Zac."

"Really? Musta worked 'cause Zac's here, too. He can come in when I leave."

"Listen," Ben said. "I want you to know . . . I've made peace with Dad and Mom. Jill brought them to visit."

While part of Michael was happy for his brother, the news didn't soften his feeling towards their parents one bit. "That's great, Ben."

"Now, I know you, Mikey. . . . I know you're still mad at them on my account. Please. For your own sake. Forgive them."

"Okay."

"I mean it, Mike . . . settle it now . . . Jesus wants you to. He told me so."

Michael felt the flesh on his arms and neck rise up as he thought of the billboards he'd seen on lately . . . *HE is coming soon* . . . and he looked at his brother. "Jesus spoke to you?"

"Yes. . . . Jesus and I have prayed for you. We love you."

Michael felt a mixture of anger, sorrow, and confusion. Why was this happening to Ben? Although he spoke aloud, he wasn't sure to whom he was talking. "This is not fair. It's not fair."

Ben inhaled slowly before answering. "Ohhhhhhh, Michael. I keep thinking of a verse saying . . . 'Better is one day in His courts than thousands elsewhere.' It's true you know . . . so true. I've freely walked into His courts now, Michael. No matter how it looks to you . . . the last part of my life . . . has been the best part."

Ben soon dozed off and Michael left the room. It was Zachary's turn.

Zac, who hadn't been to the hospital since the day they brought Ben in, stood inside the door of the metal enclosure for a while, not wanting to approach the bed. His brother looked so motionless . . . so skeletal.

When Ben's foot moved and he turned his head a bit, Zac found the nerve to get the chair and bring it around to the side of the bed Ben faced. He lowered the railing between them and waited. Within a minute, Ben's eyes opened and he slowly smiled.

"Hi, Zac."

"Hi."

The smile faded. "I'm so sorry I got you in trouble . . . but I *had* to come to the arena, Zac. The Lord wanted me there. I'd do it all again, and more, to know it spared you from this," he said, looking down at his own wasted body.

Zachary put both hands on the edge of the bed and leaned down with his face against them.

Ben spoke in a soft, sincere voice. "I'm so happy you're okay. I love you, Zac." He couldn't see his brother's expression. Zachary couldn't—or wouldn't—speak, so Ben continued, "I remember you going to church when we were young, and Dad and the rest of us making fun of you . . . and the girl dying. . . . I'm so sorry. I want so much for you to give God another chance, Zac. . . . He's waiting for you."

It became obvious Zac was crying, but he still didn't speak. He slowly moved one of his hands up to gently place it on his brother's shoulder. Within minutes, Ben fell back asleep.

At 11:02 p.m., Benjamin Gordon drifted out of the cage and beyond the reach of any disease.

CHAPTER 31

PHILADELPHIA — October 2nd

It was still early morning when Matthew North got out of his car. Before he'd taken three steps, he heard someone calling to him. A woman emerged from a vehicle parked across the street and approached him

"Excuse me, I wonder if I could speak to you for a moment."

Although he did not respond, he stopped moving toward his house and looked at her, so she came closer.

"I'm Linda Posner," she said, "I work for Channel Five. I know this might not be a good time for you, but do you think you could spare me just a few teeny weeny minutes?" She smiled and held her thumb and index finger about an inch apart to indicate she meant a really small amount.

He tried not to look exasperated. "I'm not doing any interviews."

He hadn't run into his house and slammed the door, so she continued to close the distance between them. "I know. But, this doesn't have to be a formal interview. It could even be off the record. People want to know more about what kind of person Mr. Gordon was. I've already spoken to some of his friends, but you are the one who spent so much of his last days with him. Don't you want people to understand what happened to him, what kind of man he really was?

Matt frowned. "Miss . . ." He'd forgotten her name already.

"Posner."

"Miss Posner. It's not important whether or not you or your audience understand him. What he and I have talked about is nobody's business but ours. I know you have a job to do, but I can't help you. Good day."

"So you're saying you don't care about all the rumors going around? You have no desire to set the record straight?"

Matt regretted being polite. He turned and started walking to his front door.

"Do you realize what an opportunity you're missing here?" she shouted after him.

He opened the door, entered his house, and shut the door between them. Then he went to find his kids, who were preparing to leave for school. He hugged them and told them how much he loved them.

Later, when he retired to his room, he thought about the last few nights. He'd been there while Ben drifted in and out. As some of the medication would wear off, Ben would awaken and, for a while, he'd have a lucid window. Sometimes, for more than an hour, he'd be capable of moderate thought, able to speak and to understand. As they spoke in those "windows" of time when Ben could communicate, Matt came to appreciate the man's simple, solid faith.

Ben's regular pastor came during the day, and Matt had taken the "night shift." They agreed they weren't just there for Ben, but for his family.

Ben's brother Michael, who visited often, was taking it badly. The parents came with Ben's sister and, after healing words, left in tears. His brother Zachary (once he got out of jail) visited and looked totally devastated.

In the past three days, Matt had seen God move on Ben's behalf over and over again. Sadly, few people seemed to recognize it. The most heartbreaking words he'd heard were those coming from Ben's brother, Zachary. When Matt offered to pray with him, he said Matt was delusional if he thought there was a God who cared, or heard, or moved on anyone's behalf. He said life was a joke or it was pain, nothing more.

So much bitterness, ambition, so much sorrow, he thought. *All the name-calling, all the misunderstanding. But seeing how Ben loved You, Jesus, has inspired me. Thank You for letting me meet him this side of heaven.*

Matt planned to take several days off now. He'd sleep through the day, get up after his children got home from school, then spend the entire evening with them.

He'd already crawled into bed. He felt so cool, so comfortable, but then he remembered one, last thing.

"What a wonderful Father You are," he said aloud. "I know You and the angels were rejoicing a few hours ago as Ben escaped those iron bars. I'm so thankful I got to see his victory.

# # #

Linda Posner had already traveled miles from Chaplain North's home. She'd made an appointment for an interview the night before, but would have stood the fellow up if North had wanted to talk. It would have been a nice, human interest story.

Oh well, she thought, ready to write it all off. Not only was Mr. Gordon dead, but apparently, so was the story. *Even Thad Seager has moved on to greener pastures!*

If she hurried, she could still meet the man she'd agreed to interview and only be a minute or two late.

She found a parking space and got out of her car. Only now did she feel a little apprehension. Although she'd agreed to meet a man in this little park by a lake, she honestly hadn't given the location a lot of thought. In fact, she would've told the guy to take a hike if it hadn't been for her lack of progress on the Benjamin Gordon story.

No doubt, by the end of the day, her boss, Mr. Baumgardener, would call her back to the office and she would do meaningless tasks until she got another assignment. But first, she would check into this possible lead.

A man, who identified himself as a doctor, had seen her on television and called her a few days ago. She'd taken the call in hopes he was one of Gordon's doctors looking to leak some information.

Sadly, this doctor had nothing to do with her current story. Instead, he promised to give her some bombshell information about "Regeneration Therapy." She told him she was busy, but that she might get back to him. Chances were better than fifty-fifty the guy was a screwball of some sort.

After two endless days sitting in the restaurant near the hospital, Linda decided to call the guy back and at least hear what he had to say. Even if the story seemed to be a good one, she'd take it slow. She'd been bitten before by stories that, while true, were too large for her to handle.

As she entered the park, she recalled one story in particular back in Ohio involving cloning and genetic engineering. Her rush to beat other reporters to the story ended as a bungled mess. Even though she had the "facts," her lack of status translated to lack of credibility. By the time others got around to checking the facts, the laboratory had covered the evidence. She was ridiculed and later fired.

This time, she vowed, *I'll be careful to assemble the whole thing and to show it to Baumgardener first. He's got the clout to make it work.*

She approached a man on a bench near the water. "Dr. Mehndolson?"

The middle-aged man turned. "Yes. Thank you for coming, Ms. Posner."

Linda spent three and a half hours with Dr. Mehndolson while he rattled off hundreds of bits of information from memory. If what he said could be verified, it could lead to a major scandal involving a large laboratory and a major pharmaceutical company.

According to the doctor, the Attlebury Clinic, and several others, were part of the "first phase" of bringing into the healthcare system in America. Tests were being conducted at these clinics to confirm or disprove the claims of the manufacturer and other medical institutions in Europe and China. If the tests were successful, the therapy—said to miraculously return vigor to elderly people—would then enter the approval phase.

Dr. Mehndolson, looked out across the lake. "The problem," he said, "is that nearly half the people who are actually getting the therapy at the Attlebury Clinic are showing a dramatic decrease in mental capacity. While most of them can now run a quarter of a mile, chances are good they can't tell you why they like ice cream or recall their grandchildren's names."

By the next morning, Linda had done sufficient poking around to head to Baumgarder's office with a few "facts" and seek his approval to do an in-depth investigation.

He read her summary of Dr. Mehndolson's accusations along with the list of supporting data Linda had compiled.

He whistled. "Boy. That's some story."

"Will you let me do it?

His chair creaked when he leaned back in it. He squinted at the ceiling for a few moments.

"Will you let me do it?" she repeated.

He looked at her. "How come UIG or one of the other networks hasn't taken this on? Why did he come to us?"

"He saw my story on Philadelphia's preparations for the conference that UIG picked up a few weeks ago. Maybe he thought I worked for them at first. He doesn't look like he gets out much. Maybe he just wanted to spend some time with a woman. I don't know why. But so far, everything I've checked lines up with what he told me."

"You sure this isn't just disgruntled employee stuff?"

She was getting irritated. "You think I just fell off the boat? Of course it's possible he's a lying dog . . . this is why I want your permission to dig . . . to fully develop the story before we decide to air it."

Baumgardener put his hands behind his head and stared at the ceiling again.

"I'll bring everything I get to this office first. Think of it. This could be one of the biggest stories ever."

After what seemed an eternity of silence, he sat up in his chair, faced her, and spoke. "Let me consider it. Don't do any further development until we talk again."

Wanting to appear calm and professional, she unclenched her hands and spoke with a soft voice. "How soon will you let me know?"

"Tomorrow morning at the latest."

She willed her face to relax before looking him in the eyes. "Then, I suppose I'll talk to you later. Thanks for at least considering it."

CHAPTER 32

OKLAHOMA — October 3rd

The last seconds silently ticked away on Jason's watch, and the numbers changed to reflect a new hour: Five a.m. Those who watched the dorms at Henderson's Youth Ranch throughout the night would be preparing to finish their shift. At six, most of the other adult employees on the ranch would get up. At seven o'clock, they'd wake-up the boys who lived there.

The sun hadn't come up yet, and Jason McAllister would be confined to his room for another two hours; but he couldn't sleep. Last night, because of a broken water pipe, they'd crammed him into a room with three sets of bunk beds and five other guys. It was a temporary situation, but he didn't know if he'd be able to endure it.

He tried to breathe slowly. He needed to convince himself there really was enough air in this room. The walls were far enough away, and the bunk beds had enough space between them to allow for escape, didn't they? He could hear the others breathing. They were using up the air. When he tried to leave the window open before bed time, saying he liked "fresh air," he'd been overruled by the others.

When they had me in the third floor lockup, Jason thought, *at least I was in a cubicle by myself, and the lights of the main desk came through the window of my door. Then, in my regular room, Bobby would leave the door open a crack to let the light from the hall come in . . .*

Jason had been content to let his roommate think he was allowing this one kindness, saying he "didn't mind" if Bobby needed to have the door open.

Now, Bobby is in another room, and there's no excuse. How can I get Mr. Talbot to move me out of here? What could I say to change the situation? Thoughts continued to swirl around in his brain as he tried not to revisit the question of how much air remained in the room.

Before he'd gotten into trouble with the law, Jason lived as he pleased. He skipped school and slept all day when the others were gone, then stayed up most of the night. The farther behind he got with his lessons at school, the more appealing it was to stay away.

If anyone forced him to go to school, he'd just pick a fight with another kid and get himself suspended or make such a problem at his foster home he'd be shipped off to another one.

Jason closed his eyes. *You used to do whatever you wanted. You could walk the streets with your friends till three or four in the morning.*

Although he called them "friends," they only had two things in common: Each had chosen to live life under the cover of night, and each of them believed they would die young.

He thought about being arrested with the others for burglary and drug possession. The judge read Jason's file and decided to send him to the ranch in hopes of giving him a fresh start.

What made the judge pick me instead of another boy? I'm just lucky I didn't get sent to the correction facility. Jason's eyes reassessed the room while he tried to breathe slowly. *The overcrowding in there is worse than this. My only choice there would have been to become so bad they'd put me in solitary confinement. . . . But I can't hit anyone now. He wiped a trickle of sweat off his temple.*

Until recently, he considered himself immune to any sort of lecture on bad behavior. Until recently, Jason had never admitted—even to himself—that his main motivations for almost everything he'd ever done were anger and fear. Not until Mr. Ruiz came into the picture.

Mr. Ruiz. He's too big to intimidate. He doesn't react to insults . . . and he's way too determined to get in my business.

So far, Jason had tried every way he knew to get this guy to give up on him and leave him alone. So far, it hadn't worked.

He's like my shadow, showing up everywhere. He seems to KNOW where I am and what I'm doing . . . why I'm doing it. Forever asking if I'm tired of the way I live. Why should he even care?. . . 'Cuz it's his JOB to care. No other reason. He get's paid to herd me around like some cow all day.

It was almost a month since he'd gone with Mr. Ruiz to prepare a place for the camp out. While there, Jason became so frustrated he decided he would fix his problem with Ruiz the same way he fixed most of his problems: He'd attacked the man with every ounce of his strength while calling him every foul name he could bring to mind. What he didn't count on was Ruiz's response.

Until then, the guy had dogged his every step and made sure he paid the penalties for breaking ranch rules. However, this time Ruiz acted as if nothing happened. He said it was grace—getting forgiven when it wasn't deserved. Mr. Ruiz spoke of a childhood as bad as Jason's, but then told of the way he finally closed the door to it and came to a place of rest.

Well . . . maybe he does care. But what difference does that make? . . . Perhaps he's the one who had Shawn Thatcher moved to another dorm. . . . Is it getting hotter in here?

Jason sat up on his bunk and put his feet on the floor. He had to think of something to distract himself.

Think of camp. Yeah. Think about it. Outside in the air. You could see the stars at night. . .

Three weekends ago, something really strange happened to Jason. He wasn't sure yet if it had just been a momentary weakness on his part, or the persuasive words of Ruiz, or the enjoyment of the outdoors, or what. . . . He'd actually been allowed to go on the camp out, and on Saturday night, Ruiz asked if anyone wanted to receive Jesus into their life or if they wanted prayer. Jason desperately wanted to raise his hand but could not. He'd prayed silently and hoped it would count for something.

The glimpses Ruiz continued to give him of the possibility of a different life were so appealing. But if he wanted to stay on the ranch to hear more, it meant keeping his anger in check. Any more "incidents" and he'd be shipped out. So far, he'd managed to hold his rage down but a new problem seemed to be surfacing: Fear seemed to be filling all the places anger once occupied.

Jason wiped his face on his shirt. *How can I protect myself without fighting? Shawn and others are beginning to smell something and soon they're going to get me.*

It seemed as soon as camp ended, things had only gotten worse. And now, he'd been stuffed in this room with all these people. What could he do? He might have to stay there for a week while they repaired the other part of the building. Were there no exceptions?

You see what happens when you try to change the way it is? he thought with disgust. *You're trapped in here. You can't stay awake forever. This will never work for you.*

Jason tried taking air in through his mouth and clenched his hands on the edge of the mattress. He needed to get a grip on his thoughts.

Maybe you could talk to Talbot. . . . Right. Like you could just go and say "Excuse me, Mr. Talbot, but I'm scared of tight, dark places." What if the others found out? There'd be no livin' it down.

A few weeks ago, he would have found an excuse to beat up one of his bunk mates to get himself out of such an overcrowded room. But, unless he wanted to go back to jail, this was no longer an option. He was trying to think in longer terms, to make better choices, but how long could he go on like this?

A flash of being locked in a closet with brothers and sisters—all of them crying and begging to be let out—came to his mind and he stood up. He moved near to the window and opened it a crack. After a few pulls of air, he looked at his watch.

Less than two hours. Less than two more hours.

Another hour and a half dragged by as he fought the urge to panic. Finally, around six-thirty, the sun began to light the world outside enough to slowly brighten the room. He got back on his bed.

Maybe . . . I could talk to Mr. Ruiz.

Jason fell asleep just before it was time to get up. In fact, it seemed his eyes had closed only moments before Mr. Talbot opened the door.

"It's seven o'clock, guys! Time to get up!"

Most of the boys in the room groaned before stirring and eventually getting up. Jason fell back asleep but none of them dared disturb him. He had a reputation for a violent temper, and they weren't too thrilled with having to sleep in the same room with him.

When Mr. Talbot came back to the room, he found Jason sleeping and tried to get him up without a major battle.

Jason sat up and looked him in the eye. "Please, Mr. Talbot. I don't feel good. Please let me sleep."

Talbot studied him and sensed vulnerability. Something in Jason's demeanor was different. "Okay. You've got till ten. No later. If you're still feeling bad, we'll go to the infirmary."

When ten o'clock rolled around, there were more things to consider than whether or not Jason felt good. The young man was told to get dressed and head straight to Mr. Henderson's office. Why did the owner of the ranch want to speak to him?

"Jason," Henderson said, once they were alone. "I need to talk to you about something very serious. It has been reported to me you've been involved in another fight. Is this true?"

Jason looked confused. "What do you mean? I haven't done anything. Who told you that?"

"It's not important who told me. I was told you were involved in a fight with Mr. Ruiz recently. Is this true?"

The words stunned him. He thought the fight with Ruiz was water under the bridge. His mind raced to track down who could have told Henderson. *Ruiz could have. No, he said he wouldn't tell. Talbot might have known, but he would have done it before now. But what about Bobby?*

When Jason showed up that evening after the fight, Bobby had asked him why he was all banged up. Jason had distorted the story a bit to make himself look better and said he'd taught Ruiz a few things. *Bobby must have told others who, in turn, probably added to the story even more. Bobby's got a big mouth. He didn't go to Henderson, but he's told someone who has.*

"I . . . I don't know exactly what you mean, Mr. Henderson," Jason finally managed to say as he panicked inwardly. *A month ago you could have lied to him and not even blinked! What's happened to you?*

"Did you and Mr. Ruiz have a fistfight or not?"

"Well. Not exactly. He never hit me . . . and I missed him most of the time. And it wasn't on ranch grounds anyway."

There was a knock at the door before the secretary, Myra, opened it. She looked at Jason, then at Mr. Henderson and said, "He's here. He's between classes. You want me to ask Mr. Stone to take his next class?"

Myra could have used the intercom but just had to see the way the boy looked while he was sitting there. She let herself glance at him again.

"Have him wait for a moment," Henderson responded. "I'll let you know about Stone shortly."

Once the door closed, Jason wanted to continue his explanation. "It was all a misunderstanding. I—"

"That's all I need to know for now." Henderson said. "I'll be calling you back to the office later. Meanwhile, I want you to go to class."

Leaving the office, Jason felt sick. *You're off the ranch! They'll send you to jail!* He inwardly cringed when he saw Mr. Ruiz out the corner of his eye, standing only a few feet away. He could only look at him for a moment before riveting his gaze to the floor. *He's gonna think I'm the one who buckled and ratted on him.*

Ruiz called to him in a friendly voice. "Hey, Jason."

Now he felt even worse. He'd never uttered the words "I'm sorry" before, but he desperately wanted to do so now. If only he could explain.

"Mr. Henderson is waiting for you," Myra said, in an effort to keep things moving. The event she'd hoped for had come and she couldn't wait another second. Ruiz turned and disappeared behind the door.

"What are you supposed to be doing?" she asked the boy.

"Gotta go to class," Jason mumbled before he slunk out of the room.

Myra's face softened into a small, triumphant smile. It lingered on her lips for a while as she mentally replayed the delectable morning she'd had. It started with the envelope coming from Zenith. She knew what was probably in it without being able to see inside. She'd had to work at not looking jubilant as she took it into Henderson. And then, within an hour to find out Ruiz had covered up a fight!

Mr. Henderson's voice came over the intercom and startled her. "Myra."

Her face hardened once again. "Yes?"

"Go ahead and ask Mr. Stone to take Ricky's class."

"Yes, Mr. Henderson." She turned off the intercom and closed her eyes, whispering, "Thank you, Lord." How she wished she could see Mr. Ruiz trying to dig his way out of this one.

CHAPTER 33

PHILADELPHIA — October 3rd

Linda Posner stood in the Channel Five newsroom. *Soon*, she thought, *I could be the permanent anchor of the evening news. If only I could get this story out now. UIG and all the other big networks are in town to cover the Conference blowout. If I could get out there NOW*—She caught herself. *Patience! Don't run ahead. That's what got you in the soup last time. You must keep your wits about you and it will all work out. If you do this right, they'll notice you. Pull it off, and nothing can stop you. What a story it will be!*

She could hardly contain herself as she thought about how she'd develop her secret assignment—exposing the truth about Regeneration Therapy. Of course, the better part of the story would rest on her talks with Dr. Mehndolson and a registered nurse he'd told her about who expressed a willingness to talk. From these interviews and other research she'd already mapped out, a clear picture would emerge.

Mehndolson told her all the people who entered the clinical trials met certain criteria. None of them had life-threatening health problems or diseases involving rapid deterioration. "Those who actually got the therapy," he'd said, "were easy to spot after the first few weeks of the experiment. They were virtually transforming before our eyes. The way they grew stronger every day made them easy to spot. Two months after the physical boost began, however, most of them began deteriorate mentally. While they could do rote tasks, many seemed to have lost the ability to problem solve or think creatively. . ."

Linda held the small disk containing the raw data from their interview in her hand. *Soon, you'll be—*

"Linda," she heard a man's voice behind her say, "I'm glad you're here,"

She turned to see her boss, Mr. Baumgardener, standing near the opening to her cubicle. "Do you think you could speak with me for a few minutes?"

She smiled and rose from her seat, keeping the disk in her hand. She glanced around as they walked toward his office. *Careful. Don't give anything away to the others. Let it be a surprise.*

When they'd entered the office, he asked her to close the door and be seated before he started the conversation.

"Do you have the information you've gathered so far?" he said, casually.

"Do I ever." She opened her hand to reveal the small disk, then handed it to him.

"You didn't leave a copy at your workstation or on your computer at home did you?"

"No. I have a backup disk, but I didn't put anything in an accessible system."

"I'll want the backup."

She felt her face getting hotter. "Why?"

He set her disk down on his desk. "I've done some checking, Linda. It seems your Dr. Mehndolson is quite a wacko."

She could feel her pulse pounding in her temples as her mind scrambled to pull together all she knew so far. She'd checked Mehndolson's credentials and verified his past projects. She'd made sure he'd actually worked at the clinic, thinking if he'd made it that far, he must know what he was talking about. After she'd checked on a few of the details he'd given her on Regeneration and found they were true, she'd rushed to talk to Baumgardener. How could she have made such a stupid mistake? In her desire to not repeat a large mistake she'd made in the past—doing *all* the research, then attempting to tell the story without permission from on high—she'd stepped into another pit.

"Apparently," Baumgardener continued, "he was fired from the project because of his unstable behavior."

"He seemed intelligent and rational when I spoke with him . . . and I *did* check on some of the facts he gave me before I came to you."

"Well, I did some checking, too. I'm told he threatened the director of the clinic."

She thought about how she'd met him alone in the park. Another foolish mistake. The man could have harmed her.

"You know the old saying," Baumgardener offered, "there's a fine line between genius and insanity."

She'd been foolish, but hadn't crossed any lines. She should have been relieved this was the full extent of it, but all she wanted to do was to slink off to some dark corner and hide. She held her head erect and prepared for a lecture. "I'm sorry I wasted your time. I just thought we could look into it."

Baumgardener didn't raise his voice but his firm tone communicated his disappointment in her. "Ambition can be a good thing, Linda, but you'd benefit by harnessing yours. Concentrate on pouring your enthusiasm into stories you're asked to do rather than searching for big stories on your own."

She looked down. "Yes. You're right."

He noticed the color in her cheeks and considered again how beautiful she was. "But it doesn't have to be the end of the world, now, does it? You've done well with the assignments I've given you haven't you? Trust me." He knew his next words had to be carefully chosen. Being her superior made it difficult. He said softly, "I know you're talented and I want to help you."

After a moment, she managed a smile. "Thank you, Mr. Baumgardener. I'd like it very much if you could find some time to teach me more."

He sat up straighter in his chair, looked briefly at her, and then softened the tone of his voice. "Well, I usually don't have time during business hours."

"How about dinner some time, then?"

He chanced another look at her. "I have a rule about spending personal time with employees . . . however, I think we could make an exception, couldn't we?" His phone rang but he ignored it, waiting for her to respond.

"Definitely. How about tonight?"

His phone stopped ringing when the line management system kicked in with voice mail. He looked at his watch. "I don't get off until eight."

She could see he was nervous. "Eight then."

"You sure?"

"Yes."

The phone started ringing again. He turned on his headset. "Hello?"

She got up from her chair to leave.

"Hold it a sec," he said, pushing the mute button for his line. He looked at Linda, "Just one more thing."

She paused.

"Your back-up disk. . . . We could get sued big time if it ever got out. I need you to give me the other disk as well."

Something was up. Was this actually a big story? She could continue to pursue it on her own. She quickly considered her options. Wasn't it better to walk through a door Baumgardener opened than to defy him and possibly crash her career permanently? So what if she got to the top a bit slower? At least he knew how to get there. She smiled her best smile. "Certainly. I'll go get it."

# # #

In two days, Dr. Timothy Mehndolson would vanish without a trace.

CHAPTER 34

SOUTHEASTERN OKLAHOMA

While Linda Posner retrieved her backup disk for Mr. Baumgardener, twelve hundred miles away, in Oklahoma, Ricky Ruiz described what had happened out at his friend's cabin.

When he'd finished the story, he said, "You've told me on several occasions I have discretion to decide what is a 'reportable offense' and what is not. I felt there'd been a real breakthrough, so I chose not to report it. I knew the proof would be in seeing what he did after that. If I'd read the situation wrong, he was gonna do something to get himself in trouble again anyway, and I would've only saved him for a day or two. But the truth is, he has improved. I've kept tabs on him through his teachers and Chuck. He has stayed out of trouble. When he came to the camp out, I know he came this close to praying out loud with me. I know something's happened inside him, Paul. Please, give him just one more chance."

"Well, it's gotten more complicated now," Henderson said, rooting around on his desk and locating a piece of paper.

"What do you mean?"

"I got a notice from the Zenith Corps this morning notifying us of an upcoming transfer of custody."

Ricky's hands tightened into fists. "I don't believe he signed up."

"You're probably right. By the wording, it doesn't look like he volunteered. I don't know who put them onto his trail, but someone must have turned in his name and case number, and they found a judge who'd sign him over. No one else knows yet. I no sooner opened the notice then this whole thing about him fighting came up and, since it involved you, I felt I had to address it first. If he'd been told he was signed over to Zenith, he might have tried to lie about what really happened in order to muddy the waters for you. By the way, he fessed up to it and said you never hit him."

"What are you going to do now?"

"Well, it may not help Jason, but, remember the Supreme Court heard arguments in several combined suits against Zenith two weeks ago. The fact they agreed to go ahead and hear these cases before they went through all the other appeals courts should be an encouragement in and of itself. A decision could come down any day now. We have to believe all of our prayers are making a difference in this thing."

Ten minutes later, Ricky emerged from Henderson's office looking somber. He approached Myra and asked, "Where's Jason right now?"

"Mr. Hampton's class," she said without checking.

Ruiz started walking away. "Okay. Thank you."

Myra noted Ricky's happy stride was gone. "Your welcome."

# # #

Jason never thought he'd be glad to sit in a classroom, but today he was. When Mr. Ruiz appeared at the door and asked to have him excused, the young man wished he could just stay there, safe within its bounds. It wasn't possible, of course, and he certainly didn't want the humiliation of being dragged out of the room. He got up and went to the door.

They stepped outside of the school building just as the sun came from behind a cloud. Brilliant light flooded the space between the buildings and it hurt Jason's eyes. He shielded them with one hand and kept pace with Ricky. After a few seconds he had to say something.

"I didn't mean to get you in trouble, Mr. Ruiz. I . . . I'm sorry."

Mr. Ruiz continued to look forward. "I'm not in trouble. Mr. Henderson wanted me to come get you so we could all talk."

The scrunch of gravel under their shoes was the only sound as they closed the distance to the office. Jason's mind raced around different things to say, which might entice Henderson to grant him mercy. Could he bring himself to beg? Would it help?

Once they were back in Henderson's office, Jason wasn't asked for any more details about the fight. Before he could begin any sort of plea, Henderson told him the Zenith Corps was trying to schedule a transfer of custody. It struck him speechless.

"I want you to know," Henderson said, "the fight is a dead issue. Mr. Ruiz explained it, and that case is closed now. We just want to concentrate on this Zenith thing. Did you sign up for the corps?"

Jason's voice was barely audible. "No."

"Well, we can't break the law to keep you, but we're going to follow up on every legal means we have to resist them and we're going to pray God will intervene. Mr. Ruiz and I both feel there's reason to hope for a breakthrough in the situation."

A while later, the door to Henderson's office opened. Myra looked up from her computer terminal and saw Jason looked like he'd been crying. For one brief moment, she almost felt sorry she'd done it. The feeling vanished instantly when Ruiz put a comforting hand on the boy and said something she couldn't hear. The sting of punishment was being eased away by Ruiz's soft words. She clenched her jaw. Soon, they'll both get what they deserve.

Once Jason left, Ricky turned to her. "Since I don't have to hurry back to class," he said, "have you got the requisition for sports equipment I gave you?"

"Yes. Do you need to cancel it?"

"No. I need to add a few things. I'll be getting an increase of students next semester."

Myra looked shaken, but said nothing the rest of the time Ricky was in the office. As soon as he'd gone back to his class, she went into Mr. Henderson's office.

"Yes?" he said. "You wanted something, Myra?

Her anger had simmered long enough. "I want to know where this situation stands."

"What specifically did you want to know?"

"Did you fire Mr. Ruiz or not?"

Paul Henderson closed the drawer he'd been looking through and looked at her. Two years ago, he'd hired Myra to serve as secretary at the ranch. During her initial interview, he had pieced together several facts: Her ex-husband had left her struggling to survive financially as well as emotionally. Her son, in his late teens, had run away and joined a gang down in Dallas. Her daughter was not doing well at home.

Although Myra had clerical skills, they weren't what made him select her over other applicants. He'd done it in hopes she might not only earn enough to live, but also find solutions to some of her own problems. He thought perhaps the hardness he saw in her would melt, and she would be capable of receiving and giving something that should be a basic product of Christian life: kindness. He'd hoped maybe she would, in time, be able to minister to her own hurting children.

He watched her as she stood there, clenching the back of a chair, glaring at him with hateful intensity. She was actually trembling. *What a pity,* he thought. *She's consumed with so much bitterness . . . and she thinks it's the Lord.*

"I have no intention of firing Mr. Ruiz," Henderson said.

Myra's voice became shrill. "How can you do this? Some of us work so hard to do the right thing, to set a good example, and you want to reward a man who doesn't even take his job seriously! He cares *nothing* about the rules!"

"What rules, Myra?"

"He let the boy fight with him and he lied about it."

"Whoa! Back up a second here. I myself gave Mr. Ruiz discretion to decide when to turn in a boy or not. He's never abused this authority. And after hearing all the details, I believe he made the right decision concerning Jason. There was no 'lying' involved."

One of Myra's bony hands had gone to her throat as if she were protecting it, the other remained locked onto the back of the chair. Her eyes looked as if they were going to pop out. "That's not all, though. He's done more things. He's gotten a traffic ticket with our car! And I saw him dancing in a place where drinking was going on!"

Henderson looked disbelieving. "Where was this? For that matter, what were *you* doing in a bar?"

"It wasn't exactly a bar. It was the county fair. But think of the boys, Mr. Henderson. Think of the influence he's having on them. He can't be allowed to do this."

Henderson sighed. In some sick way she was actually jealous of Ricky. "I don't think you have a clear picture here, Myra. I already knew about the ticket . . . and as far as his influence with the boys . . . I wish I had ten more men like him."

"You can't say that! Think of the ranch's reputation!"

Henderson realized she wasn't going to let this go. He looked directly at her and spoke in a calm voice. "These boys need rules and order, but rules and order will not save them. The law never saved *anyone*. I want this to be a place where a broken person can find a relationship with God. That's the only reputation I want for the ranch . . . and, next to God, I have the final word here. Is there anything else?"

Her eyes narrowed. "Either he goes or I go, Mr. Henderson," she said, her voice quavering.

"Pardon me?"

"I see you need to realize how seriously I take this. He goes or I go."

"Then I'll consider this your two weeks' notice."

CHAPTER 35

WASHINGTON D. C. — October 7th

President Don Cole ran cold water over his hands and then splashed some on his face. He needed to have his wits about him. He combed his wet hair, then buttoned his shirt.

More than an hour ago, at three in the morning, he'd been awakened with the news. There had been an accident in space. A US shuttlecraft was using an extension of the boom in its cargo hold to help deploy part of the solar array for the space station, when something went wrong. There was a collision with the oxygen tanks of the station and a very large explosion. All of the people on the station and in the shuttlecraft were presumed dead.

Within minutes of the blast, a shower of large and small fragments from the station began striking the earth's atmosphere. Some of the pieces hit at such a shallow angle they bounced back out into space, many burned up during re-entry, others managed to plummet through the air to the water and ground below. Most of the strikes on the ground were in sparsely populated areas of Russia. So far, the known death toll on the ground was nine people.

Don looked at the television screen across the room. Although he'd muted the sound, Don could see the news broadcast was about the space station. He'd been told hordes of media representatives were already outside the White House, waiting for him to give an official response to the disaster. He looked at his watch before slipping on his shoes. It was four-twenty-three a.m.

The president turned off the television and took a deep breath. *Oh, God, I see it coming. Thank You for guiding me. I know You granted me favor with Ivanov when I called him. Help him as he makes decisions regarding this. Help me to stay within the bounds of Your wisdom, no matter what things look like.*

At four-forty, President Cole walked out of his quarters. A growing entourage of men and women began to cluster around him, some asking questions, some taking orders, as he made his way down the hall.

Only sketchy information was available, so Don hoped this meeting would unite the men and women who would be working for solutions. Very quickly, they needed to access accurate information and know how to interpret it. As conclusions were reached, he would have to decide what steps might be needed to defend the country, how to respond to his counterparts in other countries, and what to say to the reporters who had gathered like hungry wolves outside.

Five workers entered the elevator with the president, but no one spoke to him during the short ride down to the floor where the meeting would be held. Two people spoke softly to each other in the back of the elevator, but Cole, lost in thought, didn't even hear them. He tried to recall all he'd read about the decade-old space station. By the time he got into office, there were so many disputes over so many different aspects of the project that many in the scientific community doubted it would ever be a "technological triumph." The more Don looked into it, the more he became convinced the Space Station *COSMOS* project was an ill-conceived idea from the start.

Several times since he'd been in office, he'd suspected the Russians and the French wanted out of the project as badly as he did, but no one wanted to be the first to withdraw. Departure from the enterprise would be the equivalent of asking for a very ugly divorce. There had been no quiet way out. What was originally hailed as a "cooperative international effort" had turned into a lightning rod for tensions over a multitude of other issues.

The doors to the elevator opened, and Don, workers in tow, strode down the hall.

Problems between the United States and the Russian Federation had been growing over the past few years. Since former President Todd had tried to make secret overtures to several Arab nations, the relations between the two old superpowers had deteriorated dramatically. Recently, there had been a sharp increase in negative rhetoric against America in the Russian press, and a number of serious accusations including espionage, sabotage, and subterfuge had been leveled against the US. Fifteen Americans (including four diplomats) had been ousted from Russia. And now this.

Everyone fell silent as President Cole entered the room and looked at the two, highly polished, semi-circular tables arching toward one another. Workers scurried around in the open space between the tables, placing clip screens and drinking water in front of thirty chairs. Preparations were nearly complete. At the far end of the room stood a podium equipped with a microphone, a computer terminal, three phone lines, and controls for video displays on the two large screens on either side of the room.

Everyone looked at the president. He consulted his watch again. "It's a few minutes early. Is everyone here?"

"General Milford is on his way but should be here momentarily, sir," someone nearby offered. "And the vice president is still in transit."

"Then we'll wait," Cole said. "I want everyone to be completely up to speed on this."

A man in uniform presented him with a clip screen. It was ready to display a briefing on what had transpired thus far.

While still in his bedroom, Cole had already been given a report by phone regarding Russian activities since the disaster and possible response scenarios. After that, Don called his counterpart in Russia, Lev Ivanov, to share all he knew concerning the accident and express sincere sorrow at what had happened. Don assured him there would be full cooperation in the investigation of the tragedy. He'd ended the call with a promise to call again in a few hours.

"Are the link-ups with the Space Agency complete?" Don inquired.

"Yes sir. They're number one on your touch menu."

Cole moved through the room and spoke to several people while they waited for the others to arrive. At five fifteen, General Austin Milford entered the room with two other men. His face looked ashen as he approached the president.

"May I speak to you for a moment, Mr. President?"

Gen. Milford motioned for two others to join them and they huddled together.

"Sir," General Milford said, "I've just been given alarming news. We've lost communications with several of our strategic satellites."

"Do you think they could have been struck by debris?"

"That's what we thought when we lost the first two of them. But two more just went off line five minutes ago. While it could still be debris, someone could be deliberately taking them out."

# # #

While President Cole conferred with General Milford, a storm of activity was taking place within Russian military headquarters. General Vladimir Gusinsky had gone to the privacy of his office to convey information to President Ivanov.

"Are you sure of this information?" Ivanov asked.

"Yes, we have lost three satellites. The Americans may have exploded the station to cover their real agenda. This could be a deliberate act. We need to prepare for the worst."

"What you really mean is that you want to go on the offensive."

There was silence on the line for a few seconds before the general responded. "Why are you fighting me on this? Why are you suddenly on *their* side?"

Ivanov considered the accusation. Was he being soft when he should be activating a plan to assure survival?. . . No. For whatever reason, he believed President Cole. He believed this was a tragic accident. "I'm not taking their side. I'm just not leaping to conclusions."

When they ended the call, General Gusinsky cursed under his breath. Everyone knew the Americans could not be trusted. Everyone knew whoever struck first would have the greatest chance. And now Ivanov wanted to wait. Wait for *what*? Wait until *all* their satellites were down?

It had been a dark day for the general when Lev Ivanov, a moderate, made it to the presidency. The man had been uncooperative at every step. This could not continue. Too much was at stake.

He would contact Uri, Yevgeny, and the others. Something would have to be done before it was too late.

# # #

At noon, President Cole made his way to his office and sat behind his desk, waiting for his cue. A man beside the camera counted down, then pointed to the monitor. Before Don spoke, he looked into the camera and listened for the words, "Ladies and gentlemen, the President of the United States."

"Doubtless," he began, "most of you have heard about the events transpiring last night, but I wanted to give you a brief account, hoping the facts will quench any rumors or misinformation. Following my remarks, experts from the US Space Agency will be standing by in the press room to answer technical questions.

"At approximately one twenty-three this morning, Eastern Daylight Time, a sequence of events may have caused the space shuttle, *Trek 1*, to collide with the oxygen tanks attached to space station *COSMOS*. While we are not completely certain of all the details, we do know a large explosion destroyed the station, the *Eurocapsule* docked at the station, and *Trek 1*. All personnel are presumed lost.

"Within minutes of the explosion, pieces of debris began entering Earth's atmosphere. While much of the wreckage burned on re-entry, a number of pieces have struck western rural Russia, leaving a large debris field. The death toll from the station and on the ground now stands at forty-two.

"After being notified of the event, I spoke with Russian President Ivanov and with Francois Montaigne, the President of France, to assure them all possible avenues were being explored to determine the cause of the explosion, and that we desired to work cooperatively in our investigation.

"At five this morning, the vice president and I met with civilian, military, and Space Agency experts to obtain all available information and order a full-scale investigation into this horrible tragedy. We hope to have preliminary findings within hours, but ask for patience both from the American people and our allies who have worked with us in this endeavor.

"At this time, there are still a number of large and small pieces of debris which may enter our atmosphere. Space Agency officials are linking with the Russians and the French to determine possible outcomes. . ."

PHILADELPHIA, PA

At Philadelphia's Channel Five, Linda Posner stood inside the news room and watched the bank of screens depicting coverage of the *COSMOS* disaster. She'd rushed to the station once she'd heard about it. She'd get a lot more data about the incident at work than she would watching TV at home.

Someone turned up the sound for UIG. Since Channel Five was the local affiliate, this was the coverage they were sending out on the air. Linda focused on the UIG screen and listened intently. Carmella Lang, their morning anchor, was speaking.

". . . high-ranking sources at the Pentagon have informed us Russia has now placed their military in a state of high alert."

For the first time since she was young, Linda was experiencing real fear that global matters were spinning out of control.

Another Channel Five reporter, Gil Rusk, seemed to be taking it all in stride. He took the last sip of his coffee and shook his head as he stood next to her. "Wouldn't you just know it?" he said loudly. "And I suppose all those screwy doomsday people will be crawling out of their dark holes and screaming Jesus is coming back and we're all gonna burn. I despise those people. Someone ought to lock 'em up."

Linda said nothing. On the way in, she'd driven by a billboard. She'd gotten a chill as she read the words on it: "HE is coming soon. Get right . . . or get left." She didn't know *what* to believe.

CHAPTER 36

REYKJAVIK, ICELAND — October 9th

Before they stepped out of the room, exhausted Presidents Cole and Ivanov had a few moments of privacy. Ivanov leaned forward and shook Don's hand. "Now to sell it to the generals, eh?" he said, barely loud enough for Cole to hear him.

Don chuckled quietly. "Yes, you're probably right, Lev."

Only a day ago, he wouldn't have felt comfortable calling the Russian president by his first name, but they'd just finished another long session of fervent talks. Somewhere in the middle of it all, they'd dispensed with formalities. Although two translators were available (one for Cole and one for Ivanov), they weren't necessary. Ivanov spoke excellent English. In their honest discussions, both men hoped they'd woven the first few threads of an understanding–possibly of a future friendship.

They'd flown to Reykjavik eighteen hours ago to meet face to face before the extremely tense situation over the space station came to an armed conflict. There had been no time to enjoy Iceland's starkly beautiful countryside, the brightly colored roofs on multitudes of sugar-cube houses, or the cold refreshing winds. Now, the two presidents would have to hurry home and convince constituents that war was *not* imminent.

The two men exited their meeting room and followed a small contingent of diplomats and soldiers down a long hall. Bright flowers in large vases stood tall, like sentries, perched atop small tables at even intervals along the walls. At the end of the corridor, a room glutted with cameras, microphones, and avid listeners awaited a announcement from the two leaders.

The assembled men and women of the international media rose to their feet as Cole and Ivanov entered the room. The presidents took their places, side by side, behind a podium.

PHILADELPHIA, PA

Linda Posner sat at her desk trying to calm herself. Perhaps if she set her priorities for the morning, she could keep herself preoccupied.

"It's on!" someone shouted.

As long as the crisis was over, as long as things would be okay, did she really need to watch? Yes, she did. Linda clicked on the computer link so she could watch it from her desk rather than stand at the bank of screens at the other end of the room.

The link came up on the screen. She saw Presidents Cole and Ivanov standing together. They shook hands.

That's a good sign, isn't it? she thought. She noted they both looked fatigued, but relaxed while they waited to address the media. Cole smiled. *All good signs.*

A short, blond man introduced Ivanov. The Russian stepped up to the microphones and cleared his throat before speaking in his native tongue. Within seconds, UIG had an interpreter doing a voice-over.

"I am pleased to announce . . . the Russian Federation and the United States . . . have reached an understanding regarding the events of the past few days. . . . While not all questions have been answered, both President Cole and I are satisfied investigations will determine the exact cause . . . of the tragic accident on Space Station *COSMOS* . . ."

Linda breathed a sigh of relief. So nobody was declaring war today. When Ivanov finished his statement, someone shouted a question. Because the reporter wasn't in front of a microphone, Linda had to focus her attention and turn up the volume to hear his query.

". . . a terrorist hacker may have accessed the codes and sent the order to the shuttle's computers, causing the rockets to fire. Is this true?"

Ivanov looked at Cole then moved aside.

Don stepped to the microphone. "We only have preliminary reports at this point, but we do know that *something* caused the computer on *COSMOS* to fire the rockets. We hope to close in on an accurate answer very soon and will pass on information as quickly as we can."

A woman in the audience raised her hand then asked, "President Ivanov, is Russia now prepared to order a stand down of her military forces?"

The Russian president moved back to the podium, and again there was a short delay before the translator began the voice-over. "I feel the talks here will result in—"

Multitudes of videos of the next few seconds would be enhanced, enlarged, and repeatedly replayed in the days to come. At the time it actually happened, no one noticed the expression on Cole's face. He looked out at a particular man in the sea of reporters, and his eyebrows came together as if a question were forming in his mind. A mere moment later, he pushed right in front of Ivanov. There was no sound of a shot, but both men were already on their way to the floor when a horde of protectors from both countries swarmed over them.

NEW YORK

Today would be Josh Thornton's day off. He'd been up a good portion of the night, praying for one of his dearest friends—President Don Cole. Josh had finally gone to bed around four, asking his wife, Carol, to wake him with any news.

When the press conference began, both he and Carol were watching it on their living room television. They sat in shocked disbelief after Don and Ivanov went to the floor.

"What happened? Did *you* see what happened?" Carol asked.

"No! I don't know."

News cameras continued to take in the scene, but a huge clump of security personnel blocked any view of the fallen men. Everyone in the room started shouting simultaneously. Several people lunged at a man in the third row of reporters and wrestled him to the floor. Agents and soldiers dove past the first two rows into the fray.

A reporter for The Banner Network tried to yell over the top of the din. "Ladies and gentlemen! Something has happened! Although I didn't hear any shots," he said breathlessly, "it appears one or both of the presidents may have been injured. People are subduing a man near the front."

The camera bounced from side to side as some people tried to rush forward and others attempted to flee from possible injury. Soldiers in full riot gear stormed into the room, weapons at the ready.

Banner's reporter continued shouting into his microphone and straining to see as soldiers began forcing the entire crowd to the doors at the rear of the room. "I can't see either president at this point. Wait! Wait!" he said, trying to momentarily hold his position. "Ivanov is standing, and they are rushing him from the room! Oh my! Oh my! I can see . . ." he said, trying to jump up and look, "President Cole is still down!" The picture went to empty, blue screen for several seconds.

Banner's morning anchor in New York appeared suddenly. "We apologize to our viewers. All links with the scene in Iceland have been lost. While we work to reconnect with Ray, we'll give you what we have thus far. Our own Ray Dodwin, reporting live from the scene, saw both US President Donald Cole and Russian Federation President Lev Ivanov fall to the floor. Before our link went down, Ray said he could see Ivanov standing and being rushed from the room, but that President Cole remained down. I repeat, Ray Dodson said that President Cole remained down. We hope to have more from the scene in moments . . ."

Although official confirmation wouldn't come for another thirty minutes, Josh Thornton knew. He knew Don was dead. He sank to his knees and covered his face.

"NO!" he cried out. "Please Lord . . . my friend . . . "

Carol knelt beside him and they embraced, both weeping.

Then, it came rushing to him. He held his wife tighter. "Oh Lord. I know what has happened. I know Don won . . . He took his place . . . but now," Josh said in anguish, "it will come."

WASHINGTON, D.C.

Many miles away, at the highest levels of government, emergency plans were already being implemented. Expressions of shock and grief would begin flooding the media and the Internet, then pour toward Washington, D.C. Those who worked closest to President Cole would have to postpone their own feelings of shock and sorrow in order to secure a smooth transition of power. Vice President Lawrence Cunningham, already at the White House at the time of the assassination, would have to be sworn in as President.

CHAPTER 37

The set had the appearance of a large office—perhaps one of a president or some other head-of-state. Bright, indirect lighting gave the room the airy appearance of a windowed, corner suite. Colors, fabrics, and furniture had all been deliberately chosen. Every detail in view of the camera communicated authority, calm, and caring.

No one would think this room actually stood on the floor of the Gulf of Mexico, more than three miles from any coastline. Although the facility's existence was common knowledge, the perception of its actual purpose varied depending upon whom one questioned. Fellow members of the world's wealthy elite privately thought E. E. Kressman built it as the ultimate "survival bunker." Environmentalists believed he would use it as a base for extensive marine research (something they'd been told was one of Kressman's private passions). Media rivals thought the man planned on using it to flaunt US broadcasting laws. Ordinary people were envious of a man wealthy enough to afford what they imagined was a mini-kingdom in the Gulf.

This would be E. E. Kressman's third broadcast from his new headquarters and he wanted it to be as perfect as the others. Until a few months ago, he'd rarely used network time to directly express his viewpoints, but recent events, he said, had forced him to re-evaluate this policy. The mood in the world outside bordered on panic. *Someone* needed to become the advocate of humanity in the midst of so many politically charged circumstances. Kressman "reluctantly" took this position, and now intended to continue with a series of short talks to be aired on UIG and all affiliates.

The media mogul entered the room and took his place behind the large desk. Camera One took in Kressman and the entire set.

"Good day," he said. "I am addressing you, once again, because the dramatic string of events in recent days continues to beg for serious attention."

Camera Two pulled in for a tighter shot. The lines around his dark eyes made him appear both tired and determined.

"As we mourn the loss of President Cole, multitudes are searching for the persons who are responsible for a string of international tragedies. These tragedies have threatened the peace of the entire world."

Kressman continued to look directly into the camera lens, speaking in a soft, urgent voice. "While our decision to air all accessible information concerning these events has been met with criticism, our motive has not been to incite panic. We have reported facts as they came to us because we have always believed that the public just as much right to know what is going on as those in high office. It is clearly time everyone had the ability to make intelligent, informed decisions, and it is our desire to empower you to do this."

His tone became more resolute. "People in a democracy shouldn't be forced to wait helplessly in the dark while decisions regarding their fate are made by a handful of individuals with vested interests. It is only fair that citizens have the information they need as they communicate with those who represent them.

"If we unite for restraint, reasoning, and justice, we will live to see these dark days behind us. I urge all of you to support the impartial investigations and binding settlements the UN has offered to mediate. Peace be with you."

On a red background with no sound, the words, appeared in bold, white text for a few seconds before UIG returned to regular programming:

"RESTRAINT
REASONING
JUSTICE"

CHAPTER 38

President Lawrence Wesley Cunningham entered his bedroom in the White House, then closed the door. Although he'd be late for a meeting with the Joint Chiefs, he felt an extreme need for a few moments alone. Normally those who knew him would say you could set a clock by Lawrence. He'd always been a stickler for details. What would they say now?

President for nearly two weeks, he'd been sworn in before Don Cole's body had landed back on American soil. Within days of the transition, movers had transferred all of Cunningham's household goods to the White House. Aware of the tremendous strain on Lawrence, his wife had labored to ensure the unpacking process went quickly, quietly, and efficiently. She'd also completely redecorated the master suite so no reminder of its former occupant remained.

Lawrence lifted a strand of hair off of the ivory-colored bedspread and placed it in a nearby wastebasket before sitting on the end of his bed. Hoping he could somehow get tense muscles to relax, he took several breaths and closed his eyes.

He'd just experienced the most awful two weeks of his life. It began with the crash of the space station *COSMOS*, the escalation of tensions with Russia, and the death of President Donald Cole. Video tapes of the event proved that Don had knowingly stepped in front of a deadly projectile aimed at Russian President Lev Ivanov.

Even now, the scenes, from a multitude of perspectives, kept replaying in Lawrence's mind. He could see the tired smile on Don's face, the questioning look shifting to recognition, and the plunge in front of Ivanov. The specialized projectile, intended for the Russian President, burst into dozens of searing fragments as soon as it entered Don's neck, killing him almost instantly.

These images continually haunted the new president. Who knew what might happen next. Could he be the next target? He kept feeling as if a giant bull's-eye had been painted on him. Even if he kept his protective vest on, what about his head and neck? It wasn't as if he could walk around in full body armor.

Lawrence took another deep breath through his nostrils. *I've got to think of something else. What would Don do? How I wish he were here!*

Had Lawrence ever expressed the sincere admiration he felt for Don? Or had his personal distaste for sentimentality always won out? He couldn't seem to remember. . . . Taking the oath of office and attending Don's funeral were just two more examples of the myriad of things he couldn't recall with any clarity.

What would happen now? Hadn't Cole tried to teach him how to keep perspective and how to keep going? Had he absorbed any of it?

At least the assassination happened after Don and Ivanov had come to an agreement and acknowledged it in front of the press. One day after the incident, an announcement had come out of the Kremlin, stating that General Vladimir Gusinsky had been arrested with several others who were involved in the plot against Russia's president.

Only a small group of people would ever know the next step in the conspirators' plan had been to launch a preemptive first strike against the US—an event narrowly averted only hours after the attempt on Ivanov's life. In fact, if Ivanov hadn't agreed to the sudden meeting with Cole in Iceland, he might have been assassinated at home, and the two countries would now be at war.

Even though the US and Russia hadn't gone to war, underlying tensions continued to run high as the media riveted public attention on the crash of *COSMOS* and the assassination of President Cole. The United Nations had stepped in to coordinate the global search for guilty parties.

Lawrence's mind raced over the myriad questions regarding US security. How had someone obtained the computer codes for Trek 1 and ordered the shuttle to collide with COSMOS? Within hours of the disaster, a number of US communication and spy satellites had been destroyed or disabled. Although experts now believed the US hardware had been hit by debris from COSMOS, what if they were wrong? What would happen if forces hostile to the US found out about her severely diminished defense and intelligence capabilities?

Lawrence put a hand on his chest. *It's happening again! That shaking . . . what is it?* It felt like someone had taken a child's windup toy and let it loose inside his rib cage to frantically leap all over his innards.

If only I had help with all of these terrible things. The Joint Chiefs think I'm a weakling. So I'm not Don Cole! Is that a crime? They're trying to intimidate me. I need people who are on MY side.

His nomination of an old friend for vice president, Derek Voss, had sparked a sharply partisan battle in Congress which threatened to go on indefinitely. Meanwhile, Lawrence could feel himself sinking fast. Should he ask Voss to withdraw so he could offer a different candidate?

Someone knocked on the door.

"Dear?" his wife, Diana, asked from the hallway.

"Yes," he said without rising from where he sat.

"You're late for a meeting, dear. Aren't you well?"

He didn't answer her. *Oh, yes. The meeting . . .*

Diana knocked again.

"Dear? Are you all right? Should I call someone?"

Lawrence got to his feet and took another deep breath before he went to the door and opened it.

"I was just about to go to the meeting. I'm fine."

# # #

Elsewhere in the White house, Trina Watson entered her office for the first time since Donald Cole had been killed.

Her plan now? To pack her things and go home. She'd certainly saved enough to take an extended vacation. She hadn't wasted any money on a social life in nearly four years.

Trina quietly closed the door of the small office, then seated herself behind the desk. She got out a key and unlocked the top right-hand drawer. On top of the neat stack of papers, she found a copy of the e-mail she'd gotten from Cole the day he'd left for Iceland. She read the words several times, wiping away tears.

"Thanks so much for all the research and the help! You'll probably never know just how valuable your work has been to me. Will let you know if I need any more info once I get there! :-D

Don"

Bob Post had asked Trina to stay on at the White House for the time being, but she'd come to the conclusion she just couldn't do it. She couldn't walk these halls knowing she'd never see him smile and wave as he passed by . . . she'd never hear his voice on the phone again . . . never get another message. It was too much.

Don's friend, Josh Thornton, gave Don's eulogy. In it, he'd said many things she now wished to consider. Not just about Don and his sacrifice . . . but about the lives of everyone still alive and able to appreciate what that sacrifice had purchased for them: time. Time to consider who had created them and why. Time to discover, as Don had, their purpose, and fulfill it.

Trina had resolved to take some time and seek the One who created her. In the time she had left, she'd let Him make her life count.

CHAPTER 39

DALLAS SUBURB — Friday, October 26th

Zachary Gordon sat at his desk biting off the last of a ragged nail on his left ring finger while his eyes scanned his morning messages. Three from his supervisor, four junk mails, one from a woman who worked down the hall, three from various other females. Nothing from Michael.

Headlines continued to track across the top of his screen:

"DESPITE COOLING TENSIONS WITH RUSSIA, US EYES POSSIBLE DRAFT OF 18 TO 25 YEAR-OLDS >>>> CUNNINGHAM TO SIGN BILL FOR COLE MEMORIAL >>>> FLU SEASON OPENS WITH RASH OF NEW CASES IN NORTHEAST >>>> CONGRESSIONAL HEARINGS TO CONSIDER ACCELERATION OF FIBERTRONICS FUNDING >>>> Universal Information Group—the global news solution...."

Zac momentarily ignored the news. In addition to sending net mail, he'd tried to call Michael the past two nights and gotten no answer. While not alarmed by this, he did feel somewhat concerned. Concerned and guilty. Could Michael have gone on a drinking binge? Now that Ben was gone, did Mike have sufficient reason to stay sober?

Zac had moved away from Philly mere days after Ben's funeral, fortunate to find a job with a decent salary on such short notice and grateful to escape the twisted mess his life had become. Had it been three weeks already? He'd found an apartment, and begun to resume a familiar tempo.

But his regular distractions no longer sufficed. He owed something to Michael and he knew it. Other than giving money, Zac had done *nothing* to help care for Ben. Michael, on the other hand, had never backed down, never walked away. At first, Zac wanted to tell himself that Michael's "Dad thing" made him stick by Ben, but now he realized this wasn't entirely true. The revelation bothered Zac. It was like a dripping faucet he could hear in the still of the night . . . an encroaching realization that, unlike Michael who endured the sorrow and the worry of caring for their terminal brother, he'd stayed at a distance. Once again, The Great Zachary had become a master illusionist and, in a puff of smoke, disappeared from the stage where the tragic play took place.

Since his arrival in Texas, the nagging drip had gotten consistently louder. He'd almost gotten to the point of admitting his failure, but now he couldn't find Michael.

He chewed on a hangnail. Perhaps, Michael would be home tonight and Zac could begin the process of rectifying his mistake. Now would be a good time. If the military started drafting people, the job pool would substantially widen for those over twenty-five. Zac exhaled loudly. Perhaps he could find a good job for Mike and help him start a new life. A good life.

He looked up at the headlines again and clicked on the FIBERTRONICS story.

> "Congress will continue meetings today aimed at accelerating the approval and funding process for the business consortium producing FIBER-TRONICS. While use of fiber optic cables has been common in the US for decades, the new, patented FIBERTRONICS system will not only carry information, sound, and pictures, it will transport energy to American homes.

> "Corporate CEO and owner of UIG, E.E. Kressman is expected to testify before the House today in favor of the system which entirely powers his NEPTUNE PROJECT, under the Gulf of Mexico. In an interview yesterday, House Speaker Shane Moffit described FIBERTRONICS as 'a nearly miraculous, oil-free, clean energy option which has come at a significant juncture in the search for solutions to Americas' energy problems.'"

Zachary closed the news story hoping America and the Gordons had passed their worst times. Everyone deserved a new beginning.

Yes, he decided, Michael needs a change and I'll help him get it.

CHAPTER 40

PHILADELPHIA — Monday, October 29th

Media people had certain privileges. Privileges and responsibilities. Even though city officials asked people to stay home and not move about, Al Baumgardener had a press chip in the tag on his car. Possibly the chip would allow them to get past police and back to Channel Five studios. Linda Posner sat in the passenger seat and he got behind the wheel. They'd drive back to the station. Her car had been parked there since Saturday night when the area around her apartment had been quarantined.

Last Thursday and Friday, patients had flocked into physicians' offices and ER's with similar symptoms: fever, headache, weakness, and cough. At first, doctors thought it merely signaled the beginning of a bad flu season. No one thought of quarantining these people. Wasn't the flu allowed to run its course every year? It traveled from person to person, place to place without any real boundaries. So did this disease, until early Saturday morning when a significant number of these people began flooding back into the hospitals with alarming new symptoms. A large number of the patients had acute respiratory failure. The tissue under their fingernails and toenails had turned blue.

Within hours, the soft tissues in patients' mouths became swollen and discolored. Early Sunday morning, their tongues started turning black. By Sunday night the death toll reached twenty percent and rising. What did these people have in common? A large number of them either worked or lived in Philly along the Delaware River. Similar cases were being reported on the New Jersey side of the river.

Linda lied to Baumgardener when she said she'd been staying with a friend and hadn't been to her apartment (near the Delaware River) since last Friday. Actually, she'd escaped just moments before quarantine barricades went up. Later, she'd found out she could have been heavily fined and imprisoned for up to a year for ignoring a quarantine order.

Everything had turned out okay, though, hadn't it? She wasn't sick. If she'd have been forced to stay at her apartment, who knew what might have happened to her? Even now, being outside scared her.

"*Real* newspeople keep going and get the story," Al said. If nothing else, a real newsman lived inside of Al Baumgardener. Other things might momentarily occupy him, but news remained his passion. He had no stomach for those who let obstacles keep them from the obligation to keep the public informed.

Shivering in the chilly morning air, Linda wondered what had made her get dressed and go with him. Perhaps his condescending tone. Maybe seeing his determination to go did it for her. She got a fleeting picture of her favorite pink sweater hanging in her closet at home. . . . Who knew when she might actually see it again?

"Al?" she asked, forgetting she'd need to get into the office mode in a few minutes and call him "Baumgardener."

"Yeah?" he responded before hitting the auto dial of his cell phone and putting the earpiece in the ear nearest to her.

She'd discovered he didn't like anyone fiddling with the controls in his car, so she resisted the urge to touch the climate controls. "We need a bit of warm air this morning."

"What?" he asked.

Her face tightened. *If they start making a surgically implanted phone, he'll be first in line,* she thought. Now that he'd "plugged in," she'd need to stick to simple concepts.

"Heater," she said distinctly.

He turned on the heater a split second before he started his first phone conversation.

"Yeah. It's Al Baumgardener. I'm on my way in. What's the latest? Wow. Give me Dave, would ya? . . . Dave, it's Baumgardener. . . . What's your lead? . . . Well, we'll want to tweak that a bit. Get with Sue and see what the two of you can come up with while I'm on my way in. Yeah, I'll see you in about fifteen."

Linda double-checked to be sure the air control setting read "re-circulate," then held on for dear life as Baumgardener sped toward the office, all the while switching from line to line on his phone. He'd been away from the station barely more than six hours, yet he was ready to go at it again. The car suddenly slowed, and Baumgardener swore under his breath.

Linda's pulse jumped when she saw the same thing he did. Huge barricades and flashing lights in the distance. Were they being held in or kept out? Police stood on this side of the barricades, so it probably meant they were keeping people out. She and Al would still be able to leave the area.

"Dave?" he said to the man on the phone. "We have a chopper up this morning? Why not? Well charter one. . . . Try New York. We need traffic reports right now. People have to figure out how to get around the quarantine areas."

What amazed her was how matter-of-fact he sounded about whole thing, as if he'd become the director of a play.

He stopped talking. Perhaps he'd been put on hold.

Linda wanted an update. "Al?" she asked. He didn't respond, so she raised her voice. "*Al?*"

He looked over at her and held up an index finger—the signal for "one more moment."

"No!" he said suddenly. "Are there any confirmations? They airing it?"

His head whipped around as he searched for a way to turn his car. He floored the gas and peeled into a U turn, obviously about to get in a big hurry. "You're kidding. . ."

"*What?*" she asked.

Now he held up the whole hand. In frightened silence, she intently listened to each word he spoke into the phone.

"How much food do we have in the building? Can we still have some brought in? . . . Yeah. Check right now. If so, get Xavier and what's-her-name on it. Then get back to me." He sped down the street in an effort to reach an alternate route as quickly as possible. He glanced at Linda. "We have to get to the station fast."

"Why?"

"They're about to close off the whole city. Wherever we are when it happens might be where we're stuck for a while. As of five minutes ago, they closed the airports and other mass transit terminals. They're just about to shut down all the I's," he said, referring to the interstate highways running through and around Philly. "The bridges are closed, and boat traffic on the Delaware is being stopped. . . . The Office of Disease Control is making a statement in fifteen minutes. It's a full-blown plague."

Baumgardener blazed his way down the road while Linda tried to keep her panic in check, her mind filling with questions. *What does that mean? What will happen to me?*

They zoomed by a billboard with one, simple message: "He is coming soon. Get right or get left."

Linda held onto the armrests of the seat. *Could this actually be true?*

By the time they got to the station, a larger picture had begun to emerge. Thousands of people throughout the region had become infected with an airborne bacteria.

Within a half hour of their arrival at Channel Five, a state of emergency was declared in the states of Pennsylvania, New Jersey, and Delaware. The cities of Philadelphia, Trenton, Willingboro, Camden, Cherry Hill, and Wilmington would be quarantined ground until further notice.

The APIC Bioterrorism Task Force had been dispatched to coordinate with federal, state, and local health departments to control the outbreak of an antibiotic-resistant plague. The bacteria responsible for the disease had possibly been released in aerosol form along the Delaware River in what would now be classified a "bioterrorism event." Any vessel traveling on the Delaware River within the past week would be located and detained. Because the Potomac River connected to the Delaware River via the Delaware Canal, the states of Maryland, Virginia as well as Washington, D.C. would be closed to interstate traffic as a precaution.

CHAPTER 41

PHILADELPHIA — November 9th

More than a week had passed since the city had been placed under quarantine. Seven miles from the studios of Philadelphia's Channel Five, Michael Gordon prepared to leave City Hospital.

A woman in a baggy bio-hazard suit set five separate forms on the counter. "You'll need to sign all of these," she said, her voice muffled by the plastic shield over her face.

He eyed all the folds of the sleeves billowing up her arms. Only duct tape kept the large suit from engulfing her gloved hands. At any other time it would be comical. At this point, however, no one would be laughing.

Michael stood in front of the counter, his clothes reeking of disinfectant. On his face he wore a crisp, new surgical mask, on his hands were surgical gloves. He picked up the pen on the counter and wondered who had touched it last.

Eleven days ago, his sister, Jill, called him from the hospital in the middle of the night saying their parents had some kind of flu thing. In a sleepy fog, he'd barely understood her words. He promised to come in a few hours.

At nine a.m. that day, doctors downgraded his parents' condition to serious. By then, the hospital had gotten so choked with emergency cases that Michael's taxi had to drop him off two blocks away. When he arrived, a nurse informed him that Jill had become ill as well.

Hours later, Michael managed to get a call through increasingly jammed phone lines and speak to brother Zachary, who actually asked for details and seemed quite concerned. As soon as everyone got better, he wanted Michael to come for a visit. Zac would even pay for the ticket.

By the time the true picture began emerging, Michael had been exposed for several hours. They placed him in a quarantine ward with others exposed to the disease. The whole thing seemed like a recurring nightmare. Hadn't he just finished a death watch at a hospital? How could this have happened again?

Holding the pen, his hand hovered over the documents in front of him. Not that his signature mattered. They'd disposed of the bodies of his father, his mother, and his sister days ago. He was just saying he'd been informed, and that he realized he couldn't have their "remains." He signed all the papers and pushed them back toward the woman in the baggy bio suit.

"And these," she said, sliding two more forms across the counter.

One of the documents stated he was being released from the hospital. The other one said he'd been quarantined, tested, and found to be—for the moment—healthy. He signed them and passed them back to her.

She set each of the forms in special boxes, then produced one more. "This is yours. Keep it on your person at all times." She pointed to a door on the other side of the room. Go out that way. Good luck."

He stepped through the door and moved down a corridor. Before the guard behind a glass panel would buzz the door open, Michael had to show him the paper. The door opened and he stepped out into the daylight.

How could this be real? Michael asked himself. Other than suffering with exhaustion, he felt hollow. He couldn't cry. No tears could do this justice.

Why had he survived? Were he and some of the others immune or just not exposed in the necessary way . . . or not exposed at the proper time?

All he knew was that he'd passed a final set of blood tests at the lab and been issued what would soon become as much a necessity in the US as money: a certificate of health. He could go home now. But how would he get home when the city remained under quarantine? He realized this nightmare had just begun.

# # #

The blue surgical mask still bothered Linda Posner. She'd gotten over the disgust of inhaling her own, hot breath over and over again. If only she could properly fit the wire at the top of the mask so it would seal above her nose. Instead, every time she exhaled deeply, a bit of steam appeared on the lenses of her glasses. She'd had to resurrect the ancient eye wear from her desk drawer when her last pair of contacts bit the dust.

Whatever the difficulties with the mask, she'd decided wearing it was much safer than not. If desperate people managed to break into the building or if soldiers came to forcibly evacuate everyone, she had to be ready.

Huddled in her cubicle at Channel Five studios, she nervously watched her computer monitor. What else could she do? She and the others in the building were virtual prisoners. Even if they could leave, who wanted to risk it? They'd lost contact with their last "roving reporter" two days ago.

Linda's eyes darted to the clock in the upper left corner of the screen showing the number of hours since the last new case of the "Philadelphia Plague." *Fifteen hours.* This was welcome news. Thus far, the disease had taken the lives of more than 59,000 people in New York, New Jersey, Pennsylvania, Delaware, and Washington, D.C. alone. Medicines used to treat it were severely depleted, and it would take weeks to manufacture more.

How much longer could she and the others hold out here at the station? Would they draw straws to select the person who would venture out for food when supplies ran out?

She blinked, then began scanning all the available headlines for any news of President Lawrence Cunningham. He hadn't been seen in several days. Was he really in a strategic command post? Why hadn't he appeared on the air to reassure people? She frowned as she thought of Cunningham's last press conference two days ago. *He looked like such a nervous little squirrel, perhaps they decided he shouldn't appear on camera. But, how can he stay silent when even greater dangers may have appeared? The whole world may be coming to an end, and he's holed up someplace! Maybe it's even worse than we know!*

Linda's hand started to cramp before she realized she was holding the stylus for her computer in a clenched fist. She let it go for a moment and shook her hand, then picked it up again, and poised it to select any headline promising new news. One headline appeared to be slightly reworded from the last time it had crawled across her screen. She tapped it, and the article popped open.

"NEW OUTBREAK CONCERN . . . outbreaks of a "potentially deadly" contagion have been reported in Ohio, Indiana, and on Washington state's border with Canada. Although this disease presents symptoms which differ somewhat from those of the Philadelphia Plague, Dr. Emil Grey of the Office of Disease Control (ODC) cautioned the public to take the new quarantines very seriously. Given recent events on the East Coast, large numbers of people near these newly-infected regions have panicked. Roads away from the Midwest and the Northwest have become completely gridlocked. An ODC spokesperson said test results and revised quarantine postings would be made available by 10 p.m., E.S.T."

Linda closed the file. *If it's a NEW plague, what will we do? Then again, we're about out of medicines for this one!* She opened and closed her fists as she fought a wave of fear. *But REAL newspeople keep going . . . . Millions of people are depending on us for potentially life-saving information. I MUST keep going.*

She focused her eyes on her screen and began watching for a story regarding the other significant problem threatening the planet: An out-of-control conflict in the Middle East. Realizing UIG's story hadn't changed in fifteen minutes, Linda rose from her seat and walked to the bank of monitors in the newsroom. Perhaps one of the other networks had more information.

"This is Saul Kline in Tel Aviv for the Banner Network," a man on the screen said in the live broadcast. "I'm here on the rooftop of our hotel, and, you might be able to see and hear some of the melee taking place behind and below me. We received word earlier that the UN, in emergency session, has 'condemned the violence,' and is 'calling for an immediate cease-fire,' but we haven't seen any evidence whatsoever that the fighting is about to stop. In the past few minutes the battle in and above Tel Aviv seems, if anything, to have intensified. Several times in the past hour, the sky has lit up with explosions."

Saul suddenly ducked just before a loud boom. "Did you get that? Are we still on?" he breathlessly asked the cameraman before continuing. "We'll try to keep sending a signal as long as we can. We are told Sharon Peltam in Jerusalem may be able to broadcast again shortly, but we've lost contact with Guy Ramsey on the border of Syria—"

The signal went to static for a few seconds before a woman in Banner's Atlanta studio appeared on the screen, looking shaken. "We've lost our signal with Tel Aviv, ladies and gentlemen." She nervously looked to the left of the camera for a second, then tried to compose herself. "New information is just coming in, and we'll try to get it to you as quickly as possible. . . . Yes," she said, reading the words now appearing on her Teleprompter. "We are now receiving unconfirmed, I repeat unconfirmed reports that nuclear devices have detonated outside Israel's borders. The Associated Press is reporting detonations in Syria, and Reuters is reporting detonations in Iraq. We're trying to re-establish communications in the region."

Back at the Channel Five studio offices, Linda's attention suddenly became drawn to yet another monitor, accidentally placed on the wrong channel. A man with a fluffy, white hairdo and a bright blue suit stood with other men and women on an ornately furnished television stage. His urgent words came through the small speaker just below the monitor.

"I'm telling you brothers and sisters, He is coming soon—it could even be tonight! What so many of us have been telling you could be mere minutes or seconds away. Jesus could be on his way right now. Just look what is happening in America and in Israel. His people aren't going to be here much longer, I can tell you that!"

Linda jumped when Baumgardener, standing behind her, yelled, "Darrel! What are you doing? Monitor eleven! Get this crap off the screen and find XNN!"

The picture on the screen quickly started flashing different satellite channels as Darrel, searched for the correct link. His frustration had just about reached maximum overload. A number of communications satellites had been damaged or downed when the space station blew up. Luckily, E. E. Kressman still had satellites up and running which UIG and affiliates could use, but Darrel hadn't quite mastered all the new signal sequences. Many specialty channels, now off the air, showed up as blue screen or snow on the monitor as he moved past them.

Linda quickly walked to UIG's monitor to catch Sharon Webb's report.

". . . and we are getting confirmation from two sources there have been nuclear detonations in Iraq. We still can't confirm Syria. We also know several Talon II rockets have hit targets in Tel Aviv," Sharon said. "Any updates at your desk, Sue?"

# # #

Many miles away, in Oklahoma, Ricky and Rosa Ruiz sat at their kitchen table while they occasionally turned up a radio to listen to the latest news. The children had been in bed for hours, but for Mr. & Mrs. Ruiz, there would be little sleep this night.

Although Rosa's parents remained safe in Miami, three of Ricky's close friends and one of his half-brothers in New York had fallen ill, and another friend had died. Damaged satellites prevented the use of most cell phones. Jammed land-line phones eventually brought long-distance updates to a halt.

Why had all this happened? Could these possibly be their last hours on earth? Even though the thought of Jesus returning and rescuing them from the world's current peril became more appealing by the moment, Ricky and Rosa knew they could continue living in hard circumstances for years to come. Many Christians had reached this same conclusion in recent times, but had chosen not to debate their more outspoken brethren who had spent millions on the "He is coming soon . . ." campaign.

All Ricky sensed at this point was the Lord warning him to be ready to take Rosa and the children away from the apartment at short notice. Getting prepared for this would help them stay focused now and not panic later.

"Are we agreed then? If we have to leave?" he asked.

She nodded her head. "Yes. Two suitcases, two backpacks. With the babies, that's all we'd be able to carry with us."

The thought they might have to abandon their apartment and most of their belongings hurt enough. Neither of them mentioned the possibility a war might necessitate an expanded draft into the military soon. Might Ricky be called for service? How much could Rosa carry if she had to travel alone with the children? Would she try to get to her parent's home in Miami? Her mother already wanted her to come as soon as possible, but the loss of some navigation satellites meant fewer planes could be in the air at any given time. Reservations for flights were booked for weeks in advance. Rosa only knew she didn't want to be apart from Ricky unless circumstances forced separation.

And then they heard the unthinkable had actually happened. Multiple nuclear devices were being detonated in the Middle East. Both Ricky and Rosa cried and prayed. The loss of life occurring in such a short span couldn't be imagined.

CHAPTER 42

OKLAHOMA — November 10th

Ricky unlocked the car and got in. He looked up to see Rosa standing in the window of their apartment with Angela in her arms, watching him. His daughter blew him a kiss and Rosa slowly waved.

He started the car and pulled out of the parking lot. Where would life go from here? Brandon Atkins, ever at the alert for a business opportunity, had been selling all sorts of specialty foods, which could be used as survival supplies. Should Ricky and Rosa spend what cash they had on these things?

After an intense time of praying they decided to be prepared to evacuate their apartment quickly if they needed to, but not to buy a lot of provisions they couldn't carry. Today, Rosa would identify essential items that could fit in two small suitcases and two backpacks. While other people might feel the leading of the Lord to stock up on supplies, he and Rosa didn't feel impressed to do this. God warned them only to be ready to leave their apartment.

Not giving into the buying frenzy got harder by the moment, given the growing distress, but they renewed their commitment to God, and to each other, not to let fear make their decisions. It got even tougher as they saw common items disappearing from store shelves. Gas prices had nearly doubled overnight. How long could they afford to drive the ranch's car?

Now, as Ricky drove, he prayed for wisdom. After a few minutes, he turned on the radio.

" . . . as possible new cases have been reported outside quarantined areas, martial law has been declared in . . ."

Static began to interrupt the signal. Ricky tapped the tuning knob on the radio and the broadcast continued.

". . . Dr. Grey of the ODC is scheduled to make a live address in two hours and may order an extension of the ban of transportation to and from the affected regions. . . . We'll return to the news after these messages." A silly jingle for a local appliance company came on and Ricky turned the radio down.

Within half a mile, he slowed down. His friend, BJ, had taken him on the rural road up ahead several times. It wasn't necessarily a shortcut to work, but for some reason, Ricky felt he should use this poorly maintained road, which had only one lane in either direction. As he eased onto it, he prayed silently.

After several minutes, he neared the highway again. To his surprise, he didn't see another car on the road. He hadn't expected bumper to bumper traffic, but usually a steady stream of cars and trucks in one's and two's hurried along. This morning, the road was empty. He turned onto it and traveled a mile before he saw police lights in his rear view mirror. His eyes went to the speedometer. He wasn't speeding. Perhaps the chip in the car had malfunctioned again. He pulled over.

When Ricky turned to look, he recognized the same trooper who had stopped him before. He put both of his hands on the steering wheel and waited to be asked to get out of the car.

Instead, the cop walked up to the open window of the car and leaned down.

Ricky looked at him. "Good morning. My chip not broadcasting again?"

"Your chip is fine," he said with an Oklahoma twang. "What I want to know is, what are you doin' on this road?"

"I work at the ranch over there," Ricky said pointing in its general direction.

"I remember. But why did you go around the barricades?"

"What barricades?"

"You didn't see all the flashing lights on top of barricades with the big sign that says, 'ROAD CLOSED?'"

"Oh. Well, I didn't get onto this road by the main road, I came on the little lane back there. But I had no intention of breaking the law. I didn't know you'd closed the road."

The officer remembered Ricky hadn't tried to lie about speeding the last time. "Well, I'll let it go this time, but you'll have to. . ."

They both heard the rumble of large vehicles coming in their direction. The trooper looked back down the road and saw a line of traffic coming toward them.

The sound of engines slowed as a military truck, the first in a long convoy, came to a stop beside them. Two soldiers in khaki fatigues emerged from the cab of the truck and approached them, and the shorter of the two addressed the policeman.

"Good day," he said, in a thick European accent. "This is road to Stilwell, yes?"

The trooper straightened to his full height and eyed them for a moment with his hands on his gun belt. An odd intensity marked his demeanor. "Yes," he finally answered.

"From Stilwell we can take highway fifty-nine to south, yes?

Again, the patrolman hesitated for several moments before answering. "Just keep on this road. There will be signs up ahead."

"Thank you," the soldier said, before turning to his taller companion and speaking to him in what sounded to Ricky like German.

They both nodded and waved before returning to their truck. The patrolman and Ricky watched as the long military convoy passed them. Many soldiers in khaki uniforms filled the trucks. After the last vehicle passed, the trooper turned back to Ricky. The look on his face emanated fear . . . and anger.

"Who are they?" Ricky asked.

The question made the trooper realize he needed to collect himself. His expression changed and he answered, "Oh . . . they've been over in the national park doing some sort of military exercises for a while. Nothin' to be concerned about." The statement sounded uneven and rehearsed.

Ricky realized the camera in the patrol car must be recording their exchange. "Oh," he responded casually. "Should I go back the way I came or what?"

The policeman watched the last of the vehicles disappear over the hill then looked at his watch. "No. You can go on to work now. The road will be officially open in another few minutes anyway."

As Ricky got back out on the road, he knew something had gone terribly wrong. He'd lived in the area for years and not seen foreign troops here before. He'd heard they were being deployed in increasing numbers to help with emergency situations, but why had they come here? Did this mean something bad had happened in Oklahoma?

# # #

Several miles away, Rosa Ruiz looked around the apartment. Normally, by this time in the morning, bright sunlight would be filling the room. An overcast sky, however, continued to muster clouds against the light, making it look like dusk. Despite the frightening events continuing to unfold, people in unaffected areas still needed to go to work or school. Life, they were told, must go on. Ricky left for work, but he'd promised to call her later.

Rosa decided to turn off the television. The constant retelling of events, along with the different doomsday projections, made it hard to avoid a sense of hopelessness. She would occasionally get an update, but she wouldn't feed on it all day.

She sat in her rocking chair, nursing baby Daniel, and letting the soft fragrance of baby powder momentarily sustain the sense everything would be okay. His little fingers stopped fiddling with a button on her shirt as he finally abandoned himself to sleep.

Certain it must be her turn for some attention, little Angela approached the rocking chair, rubbing sleepy eyes. Rosa swiftly located her daughter's favorite rag doll, Molly, wedged between the rungs of the rocker. She swiftly pulled it out as a temporary distraction, whispering, "Here's Molly dolly."

Angela took the doll, then continued her approach to Rosa's lap.

"Just a moment, *mamí*," Rosa said softly, before gently rising from the chair and taking Daniel to his crib. She expertly slipped him onto the little mattress without waking him, then glanced around the tiny room before closing the door. *How many things will he need? What will he sleep on if we leave?*

She closed the door and returned to the living room, where Angela had crawled up onto her mother's rocker, still clutching Molly. The dolly's frazzled, yellow yarn hair had been mostly "loved off." A sad smile came to Rosa's lips. *Molly will definitely have to come with us.*

"Rockin' An'gla?" the little girl asked.

"Sure," Rosa answered before she scooped up the little girl, then sat down to rock with her. How she wanted to squeeze both of her children for dear life and cry. The wonderful/horrible pain of loving children! Having them created a whole new universe where one could be thrilled, hurt, challenged, rewarded, and held for ransom.

She pulled Angela a little closer and continued to rock back and forth, humming the tune to a song she'd learned a few years ago. It was a song of God's faithfulness. How she needed to remind herself of this right now.

Soon Angela, too, succumbed to a nap and slumped back into the crook of her mother's elbow. Rosa loosened her hold on the child and studied the soft, round face with dark eyelashes. Had it been a mistake to have children? Quite a few people thought she and Ricky should have waited longer before jumping into parenthood. When she became pregnant a second time, she endured comments about how responsible people only had one child. Some wondered if people should be bringing babies into this world at all.

She reflected on something Ricky said a few weeks before they wed. They'd seated themselves on a bench in Central Park on a beautiful Fall day, and his eyes were bright with joy as he explained a revelation he'd received.

"I'd given up on marriage and children," he said. "I'd really gotten into the idea that hard things would come, and soon, maybe Jesus would return. How could there be time for anything but God's work? I got into the mindset that the Lord called some people to stay single and figured, given the dark times, this was my call, too. . . . That's why loving you was so awful for me at first, Rosa. I thought you were a distraction I had to resist. And as I saw you get closer to Jesus, it hurt all the worse.

"Even when God let me know it was okay to love you, I resisted. But now I understand. So many people our age and younger have lost all hope of a future. Whether they know the Lord or not, they've grown up with the idea they won't live to be old. They think some big event will happen, and that will be it. The world says, 'Grab all the pleasure you can! Don't make any commitments! This may be your last day!' The church says, 'He may come tonight, so don't mess up!'

"I finally saw how Satan has been using this 'no tomorrow' mentality to rob *everyone!* Although there really will be a final day—a day Jesus *will* come back—the devil has turned it all around. He's made what will be a shining moment *look* like an approaching black hole that's sucking the light out of everything. Instead of the wonderful promise it is to all who will lay hold of it, the devil has turned it into a threat the world resents and the church misuses.

"Even though I thought in terms of using what time I had for God's work, my heart often felt heavy. . . . And most Christians aren't even concerned about the work! They're thinking, 'why go out to the harvest field and possibly get contaminated by the world when Jesus might be here any minute?' They're so afraid of messing up, they've hidden their talents. They figure judgment is due, but that the world *deserves* it. They aren't praying for mercy, because they figure they'll be gone when judgment comes! They aren't trying to change anything. They're just hanging out with each other, letting the world rot, while they stay at a safe distance in an endless 'holding pattern.'

"For unsaved people, it's even sadder! Why work for anything but money, or learn to do anything other than how to get more toys? Why marry, or sacrifice, or plan for a future if you're going to be dead soon?

"Our generation and our whole culture has been saturated with this thinking! Just look what it's done. The world has gotten so sick, Rosa."

Then, Ricky's whole face lit up with the smile that could still make her heart skip. "But in the midst of all this despair the Lord wants to breathe *hope* back into people. He has spoken to me, Rosa. Our lives—yours and mine and our children's lives—are to be lived with hope every day. By our lives, we will show the world there is something to live for! We will be a picture of His love, doing His work every day until we die or until He comes for us."

Now, as Rosa rocked their little Angela, she considered these words afresh. More than any concern she had for herself, she wondered what might happen to the precious children she loved more than her own life. Come to think of it, had she ever come close to grasping how much God loved His children until she'd had her own? Would she give her life for them? In a second! Was there anything she wouldn't do for them? No. Had she ever rejoiced when one of them got hurt? No. Even when Rosa corrected Angela, it reflected a deep desire to see her daughter avoid costlier experiences in the future. She stroked her daughter's cheek and hummed the tune again before slipping a pink ribbon out of the girl's dark, silky hair.

No, Lord, I'm not sorry I had them. When Ricky and I married, we gave ourselves to You, and You chose to give these children to us. They have been Your blessing to us, Your gift, and I remind myself, no matter what, You will never leave us or forsake us. We've done more than mark time. We've lived. Even if there are sorrows ahead, they will seem like a mere blip once we're in heaven. . . . Help me to never forget this, Father.

Rosa leaned forward and kissed her daughter's forehead before putting her to bed.

She felt stronger now, able to do what she needed to do.

She retrieved two medium-sized suitcases from under her bed, then found two backpacks hanging on the back of the closet door. She'd have to try packing them at least once to see what all would fit. The sum of their whole lives might have to lodge in these four containers if they had to leave home suddenly. While it might be possible to come back to the apartment and get other things, Ricky and Rosa wouldn't count on it. They had no idea where or how far they might need to go or when. They only had the sense they needed to be prepared to leave.

What should she pack? What *could* she pack? Two changes of clothes for Ricky and herself. Several changes of underwear. What about extra shoes?

A lot of the space would have to be taken up with baby paraphernalia: Blankets, cloth diapers, liners, plastic pants. While disposable diapers remained handy, they might not be available soon, and they took up a lot of room.

She needed to consider hygiene items like soap, tooth brushes, deodorant, and shampoo. What about eating utensils? Should she take a couple of place settings just in case?

She scanned the apartment and tried to look at each object as if this would be the last time she saw it. Could she live without it? She briefly studied pictures of their wedding, the birth of the babies, and her family in Miami. Without frames, a few photos would take up very little space. . . . But the wall plaques her mother had given her . . . they'd have to stay.

What about the baby books, the bronzed baby shoes, the dress she'd worn for her wedding? With an aching heart, she realized all of these "treasures" would have to be left behind.

She looked at the top of her dresser, at all the bottles of perfumes and cremes. Most of them would have to stay. What about the small basket of jewelry? Most of it was junk, but at the bottom of the basket there were two treasures: The beautiful gold crucifix on a chain her aunt had given her when she turned eighteen, and a cloth bag with a strand of real pearls given to Rosa on her wedding night. She poured the jewelry out of the basket and picked up the crucifix, remembering the first night she met Ricky.

"Does that mean anything to you or is it just an expensive piece of jewelry someone gave you?" he asked. At the time, she couldn't believe he'd dared to ask such a thing! She had always considered herself a Christian. She'd done the classes and the ceremonies, hadn't she? Months after Ricky asked this question, she came to realize she'd spent her whole youth with a skewed mental picture of Jesus. She'd always seen him either hanging helplessly on the cross or, like baby Daniel a few minutes ago, supported in His mother's arms. Neither picture reflected Jesus' current condition.

She looked up from the necklace. *I know you're no longer hanging on the cross, Jesus. And you're not a helpless baby in a manger scene. . . . You're in Heaven right now, full of power, interceding for us . . . giving us strength to go on, to share our faith, to give hope.*

She set the crucifix on her dresser and picked up the cloth bag. The lustrous strand of pearls slid out of it into her hand. Could she part with them? What if the family needed money? Could she sell these two necklaces? She placed the pearls back in the bag and set them on her dresser when she heard someone knocking at her door.

When she opened it, she saw her neighbor, Iris. Rosa had babysat for Iris' daughter, Katie, and Iris' baby boy was only a few months older than Rosa's Daniel.

Recently, the two women had become close friends. For the last six weeks, Iris and two other young mothers had been coming over and talking about spirituality. A week ago, Iris decided to ask Jesus to become the Lord of her life. Four nights ago, Iris' husband did the same.

This morning, however, tears filled the young woman's eyes as she clutched her little boy, Cameron. Rosa opened the door wider and hugged her. "Iris. Come in."

"I'm just so scared," Iris said, before stepping into the apartment. "What if this is the end of the world? People on the television are saying it could be. Even if no one drops bombs on us, we'll all get the radiation—it floats everywhere! What about the plague? Will Jesus come before it happens? He will, won't He?"

Rosa led her into the living room. "Let's sit down," she said calmly. "Scripture says no man knows the day or the hour Jesus will physically return to earth, but the Holy Spirit is here inside us right now, isn't He? What we need to remember is, whether Jesus is coming back tonight or years from now, His Holy Spirit is able to guide us wherever we need to go."

Rosa looked Iris in the eyes before continuing. "Throughout history there have been any number of dark eras—times when people considered it could be the end. . . . But in each of those times, there were people who knew God. They made up their minds to be faithful no matter what. They delivered the faith to the lost and passed it to the next generation. . . . What we need to do is make up our minds, no matter what, we will be faithful. This may not be the end. We need to pray for God's mercy and provision for this day, and be ready to pass our faith to our children."

CHAPTER 43

SOMEWHERE IN VIRGINIA — March 1st

Nearly five months had passed since the horrors began. A clear, sunny day stretched out around him, extending the hope of an early spring. Ages ago it would've been a day to slip outside and enjoy a refreshing walk in the crisp air. But now, who would risk being outside for such a trivial thing? He'd survived the avalanche of disasters which started last October, but the danger was far from over.

Michael Gordon stood among the group of nearly one thousand men, women and children, all wearing surgical masks. At twenty-eight, he fit into the older half of the group. Being a man put him in the minority. Many had perished long before the dawning of this bright, cool day in Virginia.

Poking a finger around the edge of his mask to scratch a two-day-old growth of beard, he studied the enclosure pen he and the others occupied. The bare ground beneath their feet had been dusted with the purple powder troops used to sanitize any area where refugees congregated. Razor-wire fences on all four sides guaranteed the civilians would stay in the long, rectangular space while they continued an agonizing wait. More than a dozen international soldiers, clad in full riot armor, stood inside the pen, guarding the gates at either end of it. In anticipation of entering the outside world, the refugees all faced the ten-foot-high exit gate, secured to the fence with strands of heavy chains.

Did he hear a diesel engine? Michael turned around to search for the source of the sound. His eyes lingered momentarily on the innumerable tents filling the quarantine camp in the distance. Hundreds of refugees scurried out of their canvas hovels and rushed down to the fence on one side of the camp. Obviously, they'd heard it too.

The engine started and began revving. Everyone watched a semi, hauling a trailer, exit the north side of the camp. It turned, then accelerated along the road. Even the soldiers stopped their quiet conversations as it approached.

The driver of the rig shifted to higher gears and the truck sped past the holding pen. Michael couldn't help imagining the cargo inside: Sick people. Some, in fevered delirium, probably envisioned themselves in a favorite place or on a plane to a South Sea island. But those in the first stages of the fever would be wasting the last of their energy, pounding on the walls of the trailer, begging not to be taken away. Michael clenched his teeth and looked away. Within seconds, everyone stopped looking. They had all come to the same conclusion: The people inside that trailer would never complete the exodus to the warmer, safer environs further south.

A directional shift took place as the crowd realigned to face the exit once again. It almost seemed as if a collective mind had formed among the group. Not wanting to touch one another, yet needing to remain within the anonymous safety of a corporate body, they'd become like a school of fish—leaning, walking, and turning almost as a single unit.

They moved two steps closer to the exit gate and Michael kept his place. When the crowd packed in a bit tighter, he slipped his right hand inside his coat to touch the papers in his breast pocket. He kept his other hand on a rolled, wool blanket, tied at either end with a scrap of nylon cord and slung over his shoulder.

Like so many others, he'd been forced to abandon his apartment and his belongings long ago. His travel order had been issued yesterday, when he'd successfully completed another quarantine period and showed no signs of any illness.

If he made it south of the Demarcation Line, he'd find some way to get to the last address he had for his brother Zac, in Texas. They'd had no contact since last year when the disasters made communication impossible.

Bits of a private conversation wafted over the group. Michael and others listened in.

".... must've been right about the southeast corner of the camp," one woman said, "so stay up toward the front. . . . If they run out of room on this train—"

"They could run out of room on the train?" another female voice asked.

"I've heard that it's happened before. If they are moving troops or—"

The two women suddenly became aware of the eerie silence sucking their words further away than they intended.

They stopped speaking before a low buzz ran through the crowd.

Soon, a man began pushing his way forward. People raised their voices in protest as his increasingly insistent movement sent bumping waves through the whole assembly. When he got parallel with Michael, a gloved hand shot out of the group and grabbed the encroacher by the hair.

"Hey, you!" the large woman with the glove shouted, "Get back in your place! You're not getting out of here before us!"

Agreement echoed all around.

The man's eyes locked onto the gate and, with a motivation beyond pain, he began to lean with all his might against the fist holding his hair. More hands projected out from the collective to stop him. Some of the people were angry, others encouraged the man to calm down and return to his proper place. The altercation escalated as he attempted to escape their grasp.

A military officer outside the fences barked orders to the troops guarding the refugees. Two of them prepared to enter the crowd.

As a warning, all of the soldiers began clacking clubs on their ceramic-and-Kevlar chest plates, and shouting, "Make way! Make way!"

The two peacekeepers moved in, forcing the civilians to press back and make a pathway. With the help of several refugees, they wrestled the unruly man to the ground, then secured his hands behind his back with tie-wraps.

Once the prisoner realized they'd be taking him back to the quarantine camp, he put up greater resistance. Another soldier joined the effort. They got him on the ground and tie-wrapped his feet.

Writhing out of their grasp, he shouted, "No! No! You can't do this to me! I have papers! I have to get on the train! I have to get on the train!"

The three uniformed men piled on top of the prisoner while a fourth slapped a long piece of tape across the man's mouth. Wordless screams and amazing physical resistance continued until the crunch of clubs brought limp silence to his body. They dragged him over by the fence and left him there. No one protested. The man had sealed his own fate.

A female voice came over a bullhorn and they all intently listened to her message: "The train will be arriving in fifteen minutes," she said with an accent. "Have your travel orders and your health certificates ready. If you do not have these items, you will not be processed."

Michael thought about the close call he'd had yesterday. International soldiers came to the tents of those who'd completed the quarantine period. A woman introduced to the refugees as an "official observer of the US government" stood with the soldiers. She informed the refugees that, under the most recent Emergency Powers Act, civilians could be compelled to assist any federal officer or any agent designated by the federal government. The civilians were to consider the soldiers "designated agents."

Of course, no one had to tell Michael why they'd come. They'd come to commandeer people—to "compel" them to work in a contaminated area where they didn't wish to go.

The "observer" thing is a new twist, Michael thought at the time. *Does anyone really care if we live or die?*

The soldiers had a list of names. Anyone called would be forced to serve as a laborer on a squad for "as long as deemed necessary." A sergeant called the names, last name first.

In the middle of the roll call, Michael heard, "Mandheim, Adam . . . Michaels, Gordon . . ." and his blood stopped in his veins. He didn't move an inch. He'd already finished one term on a "squad" a month ago. Only four people survived the entire term of service.

Again, the name "Michaels, Gordon," rang out, but Michael stood silently among those who hadn't been called.

"Where is Mr. Gordon Michaels?"

No one responded. Soldiers dispersed to check everyone's papers.

Slowly, they worked their way toward him. He tried to stay calm.

"Papers," a man with a thick accent finally said to him. Michael handed the soldier his health certificate and his newly issued travel card.

"This is you," the soldier said. "Gordon Michaels."

People nearby moved away but kept their eyes on the situation.

"No," he said, matter-of-factly. "Look at the certificate. My name is Michael Gordon."

"Yes. But this is you, no? Someone just made da error wit two first names."

He had to be bold. "How do you know that? Maybe there really is a Gordon Michaels in this camp. All I know is my name is Michael Gordon and if you don't have orders with my name on them, you shouldn't be taking me anywhere. It would be illegal."

For whatever reason, they were in a serious time crunch. The soldiers reluctantly looked at the observer. Without her, the name glitch would have been penciled over, or ignored altogether.

The woman looked at the list, then at Michael's papers. Her gaze met his for a split second. Did he see any humanity there? He couldn't tell. She turned her back to Michael and faced the soldiers while she considered the matter further.

Finally she spoke. "He's right, you know. You only have legal access to those on your list and, technically, his name is not on your list."

As it turned out, they settled for leaving, minus one man— and for the first time in his life, Michael rejoiced at having two first names.

Now, as long as he showed no signs of illness, he'd be allowed to get on a train and escape south. Getting there remained all he wanted to think about . . . not his mom, dad, and Jill lying in a common grave. A fleeting memory of embracing his parents for the first time in years at Ben's funeral tried to work its way forward in his mind, but he shoved it back down. He didn't want to think about *anything* that had happened in the last six months. Not right now. Right now, he wanted to get on a train. For some strange reason, he wanted to live.

Outside the fences, a soldier walked toward the exit gate and the refugees turned around to watch him. He moved past the gate without touching it.

Michael became increasingly aware of an unhappy toddler in the arms of a woman in front of him. Awakened by all the jostling and yelling, the little girl pulled off her mask and looked around in sleepy-eyed confusion. The woman, who had turned around during the altercation, didn't notice her daughter's missing mask. She also seemed oblivious to the fact that she was now facing the wrong way. The little girl's whining grew louder.

"Shhhhhh," the mother said. Despite the glare, she made no effort to shade her eyes or turn her head as she vacantly stared toward the bright, morning sun.

Michael looked down and saw filthy bedroom slippers on the woman's feet. The mob shifted, briefly shoving him against mother and daughter. She didn't notice.

"I want Smudges, Mommy," the little girl whimpered.

Mom stroked the back of the girl's head. "We'll get you another kitty soon."

More soldiers outside moved toward the exit gate and the crowd inched forward. Mom got bumped along in the current of their movement.

"Remain where you are," the voice on the bullhorn said. "Anyone not cooperating is subject to arrest. Stay calm. Your turn will come. Make sure you have your travel orders and your health certificate ready. . . ."

Keeping his hand on his shirt pocket, Michael briefly looked beyond mother and child to watch the soldiers outside the gate.

"Any person," the voice continued, "found with anything which could be used as a weapon will be arrested and detained."

Michael heard the thud of something hitting the ground nearby.

"Where's Daddy?" the little girl whined.

"I don't know," Mother responded in a monotone voice.

The girl began to cry. "I want my Daddy."

"Shhhhhhhhhhh. We'll get you another kitty soon."

Michael bent down, putting his face in the center of the mother's stare before he spoke quietly and firmly. "You need to turn around." He pointed toward the gate. "That way."

A dark-haired woman nearby changed places with her husband so she could help. "Here, dear," she said, taking one of mom's shoulders and gently pulling her around. Mother did a slow turn.

# # #

Twenty feet ahead of Michael, a blond woman held onto the remaining handle of a small, scuffed purse. She'd managed to keep her place in the crowd for what seemed like hours. All of the remaining pockets in her clothing had large holes, forcing her to carry the hideous handbag. In it, she'd placed her papers, two faded photos, and the remnants of her only pair of eyeglasses. The shredded hems of her baggy pants dragged on the ground and her blond hair hung down onto the shoulders of her oversized coat in long, oily strings. So what if she used to be Linda Posner of Channel Five news in Philadelphia? The only thing people wanted to know now was that they'd be going south.

She squinted at a movement near the gate. Was someone unlocking it? Another dizzy spell swept over her and she nearly panicked. Fearing exposure to the fever rumored to be starting in a corner of the quarantine camp, she hadn't risked going to get any food rations since yesterday. Because Linda had no fat reserves, a day without food took a huge toll. She inhaled slowly and tried to ease the immense weight of her coat by grasping the lapels and lifting up. She closed her eyes and willed herself to have the strength to walk through the gate.

In preparation for processing, soldiers inside the pen began to push at the front corners of the crowd, squeezing the first few rows to a mere six people wide. Linda and those around her were forced to take several steps back to accommodate the shift.

Just another hundred feet or so, she continued to tell herself. *There'll be some food outside or on the train. You'll be okay. A good reporter keeps going. Wouldn't Al be proud of you if he could see you now?*

The woman next to Linda suddenly turned to a man behind them. "What did you say?"

The frail, wrinkled man shrunk a little. "I was just talking to myself," he quietly answered.

"No!" the woman insisted, "I heard you calling on 'the Lord'!"

A collective grumble went through the listeners while the offended woman got even louder. "Haven't all of you religious fanatics caused enough trouble? . . . We were all going to be punished while you disappeared with God, eh? Well, what happened?"

The man turned red but didn't reply.

The woman trembled with anger. "I'll tell you what happened! HE DIDN'T SAVE ANYBODY! He's NEVER coming so just shut up!"

Soldiers at the perimeter prepared to move in. One of them spoke through a bullhorn, "Remain calm. People inciting altercations will be kept off the train and incarcerated."

The woman, still shaking with rage, reluctantly turned away from the man. She lowered her voice but continued to rant quietly. "*I'm* not the trouble-maker . . . how dare he say that after all we've been through . . . stupid, stupid idiot . . ."

The officer outside the fence motioned to the troops inside. They allowed a few people in the front to spill into the small, empty space near the gate and began checking papers. The people on Linda's left started pressing forward, but she didn't dare try to slide over into the flow. Blurs of brilliant sunlight reflected off every surface in front of her as she waited. Keeping her eyes open became increasingly difficult. Another wave of dizziness came and, without thinking, she steadied herself by leaning against the man in front of her.

"Hey you!" he warned in a low voice, "Stop that!" To make his point, he backed up a step to shove her away.

Linda lost her balance and started falling. She didn't dare to grab anyone as her view of heads and shoulders turned into streaks of clothing. The streaks of clothing turned into legs, and finally to shoes . . . and then, to purple clouds of dust. Someone stepped on her before darkness momentarily set in.

She awoke with a start. *Get up! Get up!* her mind shouted. Weak and now trampled, she couldn't rise from the ground. *They'll say you're sick, they'll take you back!*

She forced her eyes to stay open and saw a widening circle of light as people moved away from her. Soldiers were already pushing in her direction, shouting, "Make way! Make way!" with the now-familiar *clack clack* of clubs on armor.

A man crouched down beside her. Blue eyes above a masked face moved into her narrow field of focus. He wasn't wearing a uniform.

"Are you all right?" Michael asked.

The left side of her face, her eyelashes, mask, hair, and both her hands were now coated with the sanitizing dust from the ground. Still clutching her purse, she grabbed his coat with her free hand and pleaded for her life. "I'm not sick. I swear it. I just haven't eaten. I fell and people stepped on me. Please . . . don't let them take me back."

Two soldiers continued marching toward her. "Make way! Make way!"

Just before the circle parted to let them in, Michael hauled Linda up off the ground and stood her on her feet. The soldiers, a female and a male, arrived and surveyed the scene.

"She's okay," Michael said. "Someone accidentally knocked her down and she got stepped on." Behind her back, he had a tight grip on her belt so she wouldn't fall again. He shrugged and continued his explanation, "She's shaken up, but she's okay. I'll make sure she gets on the train."

"You want to see if they can do anything for you at the medical tent?" the female soldier asked Linda.

Linda's eyes widened. "No, no. I'll be fine."

"Suit yourself," the uniformed woman responded, then nodded to her companion.

The male soldier turned to address the onlookers, banging his club on his armor to accentuate the warning. "Everyone *stop pushing!* If we have to come back in here, *somebody* is going to join the man by the fence over there. Is that clear?"

All the eyes above the masks gave silent assent by looking down at the ground.

The female soldier faced the couple again. She studied them for a moment. Michael appeared alert but composed. Linda looked frightened, but not ill.

Large links of chain *clunked* as someone pulled them loose from the gate. With the two soldiers in their midst, the crowd remained still.

The female soldier motioned to Michael and Linda. "Both of you. This way." She and her partner turned and began shouting, "Make way! Make way!"

Refugees began making a pathway. After Linda attempted several wobbly steps, Michael picked her up and caught up with the soldiers. When they emerged from the crowd, he set her down again and they proceeded to the exit gate.

The male soldier addressed the couple. "Give me your papers and I'll clear you through right now."

Within a minute, Michael and Linda passed through the gate. The dirt on the ground gave way to gravel, which filled the entire clearing around the tracks. A small shack for soldiers and two tents used by vendors stood fifty yards to their left. Two outhouses were almost the same distance away to their right. Purple-stained pathways in the gravel went both directions. Michael and Linda headed for the vendor's tents, but she needed to stop before they got there, so he helped her to sit down on the gravel.

"You gonna be okay?" he asked, crouching beside her.

Her eyes welled up as she tried to move her limbs. "Yes. I'm just real sore."

"They'll have water in the tents. I'll go get some before they run out." He stood up and started to walk away.

"Wait. What's your name?" she asked

"Michael. Michael Gordon."

"Thank you, Michael," she said, pulling her legs up into a fetal position.

When she did this, he saw the tops of her socks flopping loosely around her stick-like legs. After pausing a moment, he reached into his pocket and pulled out a package of crumbled wafers. "Here."

She stared at the package as if it were a mirage.

His eyebrows went up. "What . . . you're waiting for something fat free?"

She reached out and slowly grasped it. It was real. "Where did you get this?"

He started walking away. "Don't ask. I'll be back in a minute."

Linda quickly bit off the end of the wrapper, picked up the bottom of her mask, then poured the crumbs into her mouth. With such a dry tongue, she could barely swallow, but she couldn't wait for water. She managed to get every tiny morsel out of the package and devour it.

When Michael returned, much of the area around Linda had filled in with fellow passengers. He squatted down and unscrewed the cap before he handed her one of the bottles of water. "These were probably filled with a dirty hose by the vendor's scabby sister, but we won't think about it, right? Your water is supposed to have some glucose in it so it'll give you a boost."

She plugged the bottle in underneath her mask and took a long drink, then stopped to catch her breath.

"Look at you," Michael said, reaching over and brushing the purple dust off her face. "Oh, and the water guy told me we should take these off whenever we can." He grasped the band holding her mask on and pulled it loose. Several people nearby looked on in amazement.

For a moment, he seemed larger than life, so she let him take off her mask and watched him remove his own. Within seconds, however, the magnitude of it sunk in. She'd had a mask on her face for months, moving it to the side only to eat or drink. She quickly covered the exposed skin on her face with her hand.

"It's okay," Michael told her. "Everyone out here is supposed to have a health certificate, aren't they? If you want, you can put it back on." He placed her mask on one of her knees, and she gazed at it for a moment. They probably were safer out here than anywhere else, but the cool air on her exposed skin and in her nostrils felt so scary, the urge to put the mask back on was almost overwhelming.

When she finally took her hand away from her face long enough to get another swallow of water, Michael chuckled and said, "Oh boy . . . the water guy was right. We've all got dark, chapped skin—except where our masks covered our noses and mouths. When we get south, it'll make us easy to spot. Even though we're clean, people are a bit paranoid about somebody fresh out of a quarantine camp. The water man says they call us 'chimps,' because of the monkey look we've all got." He smiled and pointed to the light oval of skin around his own nose and mouth.

Despite his handsome features, she realized he did have a distinct, chimp-like appearance. It made her smile, too. She decided that, perhaps, she could leave the mask off for a minute or two. She took her hand away from her face and slowly inhaled.

His smile disappeared when recognition set in. "What's your name?" he asked.

"Linda. Linda Posner."

He looked away and, after a few seconds of chilled silence, he spoke again. "Drink up, Linda."

Did he know her? Possibly he'd seen her on the news, but why would this make him unhappy with her? Surely, they'd never met. Something did seem familiar, though. What could it be? She tried to concentrate. *Perhaps it's his name.* She took another sip before it came to her.

"Gordon. Michael Gordon!" she blurted out. People turned to look at them and she lowered her voice. "I know who you are. You're that guy's brother."

He took another long pull of his water before putting the lid back on the bottle shoving it halfway into the gravel between them. "Yeah. And I remember you, too."

Memories flashed through her brain. She saw herself standing with the swarm of reporters outside the hospital, shouting questions at Michael about his brother. Her mind replayed the voice-mail she left on Michael's phone before he blocked access to the line.

She took a breath before trying to explain. "You must understand. It was a big story. It was an opportunity for me to be seen by national . . . media," her voice trailed off.

He sucked his teeth in disgust and shook his head.

She straightened up and pushed her hair behind her ears. "People always want to blame us. But the same people who want their own privacy, relish every dirty detail they can get about others. It's the *public* who drives the media to such extremes."

He started to get up, but before he could stand, Linda grabbed his sleeve. When he turned to look at her, his eyes flashed with anger. She quickly let go of his arm.

"Please don't hate me," she said in a desperate whisper. "I'm so sorry. If I could go back and change things . . ."

His eyes swept over her frail form once again and the expression on his face softened somewhat. He tucked his mask in his pocket and peered into the distance for a few moments before he spoke again. "Let's forget what was back there. That life has passed away."

They heard a train in the distance.

"Drink your water," he said, "and we'll see if we can get on the train."

CHAPTER 44

Ricky came back to the clearing with a brilliant smile. "Look what I found!" he said. He held out his hands and showed everyone five small eggs nestled between them.

A round of "Ohhhhhhhhhhhs," followed as twenty-two people all pressed closer to see the small, oval treasures.

Rosa clapped her hands with delight, then produced five bouillon cubes in a small plastic bag. She'd slipped them into her pocket days ago when soldiers forced them off the ranch.

"Egg drop soup!" she said.

"Enormous idea!" spouted one of the teens while the others applauded.

Ricky handed the eggs over to Jack, then turned to Jason and gave him a playful sock on the arm. "See that? Didn't we pray for some more food?"

The young man nodded and smiled before asking, "What's egg drop soup?"

"Let's make a fire and you'll soon see!" Jack declared.

They'd selected this old picnic area as a spot to camp for the night, then discovered it had a functional, hand-powered water pump—an unexpected bonus. Well water might be safer than water in nearby lakes and rivers.

Not far from the pump, some unknown traveler's push-cart had suffered a broken axle. The owner had been forced to abandon the cart, still loaded with most of its contents. Other travelers had ransacked it in search of food or valuables. Dishes and other household objects remained where they'd been flung during repeated rummaging.

At first, when Ricky and the others came upon the strewn debris, everyone stood in silence for a few moments, as if honoring the dead. Scattered remnants of an existence they'd all had to leave behind littered the ground around them, reminders of a life filled with transportation, food, and entertainment . . . a life with hot water, indoor plumbing, clocks, and telephones. While the group probably wouldn't keep any of these items, they could make use of them for the night.

Several in the group had hoped to make better time. Despite their wishes, traveling with small children and people still weak from a recent fever made for a slow journey. The group barely eked out ten miles a day. Those who wanted to go faster didn't dare break away from the assembly. People walking alone or in smaller clusters became easy targets for armed robbers. It was better to travel slower and arrive alive at their intended destination. Tomorrow afternoon they'd finally get to a large military encampment. As long as the promised food and supplies were there, all would be well.

Men and women collected dishes and took them to the pump to rinse them off. Ricky sent Jason and other young men into the surrounding trees to find dead wood for a fire. Several adults in the group warned them to look out for snakes. Rosa found a cooking pot, much larger than any of the small ones they carried, and showed it to Jack. He did a little jig over it.

Two days ago, soldiers had forced them from Henderson's Ranch, taken them to a road, and dropped them off with orders to head south. Troops sporadically patrolled the roads, and anyone caught traveling the "wrong" direction—north—could be arrested for "non-cooperation."

The smaller children had eaten the last remnants of their military rations at midday. The group's destination, an encampment near Interstate 40, was still a day's walk ahead of them. Tonight, however, they'd all have some soup.

Rosa looked up as Jason and other young men returned to the camp, reporting they'd found the "mother lode" of firewood (a dead tree) nearby. She watched Jason disappear back into the woods and marveled, once again, at the change in him. Hostile, violent, and solitary in the past, he was now animated and eager. Just before the disasters started, he'd made a commitment to Christ, and despite the hardships they'd all suffered, he'd blossomed.

Soon the large pot, filled with water, sat over a crackling fire. Most of the people rested or took the time to wash off dust from the day's travel, while the water heated. Rosa knew she'd have trouble keeping Angela away from the flames. "Too hot!" she reminded the little girl before a wet and hungry baby Daniel started to cry.

"I'll watch her for a few minutes," a teenager named Traci offered. She bent down and spoke to Angela. "Hey girl, why don't you and Molly dolly come with Aunt Traci and Katie?"

After being carried most of the day, Angela needed to spend some energy. She grabbed her dolly and happily ran to Traci.

Once freed from watching her daughter, Rosa quickly spread a small blanket on newly sprouting grass at her feet. She slipped Daniel out of the sling she used to carry him, and set him on the blanket. The cold water on the washcloth she used to clean him made his little jaw quiver as he cried.

"Oh, I'm sorry you're so cold, little one," Rosa offered in a comforting voice. You'll be warm again in a moment. I promise."

She quickly dressed him, picked him up, and shook out the blanket. When she spotted several large, brown stones about fifteen feet away, she sat on one, facing the trees nearby. She draped the blanket over her shoulder and nursed Daniel, speaking softly to him while she rocked back and forth.

A year ago, she would have delighted in spending the day outdoors with such pretty scenery. Surrounded by rolling hills, large trees just starting to bud, and sparkling water gliding past scenic rock bluffs, the family would have had a lovely picnic.

Her eyes focused on some distant spot. *Yes, with chicken. And rice with black beans. Sticky rice, just the way Ricky likes it. Oh yes, and—*

Rosa quickly shook her head, as if the chicken and rice thoughts would fly out one of her ears, and be gone.

Of course, the alternative to her flight of imagination had little appeal. In the real world, her body ached all over and she didn't even want to *think* about washing diapers and washcloths in cold water. Still, it would need to be done before she could sleep tonight. The dirty clothes they'd worn for three days could wait until they had a day when they didn't have to travel. Maybe after dinner she and Iris could heat some water in that large pot and wash diapers. What would happen when the soap ran out? She remembered her great-aunt telling her how "in the old days" people tried to potty train kids not even a year old. No wonder!

Rosa turned to see Jack holding her bouillon cubes and felt a twinge of regret. She'd gotten so excited when she saw the eggs Ricky found, she'd let herself get carried away. Those cubes had been her stash, a final hedge against starvation. Shouldn't she at least have waited until tomorrow to offer them? *They're Yours now, Lord*, Rosa thought. *You provided when we had so little. I guess this is the next step . . . trusting You when there's nothing left. Please help us.*

Ricky came up behind her and squatted down so he could put his chin on her shoulder. "Okay?" he asked softly.

She would cry if she attempted to speak, so she just nodded.

He lingered a moment, then picked up the bag with the wet diapers in it. I'll go wash these out. Do we have any more soap?"

"Yes. Just a bit. In the top of my bag." She swiveled around on the rock so she could look her husband in the eye. She tried to give him her best "I love you" look.

He gave her a tired smile and kissed her on the end of the nose before departing with the diapers and the soap. She finished feeding Daniel, who then wanted to climb down and try his best to walk unassisted.

Iris, carrying her own son, Cameron, came over and handed Rosa a cup of heated water to drink. Spotting a rock near Rosa, she perched on it before letting Cameron squirm loose and toddle over to Daniel. Rosa let the warm cup soothe aching hands, then brought it close to her chin, allowing the rising vapor to waft up over her dry skin. Every cell in her face whispered, "thank you." Then, the fragrance of something wonderful filled her nostrils.

"Lemon!" she said with delight.

Iris smiled. "You inspired me with the bouillon cubes. A soldier gave me the lemon last week, and I've been hoarding it since then. When I saw you pull out those cubes, I thought, 'How could I be so selfish?' What would've happened to Jack and the children and me if you and Ricky hadn't taken us with you to the ranch that day? What if Mr. Henderson hadn't let us stay? And later, when the soldiers took all of the guys to repair the railroad while it was so cold. I don't know how I could have survived without being able to pray with you every day."

Rosa sighed and closed her eyes for a moment. What would any of them have done if Mr. Henderson hadn't been so generous? When he died of a stroke two weeks ago, they'd been torn between sorrow at losing such a precious friend, and joy that he could actually embrace Jesus and rest from his labors. Rosa set the cup down and reached over for Iris' hand before looking up.

"Thank You, Lord. We've had all we need. Thank You for companionship, and eggs, and lemons . . . and water and bouillon, and even dry wood for a fire."

Jack, the official cook for the group, began the soup-making activities, and the air swelled with the delicious odor of the bouillon. Even if it ended up being mostly water, they'd savor every drop. Hopefully, everyone would get a whole cup of it.

Twilight lingered over them as Jack stirred the last bit of egg into the broth. He looked up at his audience then stepped back from the cooking pot. Without anyone being told to do so, they all held hands and bowed their heads.

"Father," Ricky said, "We acknowledge that all good things come from You. We thank You for so much today. It was another good day to walk. You kept those thunderstorms west of us. . . . No one tried to harm us or steal from us. You led us to good water and gave us this food. We boast before heaven that God has provided for us. You've been a good Dad. Thanks for the hot meal, Father. Sanctify it for our bodies to use. Amen."

When they opened their eyes, they realized visitors had arrived and were watching them. Twenty men, women and children stood with a large, brown dog where the path cut through the trees to the road.

Ricky looked at the balding man in the front of the group for a moment, then said, "Your name is David, isn't it? You brought donations to Henderson's Ranch before didn't you?"

"Yes, yes. I remember you, too" the man said, visibly relieved. He grasped the hand of a woman in his group. "This is my wife, Alyssa, and these," he said, nodding to three boys nearby, "are our children, Austin, Kyle, and Eric." He continued, calling out the first names of people in his group. Finally, he pointed to a woman with two boys, ". . . and these people just joined us this afternoon. . . . I hate to admit that I've forgotten your names. Perhaps you can introduce yourselves?"

"My name is Ana," the woman said, "and these are my nephews, Doug and Jesse. And this," she said rubbing the dog's head, "is a new friend. He found us a couple of days ago and has watched out for us ever since. The boys decided to name him Tracker. He's a good watch dog, and he behaves."

As if to prove her point, Tracker sat down.

Once they had all exchanged introductions, David took another step forward. "We'd already decided to stop for the night, when we saw your fire through the trees."

No one knew what else to say for a few seconds. Merely standing there together in such a large group could get them into trouble. The new government had banned any civilian-led gatherings in excess of twenty-five people.

A log in the fire popped and sent sparks flying before Ricky looked around at the members of his own group, then stepped back to the cooking pot. "We just finished thanking the Lord for food. He has given us a feast tonight—including dishes. He must have known you'd be coming. Would you like to join us?"

David untwisted the knot on top of his bundle with shaking hands. "Could we? We still have a bit of cornbread here, don't we Alyssa?"

The adults backed up and let the younger children get soup and a hunk of the hard, crumbling cornbread, first. Next, the teens and the women got food. Last, all the men stood in line with cups. Jack kept scooping out soup until everyone had some, then looked down into the pot. It wasn't even half empty, and two inches of corn bread remained.

Everyone ate, too hungry to talk and eat at the same time, the warm liquid soothing their souls and feeding their bodies. They all had seconds, and thirds . . . yet more soup remained in the pot. When all had eaten their fill, Ricky and Jack looked in the pot again. A couple of cups of soup remained in the bottom. Ricky looked up and smiled, then spoke to all the others gathered at the fire.

"Let everyone bear witness. Once again, God has fed us."

Many said "Yes," or, "This is so."

"Thank You, Jesus!" one little girl said loudly, with several adults adding "Amen!"

Ricky noticed one of the new boys standing near the trees with his dog, trying to hide the fact that he was letting it lick his cup.

"It's okay," Ricky said, approaching the pair, then bending down to pet the animal. "He can have some. He's kept a good watch on you guys. That's worth some wages isn't it?"

He sent the boy to get some more soup for the dog.

Everyone sat for a few minutes, letting their meal settle. The boy's aunt raised her hand as if she were in a class, waiting to be called before speaking.

Ricky smiled and spoke to her. "Ana is it?"

"Yes."

"You wanted to say something, Ana?"

"My husband, and his brother," she put her arms around the boys at her side, "their dad, got taken by soldiers to work on a squad months ago, and we don't know what happened to them." Her eyes welled up. "Then their mama died of pneumonia a few weeks ago. . . . The Army made us go, and it's been hard.

"Day before yesterday, another group put us out so they wouldn't have to give us our share of the food rations the Army gave them," she said, tears now streaming down her cheeks. "We're so grateful David and the others let us travel with them and shared some food with us. They've been kind to us all afternoon. And now you let us eat the soup." She covered her face with her hands and spoke with difficulty. "We've never been church goers, but God must have taken pity on us today."

Just about everyone started to cry. Ricky looked at Rosa before they both moved to sit in front of the woman and her nephews.

"You're right, the Lord helped you today," Ricky said. "All David and the rest of us have done is show you His goodness. The Lord invites everyone to 'taste and see' that He is good. And tonight, He worked a miracle by feeding us all. The God of the whole earth has taken this opportunity to show you how much He loves you, Ana. He wants to be your Father. Now that you've tasted and seen, would you like to accept His offer?"

"Yes, I would," she responded, wiping her face.

Rosa offered Ana her hand.

Ricky asked, "Anybody else?"

Both of Ana's nephews and another man from David's group said, "yes."

"I came to a place years ago," Ricky told them, "when I finally admitted to myself that I could never bridge the gap between myself and God. I could never make myself good enough for God." He looked at Rosa. "My wife had to come to the same conclusion."

Rosa squeezed Ana's hand. "It's true. Compared to Ricky's life—mine was almost spotless. While I would admit to a few flaws, I thought I was nearly perfect . . ." she blushed and looked down. "Nearly. But one day, I realized that 'nearly perfect' was still not perfect." She again met the gaze of those in front of her. "How could I stand before God? In my heart I, too, had to admit I'd fallen short."

Ricky spoke quietly. "Do you know in your heart that you've fallen short? Do you feel as if you're separated from God?"

They nodded.

"Then you've taken the first step. Do you realize there's nothing you can do to fix the problem?"

"Yes," Ana said, wiping her face again.

The others agreed as well.

"Good," Ricky said. "Then you're ready to be adopted. A light has come on in your heart to show you where you stand. That same light has started shining on the way of escape. The way is to believe in Jesus—the only person who was ever born God's son. He lived a perfect life here on this planet and, when He was just a little older than me, He allowed Himself to be executed for offenses He never committed. The whole reason he came to Earth was to pay the penalty for our flaws, our imperfections. He came to die for our sins—to open the way back to God."

When Ricky paused, they could hear the snapping wood in the flames and crickets in the surrounding darkness. The warmth of the campfire seemed to grow more intense, pushing back the chill in the night air.

"After three days in a grave, Jesus came back to life and will never die again. He's with the Father now, watching us. Even now, all of heaven is listening, waiting for your decision. You see, it's still your decision. You're free to believe whether or not I've told you the truth. You can say you don't believe it and God will still love you, He will still be reaching out for you, wanting you to experience more of His great mercy, His deep friendship, His infinite love. He'll still want you to be His daughter, His sons."

"I'm not saying that if you choose to believe what I've said, everything will go well for you. As long as you're here on this earth, you will have sorrows and hardships. But if you choose to accept Jesus as The Way to the Father, you will have a Friend who will *never* leave you or forsake you. No matter what you face tomorrow, God's Spirit will have come to live right inside you. He will guide you, if you let Him. And when you pass from this earth, you will live forever with the Lord in Heaven. Do you want this?"

They nodded.

"Then you need to say it to the Lord. Repeat this prayer after me." Ricky bowed his head and said, "Jesus . . . I believe You came into the world to save me. . . . You died and rose again . . . so I could be adopted by Father God, and live with You in Heaven forever. . . . I invite You into every part of my being, every part of my life. . . . I want You to be my Lord, my Savior. . . . I turn away from my old life . . . and offer the rest of my days to You. Teach me Your ways, Lord. Help me to be Your witness for the rest of my life. Amen."

Ricky briefly placed a hand on each of those who prayed, then said. "Father, I bless each of these. I bless my new brothers and my new sister. Grant them strength now to fulfill all Your good plans for them. In Jesus' mighty name, Amen."

Although many of the men and women had been strangers just hours ago, they now felt kinship with one another. Ricky, Rosa, Jason and many others spent a while encouraging the new family members.

Eventually, people collected the dishes and rinsed them in the cooking-pot-turned-sink. After that, the adults and oldest teens gathered in a circle around the fire. Some sat on the ground, others sat on stones. While the children moved around them, playing games, they would swap the latest "news."

With the breakdown of electronic communications, nearly all information traveled by word of mouth. The problem came in deciding what to believe. Accepting and repeating every story could lead people to a greater sense of doom or panic. Ricky and Rosa had decided to rely less on unproven "stories," and encouraged others to listen for eyewitness accounts.

They'd all heard stories about chemical and biological contamination back east and to the north. Casualties from these disasters might number in the millions. One tale said President Lawrence Cunningham had gone insane and locked himself in a closet during the worst of it. This, people said, was what triggered his removal from office.

Some had friends and relatives who froze to death when oil dependent utilities failed. The number of people being forced to retreat from the contamination and the cold was in the tens of millions. Large numbers of international troops had flooded the country. Why were they here? Their official task was to facilitate evacuations. Many believed they were also plundering whole cities after they forced civilians to leave.

One woman brought up the "resistance movement" and a lively discussion followed.

Rumors of armed conflicts abounded. Unwilling to leave their homes and all they had, some people flatly refused to move south. In some areas, people said, defecting US troops had joined civilians to fight against UN controlled forces.

David, the man who had brought the cornbread, spoke. "All I know is that foreign soldiers came to the house to confiscate our weapons early on. By the time they told us to leave, the phones were down, the power was off, we had no gas for the cars, and we had no food. We didn't have much choice. I did overhear two soldiers talking about a big standoff in Tulsa, though."

"The way I figure it," a man in a blue shirt by the name of Cody said, "rich people made deals to avoid walking south, and criminals knew how to hide and fight. It's the poor and the middle-class who've been easiest to rout out."

How many more people would still pass down the hundreds of designated pathways south? Only one thing seemed clear: Any who managed to delay their exodus would have to walk farther. By all accounts, oil supplies continued to dwindle, so transportation would diminish as well.

"What I wonder," David said, "is where they're going to house all these millions and millions of people. Where are they going to put us all?"

"Before troops took my short-wave radio" a blond woman by the name of Laura said, "I heard they were forcing whole families to live in one bedroom of a house or apartment down south. The people who own homes have to share. And some refugees are forced to sleep on the floors of government buildings or in temporary huts, or tents."

"Right now, I'd be grateful for a place with a covering over the top of it and someplace to shower," an older man from David's original group said. "Amazing how our priorities have changed, isn't it?"

Most nodded in silent agreement.

"Lord knows," David said, "none of us really appreciated how much we had before. And, how much of it did we really need, anyway?"

Silence encroached on the group.

Jason and others decided to take torches and fetch more firewood. Meanwhile, the younger children wanted some attention. Couldn't everyone stop and play for a few minutes before bedtime?

"How about a game?," David asked loudly.

"Yes!" they responded with hopping and clapping.

"Okay, a game it is," he said. "I want all you kids to look around at the stuff people threw on the ground here. I want to see which one of you can find the most useless item. If you wander outside the light of the fire, you lose. You have to stay where we can see you to win . . . okay? You have until," he said, putting a stick across the stones which had held the cooking pot, "this stick falls into the fire."

At first, only the younger kids wanted to play, but shortly, the teenagers became interested as well. After several minutes, the stick fell into the fire and David declared the judging must begin. Adults would vote for the most useless object.

The younger children went first, and the grown-ups showed amusement at the found objects: bent spoons, a fancy feather duster, a cup with no handle, broken plates, and a high-heeled shoe.

Some of the teenagers, however, turned the game into a real "hoot." They *demonstrated* the difficulty of using their items.

Traci, a fourteen year old, produced an electric curling iron, wound it around a lock of her hair then looked shocked when it didn't work.

"Oh!" she exclaimed, grabbing the plug at the end of the cord. "No wonder!" She moved from rock to tree to stone looking for a place to plug it in.

Everyone chuckled and applauded. With each performance, the applause and laughter increased. Jason, with a golf club, wondered when he'd ever find the green. Mariah had a cell phone and wanted to order a pizza. Bryce perused a book on staying slim, Alexandria filled an ice cube tray, Joe stuffed a "rush mail" envelope with several CD's and wanted to mail them. A young man by the name of Ken decorated a rock with Christmas lights. Tim pretended to be slicked up for a date, needing only to find his front door, so he could lock it with a key.

But Carlos won the game. "Woo hoo!" he shouted when his turn came. "Some idiot left his credit card here! It's mine now, baby!" The audience roared with laughter, and the dog barked while Carlos jumped around like a football player who'd just made a touchdown. "I'm outta here! . . . I'll get me some cool clothes . . . and a set of wheels!" He stopped and looked around, scratching his head. "Any set of wheels. And then I'll go to the nearest gas station . . . oh . . . doink."

The humor brought healing to weary travelers. The losses they'd encountered during the past months had become incalculable. In the midst of war, contagion, and cold, the life they knew had vanished. The "useless item" game had provided a window where they could view some of the losses they'd endured, and laugh instead of cry.

For most of them, this evening had been the first time they'd had full stomachs or laughed in a while. All were witnesses to the fact that God had fed them and made their hearts glad out in the middle of nowhere. As they prepared to spend the night, each felt a renewed sense of hope. Perhaps tomorrow would be the beginning of a turn for the better.

Less than a day's journey away lay their destination: a military encampment. After they passed through the quarantine process, they'd be scheduled for transport into Texas by truck, train, or bus. Once they reached Texas, they'd have the possibility of relocating elsewhere in the south. Each person could resume a life which, while difficult, would be far better than what they'd endured this past winter.

Ricky prepared what he called "the nest" for Rosa and the children. He found a place where the ground seemed relatively smooth and unfolded a sheet of plastic to put there. The old tarp had a couple of small holes, but would keep a lot of the dampness from the ground out of their bedding.

Next, Ricky rolled out a blanket on top of the plastic. Lastly, he placed the two backpacks at one end for pillows and the two small suitcases on either side near the head of the bed so the children wouldn't roll off the blanket. Once Rosa and the babies settled in the nest, he put two more blankets on top of them, then kissed each one.

Angela had already fallen asleep, but baby Daniel expressed his displeasure until the warmth of being under the covers and his mother's soft singing finally relaxed him. As Rosa lay there, snuggled up to her babies, she looked up at the stars and started thinking about her parents. Were they able to look up and see these same stars? Were they okay? It had been months since she'd been able to communicate with them.

Just think of how people lived hundreds of years ago, she reminded herself. *They'd lose track of each other for years sometimes! What's a few months compared with that? Perhaps when we get south, we'll be able to find some way to contact them.*

She searched the night sky. *Lord, You fed all of us here tonight, just like in the Bible! You have made a way in the wilderness for us. A few years ago, would I have believed You still did such things? We have tasted and seen, once again, that You are good.*

She could hear people softly talking while others snored. The dog, Tracker, rested by his little family.

Rosa closed her eyes. *You are a good Daddy. I love you.*

Not far away, Ricky and Jason sat together on the ground, with their backs to the camp. They would take the first watch along with four others, stoking several small fires around the camp's perimeter to take some of the chill out of the night air. They would also keep an eye out for any danger.

"You think we'll really get there tomorrow?" Jason asked.

"Oh yeah," Ricky answered. "Maybe by the middle of the afternoon."

CHAPTER 45

SOMEWHERE IN NORTH CAROLINA — March 1st

She heard the soldiers coming but couldn't get up. Boots and riot gear sounded the approach of certain doom. *Clack clack, clack clack!*

People called out "Make way! Make way!" yet she remained frozen to the ground.

Linda opened her eyes. Startled, she jerked and leaned forward, gulping for air.

"Hey, welcome back," a man said.

She quickly turned to look at the person speaking to her.

"Bad dream?" Michael asked.

She felt for her mask, then exhaled and leaned back next to him. Everything around them reflected the strange, green glow of chemical lanterns on either side the railroad car. The clacking sound she'd heard in her dream came from the metal wheels along the rails.

After being given tubes of rancid tasting "protein paste" to eat, and waiting for hours, they'd been jammed into this empty railroad car like cattle. Once they boarded, they endured more waiting before the train started moving. She'd been so grateful Michael had found a place in a back corner where they could sit down on the floor and have something to lean against. Exhausted, she must have fallen asleep after the train started moving. The crick in her neck told her she must have slumped over and stayed in an awkward position for quite some time. Even now, the rocking of the train made her head bob back and forth painfully. She extended her arms to get her hands out of her coat sleeves and rubbed her neck while she rotated her head around.

She tried to stretch and winced. "Where are we?"

"Probably North Carolina. There's no way to tell, really. Even if they opened the door, it's dark out now. Besides, I wouldn't know one state from another. They might stop soon, though, and let us get off for a few minutes. Think you can at least hobble around? We'll have to take turns saving this spot or we'll lose it."

She pulled her knees up to her chest and tried to push down on her feet. "I hurt a lot, but I think I can get around."

A man who'd been scrunched up on the floor next to her legs now expanded into the space she'd left.

Michael looked at her. "See what I mean?"

They sat in silence while the train continued down the tracks a few more miles.

Once she'd fully awakened, she looked down at herself and realized what a horrible wreck she must look. "I can't believe how long I've worn this," she said, opening her coat to expand it around her legs. "And I can't believe how bad all of us smell. You'd think they'd open the door a crack."

"It's too cold," he said.

She looked into his blue eyes. In the camp, fear had kept her mostly to herself. Now free and feeling a little better, she realized how much she'd missed simple human companionship.

"What do you think it will be like when we get south?" she asked. "You think it will be anything at all like life used to be before?"

He shrugged. "I doubt it. How could things ever be like before? They'll be better than what we left, though. I've heard, they only had a few minor outbreaks in the beginning, so they probably won't have everything quarantined. People are living indoors, but it'll still be dark and cold at night. I heard electricity's only used for hospitals, factories, pumping water— things like that. The oil not used for electricity goes to fuel things like this train and military vehicles. Nobody's going to be allowed to use cars anymore, at least not ones that need gas."

"Didn't you hear about the new fibertronic technology?" she asked. "I heard it works and we all can have it."

Michael *had* heard the stories about the fiber optic threads, capable of carrying not just information or voices, but energy as well. He remained skeptical, however, about Fibertronics having any immediate impact on life. "It may work . . . but who's set up for it? Everything in this country runs on electricity, and the fibers don't carry electricity. Even if the technology works, it'll probably be a long while before any of us get to use it. Don't get your expectations up."

He'd been staring at the ceiling, but when he glanced down at her again, he realized she looked like a fragile, porcelain doll dressed in some homeless person's clothes. She appeared too frail and frightened for his pessimistic views. "I don't know what it will be like," he said in a softer tone, "but, hopefully, it'll all work out in time."

While she'd been sleeping, other people in the car shared the latest news: Something had gone wrong with genetically altered seeds and a large part of the winter wheat crop in the US had failed. . . . Perhaps this was just a crazy rumor. How could anybody know for sure? Why tell Linda? If it were true, everyone would know soon enough.

A large man wearing a dirty eye patch scooted closer to them and appeared to be chewing something. A few moments later, another man jumped up and shouted, "That's mine! That's my food! Stop, don't eat it!"

He leaped on the man with the patch and they started grappling with one another. They rolled over the top of the man lying by Linda's feet. The accuser hit his head on the side of the railroad car. There were no soldiers riding in the car, and no one tried to separate the combatants. All of them had witnessed, or experienced, this same scenario many times. Unless it involved one's own personal property, a smart person stayed out of such brawls. The struggle continued for a few more moments before the accuser, a much smaller man, quit the struggle.

The man with the patch moved to another part of the car, making all sorts of grunting noises. Those nearby quickly yielded and let him have it for himself, while a few people near the loser tried unsuccessfully to comfort him.

"But that was my food!" he kept saying.

Linda started shivering uncontrollably, so Michael opened his blanket and bid her to move closer. Cold and scared, she scooted closer to him, and he put his arm around her.

After she'd calmed down, she spoke again and asked what would become a common question in the future. "What made you want to live?"

He closed his eyes. "I don't know. I got dragged off for 'temporary service' in December. I didn't care at first. I didn't care if I died. They made us do food drop-offs in contaminated places. Later, they made us cart frozen bodies to pick-up points. It was so cold, it seemed like it would never end. Most of the people on my squad died–but not because they got contaminated. They froze to death. . . . Then one day it was over. They said I was done. If I could pass isolation for six days, they'd let me into a quarantine camp, and then I'd be free.

"I made it to the camp, and after a while, I realized I wanted to live. I couldn't have survived all that for nothing. There had to be some reason, some purpose for it." Michael leaned his head sideways so his jaw rested on the top of her head. "What made you want to live?"

She thought about the days she'd spent since last November. "I never wanted to die. I was terrified I'd get it the whole time. Seventeen of us stayed holed up at the television station for two weeks when it was first raging, and none of us got it. We kept going, we stayed on the air longer than anyone else. Even when we had to leave, we were able to get health certificates, so a couple of us went down to where UIG had studios outside of DC and stayed near there. We got robbed a couple of times, and we went hungry for a while, but we made it through . . . and then he slipped and fell. My boss. After all we'd lived through, he fell and hit his head, and they took him, and he died." She shuddered. "When I fell today, and everyone just stood there looking at me, I thought, 'This is it.' I was so scared they'd take me away." She leaned against Michael and started to cry quietly. "I don't want to die. I don't want to die. I want to live and to do things again."

He held her close. "Don't be afraid. We've both made it this far for a reason. We're going to live."

CHAPTER 46

EASTERN OKLAHOMA — March 2nd

Ricky and the others presented themselves at the north gate of the encampment at three in the afternoon. Everyone traveling south via this route had to pass through this quarantine camp before proceeding south.

On a long, slow rise of ground before them, within a huge, fenced enclosure, they saw hundreds of tents, Quonset huts, and an odd variety of portable buildings. Their eyes drank in the scene as if it were a beautiful piece of art.

None of the refugees wore masks. Medical garments had become so scarce in the region, only military and medical personnel were permitted to wear them.

US Army soldiers checked the travelers for ID's, then searched their belongings for contraband. Several pocket knives, permitted while walking south, were confiscated. No weapons would be allowed beyond this point. A military physician briefly checked each person for signs of illness.

Having completed the check-in process, they were escorted through another gate and made an immediate right turn. Along the left side of the lane in front of them stood six separate, double-fenced enclosures. Each of the enclosures, a quarantine "pen," contained as many as seventy small tents. The tents had large numbers painted on the sides and would be "homes" for new-comers for six days before they could enter the main camp. They were shown to pen "A" and locked in.

Ricky and Rosa looked for the family's assigned tent, number sixty-seven, in the back row of the pen. Once they reached the final row of tents, Rosa could hear someone calling her name.

"Rosa! Rosa! Rosalinda Ruiz! Look up here!"

Rosa looked up beyond the double fences at the back of the pen. Inside the main encampment she saw one of her dearest friends running toward the fences. Rosa set down her suitcase and ran to the end of the enclosure, yelling, "Sara!"

Sara Reisling quickly reached the fences. Between the two women lay a ten-foot strip of "no man's land" which separated those in quarantine from those in the main camp. "Rosa! Ricky! Thank God, you and the babies made it!"

"Oh, Sara," Rosalinda cried, "It's so good to see you! How long have you been here? Have you heard about anyone else?"

Before Sara could answer, Ricky joined his wife at the fence, "Hi! Look, Angela," he said to the girl in his arms, "it's Sara!"

"Oh, I'm so happy you made it!" Sara said. "My group arrived here last week. We just got out of quarantine yesterday. Listen, you guys, there are a lot of people you know here!"

"Really? Who?" the couple said in unison.

"Some boys from the ranch. And people from church. Tell you what, you get settled and I'll meet you back here in about fifteen minutes or so."

Rosa, bone tired a few minutes ago, hurried with Ricky to the tent, chattering the whole way.

"Isn't it wonderful? This is so wonderful—to know Sara and some of the others are safe. Who else do you think is here? If we have to stay in here for six days, does today count? Oh, I look so awful, do you think I have time to change my blouse?"

Ricky just smiled.

Fifteen minutes later, the Ruiz family, combed and wearing their cleanest shirts, stood at the fence facing the camp. Jason and two other boys from the ranch stood with them. Soon, they could see Sara, with several young men in tow, walking down the road leading to the fence.

"That's Pete!" Jason said.

"And Lonny . . . and Seth!" Ricky added. "Hey!" he yelled at the boys.

Pete, Lonny, and Seth trotted to the fence. "Hey, Mr. Ruiz!" they answered back.

Sara and Rosa moved down the fence a few yards so they could have their own conversation.

"Oh Sara, I'm so glad you're here. I've missed you so much. Are you okay?" Rosa asked.

Sara smiled. "I'm so happy you've made it, too! Yes, I'm okay. Our group got here in two days. It was a little cold, but it wasn't so bad."

"Who else is here?" Rosa asked.

"Paul and Rene Winford from church . . . and you probably haven't heard about Brandon and Cassidy."

"Heard what?"

"You know how Brandon always tried to sell those provisions and things."

"Yes, what happened?"

"Well, after you guys got stuck out at the ranch, soldiers showed up in town and wanted to confiscate everyone's food for common distribution. Brandon just kept quiet about all the provisions he had. When people got hungrier they figured he had food and they wanted it. But he wanted to sell it, and they didn't have money to pay for it. He gave some to a few people on credit, then wouldn't let any more of it go. A bunch of men showed up at his house one night and broke in. Brandon tried to fight them off . . . and they killed him."

"Oh no!" Rosa gasped.

"Isn't it awful? Cassidy is here with us. Please pray for her. She has family in Louisiana, but she'll go with me to Texas first until she can arrange for a way to get home. My heart is so broken for her, Rosa."

"How long do you think it will be before they ship you out?"

"I don't know . . . there haven't been any transport trucks or buses here in several days. There seems to have been some sort of delay, but they don't tell us anything . . . I have to go in a minute or two. It's my turn to work in the laundry."

"*Laundry?*"

"Yes. You have one, too! Go back to the front of your pen, by the gate. On your left you'll see a square tent with several black metal barrels sitting on a stand next to it. That's the shower tent, and the sun heats those barrels up during the day to give you hot water!"

Rosa thought she might cry.

"Yes! You'll get to take a short shower and they'll let you wash a few things in a tub. They even have soap! Just make sure you get there early, before the hot water's all gone."

"Oh, it sounds wonderful."

"I gotta run, Rosa, but I'll meet you back here tomorrow after breakfast if I can, okay?"

"Yes. Tomorrow, God willing. . . . Wait! What if you get shipped out? How will we ever contact you?"

"You don't have my parent's address anymore?"

"No, we lost our address book."

"And, I suppose you don't have any paper or pens with you."

"No."

"I'll find something to write on and send you my address later tonight. Keep it with you. Do you know where you'll be going when you head south?"

"No."

"Come to my house in Texas and we'll help you."

"Oh, wouldn't it be great?"

Sara started up the hill, walking backward to be able to shout a few more words to her friend. "Yes! You and Ricky pray about it—you'll have my address—come when you can. I haven't left yet, though. I may be stuck here a while. Who knows? We may get to leave together. I have to run now! Love you!"

Rosa joined Ricky, who still lingered at the fence, talking with some of the ranch boys. Although not quite as emotional about it as Rosa, she could tell he was thrilled to see the young men had survived.

Baby Daniel started squirming in Ricky's arms so Rosa took him, and set him down to let him scoot around with his sister for a few moments. She pulled on Ricky's sleeve hoping he'd save any prolonged discussion for later. Her mind filled with thoughts of hot water, clean hair, and clean clothes.

Before winding up his conversation, Ricky noticed a woman in a baggy blue dress, walking behind the boys. The tight bun at the back of her head accentuated her severe features. He recognized her immediately. She did a double-take when she saw Ricky, then stopped in her tracks as her whole face contorted.

"Hello, Myra," Ricky said.

"You!" she spat out before storming off.

"Yeah," one of the boys said when she'd gone. "We forgot to tell you. Ms. Ballardi got out of quarantine yesterday."

Later in the evening, once they'd showered, everyone in quarantine felt much better. Only one thing dampened their mood. About an hour after Ricky's group arrived at the camp, David's group underwent the entrance process. Within moments of their arrival, they found out the dog, Tracker, who had come with Ana, Doug, and Jessie, wouldn't be allowed to enter the camp. Due to sanitation and other concerns, refugees were forbidden to keep any pets.

Normally, the military confiscated animals and "put them to sleep." Tracker appeared to be in good shape, though, and the boys insisted the dog could hunt. Soldiers at the gate consulted with a superior officer who decided that Tracker could be an asset to the search and reconnaissance team. Knowing the dog would survive and be cared for kept Ana and her nephews from total despair, but the loss of his company still hurt them deeply.

Because David's group came in on the same day as Ricky and Rosa's group, they'd all be spending their quarantine time in the same pen. As soon as word about the dog got around, many gathered around the little family and prayed, not only for Ana and the brokenhearted boys, but for Tracker, who'd been a faithful protector. David reminded them the dog had been yet another provision for them along the way. Who knew? God might use Tracker to help other families survive.

CHAPTER 47

EASTERN OKLAHOMA — March 10th

Transport trucks and a bus had arrived at the quarantine camp for the first time in more than three weeks. A buzz of excitement went through the refugees. Who would get to go this time? Pregnant women, and families with small children had first priority. After these people had been assigned space, a random "lottery" decided who got the remaining seats.

At a distance, Sara Reisling and Rosa Ruiz stood together watching the door of the information shack. Sara held onto little Angela's hand, and Rosa carried Daniel. Soon, a soldier would come out and post a notice with the name of everyone leaving camp.

"It's sure is taking them long enough," Sara said. "I have to keep telling myself: If not today, then soon. We're getting such a backup of people, you'd think they'd be running extra busses just to make more room in the camp. You've memorized my address in Texas now haven't you Rosa?"

"Yes, I've memorized it," Rosa said.

A soldier came out of the shack with papers and a staple gun in his hand. He started stapling the new list on top of the old ones. People began converging on him.

"Just wait till I'm done," he said, without even looking back at the crowd. "If you swarm me, I'll stop and go back inside. I'll be through in a minute and then you can all see."

When he'd finished, he quickly stepped back into the shed before the giant surge of readers swept forward.

"Are they alphabetical?" someone asked.

"Yeah," an older man answered.

"Then we'll be in the second half of the list," Rosalinda said.

"You stay back with the babies," Sara warned. "I'll look for our names."

Rosalinda moved off to a safe distance to wait with the children. Within a short while, Sara emerged from the crowd and walked toward her.

"Tell me," Rosa said.

"I'm on it."

"Oh Sara! That's wonderful!"

"And *you're* on it."

Rosa bounced up and down, then hugged her friend.

"Wait, Rosa," Sara said in a somber voice. "You and the babies are on it, but Ricky isn't."

"What? It must be a mistake. They just accidentally left his name off the list." Even while Rosa said it, however, she got a terrible feeling.

Within minutes, Rosa located Ricky and told him. "You must go and tell them that they made a mistake. Families are supposed to be kept together," she said.

Before he could reply, a soldier appeared. "Are you Enrique Ruiz?"

"Yes," Ricky replied.

"Come with me, please."

"You go to our tent," Ricky said to his wife. "I'll come back as soon as I can."

Now she feared they might take him for a squad. "No. I'm coming with you. Sara," she called to her friend, "take the babies. We'll be back soon."

When Ricky and Rosa got to the camp's headquarters, soldiers told Rosa she'd have to wait outside. She stood outside the wooden building on the rutted, dirt road, praying inwardly. She told herself not to focus on fears, but on the Lord. Soon, she couldn't hold still, so she paced back and forth in front of the building.

Finally, Ricky emerged. She ran to him and looked him in the eyes. "Tell me."

"You know how they've been looking for doctors and nurses among the people here in the camp."

"Yes. But what does that have to do with you?"

"They still need more . . . and someone told them I used to be an emergency medical technician back in New York."

"Who told—" Rosa's eyes darted to a movement beside a building nearby. A dark-haired woman had been watching them, but now turned to walk away. "Myra! She did it!" Hot tears of rage burned in Rosa's eyes. She wanted to run and catch that woman, then possibly knock her down before demanding to know why she'd done such a thing.

Ricky grabbed Rosa and embraced her tightly. "It doesn't matter, Rosa. Let go of it. We will pray. If we embrace God's will, what can anyone do to us outside of it?"

March 11th

The time had come. All those scheduled for transport needed to start boarding the bus and the trucks. Since the bus had seats, women and infants on the list would be allowed to ride it on a first come, first serve basis. The trucks were tractor trailer rigs originally built for livestock. People would be allowed to ride them thirty miles west to the train which would take them to Dallas. Many gathered by the gate to say last goodbyes.

Because Jack and Iris had baby Cameron and Katie, they'd be allowed to leave before many people who had been in the camp longer. Ricky and Rosa hugged them and bid them safe journey.

Cassidy, the young woman whose husband, Brandon, had been killed, stood near Sara, waiting to board a truck. Sara looked at Ricky and Rosa, fearing she might never see them again. She hugged Ricky, then Angela, then Daniel, and lastly, Rosa. "Are you sure you want to do this?" she asked.

"Yes," Rosa said, calmly. Peace had come to her heart. "No matter what, we want to stay together."

"And you've—"

"Memorized your address," Rosa finished the sentence. "And when we come south, we'll head right to your door. Meanwhile," she said, missing her friend already, "you and Cassidy will be in our prayers."

"And you will be in ours."

A soldier called out, saying all passengers had to find their seating.

Sara embraced Rosa one last time. "You know, we'll laugh about all this when we're in Heaven."

"Yes, we will."

# # #

As the sun set that evening, Ricky, David and a large group the other Christians remaining in the camp stood together. Many of them looked very downcast. Who knew when the transport trucks might come back? Maybe tomorrow, maybe weeks from now.

"What if we're stuck here for a long time?" Ana asked. "I don't know how much longer we can live like this. . . . And what if an outbreak hits the camp? We would've come all this way, just to die in one of these tents."

Ricky spoke, not just to Ana, but to everyone who might be thinking the same thing. "Listen. Remember the New York riots? Friends and I got stuck right in the middle of it when the city all around us was on fire. We were threatened—moment by moment sometimes—with death. It was hard not to be scared, but Rosa" he said, clasping her hand, "and others were praying for us. The Lord gave us a word and I chose to trust Him.

"Here I stand today—not because I was clever, or good, or strong, but because the Lord placed me in His hand and I've stayed there. You have to know there are Christian brothers and sisters out there," he pointed south, "who are praying for you. Seek God, allow Him to place you in His hand, and don't crawl out of it. No one who does this will be ashamed when they meet Him face to face."

CHAPTER 48

MONTGOMERY, ALABAMA — March 16th

Ignoring the pain in his shoulders, Michael walked down the street carrying the small canvas bag containing his work clothes. He'd just been to the ScrubMat where he'd showered and shaved after another hard day as a laborer, mixing cement at the site of a new apartment complex.

Tiny one—and two-bedroom flats couldn't be built fast enough to accommodate the mass exodus from the north. The government continued to hire tens of thousands of men and women for construction and manufacturing projects in an effort to stay afloat in a sea of unemployed, homeless, hungry people.

Once Michael had accumulated a few dollars, he scheduled an appointment at a phone center. On the scheduled day of the appointment, he was allowed to use a phone and attempted to call Zac. Amazingly, on the second try, he connected with his brother's voice mail at work. Limited to less than a minute, his message consisted only of essentials. He told Zac he had survived, that he would try to get to Texas as soon as he had the money for transportation, and that he'd be bringing someone with him. Even though he'd only gotten a recording, it was good to hear his brother's voice.

Michael had worked hard to save money for travel, but today he'd been presented with an opportunity to spend some of it on something else. He didn't think he could resist it. Walking down the tree-lined street toward home, he tried to calculate just how much he'd allow himself to spend.

All the formerly middle-class houses along the street had been "sectioned out" so that uprooted northerners had places to live while they awaited new housing. By the time Michael and Linda arrived in town, all bedrooms, attics, basements, and garages were already filled to capacity. After several days in a dirty, noisy "tent city," they received a lodging assignment. Compared to a tent, the shed behind the yellow house Michael now approached seemed like heaven.

Because the shed had no running water, he and Linda showered and did laundry at the ScrubMat, a block and a half away. Specially built outhouses, strategically placed in every neighborhood and plugged directly into city sewer lines at curbside, accommodated the sanitary needs of the multitudes who lived in yards, garages, and sheds.

Michael walked up the driveway of the house and walked around to the back. Linda, home from a day of "temp" work in a government office, sat in the doorway of the shed. She looked up when he entered the yard.

"Hi! What's for dinner?" he asked.

He meant it as a joke, but she didn't smile. "You ever get tired of asking that?"

"No," he said, reaching over her to set his bag down inside the shed. "I figure, one magical night, you'll say, 'steak and baked potatoes!' Even a fresh hunk of bread would be nice. Can I help it if I can't forget what real food was like?"

"I suppose not," she said, a bit sadly. It had been so long since they'd had a hot meal. While packaged rations served the purpose of keeping people alive, the reconstituted powders and pastes had virtually no flavor, color, or texture.

She stood and Michael slipped his arms around her. "Still, you have put on a few pounds. I should be grateful you don't look like a stick woman anymore."

She smacked him lightly on the back. "Hey. Be nice."

"I thought that was a compliment. . . . So what's for dinner."

She smacked him again. "Guess."

"I'm guessing I got paid today," he said in a low voice, "and that one of the guys told me where to get some real food on the sly."

Linda's eyes got wide but she lowered her voice as well. "Real food? Like what?"

"Strawberries and maybe some carrots."

"Strawberries! How much do they cost?"

"Does it matter?" he asked. "Just this once, we're gonna have some real food for dinner. What do you say? Wanna blow some Texas ticket money on food?"

She hugged him. "Strawberries!"

"Then as soon as you're ready, we'll sneak into a dark alley and," he said, looking around before whispering in her ear, "buy some strawberries."

An hour later, Michael and Linda stood inside a small building in a nearby business park. The seller, satisfied they weren't government agents, offered the goods.

"How much?" Michael asked.

"Fifteen dollars a container."

"How many are in a container?"

"Around ten."

Michael thought a moment. "How about bread? You got any bread?"

The man gave a loud laugh. "Even if we had flour for bread, where could we bake it so that a hundred thousand people wouldn't smell it, then come and kill us for it?"

"How much are the carrots?"

"Sorry, they're all gone."

Michael reached in his pocket. "We'll take three containers of strawberries."

After paying for the berries, they placed all three containers in Michael's canvas bag and left the premises. Walking swiftly down the street, they passed a burned out church. Linda could see the sign for it in the fading light. *Another "fundamentalist" church*, she thought.

"Huh," Michael said. "Look at that. Another one. People are really getting into burning these things."

A chill went through Linda. After the war in the Middle East had gone nuclear, she'd gone online and found one of the "He is coming soon" websites. She read through the reasons why Jesus might appear any minute, and the descriptions of what would happen to the "unsaved" people who got "left." She'd almost responded. All she would've had to do was click on the "salvation link," where she could read through a prayer and respond by typing in her name and city, which would then be posted as a public "confession of faith." She almost did it, but after a few moments, the urge receded and she started thinking, *Wait! This is nothing but a scare tactic. How many people are rushing to do this, solely as a kind of "fire" insurance? If the world survives, they'll all look like fools. If my name gets posted here, everyone will know it! It could ruin my credibility as a reporter! Why not wait and see if*

Jesus really comes? I can always decide to do it later if it's true.

Linda glanced a last time at the burned out shell of the church and shuddered. What if she'd given in? I'd be feeling like a total fool right now.

The sky continued to darken as the couple rounded a corner and entered a small, empty playground. They intended to cut through the little park on the way home, but only got half way through it before the call of the strawberries overwhelmed them. Couldn't they stop a moment and eat just a few? They stopped in the shadow of a large tree and sat on the ground facing each other before Michael looked around, then reached into the bag. He wouldn't pull out the container for fear someone would see they had food. "Man," he said, starting to laugh, "you'd think we had heroin or something the way we're acting."

She looked around. "Hurry."

He rooted around in the bag for a strawberry. He couldn't see well in the shadows, but didn't care what the berries looked like or even if they'd been washed. He placed one in her hand and got another out for himself.

Linda took a moment to smell hers, then began nibbling it. By old standards, the not-completely-ripe fruit would have been considered so-so, but to her deprived taste buds, it was exquisite. Though she wanted to eat it slowly, she couldn't help devouring it. Perhaps she'd even eat the leafy top later. She put it in the canvas bag and got out another strawberry.

Michael hadn't bothered with nibbling. He popped the whole berry in his mouth then, after several chews, he smashed it between his tongue and the roof of his mouth trying to get every molecule of juicy flavor out of it before swallowing.

They both devoured another, then a third before they heard the first siren, signifying curfew would begin in fifteen minutes.

Was someone walking by? They closed the bag, quickly stood, and began heading toward home.

Making their way through the park, they became aware of someone groaning. Linda, frightened by the sound, grabbed hold of Michael's arm and kept close. A solar powered lamp on a post up ahead came on and provided some illumination.

Several yards off to the side, they could see a man kneeling down with his back to the lamp. He cried out loud. "I can't go on. I can't go on anymore," he sobbed. "I can't."

Michael slowed down and Linda pulled on his arm. "Let's get out of here," she insisted. When he stopped, she said his name in a panicked whisper. "Michael! He could be a robber!"

"Excuse me," Michael said to the man. "Excuse me."

When the man turned, they could see his bony "chimp" face.

"You just got here didn't you?" Michael asked.

"Yes. And they have no more food tonight, no place to sleep." He wiped his face with both hands. "I just can't live like this anymore. What's the point?"

"Go that way," Michael pointed left. "In a few blocks you'll find a tent city. Since there's a curfew, they *have* to let you in. It isn't going to be cold tonight so you'll be okay even if they're out of blankets. Tomorrow, they'll show you how to get to the employment office. It's not far and they have plenty of jobs with daily rations. . . . Meanwhile, " he said, opening his bag, "take these." He pulled out a full container of strawberries and tossed them to the man. "Eat them now, then go to the tents. You'll be okay."

Before they got a few steps away the man popped the lid off the container, scooped nearly all the strawberries up in one handful, and shoved them into his mouth.

As soon as they'd gone a safe distance, Linda jerked his arm. "Why did you do that?" she fumed.

"Don't you remember how cold, how hungry, and how scared you felt? I remember when I thought I couldn't go on. Some man gave me his rations and said, 'there's still hope. Don't give up.' It made me think I *could* live, Linda."

"But you didn't have to give him our strawberries! What's wrong with you?"

He didn't answer, and they walked the rest of the way home without speaking. When they got to the shed, he opened the door and set the bag inside. "You eat the rest of them. I've lost my appetite and I need to walk for a while."

She stepped inside and slammed the door, not caring if he went for a walk or not. Michael returned to the street and started in the direction of a place where he could buy some homemade booze. He still had some cash left and planned on spending all of it.

By two in the morning, Linda's anger had disappeared. Scared Michael might not come back, she'd stayed awake crying for hours. Although she'd lived alone for years before the disasters, everything had changed now. It wasn't just a case of depending on Michael, she felt some sort of bond with him. All her previous relationships had been fair exchanges; if she needed something from a man, she got whatever she wanted, and he got the pleasure of her company for a season.

But Michael was different. He'd just appeared and saved her when she looked her worst and had nothing to offer. He'd showed kindness to her, kept her safe when she lacked the strength to look out for herself, and had never forced his attentions on her.

Unlike most of the men she'd known (who were clueless outside an office environment), Michael proved to be adept at many things. He could make clever adaptations to common objects and knew how to fend for himself. In a world where technology had crashed, his manual skills might give them a definite advantage. His intelligence, given a chance to bloom, might allow him to be somebody in the future.

But what if he got arrested for breaking curfew? What if he kept walking and never came back to her? She heard the sound of his key in the lock and melted with relief. He came through the door and she rushed to him.

"Please don't be mad at me anymore," she said, hugging him tightly. "I know it seemed mean, but I was truly frightened."

"Thasssssokay," he slurred. He'd drowned all his anger and currently felt no pain. As soon as she loosened her grasp, he got down and crawled onto their sleeping mat without even taking off his shoes.

She got down next to him and tried to explain.

"You don't understand, Michael. We walked by the burned out church and it reminded me of something awful. Then, when you gave that man the strawberries, I just freaked. You asked me if I remembered being hungry and said a man helped you when you got to the camp. . . . Well, it was like you were trying to make me feel guilty—and it made me mad. But I'm not hard hearted, Michael. It's not about me, it's about us. After all we've been through, don't we deserve to live? Is wanting to survive a crime?"

She heard the sound of his deep breathing and realized he hadn't heard a word. She shifted around and thought for a few moments.

"The truth is," she said softly, "I *do* feel a little guilty. You weren't the only person who helped me at the camp. When I first got there, I was near starvation, too, and so cold. This woman in my tent was very kind to me. She let me have her cot so I didn't have to sleep on the cold ground. She even shared some of her rations with me. . . . She said she was doing it for Jesus . . . she was giving Him her bed, sharing her food with Him. But when some people found out she was a Christian, they started tormenting her—and anyone who hung out with her. Somebody from our tent told the soldiers she was a troublemaker. She and a few of her friends got taken away, but I don't know where. . . . And, you know who it was?" Linda still marveled at the thought. "It was Trina Watson. You probably wouldn't remember if you'd ever heard of her. She was an assistant to President Cole . . . and just look what happened to her."

Linda had tried very hard to forget the camp. Recalling Trina Watson now made something inside Linda ache. If only she could make it stop.

"I can't help her, I can't pay her back, but I'll try to do better. I'll try to be more like you, Michael." Linda rested her head on his shoulder. "Maybe when we have more, when things are better for us, we can give to charities who distribute things to people in need. That would be good, wouldn't it?"

Hours later, when daylight came into the shed, he awoke with a huge hangover. He squinted up to see Linda, already dressed and ready to leave for work.

"I'm really sorry," he said, barely above a whisper.

"Me too," she answered softly.

"I haven't done that since . . . well, it doesn't matter. I'm sorry. I should have put the money away for our tickets. Won't happen again."

CHAPTER 49

DALLAS, TEXAS — March 28th

Edith Todd took a few cleansing breaths and tried to relax. The day began with a meeting in Atlanta, then a bumpy trip in a car to a remote location where she boarded an airplane, flew to a private airstrip in Texas, then endured another long ride in a truck to this television studio in Dallas. Now, in a few seconds, they'd begin taping her interview.

Although she'd not spoken with E. E. Kressman in person (who ever had?), his personal assistant, John Klost, assured her the man had been inspired by her vision.

"Mr. Kressman feels the time is now," Klost said. "And he wants to help you take your vision to the people. Your message may lead millions of frightened, disillusioned people out of darkness and division."

Her heart leaped at the thought of inspiring Kressman—a man who was bringing so many threads in the tapestry of the world together. He'd even let her fly in one of his personal jets today! Over the whole earth, how many planes might have been in the air? Ten? Fifty? In any case it would be a small number. What an incredible privilege to be able to fly again.

Mr. Klost justified the expenditure of fuel to fly her around this way: "Isn't speeding your message of hope to desperate people one of the most important things we can do at this time? The sooner they respond, the sooner our future will begin."

Edith looked around the studio. *What a victory this is.*

"We'll begin in fifteen seconds," a woman near the camera said.

Edith took a few more breaths, and straightened her posture. Her creamy-white turtleneck and pants accented her excellent physique. Near her left shoulder, she wore a gold pin with three interlocking triangles. Mr. Klost said it was a gift from Kressman. Would he notice it?

"Ten seconds."

Today's interview, to be played both in its entirety and in short, commercial clips, would appear in as many venues as possible. The man doing the interview, Terence Topps, became famous for his nightly UIG interviews years ago. The catch phrase for the show had been, "Terence Topps That!"

"Five, four . . ." The woman finished the countdown with her fingers then pointed to Mr. Topps.

"We're here today talking with former First Lady, Edith Todd, pioneer and visionary. Welcome to our studio, Edith. Nice to see you."

"Thanks. It's nice to be here, Terence."

"I could waste a lot of time with pleasantries and biographical info, but everybody already knows who you are— couldn't we just cut to the good stuff?"

She laughed. "Why not?"

"In just a moment, we'll play a clip of your speech at the World Conference on Spirituality last year, but before we do— when you shared your vision there, did you have any idea it was so close to happening?"

"I think maybe I did. I had an incredible sense of destiny that day. I can't describe the energy flowing through me while I spoke the words."

"Wow," Terence said. "Let's play the clip."

Edith watched the segment of her speech at the convention on a monitor. Each time she'd seen it, her own words made more sense to her. The clip ended, mercifully, before the chaos started.

Terence looked at her again. "I get goose bumps watching it."

"Me too!" she said.

"And within seconds of saying those words, the attack happened, didn't it?"

"Yes. And, since then, I've come to think this was just the beginning of the 'war in the atmosphere' I saw in the vision. Forces of darkness are trying to thwart enlightenment, trying to stop the liberation coming to every man, woman, and child on this planet."

"Well, they may have tried, but you're a hard woman to keep down, aren't you?"

"You bet!" she said, "What the people inside the arena went through that day proved to be a foreshadowing of what would happen everywhere within days of the convention.

Soon millions would know sudden panic, and loss of the 'normal' things in life. The whole world would feel the war being waged for the soul of this planet."

Terence looked at Edith with a mixture of astonishment and admiration. "And who is winning now?"

"I invite people everywhere to look around," she answered, extending her arms, holding her hands outward. "The world hasn't come to an end, has it? If the people of Earth will unite and cast aside all the old barriers, we can leap into the future. Instead of sliding back to being Neanderthals with stone axes, we can very quickly achieve a new realm of technology—a realm far beyond that which we enjoyed a year ago."

"You make it sound as if this could happen tomorrow."

"Well," Edith said with a grin, "it's almost that close. Even as we speak, nearly thirty-five percent of the population in the US is working on the conversion process."

"You mean, converting to Fibertronics?"

"Yes. But, you know, it's more than technology. It's converting to a whole new state of mind. It's erasing all the borders on the map and throwing down all the old superstitions. It's realigning yourself with what's to come and letting it pulse right through you . . . letting it bless every part of you."

"How do we go about doing it?"

"Centers either have been or are being built in every metropolis in this country and around the world. These centers will be the beachhead for the new technology. Appropriately named 'Centers for Tomorrow,' they'll be the contact point for every person who wants to connect with the future. In fact," she said, leaning toward Terence, "this afternoon, and tomorrow, I'll be dedicating some of the first Centers for Tomorrow in Dallas and the surrounding areas! These are places where people can come in and see how close 'tomorrow' actually is. They can sign up on the spot and be the first in their communities to get not only *Fibertronics*, but all the latest developments. Within months, some of the people who watch this and respond will be able to step right into the future."

Terence broke in at this point. "Did you say *months*?"

"Yes I did. It's that close in urban areas . . . less than a year for those in outlying areas. I got an update from the

Office of Information just today, and things are looking up. Since President Moffit signed the commitment to transfer to Fibertronics on a national level, steady progress has been made on all fronts."

"And it's just as simple as going in and saying you want it? There's no catch?"

"Well, I wouldn't call it a catch, but there is more to it than just saying you want something . . ." Edith focused on the camera lens and tried to imagine she could look right into the eyes of the viewers. "Again, what I've been talking about here goes beyond the natural, beyond the physical. The whole world needs a change, so that we'll never again experience the devastation we've just endured. Each and every person needs to make a commitment to cast off the old and receive the new. It's a commitment of body, soul, and spirit for a better world. Of course, the first ones to make the commitment will be the first to know its benefits."

Edith's eyes sparkled with obvious delight as she continued. "Just think, lights, hot water, television, E-mail, telephones, and more are so close! A step behind those things will be new appliances, transportation, medical advances, and the restoration of a whole food diet. In the middle of it all will be an ever-expanding door into a glorious spiritual life, more fulfilling than anything you've ever imagined."

Terence leaned forward in his seat and asked. "So you're not just talking about air conditioning and better food, you're not just talking about peace and safety, you're speaking of spiritual things as well aren't you?"

"Exactly."

"Well, what if I've always been a Buddhist or a Baptist or whatever?"

"This is the best part, Terence!" she exclaimed. "We want to live in a world that reverences culture. We're not asking people to forget who they were, we're just asking them to let those things be placed in the historical museum of their hearts. A person's roots can be given honor, yet not be the guiding force of their existence. It's just like—when I was a little girl, we used to celebrate 'Columbus Day.' I commemorated it, I marveled at the man's accomplishments, but I've never said to myself, 'now, what would Columbus do in this situation?'" She laughed. "You know?"

Terence laughed as well. "I get it. It's not about losing respect for the past, it's about letting go of the things holding us back and putting us at odds with each other."

"Exactly," Edith responded. "What happened this past year is a perfect example. The spiritual has been reflected in the physical. The old ways, the old religions, the old barriers are what caused so much pain. The lessons have been costly and difficult, but hope is here. New life is springing forth . . ." Again Edith looked into the camera, "Won't you take some time right now to consider what the old ways have cost you? Why not turn over a new leaf for a new life? . . . What are you waiting for? Get your information packet today and see how simple it is!"

CHAPTER 50

DALLAS SUBURB — March 28th

Zachary Gordon started up the steps to his apartment.

"Hi Zac," a woman in a first-floor doorway called to him. "I got some extra rations today. Want to come to dinner?"

"Uh . . . sorry," he said, leaning over the railing. "I promised myself several times today I'd just crash tonight. You wouldn't want me to break a promise now, would you?" He smiled his best smile at her. "Rain check?"

"Sure. Tomorrow?"

"Deal," he called out, then quickly mounted the stairs before she could extend the conversation.

When he got to the second floor, a door opened. "Hello," the brunette in apartment 201 said. "I was just thinking about you. Wanna come over later?"

He looked at her. "Uh . . . "

"Zac?" a man down the hall said.

Zachary peered down the dimly lit corridor to see a tall, slender man standing with a small woman. Several bundles rested on the floor beside them. The man had long, blond hair and a beard. *Could it be?*

"Michael? Is that you?" he asked.

The man started walking toward him. "Yes. It's me."

Zac completely forgot the woman in apartment 201. He ran and embraced his brother. "Michael! When you left that voice mail for me, it was like hearing from the dead. I can't believe you're actually here."

Michael's companion left her spot by the bundles and approached. Once the brothers finished their bear hug, Michael introduced her. "Zac, this is Linda. Linda, this is my brother, Zachary."

Zac didn't know if he should shake her hand or hug her. He studied her face for a moment, thinking perhaps he'd seen her before, then discarded the idea. He decided to hug her. "Welcome," he said. "Come, let's get inside where you can relax."

# # #

About fifty miles north and west of Zac's apartment, Sara Reisling sat on the back porch of her parent's little house. The home had also become a shelter for Brandon Atkins' widow, Cassidy, and another refugee family. Four days after their arrival, Cassidy and Sara still felt as if they'd stepped through a time warp. Each wore a clean dress that actually fit. Although the house didn't have electricity, it did have running water. The walls and roof didn't puff around in the wind either . . . and the upstairs bedroom they shared seemed so large for just two beds. Even in this quiet neighborhood, when she dreamed, Sara still heard the sounds of hundreds of people moving about and talking.

The two women sat in a large, wooden porch swing and rocked for a while in silence.

"How long do you think it will take for my brother to get here?" Cassidy asked.

"Daddy says it takes weeks to get anywhere. I'm so glad you could actually get in touch with your brothers, but I'll be sad to see you go."

Cassidy looked down. "I'll be sad, too, but I feel like I should be with my family now."

Sara squeezed her friend's hand. "We've been through so much . . . you've become such a dear friend." She stopped for a moment, then spoke in a happier tone, "Daddy is gonna hate losing such a killer opponent at checkers."

Cassidy's face warmed at the thought. "Yeah. I do defend womanhood pretty well, don't I?"

They heard the squeak of the screen door at the back of the house.

"Supper, girls," Sara's mother called to them.

They slowly rose from the swing and went into the house. Tonight, the other family sharing their home would be out for the evening. The Reislings and Cassidy had the table all to themselves. After they sat down, everyone grabbed hands.

"Oh Lord," Pete said, closing his eyes. "You know how full my heart still is. Words can't say how grateful we all are to have our Duchess back with us. We continue to ask You for Your plan for Cassy. Thank You for this food. Bless it, Lord. In Jesus' name,"

"Amen," they all added.

There were real peas this evening so everyone except Sara wanted to save them for last. Sara, on the other hand, took a gray protein cube off her plate and smashed peas into it before biting off a hunk.

"*Mmmmm*, this is good," Sara said.

Her father, mother and sister looked at her as if she'd lost her mind.

"No. Really," she said. "Compared to what we got in the camp, this is pretty tasty. I mean, at least we can put salt on this. Go ahead. Try the cubes with the peas. Makes 'em better."

The others tried it.

"Well," her sister, Noel, said, shrugging. "The peas do make the cubes more palatable."

"You've gone and invented a new dish," her father announced. "We'll call it Duchess Surprise."

"Thanks, Daddy. I always wanted to be famous."

"Change of subject," her mother said. "Are you still planning on going to look for a job tomorrow, Sara?"

Sara swallowed a bite. "Yes. There are more students in the area than ever. It should be easy to get a teaching position."

Naomi glanced at Pete then said, "It's just that we want you to be careful."

Sara set her fork down. "I've heard all that you and Daddy told me about how things are right now. Don't worry. While I'm not going to hide my beliefs, I'm not the same woman who picked a fight about faith with the principal during her first teaching job, either.

"It's just," Pete said, "we heard they burned another church last night. People are really angry. Some want to blame us for the war."

"But that's stupid! We didn't start the war. We weren't even there!"

"It doesn't seem to matter right now. They lump Christians who believe the Bible with radical Muslims and it suits their purpose. And there's another serious problem. A lot of Christians have fallen away because they're angry, too. Last year, they convinced themselves Jesus was coming back. He didn't, and now they're stuck here—in the world they pronounced so much judgment on. Right now, they're as hostile as the others. We just want you to be wise about what you do, Duchess."

CHAPTER 51

EASTERN OKLAHOMA — April 15th

Because he couldn't knock, the soldier called softly, "Inside, hello inside," before opening the flap to the tent.

Ricky sat up. "Yeah?"

"I'm sorry, Mr. Ruiz. Could you come with me?"

"What time is it?" Ricky asked. He recognized the soldier standing outside under a full moon, a young man by the name of Norris. He'd been sent to fetch Ricky late at night on several occasions. Soldiers weren't allowed to mingle with civilians, but Ricky had noticed him lingering at the periphery of prayer meetings.

"It's four o'clock," Norris answered.

Rosa stirred and rolled over to face Ricky. "What is it?" she asked quietly.

Ricky cleared his throat and spoke to the soldier first. "Okay, okay. Just give me a second." Once the flap closed, Ricky gently patted Rosa on the hip. "Gotta go, *mi corazón*," he said softly. "I'll be back later."

The soldier stepped back from the doorway, trying not to listen to the soft exchange between husband and wife. In actuality, there were few, if any, private words among the tents.

Military medical personnel continued to be drained away from the camp despite the constant flow of refugees coming in. Because medical needs kept rising, the leadership at the camp increasingly called upon Ricky's skills. He could accurately assess needs of patients and perform minor procedures. Often, they'd awaken him at odd hours to look at new cases so medical officers weren't needlessly roused.

A bedraggled Ricky emerged from the tent. He glanced around and realized no one but the soldier waited for him. Good. The fact they hadn't rousted Jason out of the single men's tent meant this might be an easy deal. If several cases awaited, or if someone needed to be held down in order to get stitches, they would've enlisted Jason's help. Ricky started down the hill toward the medical tent.

He heard Norris' voice behind him. "Not that way, Mr. Ruiz."

Ricky turned. Perhaps they needed to go directly to someone who'd been injured.

"This way," the soldier said, before heading toward the top of the hill. Ricky caught up with him, and they passed between the rows of tents in silence. They topped the rise, then headed down into the south side of the camp where few civilians ever set foot. Finally, the two men reached a small, wooden building standing apart from the others.

Norris knocked on the door. Someone opened it a few inches, allowing the lamp light inside to spill out onto the ground. Once the silhouetted man inside the doorway recognized Ricky, he opened the door all the way and bid him to enter.

Ricky mounted the two steps into the quarters leaving Norris behind. Ives Yurich, the camp commandant, quickly closed the door and spoke in a hushed voice. "Thank you for coming. I'm sorry to call you here so late."

"No problem. What do you need?"

A low moan came from the other side of an accordion-style divider, and a look of torment filled the commandant's eyes. "She's very sick."

Ricky knew who it must be. Although he'd never seen her, the whole camp knew the commandant had a woman. With shortages of supplies and problems with transports south, hostile sentiments against the troops continued to mount. Had someone harmed the woman in an attempt at revenge?

"If she's seriously ill or hurt," Ricky said, "perhaps you should get one of the officers to look at her. I'm not a doctor. I'm an EMT."

"They've looked at her," Yurich said, staring at the room divider. "They say she's dying." He clenched his jaw, unable to speak for a few moments, then turned to face Ricky. "But I've heard you might be able to do something. I've been told that, several times, when you've been sent into the pens among whole groups of sick people, they all recovered. . . even when there was no medicine . . . and that when *you* tend critical patients in the hospital tent, they almost never die."

Another moan came from the other side of the room.

Yurich took a deep breath and continued. "And I've heard other things. If you have some sort of . . . power . . ." he said in a hushed voice, stepping closer to Ricky, "I beg of you. I'll pay you any price. I can get you and your family away from here. Just please," his voice cracked, "don't let her die."

"Let me see her," Ricky said quietly.

The commandant quickly moved to the divider and folded it out of the way, revealing a red-haired woman lying on a bed, her pale beauty overtaken by swelling in her face, abdomen, arms, and legs. Ricky walked to the left side of the bed and took hold of a puffy hand. Dazed with painkillers, she slowly opened her eyes and stared at him before speaking in a thick voice. "You're him, aren't you?"

"My name is Ricky. What's yours?"

"Briana. Briana Saunders. Please . . . don't judge me . . ."

Ricky looked at the commandant, who stood at the corner of the bed, then turned back to the woman and spoke softly to her. "I'm not here to judge you, Briana. I'll be right back. Okay?"

The two men moved away, toward the door of the cabin.

"Tumors?" Ricky asked.

"She's full of them," he said, flexing his fists. "And now her kidneys and her heart are failing."

Ricky pointed outside. "Have Norris go get my wife and my assistant, Jason. He knows where to find them."

Within twenty minutes, Norris returned with both of them. Once Rosa and Jason stepped inside, Ricky spoke to the commandant again. "You have to leave now."

"I won't interfere."

"It's a matter of faith. We believe God can do this. Go outside."

Though not accustomed to taking orders from civilians, Yurich's desperation outweighed his pride. "Can I stay right outside the door?"

"Yes, you can wait there. But don't come in until we call you."

Yurich stepped outside and closed the door, oblivious to the sound of crickets filling the cool night air.

"Keep everyone away," he told Norris. "I don't want to see anyone within twenty feet of this cabin."

As soon as Norris moved away, the commandant turned to stare at the closed door of his quarters. The urge to go back in remained very strong, but he froze his body in place, facing the door.

Everything around him grew slowly darker. Long shadows from the sinking moon slipped along, overtaking the space between the buildings, slowly covering the camp in a black shroud. The commander didn't care. He needed only to hear. All his energy became riveted on sounds coming from inside his quarters.

He could hear them walking, back and forth on the wood floor . . . and voices. Perhaps they were praying. But it was taking far too long. Her last minutes might be ticking away. The fear he might never see Briana alive began rising like a choking flood, and he struggled to keep it at bay.

Nicknamed "the machine," Ives Yurich had been raised in military schools, graduated from West Point, then risen through the ranks of the Army. He'd learned how to fight every adversary. He'd never retreated, never been vulnerable. Until now. His whole body began to shake. He loved Briana more than he loved his own life—and he could do nothing to save her.

This was taking far too long. His strength left him and he fell to his knees. A sound made his head jerk. *What was that noise? Briana!* Was she crying out? In pain? Dying? How much longer could he bear to stay away?

Then came a long, awful silence. What did it mean? A terrible certainty finally broke through the last barrier in his mind: *It's over.* He collapsed onto the ground, his heart dissolving and draining out of him in a long, low howl.

# # #

Finally. The eastern sky started to lighten.

Norris turned for a quick glance just as the door to the cabin opened. After one look, he knew. He resumed his stance.

Yurich didn't hear the door open or even the sound of Rosa's approach, but felt her warm hand gently touch the back of his head.

"You can go in now," she said to him.

Yurich looked up at her. Perhaps the first rays of morning light were what made her skin seem so radiant. He got on all fours, then stood up as the door swung open wider. How could this be? There, just inside, stood Briana, arms outstretched.

The commandant took the first few steps slowly, then leaped through the doorway. He carefully touched her face, then her neck. Yes. The swelling had disappeared . . . and her eyes were shining.

Outside, Norris, still with his back to the door, could hear joyful cries. His own heart had already filled with thanksgiving. When the three refugees finally came out of the house, they stopped and gathered around him.

"I have something to say, and something to ask of you," Ricky said.

Norris looked at him. "Yes sir?"

"We did not heal that woman. God did. If anyone asks, that's all you need to say: 'The Lord healed her.' I've seen you standing near the meetings and outside the tents when we pray. I can see the Holy Spirit is in you. Please, don't grieve Him by giving credit to us. . . . Couldn't we just let Him keep doing miracles any way He wants to?"

"Yes sir."

April 25th

Nearly a month had passed and many transport trucks lined up at the gate on the east side of the camp. They would pick up troops and equipment, then haul them to the train tracks which ran east of the camp. Civilians never traveled in the trains running along those tracks. Those trains took troops north, or further east into Arkansas.

A female soldier came to the medical tent requesting Ricky's presence at the commandant's quarters. On the way, they moved through a small, open area in the compound. Children appeared from everywhere to grab onto Ricky. Many of them considered him a human jungle gym, and he indulged them for about ten seconds before telling them they needed to let him go. One little boy stubbornly clung to a leg.

"Max," he said, looking down at the child. "You wanna be on my team tonight?'

"Yes!"

"Then you have to let go, so I can get back in time for the game."

Max complied and Ricky tousled his hair. "See ya."

A few minutes later, Ricky stood outside the commandant's quarters. Ives Yurich and Briana, his new bride, both came out. Briana gave Ricky a big hug.

"Okay, okay," Yurich said, smiling. "Go find Rosa so I can speak with her husband."

Briana, glowing with health, left the two men.

Yurich watched her walk away, then looked at Ricky. "Every time I look at her, I think I must be dreaming."

"And I hope you're still thanking God every single time, Ives."

"Yes. He has saved us both," the commandant said.

A lieutenant appeared, and Yurich returned his salute. "Wait here," he said to the soldier. "I will return shortly." The young lieutenant took up a waiting stance before his commanding officer turned back to Ricky. "I have many things to do, but first we must talk. Come with me."

The two men strode down the hill toward the south until they reached a gate Ricky had never seen before. A private at the gate saluted and opened it when ordered. For the first time since the day they'd arrived, Ricky stepped outside the fence of the camp. Yurich led the way out into the open field before speaking.

"Well, my friend, how's the air out here? Have you really considered what it would be like to leave? I need to know. You see, new troops will be coming and all of the US soldiers will be deployed elsewhere within the next few days. You're not supposed to know this, but I couldn't go without doing something for you.

"Where are you going?"

Ives laughed. "You really like to push it, don't you?" He looked around, then spoke again. "Briana's going south. She doesn't know it yet, but I won't be going with her. I'll be going north."

"Is there fighting?"

Ives looked across the field toward a deep blue lake in the distance. "I can't say." He seemed lost in thought for a moment, then spoke again. "I could send you and your family down with Briana tomorrow. You mustn't let anyone know, though. They'll figure it out when you're gone."

A sad look came to Ricky's face. "Why can't *everyone* go?"

"There are problems. For one thing, they can't absorb any more people for a while. Not with the old governmental systems. But soon, I'm told, a more efficient system will be fully in place. It won't be long. Everyone will be going south shortly. You'd just be going a bit sooner than the others."

"Why are they making everyone leave their homes if there's no place to put them down south? Why are we forced into these camps instead of staying in cities and towns along the way? Is it because there's fighting in some of the cities? Or is it that, as long as a town is empty, it can be looted? Is this how the government is finding the resources to pay for everything?"

"That shouldn't concern you," Yurich responded. "You and your family will be taken to a good place. I will see you get whatever you need to start over."

Ricky took a deep breath. "Rosa and I have prayed about this, Ives. We can't leave while all the others are trapped here."

Ives frowned. He wanted very much to convey the seriousness of the situation. "Listen to me. I will only say this once. Shortly it will become more *difficult* for people like . . . us. For people who believe the Bible. What you profess—what we've seen and touched—may be classified as a "fanatical fringe religion." It may soon be considered 'unacceptable' in the new society. . . . Listen to me, Ricky. Word has already traveled outside this camp about how it's spreading here. I can't guarantee your safety or your freedom once I'm gone. You need to relocate now."

Ricky realized the time the Lord had warned them about might soon be upon them. Looking up, he saw a flock of birds tracking across the sky, and watched them for a few seconds before speaking.

"You know, Ives, Rosa and I received a word from the Lord years ago. He called us to display His life and to give hope wherever we went. The life of God isn't mere affluence or brief, happy moments. Life is what goes on in here," he said, pointing to himself. "Rosa and I are showing these people not to be afraid, we're showing them how they can be free no matter where they are. Outside of God there is no freedom, Ives. We have been placed here to walk with these people, and we can't just disappear in order to save ourselves from the hardships they will face. Whatever their fate is, we will share it. Whatever cup they drink, we will drink as well."

Ives nodded. He understood, he'd had to make a similar decision regarding the young soldiers under his command. "So what *can* I do for you?"

"Several things: First, Rosa and I want something that says we have custody of all the children given to us. They've lost their families, and we don't want anyone to be able to just take them away."

"How many are there?"

"Nine. And Jason. That would make ten. We know other families who've taken in children as well."

"Get lists to me immediately. I'll see what I can do. What else?"

"Couldn't we set up some sort of way for people to leave a lasting record of passing here? Thousands of people have been separated from loved ones . . . how will they ever find each other?"

"We keep records."

Ricky blew air between his lips. "Oh yeah. Like the military is going to give us access to their records. No. We need to be able to leave messages here. . . . A friend of mine has a great idea about a place where the messages could go. I know you have the surplus materials for it. Couldn't you let us do this?"

"Bring this proposal and the names of the children directly to me this morning."

"And one more thing," Ricky said.

"Yes?"

"Let the soldiers come to prayer if they want to. They may be going into dangerous places very soon—let us touch them and pray for them."

Word of all the "unexplainable" things taking place in the camp recently had swelled the numbers of civilians coming to prayer meetings. Soldiers, however, had to meet discretely among themselves, or secretly with refugees. Even Yurich and Briana had met privately with Ricky and Rosa on several occasions.

"Well," the commandant said, looking up toward the camp, "You know what the orders say: No fraternizing with refugees. No large gatherings." He seemed lost in thought, then spoke again. "So, make sure the meetings stay small. . . . Perhaps you should have more of them. I'll send soldiers, like

Norris, to monitor the situation. I couldn't stop you from praying for them."

Ricky smiled. "Thanks."

Yurich still felt a deep stirring inside, a need to protect the man who had done so much, yet wanted so little in exchange. He looked directly at Ricky. "Just be careful. There are those who oppose you . . . not just in the military. You have enemies, Ricky—among the refugees. I'll be gone soon and I won't be able to help you."

NORTHWEST OF DALLAS — May 3rd

Pete Reisling came down the stairs to open the door. Who could be knocking so early? He looked out the peephole. A pretty, red-haired woman stood with two soldiers. And was that a jeep parked out in the street? Pete's pulse quickened a few beats. He had no idea what this might mean, but he opened the door.

"Hello?" he asked.

"Is this the house of Sara Reisling?"

"Yes," he answered cautiously.

The woman gave him a sad smile. "I know you don't know me, but my name is Briana Yurich. I've come with a message for Sara from Ricky and Rosa Ruiz."

Sara had been standing on the stairs holding her bathrobe closed, listening to the exchange. When she heard the names of her friends, she lost all caution and flew down the stairs. "Oh! That's me! They're my friends! Where are they?"

"They're my friends now, too," Briana said before her smile faded a bit. "They're still at the camp . . . but Rosa asked me to give you this," she said, reaching into her purse for several small, folded pages.

"Where are my manners?" Sara suddenly said. "Please, come in."

Briana looked at her uniformed escorts. "Well, I only intended to stay a few moments."

"Oh, please," Sara begged, taking the woman's hand. "I must hear all about them and what is happening . . . couldn't you stay for a while? Perhaps the men could come in as well, or maybe return for you later today?"

In the end, Briana did agree to stay, sending the soldiers away to return later. She drank a glass of water and allowed Sara to read the letter first.

Rosa had written it in tiny print, leaving almost no margins to maximize the use of the paper. Sara devoured the letter quickly.

> *"Dearest Sara:*
>
> *I'm writing this in haste, hoping to convey so much in so little space! How I miss your company.*
>
> *Ricky and I have been very busy here at the camp. God is doing such awesome things, I don't have the time to tell even a fraction of them, so will try to summarize our lives in hopes you'll catch a glimpse of us and be spurred to continue praying for us.*
>
> *Our worst day happened just a few days after you left. Soldiers brought a fever to the camp and several people passed away—one of them was a little boy who died in Ricky's arms. I don't have words to describe how it devastated Ricky. In the coming days, he thought perhaps he'd been wrong to let me and the children stay.*
>
> *But, one night, a group of us were praying and the presence of the Lord overshadowed us. With the glorious awareness of Him came a conviction about something we had all done. Until the disasters, we'd given virtually no thought at all to those in other countries who suffered. What did we care about many who sat in prisons for years, who had been tortured, and even put to death for their faith while we sat in our nice homes, safe from real suffering or persecution? Now that we live in such harsh surroundings, we beg for relief. But what about the millions we never prayed for, never helped? We felt so sorry, so broken about it. How could we have done this? As we cried out to God for forgiveness, something wonderful happened, Sara!*
>
> *Since that night, the Lord has been visiting us with signs and wonders! We can see now—no matter what happens—we were born for this time.*

Sometimes, when people come to meetings to pray, they are healed just stepping inside the tent! Other times, it happens when everyone lays hands on them, other times it's while everyone is worshiping and no one is touching them at all.

Sometimes, the water tastes like grapes, or we'll smell roses in the middle of the night. . . . Sara I can't describe it all. Conditions stay the same, but we sense God standing with us every day and people (including soldiers!) are getting saved.

Sadly, the number of orphans coming into the camp is increasing. All of us are taking them in. In addition to Angela and baby Daniel, we now have ten children (including Jason). Please pray for these dear ones. One of them is a little girl of six or seven. She was brought to the camp a couple of weeks ago after they found her alone in the woods, screaming her lungs out. Even after they got her to the camp, she kept screaming despite the sedatives they gave her. Long story short—Ricky was certain she wasn't ill. The soldiers let me (and the kids) live with her in an isolated tent for six days. After the first few hours, she stopped screaming, then finally fell asleep in my arms. For twelve hours. When she woke, she was calm, but she's never made a sound since—and she almost never lets me out of her sight. In fact she usually has to be holding onto me or my clothes.

The day after they brought her in, a small group of adults was found, murdered, about a mile from where they found her. We're all assuming her parents are among the dead. Whatever she saw is locked inside her. She has dark hair and eyes, and such a beautiful little round face that Ricky says she reminds him of a Daisy—so that's what we're calling her. Pray Daisy can open up to the presence of the Lord, so her heart can be healed of this awful thing, and she can be free.

I'm running out of paper. A change is coming to the camp, and the Lord has warned us persecution is at the door. Please pray we stay strong and keep our eyes on the Lord.

> *How I miss you! We still hope to see you again, dear Sara.*
>
> *Love, Rosa"*

Sara wiped tears from her eyes and looked up at Briana. "How can I ever thank you for bringing this to me?"

Briana reached over and put her hand on Sara's. "Truly, it's been my joy. I would've walked here if I had to. Now I'd like to tell you about the circumstances which brought Ricky and Rosa to me, and allowed me to be here . . ."

EASTERN OKLAHOMA — May 22nd

It had been a month since the US soldiers left the camp. United Nations forces under the command of Col. Juanita Ortiz now controlled the camp. Although the government's new system had been delayed, one more large transport had taken hundreds of refugees (picked by a random drawing) to southbound trains.

Because it seemed to keep morale higher, Col. Ortiz continued to let remaining refugees go "out to the rocks to leave messages." Small, escorted groups could go out in the morning and in the evening with paint brushes and cups of the olive-drab or tan paint used on the camp's buildings. A short distance away, a small canyon proved to be an excellent location for any who wanted to leave a record of their journey past this point and/or a message for loved ones to find.

In addition, supervised crews of refugees had been allowed to plant and maintain food gardens outside the camp. Soon, edibles from these gardens might help ease the food shortage.

On the north side of the camp, Ricky Ruiz walked among the tents, trying to stretch out his back and legs during the remainder of his morning break. A movement caught his eye, and he spotted his wife in the distance, gliding along with a flock of children. Even with stained, mismatched clothes and no makeup, how lovely she seemed to him.

She hadn't seen him yet, so he hid between two tents and waited for her to pass. He pulled off a large handful of the grass by his feet and, when she walked by, he tossed it at her. She quickly turned, then smiled up at him. The children, delighted with the green shower, mobbed "Papa Ricky." All of them, that is, except Daisy, who almost never let go of Mama Rosa's skirt.

Before Ricky hoisted baby Daniel up on his shoulders, he kissed his wife, hugged Angela, and smiled at Daisy. "How is everybody today?" he asked.

"Most of us are pretty rowdy," Rosa said before turning to stroke Daisy's hair. "But some of us are still quiet."

Although Daisy could occasionally be left with the Ruiz's oldest "daughter," a fifteen-year-old girl named Amanda, this was the only exception to Daisy's "Rosa only" rule. Before he left, Yurich had given Mr. & Mrs. Ruiz official custody of the little girl and, since they didn't know her name, they'd given her a new one: Daisy Ruiz.

A soldier passed by and Daisy hid behind Rosa, who gave her husband a sad look about it.

Ricky pulled a blade of grass out of Rosa's hair then brushed a few off her shoulder. "Have I told you what an incredible woman you are?"

"Not today," she answered, looking at the ground. She'd seen her reflection in a small mirror earlier and been a bit saddened by how worn and old she looked.

He got her to look at him again. "Well, you are. In fact, I may just sing the Rosa song, right here and now."

She bit her lip and blushed.

"Ha!" he said. "You thought I'd forgotten the Rosa song, didn't you?"

"What's the Rosa song?" several children said at once.

"It's a song," Ricky said proudly, "I personally composed to describe the great beauty and deep qualities of the woman I love." With one hand making sure Daniel didn't fall from his shoulders, he put the other to his chest, then drew a deep breath so he could gain the proper volume for the song.

Several expectant eavesdroppers appeared at the entrances of tents.

Rosa's eyes darted around. "Not now, dear."

He could see the color flushing her face and this pleased him. "As you wish, my queen," he said with a flourish. "I'll sing it later. Meantime, I'll let you and your subjects move on, and I'll see if I can find Dr. Schultz. I happen to know he's obtained a small stash of candy, and that, in honor of Daniel's first birthday last week, he's gonna give each of us a piece of it."

Most of the children squealed and Daisy looked around from her hiding place, eyes wide.

"Well," Ricky said, setting his son down and crouching low to be eye to eye with the girl, "we don't say much, but our hearing and comprehension are working just fine, huh?" At least she'd stopped hiding when he looked at her. "That's okay, Daisy. I know you're just storing the words up so you can say 'em later." He slowly offered his hand. "You want to bless me before I go back to work? You don't have to talk out loud, you can pray in your heart, right?"

Rosa bent down, too, and the other children gathered around, each putting a hand on Ricky. Daniel patted his father's hand, speaking mostly gibberish while several of the children took turns speaking. Of course, Ricky's ability to find Dr. Schultz got the most fervent prayer. When they were almost done, Daisy inched closer, reached over, and quickly touched Ricky's arm before retreating.

Rosa and her husband exchanged a thrilled look before Ricky beamed at the little girl, then hugged all the kids who would allow it. "Wow! I feel like a new man now!" he said, standing and stretching. "Thanks!"

He started to walk away, then turned and called out, "I love you, Rosalinda Ruiz!"

Most of the girls around Rosa giggled, and several onlookers laughed.

She went her way for about an hour, then Jason, looking as if he had urgent news, found her.

"Do you know where Ana Dashe is?" he asked.

Rosa thought about the woman they'd met during their last night outside the camp. She and her nephews brought Tracker the dog to the dinner the Lord provided. "Uh . . . perhaps. Is everything okay?"

"There's a guy in quarantine right now looking for her. We hear he came by *himself*."

Rosa looked shocked.

"Yeah. He's pretty determined. Anyway, we think it's her husband!"

Rosa bounced up and down a few times. "Oh! Let's go right now and find her!" Over time, the refugees had given every little alley and pathway between the tents a name. "You look over on Green Street. She lives in the second or third tent on the right. I'll go to the laundry . . . and I'll send Amanda by some of Ana's friends to look for her."

Before he reached her tent, Jason found Ana. When she heard her husband might *possibly* be in quarantine, the woman dropped the laundry in her arms and bounded down the hill toward the pens. When she got to the double fence, she ran along it shouting his name at the top of her lungs.

"Jeff! Jeff! Jeff! Where are you?"

As she passed the middle pen, he ran to his side of the enclosure. Soldiers had to restrain her (and threaten Jeff), to keep them from climbing over the barriers and meeting in the "no man's land" in the middle.

When they pulled Ana down, she struggled free, then grabbed the fence. "I thought I'd never see you again!" she sobbed.

Tears streamed down his face. "I never gave up looking for you, honey. I never gave up."

Within a few minutes, it was decided. If Ana wanted to go through the six day quarantine again, they'd let her over into the pen. She went gladly, and the news traveled through whole camp like a flash flood. The messages had worked! Someone had been found!

Later, after dark, the Ruiz's oldest daughter, Amanda, watched the sleeping crew of kids so Ricky and Rosa could sneak out and have a few moments alone.

"It's warm this evening," he said as they entered a small open space at the edge of the camp. "Going to get really hot soon."

She slipped her arm around him. "Well, I guess the pioneers way back when survived the weather, so it's been done before."

He'd brought a scratchy, olive-green army blanket to spread on a small patch of turf between the last tents and the fence bordering the camp. They sat on the blanket, looking up at the sky, ignoring the fence in front of them, pretending they were the only two people for miles. They'd been sitting there for a few minutes when several bright streaks began blazing across the heavens.

"Look at that!" several people nearby exclaimed at once. People all around piled out of their tents to see the spectacle. "Up there!"

Several more balls of fire raged along the same course as crowds gathered outside.

"What are they? What are they?" many wanted to know, almost panicking.

"They're missiles!" one man yelled.

There were a few exclamations before one woman said, "No! Maybe it's . . . maybe it's Jesus!"

Everybody seemed to take in a breath as they watched in silence for a moment. Ricky put both arms around Rosa. The phenomenon disappeared.

By then, a man had worked his way forward through the spectators and grabbed the arm of the woman who had spoken last. "Come home . . . *now*," he quietly commanded.

"But, Carson," she said as he began pulling her back through the group. "The whole sky lit up just like–"

"Shut up!" he shouted as they disappeared down a path between tents.

"Perhaps we'd better go," Rosa said. "If all this racket wakes Daisy up, we'd better be there."

"You're right," Ricky said.

They picked up the blanket and started squeezing through the swarm of people.

"You know what I think?" One man said loudly. "I think we're being visited."

"Visited?" someone asked. "By whom?"

"Intelligent beings from other planets, or other dimensions. They're coming to help us. They're going to stop us from destroying ourselves."

Rosa stopped and turned to look at the man, then at her husband. Ricky motioned for her to move on. Once out of the crowd, Rosa leaned close to him and asked, "What do you think they were?"

"Who knows? Maybe more pieces of the space station coming down."

They reached their tent and went inside. Amazingly, Daisy still slept, but several of the other children had awakened and been frightened by the commotion. Ricky and Rosa cuddled with them in the center of the tent, assuring them everything was okay.

Then they all heard loud voices coming from a nearby tent. Both Ricky and Rosa recognized the voice of the man who had dragged his wife away from the group looking at the sky.

"And you were wrong AGAIN!" he bellowed at the top of his lungs. "Your big mouth is gonna get us in big trouble if you don't stop it! And, if you don't stop it, I swear I'm leaving you."

"But Carson," she pleaded, "He could be here any minute."

There was the sound of a slap and crying. Ricky started to get up, then sat back down when he saw soldiers outside, ordering the noisy couple out of their tent. Before being hauled away, the man became even more abusive.

Daisy awoke during the melee, and ran to the clump of children huddled around Rosa and Ricky. The others grudgingly moved aside so Daisy could squeeze in near Rosa. This time, instead of gravitating to the side farthest from Ricky, she wriggled into a spot just between them and shivered. They all put arms around her and prayed.

DALLAS, TX

Two hundred miles away from the Ruiz tent, just before the fiery show in the sky, Zachary and Michael Gordon stood on the roof of their building with Linda and a lovely lady named Sierra. Zac had discovered a way to get on the roof weeks ago, and, with no television and no air conditioning, it was a great place to sit in the evening.

Michael and Linda moved away and stood near a corner, leaving Zac and Sierra to themselves.

"So, how was your first day on the job?" Michael asked.

She leaned against him. "It was good . . . I had the jitters for the first couple of hours, but once I got into it, I was okay."

"So what do you do, anyway?"

"Well, it's the dissemination department. . . . It's like a newsroom, sort of, only the government does it. I mean, we're collecting and dispersing information. Some of it goes out over the radio, some gets printed on flyers, some of it will go on billboards," she said, nodding to a giant, lighted sign in the distance. Though quite far away, it stood out well in a city with few lights. These "live" billboards were about to pop up everywhere. Michael knew this, because his construction team's newest assignment would be to put up the structures for over a hundred of them in the region. The billboards were, in essence, giant television screens with the capacity to be viewed by hundreds of people at the same time. Powered by Fibertronics, they'd be huge samples of the "new technology for the new day."

"Today," Linda said, "I helped work on a live billboard campaign with video clips from Edith Todd."

"Clips of Edith Todd? Saying what?" Michael asked.

Linda poked him in the ribs with a finger and teased, "Goodness, Mr. Gordon, are you turning into a newsman? Are you trying to interview me?"

"Uh . . . I thought I was just doing what you women are supposed to want . . . you know, showing an interest in what you're doing."

"Okay, okay," she conceded, "Since you're so interested, I'll tell you. Basically, it's quotes from Mrs. Todd and others on coding—you know signing up and getting onboard for how things will be in the future."

"So, people just go sign up for all this? Like you do to get a credit card?"

She didn't know why, but Linda suddenly felt uncomfortable. "Well it's not like that exactly. . . . To be honest, it's not like that at all."

"What do you mean?"

She didn't want to sound negative. After all, wasn't she trying to help sell the idea to the public?

"It's more like an agreement, actually," she said. "Yes. It's like that." She sat down and waited for him to be seated next to her. "Before now," she continued, "life got all jumbled up because people had unhealthy loyalties and worked only for their own causes. The solution is to make unity the goal. . . . So, now, they want us all to put unity first."

A harsh laugh came from Michael. "You mean, like the pledge of allegiance to the flag, only now it's about world peace? I can see what a hit this could be at sporting events. We'd all get misty-eyed and talk about unity, then the two teams could do a group hug, skip the competition, and leave together on the same bus. Gosh, I get all warm and fuzzy just thinking of it."

"Don't be sarcastic." She picked up a small piece of gravel and threw it off the roof. "It's like a marriage contract."

He cocked his head to one side. "You're kidding."

"No, I'm not. When you marry, you have to vow that you're forsaking all other lovers and pledge yourself to your spouse don't you? It's like that. You have to renounce the old ways and embrace the new. Once you do that, you're in. You get an implant—a code—and then you get all its entitlements."

He ignored the new terminology. He had other questions at the moment. "'Give up old ways.' Like what?"

She gave him an irritated look. "Are you trying to pick a fight with me?"

"No. I just don't know what it is you're saying. Be more specific about what we renounce."

"Well, like nationalism, racism, sexism . . . and fanatical religious beliefs."

"Fanatical religious beliefs," he repeated. "And what would those be?"

"I understand how this might make people nervous," she said, trying to keep in mind Michael's soft spot for Christians because of his brother, Ben. "I'm still a bit unsure about it, but, maybe it's like Edith Todd says. Maybe it's that Americans are just stuck in a western mind set. Many of us claim to be Christians, even when we don't really practice it. Lots of Jews and Muslims do the same thing. It's an outward form—like belonging to a country club. It only fosters a sense of superiority."

Linda pulled her knees up to her chest and put her arms around her legs. "Edith challenges us all to look at how little it's done in our lives. Insisting there is only one path to one God is a vain tradition, a superstition that's caused horrible turmoil. I, for one, will never forget those scary 'He is coming soon' threats as long as I live. Faith hasn't gotten me anywhere." The sight of Trina Watson being taken away flashed briefly through Linda's mind. "And I don't think it's gotten any of them where they wanted to go, either."

Just then, streaks of light started burning across the sky.

"Perhaps," Michael said, "it's a matter of perspective."

NORTHWEST OF DALLAS

Fifty miles away from Michael and Linda, Sara sat in her back yard with twenty other people. They all stopped talking when the sky lit up.

378 / Terry L. Craig

Once the sky darkened again, a woman said, "I wonder if that was old debris or shooting stars."

"I suppose either is possible," Pete, Sara's father, answered. "We spent so little time outside noticing these things before . . . who knows?"

Naomi, Sara's mother, tried to get things back on track. "It's getting late. We need to finish up soon."

"Well," a man named Chet suggested, "if what happened to Sara, Nick, and Ashleigh is any example, we'll all need to find ways to get by soon. No one has told me I have to get coded in order to keep my job yet, but it may only be a matter of time."

"And in answer to that," Sara said, "we believe the Lord has given our family an idea, and maybe each of you should consider something like it. We're going to try to open a small store. We'll end up selling mostly to people who don't want to get a code. There are lots of small businesses each of you could have, helping other people, like us, who won't sell out God for modern conveniences. Some of you can grow or make things to sell, others have skills you can sell. We'll deal in cash or we'll barter with each other. Right now, we're being given a choice, but someday, that may change. I know God will provide if we put Him first."

EASTERN OKLAHOMA

Hours later, in the refugee camp, a huge thunderstorm pounded into the area, shaking buildings and threatening to flatten tents. Even though the flap had been tied shut, high winds whipped rain into the Ruiz's tent as thunder sounded all around them. The family stayed huddled in the center of the tent. What if the storm spawned tornadoes? What about radiation or other contaminants that could be carried in the rain? When would it end?

CHAPTER 52

EASTERN OKLAHOMA — May 29th

Col. Juanita Ortiz, in charge of United Nations forces stationed at the refugee camp in eastern Oklahoma, looked across her desk at the woman who had been sitting there for nearly an hour. A late-night meeting with this refugee had, once again, proven informative.

"Well," the Colonel said, "I want to thank you, Ms. Balardi, for your help."

Myra wanted to make sure she'd been heard. "I've only seen it as my duty, Colonel Ortiz, to inform you about the continuing defiance to your authority. Your predecessor didn't represent government interests or those of us in the camp who wanted order. We want you to know we appreciate your active role in bringing things back under control, and we want to help you."

"Thank you, Ms. Balardi. If that's all—"

Myra's bony hands tightened on the arms of her chair. "When we see this man, Mr. Ruiz, and the others constantly rebelling against you, we feel it's our duty to inform you. Despite your orders limiting the size, duration, and frequency of meetings, they continue to cram people into tents for long periods of time. And, contrary to your most recent command, they're secretly meeting with your soldiers."

The refugee was repeating herself and Ortiz needed to wrap things up. "Well, Ms. Balardi, thank you for the list of civilian and soldier names. Since these meetings don't seem to have any sort of schedule, it might take some effort to get a lid on all of them, but rest assured, we're working on it. Just continue what you're doing in the meantime."

Myra wanted the Colonel to see her as an asset. This constituted a recognition of sorts, didn't it? She gave the officer a grim smile. "Some of us are so glad you're here to set things right."

Ortiz rose from her chair. "Yes, yes. You're welcome. Sergeant Polanski will see you safely back to the other side of the camp."

As soon as the sergeant and Balardi stepped out the door, Ortiz logged the meeting and made a notation:

> "Will order soldiers listed to report tomorrow for discipline and possible reassignment. Re Myra Balardi: while other sources confirm her information, she appears unstable and is not to be trusted beyond controlled circumstances."

Sergeant Polanski walked Myra to the edge of the civilian section of the camp. Another soldier made sure the coast was clear before Polanski sent her on alone. To escort her farther might arouse suspicion.

He shook his head as he watched her disappear into the camp. *When a woman is ruthless, truly, she's harder than a man. Between her and Ortiz, I don't know who would prove more merciless. I bet this little Balardi woman could claw somebody to shreds.*

Back in her office, Col. Ortiz considered her own limitations. How far dare she go to halt the activities of the fanatical religious group which had such a strong presence in the camp? If she arrested Ruiz and some of the other ring leaders, not only would she be out some valuable medical personnel, but radical followers might riot. Yet this man's influence, if allowed to grow, might create more trouble in the long run.

Ortiz cracked her knuckles and considered how much of her own fate balanced on her performance here. The camp couldn't continue to be seen as a breeding ground for religious fanatics. Hadn't this been the reason for the transfer of the previous commander?

This assignment won't crash my career, the colonel vowed to herself. *But things need to turn around. No wonder so many international reinforcements have been sent to this country.*

Americans, always difficult and independent, might break the back of the whole movement if allowed to run amok. While severely humbled by their circumstances, they still hadn't been beaten down sufficiently to become docile.

Freedom remained entrenched in their memories. They could still rise up and make trouble.

Ortiz went to the doorway of headquarters and surveyed her dimly-lit domain. Within weeks, a full schedule of transports would resume—under new regulations. What could she do? Looking out over the camp, it came to her.

Life has been too easy here. To accomplish this mission, I must make them so sorry they're still here they'll do anything to get out. I've only got a few weeks to choke out their determination. Desperate people will be much more willing to sign anything put before them. Her face hardened to a look of resolve. *And those who won't sign will get passed over until they do.*

DALLAS, TX,—7 p.m., May 30th

Michael Gordon made his way up to the apartment he and Linda shared with his brother, Zac. He walked down the dingy hall, unlocked the door, and entered.

"Hey stranger," Zac said from his seat at the table. "Linda came through looking for you about an hour ago, then went out."

Michael frowned. "Yeah. I got let out of work an hour early for one of those special presentations they've been giving everywhere. By the time the question and answer part was over, the stupid thing ended up taking an extra hour and forty-five minutes."

Zac had been leaning back, balancing on two legs of a kitchen chair, but leaned forward for a soft landing and rested his forearms on the table. "So what did they say?"

Michael sat down facing him. "Man, Zac, it's scary. They not only want you to sign that Notice of Allegiance thing—you have to give them blood as well."

Zac's mouth fell open. "What?"

"It's just a drop—like they used to do for testing diabetics. After you sign, they stick your finger and have this little slot where you put a drop. They say it's a DNA sample that'll be on your permanent ID record in the main data banks. It's part of the registration for the chip they put in your hand. That way, even if someone dug the chip out of you and managed not to disturb the transmitter, the DNA info they have for the chip will prove it's stolen."

"That's creepy, Michael."

"I know. Are you going to do it?"

Zac shook his head. "No way, man. There are plenty of ways I can get what I want without doing that. I'm not going to let them track me around like some sort of lab rat. How about you?"

"Absolutely not. This thing has gone too far. They can't make me do it, and I'm not going to."

"What about Linda?"

"She's got connections, too. She's not doing it either. As long as we can get by without it, why should we?"

Linda came in the door with a small shopping bag. The happy expression on her face said she'd found something nice to buy.

Michael smiled at her. "Hey, I just got home. Been shopping?"

"Oh yes," she said quickly. "I got a promotion today and I'm a third assistant now!" She moved over to where the two men sat. "And I got the most beautiful outfit to mark the occasion." She gave Michael a kiss, then pulled his hand to get him out of his chair. "Things are looking up and I want to celebrate. Want to go and find some real food tonight?"

Despite the dark feeling he had, Michael managed another smile. "Okay."

Within minutes, Zac sat alone in the apartment. The new information about coding had really given him a jolt. Who would have thought things could progress this far this fast? Of course, no one at his job had insisted that he go to one of those seminars on coding yet, but it might only be a matter of time.

Then again, he considered, *all this might be an idea the government wants to promote, but won't be able to fly if the majority of people resist. How many people will actually do it anyway? Even LINDA doesn't want to do it. . . . The whole thing will be a joke a year from now.*

Reluctantly, Zac gave some thought to the larger issue. He'd memorized too much Scripture as a young man to blithely accept the demands of the new order. He rubbed the stubble on his chin and considered it. Christians will have fits over this. Although he had no intention of getting vocal over the issue, the belief that other people would gave him comfort.

Yeah, he thought, *millions of them will reject it. They'll make such a racket, the whole thing will blow over in a year and it will have been a big deal about nothing. The government will realize they can only push people so far and that will be it. Why join the argument? It's not as if they're forcing people to do it. Life will go on . . . I'll go on.*

Like Michael and Linda, Zac had learned to live with "less." It wasn't so bad.

He leaned back in his chair again and considered his choices for evening activities. . . . *Cindy, Sheryl, Sierra? Yes. Life will definitely go on.*

CHAPTER 53

REFUGEE CAMP IN EASTERN OKLAHOMA—10 a.m., June 13th

For the first time in more than three months, trucks and busses sat in line outside the fence, waiting to be filled with passengers. This time, soldiers told the refugees, seating would be decided by a new method: First-come-first-serve. Anybody could report to the large, newly renovated processing center (a giant Quonset hut on the west side of the camp) and complete the necessary procedures. Today, the first three hundred fifty-three individuals completing processing would obtain seating on departing vehicles. And, soldiers told refugees, transports would be returning in two days to repeat the process. The new system would finally allow the camp to be emptied. With a little cooperation, *all* of them could soon be resettling in the south.

Col. Juanita Ortiz stood in the doorway to headquarters looking down at the long line of people waiting to go into the building where they'd be processed. Two huge, diesel generators, providing power for the new equipment inside the building, droned in the distance.

She watched a shoving match between two refugees in the line and a feeling of satisfaction arose in her. She'd played it perfectly. In the past two weeks, after declaring a ban on all gatherings, she'd intentionally made life twice as miserable for the civilians. She'd sent soldiers out by night to kill the plants in the garden. She'd made sure refugees had only the bare minimum of provisions to survive, and that medicines (including pain killers) had "run out." Even in the sweltering heat, all civilians had to be in their tents by sunset with the tent flaps closed. By now, going south had to be the paramount thing in the mind of every refugee.

This time, she ordered drivers to park the trucks and busses closer than before, in plain sight of anyone who walked to the west side of the camp. She wanted the refugees to see those vehicles waiting . . . she wanted them to see transportation to the real world had come *this* close. Then they could face the decision.

Col. Ortiz had made certain the refugees learned nothing about the processing before today. They'd be caught without preparation. The first refugees willing to sign the Notice of Allegiance would be taken, along with their underage children, directly to southbound trains. Once they arrived in Texas, they'd present a certificate verifying they'd signed the Notice, and be implanted with a coded information chip. The "code" (chip) would allow them privileges which, although modest by old standards, would seem like heaven compared to life in a camp.

Any who balked at signing the Notice would remain in the camp. They'd stay and endure another spate of spoiled rations, unbearable heat, and head lice. Each time they refused, they could watch the others—those smart enough to sign—leave for the comforts awaiting down south.

The sooner Ortiz set this camp in order, the sooner she could see it in a rear-view mirror. She'd been sent here to prove she hadn't grown too soft. Some said she'd failed when it came to removing resistant people from several small cities in Colorado during last winter's bitter cold. She'd been told to do "whatever it took," and thought she had. Hadn't her troops rousted people, even those without proper shoes or coats, and sent them packing down lonely roads south? Hadn't they interrogated, then shot, all the resistance fighters they could catch? Despite her efforts, snipers continually picked away at UN forces in her assigned area, and six international soldiers were killed in a booby-trapped bank. Ortiz was the convenient scape-goat.

She straightened her stance. She'd show them all she wasn't the weak link in the chain. For this assignment, the important thing was signing the Notice. And sign they would. While the refugees still had "rights of refusal" they weren't exactly in a position to know those rights, were they? Besides, to whom would they complain if they didn't like the treatment? Colonel Ortiz. Nobody was leaving this camp unless they signed.

NORTHWEST OF DALLAS

Sara Reisling made an effort to unclench her teeth. In order to get a licence to open a small store, she had to go to a "Center for Tomorrow," to obtain yet another certificate stating she'd sat through an entire presentation and received counseling on coding. Being forced to travel to a Center for Tomorrow and endure this procedure again irritated her, but she reminded herself to relax as she sat down facing a middle-aged woman in the small, well lit cubicle.

"Hi!" the woman said warmly, offering a hand. "I'm Celeste."

Sara shook her hand. "Sara."

Celeste entered some initial information into her computer before addressing her again. "So . . . Sara . . . did you watch the video?"

"Yes."

One click on the keyboard. "Did you understand it?"

"Yes."

Another click. "And do you have any questions?"

"No."

A scroll and a click before Celeste looked up at Sara. "And your decision?"

"I decline."

"You've chosen to decline?"

"That's right. I'm exercising my right to refuse coding."

All ten of Celeste's nimble fingers perched on the keyboard, ready to record the response to her next question. "What is your reason for declining?"

Sara cleared her throat and folded her hands in her lap. "Well, Celeste, I happen to believe Jesus Christ is the *only* Lord and Savior for the whole world. I have no intention of renouncing Him."

Fingers flew on the keys. Sara figured this would be it. They'd give her the certificate and she'd and go home.

"I see." Celeste said. "You don't feel you've misinterpreted what we're doing?"

"What do you mean?"

The woman opened a drawer in her desk and pulled out a small, clear plastic case and a magnifying glass, then handed them to Sara. "Now Sara," she said, as if talking to a first grader, "Inside this little case is an actual chip . . . just like the ones we use for coding . . . I want you to take that magnifying glass and look at it, then tell me what you see."

Sara, looked at it, then set the case and the magnifying glass down. "It's a chip, Celeste."

"Did you see any numbers or marks of any kind on that chip?"

"No, I didn't."

"Exactly. It really isn't much different from the smart chip they placed in ATM cards years ago. This is a safe, theft-proof way to keep all your documentation with you at all times. It's the ultimate in security and convenience, actually."

Sara shrugged. "I guess I'm not willing to give up that much for security and convenience."

Celeste realized that dancing around the issue wouldn't do. She needed to cut to the chase. "It goes under the skin. If it has no marks or numbers on it and it goes under your skin, it couldn't be called a 'mark' on you, could it?"

Apparently, there had been a growing problem with people accepting the chip. Sara spoke in a calm voice. "The chip isn't the main issue for me right now. Even if it isn't 'the mark,' the bottom line is: I won't sign or agree to any statement saying I deny the one true God. He is the Lord of the whole earth, the universe, and of all that is, was or will be."

A soft peal of laughter came from Celeste and she called over a fellow worker. "Jimmy. Come here." Jimmy, a nice looking man with dark hair and banker's clothing arrived in the booth before Celeste looked back at Sara. "Now, say that again."

Sara looked at the two of them. They do this so well. How practiced, *how studied they are at using ridicule as a weapon against people. I wonder how often it works?*

After a long silence Celeste patted Sara's hand and spoke again. "You know you're just being plain old silly, don't you?"

Sara moved her hand away before Celeste retracted her own and continued. "If I recall correctly, all of you said Jesus was coming any second to whisk you away." She glanced at her cohort. "Didn't they, Jimmy?"

He kept his eyes on Sara. "Sure did. But I never saw him."

Celeste pressed further. "So, where is he? Where'd he go? On vacation? You're still *here*. . . . Why? Because you had a false hope, you had a wrong concept. Can't you see it? Instead of the huge, horrible, apocalyptic ending you predicted—the one religious fanatics *almost* brought about—the entire world stands poised to enter the greatest period of its history!"

Sara fixed her gaze on Celeste. "I didn't predict any ending. Jesus may not come in my lifetime. Meanwhile, I won't deny Him. May I have my certificate now?"

Celeste gave Jimmy a slight nod of her head, signaling him to go away. Once he'd gone, she tried a new tack. "Here's what I want you to see, Sara. No one's asking you to deny God. Getting coded doesn't mean you're joining a godless world! It's not even a world without Christ! Many Christian denominations are endorsing the movement, because they've recognized we believe in Christ, too . . . we've just let him escape out of the tight little definition that's caused so much grief." She leaned forward, speaking in a friendly, confidential tone. "Trust me, a deep spiritual life will open to you once you look past your limited concept of God."

Sara leaned forward as well. "Do you have anybody, Celeste? Does anybody really love you?"

"What?" The unexpected question had several possible trap doors. "Well. Of course. The movement brings a lot of love into my life."

"No. I mean, do you have a special someone? Are you the light of someone's life, the reason they live?"

Although it had been more than a year since he'd walked out, Celeste, once again, felt the stab of loss. "No. It's not very realistic to think in such terms . . ."

Sara looked her in the eyes. "Someone loves *me* that much, Celeste. . . . In order to come here for me, he gave up incredible wealth and status. Even after he got here, if he would've been willing to forget me, he could've lived a long life, worn expensive clothing, kept a fine mansion. . . . He gave them all up for me. And, for my sake, he never had physical intimacy with another, he stayed pure. . . . Sometimes he went hungry and had no place to sleep, so he could keep working for my release from captivity. For me, he endured rejection and ridicule . . ." Sara closed her eyes and pictured it. "He could've decided I wasn't worth the all the pain—but his love was so great, men couldn't beat it out of him. He loved me so much he gave up his life for me . . ." She looked at Celeste again. "When Jesus stretched out His hands on the cross, He was reaching through time and space—for me. And the power of His love was so great, even the grave couldn't hold Him. How could I sell out such love?. . . No one who's ever known it could just throw it away."

A slight shiver ran through Celeste. She quickly rolled back her chair, then turned her head and raised her voice. "Jimmy!"

"Yes?" he answered from somewhere else in the room.

"Come give this woman her certificate, then let her out. I need to go upstairs and take a break."

EASTERN OKLAHOMA

Hours after Sara had left The Center for Tomorrow in Dallas, the last of the trucks rolled away from the refugee camp in Eastern Oklahoma. Night had fallen on the camp, and more than three hundred of its residents had departed.

Even though housed in individual tents, refugees knew the concept of personal privacy was a joke. Only two pieces of canvas and a few inches separated one small group or family from another—on three sides. Anyone walking by the flap of a tent could stick their head through it and see what went on inside.

Despite the danger of being punished for having "a banned gathering," the Ruiz family and others, had a constant flow of visitors to their tents. In a few minutes, curfew would stop any refugee movement in the camp, but until then, friends came in two's and three's to talk or pray.

A woman, the one who thought perhaps Jesus was coming back the night they all saw the fiery streaks in the sky, stood next to Rosa, crying. Rosa and several other women moved closer and hugged her.

"He left me. He left me," she lamented over and over. "How could he leave me?"

They continued to hold her, letting her talk. All of them knew this might become a common scenario soon. One spouse willing to get coded, the other not—one spouse leaving camp, the other not. The pressure to give in was enormous.

What would happen in cases like Ana and Jeff Dashe? Ana and her nephews had only been Christians for a matter of months, Jeff for a few days. Would they have the strength to refuse?

Today, it became crystal clear no one would leave the camp without signing the Notice of Allegiance. For each person, it would come down to personal conviction—one which would be sorely tested.

ATLANTA, GA—7 a.m., June 15th

Noted psychic Tony Bensen opted to skip breakfast with friends in order to spend a few more minutes alone in his apartment. Although he'd have to get going soon, he wanted to delay it as long as possible.

Walking through the streets was becoming an increasingly difficult task for him. All the turmoil, fear, and depression he sensed when he passed through crowds really got to him. Being so spiritually in tune definitely had its drawbacks. A few more minutes preparing himself for the day would be better for him than having breakfast.

He opened the door to the little ten-by-ten-foot room he used exclusively for meditation. Softly lit and receiving a continuous flow of inspired, instrumental music, this room expressed his heart. He inhaled the faint scent of fragrant oils as he sat down in the middle of the floor, crossed his legs, and closed his eyes. Perhaps today, with some effort, he'd be able to keep his sense of serenity.

Although he wanted to believe America had seen her worst days, a staggering number of suicides still occurred every day. Even now, the cries of innumerable anguished souls encroached on his thoughts. He opened his eyes and looked around for a moment. Long, white gauze curtain panels, hanging around the room, gently swayed in response to an oscillating fan.

He closed his eyes again and tried to count down. He had to find a way to cancel these disturbing thoughts and focus on the positive. Many prophets in the upper echelons of the movement could see the twin blessings of peace and security just ahead. Why couldn't he? Because he'd gotten stuck in the now. The world writhed in Transition and he felt its pain. . . . When would ordinary people be rescued from the sea of sorrows?

I must fight this depression, he told himself. *Soon, new life will spring up. The world will see the New Day dawning.*

But if that's true, why can't I see it? What about all this makes me feel so dark?

The fact that a wealthy patron had given Tony a nice apartment next to her own large home hadn't helped. Just last night, he'd dined on a smorgasbord of lovely, organic foods she'd provided. *Perhaps*, he told himself, *I merely feel guilty because I have so much compared with others. I didn't even have to get coded to obtain them. Is that fair?*

Now he came to the crux of the matter: Coding.

"So, what's my deep, abiding problem with this?" he said aloud.

An answer shot into his mind. *Because, if everything is the same . . . if, as I've been taught, all faiths just express different facets of the same God, then that means we are all brothers and sisters. If some Christians and others see it differently, does that make them any less my family? Does it give people the right to harm and persecute them? Can I swear loyalty to a movement which encourages such cruelty?*

He thought of Edith Todd and others, sitting behind closed doors and relishing the pain of the "mindless monotheists" and it sickened him. *They worry over their pets, they weep over trees, and turtle eggs, but people who oppose them "deserve" to suffer.*

No, he couldn't stand with them on this one. He wouldn't sign a Notice of Allegiance. He wouldn't get coded. Not yet. Not until both sides saw the truth.

"So what will I do?" he asked himself.

A light seemed to shine into his soul.

I will go out there and prove there's a better means of going about this. I'll find a way to bridge the gap between monotheists and the new order. I will let myself be used to bring out the truth . . . so all can live in peace.

CHAPTER 54

OKLAHOMA REFUGEE CAMP—10 a.m., Thursday, June 18th

A searing sun continued to plow into the sky, promising another day of unrelenting heat. Soldiers finished the new line of fencing behind the large Quonset hut. The building had served as the processing center where more than eighteen hundred refugees had already signed the Notice of Allegiance prior to shipping out.

In a building near the processing center, Col. Juanita Ortiz looked over the documents in her hands before signing them, then sliding them across the desk. "Here," she said. "These will be all you need. You and the others must be ready in one hour. Report to the sergeant at the west gate, and he'll make sure you get on a vehicle."

Myra Balardi picked up the certificates and folded them carefully before putting them inside her blouse where no one would see them. What an intense satisfaction she felt. She'd won. Ricky Ruiz would stay here and rot while she and the others left—without signing the Notice. A few times, she'd begun to doubt, but vindication had finally come. "Thank you, Colonel. The others are appreciative, too."

Ortiz busied herself with other papers on her desk. "Yes, yes. Goodbye, Ms. Balardi."

As soon as Myra left, the colonel finished another report on the outcome of the meeting. Ortiz hoped this would be the last time she'd have to deal with the woman and her small band of wacky followers. In exchange for intelligence information, Balardi had obtained a release for herself and ten others.

The colonel had given up the hope that all the refugees would give in and sign the Notice. In the final analysis, she decided, this looked better anyway. Now she had some credibility should accusations of force arise later. She could point to Balardi and the others and say, "*See?* Those people didn't want codes and we let them leave."

So what if Balardi was a screwball? She'd win few converts in the South.

DALLAS, TX

At about the same time Myra walked away from camp headquarters, Michael Gordon had fallen back asleep. He'd temporarily forgotten that today would be a big day. He and Linda would finally be moving into their own apartment.

The curtains suddenly flew open, allowing the uncovered window to bombard the room with sunlight. He pulled the covers over his face before Linda pounced on the sofa bed.

"Time to get up! Time to get up!" she said cheerily. She bounced the bed a few times.

How he hated cheery people in the morning. He grunted to indicate he'd heard her. If he remained silent, he'd become the victim of relentless bright chatter and more bouncing.

"C'mon! Our new home awaits!" she said, grabbing his foot and pulling him toward the end of the mattress.

"I'm almost up," he said in his own defense. "Just give me a second. You've nearly blinded me. I need to adjust to the light."

Within minutes, he got up and dressed for the day. Although unsure as to why Linda had to get going so early, he knew it would be best to placate her. The few things they owned fit into a mere fifteen boxes. The only hassle would come in carrying them several blocks to their new apartment. They'd probably be done in a few hours.

"Why don't we have a party tonight and celebrate?" she asked.

"Sure," he said in a groggy voice. "Why not?"

She grinned and hugged herself. "Aren't you excited?"

He raised an eyebrow. *Am I excited? No.* No matter how hard he tried, Michael couldn't seem to feel excited about anything. *Did I survive all that just to occupy space on this planet?*

Linda's smile disappeared and she moved closer to him. "C'mon. You can be happy. It's not wrong, you know."

He ran his fingers through his hair. "I wasn't trying to make you feel guilty, Linda. I'm just not . . . I'm just not . . . ready. So many people died, but we didn't, and I can't seem to figure out why. I mean, did we go through all that just to get plugged with a chip and become 'one' with the big cosmic machine? And, if not, what else is there?"

Linda plopped down in a ratty old chair and pulled at the stuffing protruding from the armrest. "For goodness sake, Michael, get over yourself. Does *everything* have to be so deep? Give it a rest!"

He frowned. "I'm sorry."

He turned to face her and the reddish-blond stubble on his jawline shone in the light, accenting his angular features. He'd put on the shirt she'd given him, and it was the exact same shade of blue as his eyes. Even with his surly look, she found him devastatingly handsome. If only he'd change.

"You know what I think?" she said. "I think you ought to go to that counselor I told you about. One of the gals at work used him and she feels much better. He has 'no drug' alternatives for depression."

Michael moved to the window and looked out at some children playing in the parking lot. "Perhaps you're right. . . . I'll go."

She sprung up from the chair again. "Excellent!" she said before giving him a big squeeze. "Just wait, Michael. It'll get better, I promise. We're getting into our own place today. We'll be able to furnish it with nice things—one at a time—and we'll be able to do what we want. Before you know it you'll be feeling good again."

OKLAHOMA REFUGEE CAMP

Miles to the north, Myra Balardi approached the gate with three men and seven women in tow. Each of them carried their few belongings and the certificates permitting them to be placed on a small transport truck going west to the train station.

The sergeant checked their papers, then nodded to the man at the gate. White dust rose in the sweltering heat as the soldier opened the gate to let them pass.

"Go to the second truck in the line," the sergeant said, referring to one of three waiting to depart.

The ex-refugees stepped out into freedom and began the short walk down the path to the transports. Myra looked back at the camp one last time. Could he see her? Did he know yet? Her gaze then moved behind her, to the small band of the faithful who'd endured such hardship with her. In the rear of the group, Sebastian suddenly pointed. In the path ahead of her, the dirt had eroded away from an old tree root. Before he could speak, Myra caught her foot on it and fell headlong. In an unsuccessful attempt to stave off impact with the ground, she scraped both hands, then slid sideways into a pile of rocks.

She heard a collective gasp before they all said, "Are you okay?"

Sebastian and Isaac rushed to her side. Her knees and hands hurt. Her teeth, jarred when her chin smacked onto the rocks, registered pain as well. To make it even more humiliating, she could hear soldiers at the bottom of the hill laughing at her clumsiness.

"I'm okay," she said, not wanting them to help her up. "I just lost my footing." She swept a lock of hair out of her face and prepared to stand up. A movement caught her eye. Something among the rocks, right in front of her face. As the patterns on it moved and rearranged, her eyes refocused to assimilate the image. She barely recognized the snake before it struck with lightning speed at the center of her face.

Minutes later, Col. Ortiz stared at the soldier standing in front of her desk and asked, "Say again?"

"A snake bit one of the women in the group, Colonel."

"What's her name?" Ortiz quickly asked.

"Uh, I believe her name is Ballard—something like that. Sergeant DiMarco sent me to obtain orders from you. The group's already officially checked out of the camp. What do you want us to do?"

Ortiz swore in Spanish before addressing the young private in English. "Is she still alive?"

"When I left? Barely. It bit her in the face, ma'am."

Ortiz stood and turned her back to the soldier. *Is there no end to the problems? If they bring that woman back into the camp, word of it will hit every tent within minutes. . . . And all those stupid fanatics will see this as some sort of retribution. . . . The ones who are close to buckling will be scared off.*

The Colonel spun around. "I'll call DiMarco directly. Speak to no one of this. You're dismissed."

"Yes, ma'am."

When he exited, she picked up the phone on her desk and rang her assistant. "Corporal," she said when he answered. "Call down to the transport shack. I want to speak with Sergeant DiMarco immediately." She hung up the phone. Within seconds, it rang and she lifted the receiver.

"Sergeant DiMarco?" Her posture tensed as she rapidly fired off orders. "The injured woman is to be taken inside the shack near the trucks. Tell the others in her group I've called for a doctor and then load them onto the transport. Tell them she'll be sent on later if she recovers. No one, I repeat, no one from that group is to be permitted back into the camp for any reason. When the woman expires, notify me without delay. Have you got all that?" After a pause, she said, "That is correct, do it now," and hung up the phone.

She sat down at her desk until the phone rang a few minutes later. "Ortiz," she said into the receiver. "Yes, Sergeant. . . . She has? Have the others departed? . . . Yes. How many soldiers are aware of what's happened? Inform them immediately that they are to share this information with no one. Consequences for any breach of secrecy will be swift and severe. Is that clear?. . . The body? Keep it in the shack. I'll send a detail with a bag for it after curfew. . . ."

Ten miles away, ten refugees, still in shock, bounced along in a transport toward the train station. A few of them still hoped Myra would join them in the days to come.

NORTHWEST OF DALLAS

In her home, Sara Reisling surveyed the day's progress. Most of the furniture had been moved out of the lower floor of the house. Her father and a couple of other men had been building shelving to fill all the front rooms and the basement. With pooled resources, the family would soon open a small, neighborhood store.

She closed her eyes. *We're embarking on a new way of life, a new walk of faith. . . . God has provided a way for us.*

"You'd better change out of those sweaty clothes, Duchess!" her mother said from the doorway. "It's almost six. People will be arriving any minute now."

She kissed her mother and quickly mounted the stairs to her room. What would she wear? She opened the closet door and browsed through four clean dresses, selecting a pretty cream-colored one with small roses printed on it.

Soon, she'd washed up, changed into the dress, and made her way to the kitchen to help with the final preparations for the meal. People from the neighborhood arrived in small groups. Each person brought a dish of food to share. While women arranged the food on the counters and got out plates, several young girls ran out the back door to play in the yard for a few minutes before the meeting started.

"Stay in the yard now, mind you," one mother admonished.

Within another fifteen minutes, everyone had arrived. It was time for the meeting to begin.

All of them gathered in the converted living room and stood together for prayer.

"Tonight," Sara said, "I want to thank the Lord for all He's done for us, and I have a request. The Lord has put a real burden on my heart to pray for our brothers and sisters elsewhere who are suffering. . . . I know there are many, but in particular, my heart is heavy for those who've never made it out of the camps."

Several people sounded agreement.

Sara continued, "Those of us who passed through camps should never forget. If we're being persecuted here, what must it be like for them? If meeting together is getting tough for us, what can it be like for them? Scripture says the effectual fervent prayer of the righteous avails much. We need to keep praying for those who haven't been allowed to come home to us. We need to keep lifting them to the Lord and asking Him for their release."

OKLAHOMA REFUGEE CAMP—Sunday, June 21st

Another three days had passed in the camp. Four hundred forty-three refugees had chosen not to sign the Notice. Many of them had children, so the number of civilians still inside the camp numbered over eight hundred. None of the adults had any delusions about their situation.

Only Ortiz and the senior officers knew all the soldiers would be pulling out tomorrow. They would be abandoning the camp, and heading south. Any materials they couldn't transport but which might be of value to small bands of opposition forces or roaming scavengers would be burned.

The fighting up north continued to wind down while the population in the south mushroomed. More help was desperately needed to maintain control where so many civilians had migrated. Now that people had gotten over being grateful to have survived, some were becoming more difficult to restrain.

In a private meeting last Friday, Colonel Ortiz met with General Chang. The general gave her orders, then advised her how she could prevent any future accusations. To keep refugees from "acts of desperation" before their departure, Chang also left her with one hundred additional soldiers.

On Sunday, at sunrise, all the remaining refugees and their children were assembled, as ordered, outside the Quonset hut where processing took place. Soldiers made sure Ricky Ruiz and other leaders stood at the front of the group.

Prior to the day's end, each person would be required to go into the building, hear the presentation on coding, then attend individual counseling. Perhaps some, outside the mob rule, would avail themselves of the offer to sign up. The ancient tactic known as "divide and conquer" might bring victory where everything else had failed.

Regardless of the decisions made, eight transport trucks stood ready to haul all refugees away from the camp. As soon as each truck filled to capacity, it would leave. Trucks would run continuous trips until the camp had been emptied.

Until now, if someone refused to sign the Notice of Allegiance, they came back out the front of the building. Those who signed exited to a path behind the building, which took them down to the transports. Today, however, no refugee would go back into the camp.

Jason McAllister and Amanda, the two oldest "children" of Ricky and Rosa Ruiz, were considered of age—over sixteen—so they'd been forced to stay at the back of the crowd, away from their parents. Jason could see two female soldiers take Ricky and four of the smaller children into the building with other leaders.

"They're taking Ricky in. He's got Angela, Tyler, Maria, Marcus, and Erica."

"Can you see Rosa?" Amanda asked.

Jason tried to keep his balance while he stood on his toes. "No. She must be in the crowd up there with the rest of the kids."

When Jason relaxed his legs to stand flat-footed again, he felt a small, pocket-sized book fall out of the floppy cuff of his sock. He quickly knelt down and inserted it into the sock again, then tried to twist a knot in the top of the sock to keep it tight against his leg.

Last night, before people were parceled out to tents and told not to leave them, Ricky gave him the little book. As Jason shifted it to rest against the inside of his ankle, he remembered how awed he felt by the gift.

"But . . ." he'd said in protest, "this is your Bible. I can't take this." He'd pushed it back toward Ricky.

"Listen, Jason," his father answered, "who knows what will happen to us now?"

All of the refugees sensed drastic changes in the works.

Ricky pointed to himself. "Rosa and I have stored God's word in our hearts. You must keep doing the same, because what you have in here," he said, now pointing to Jason's chest, "they can never confiscate."

With that, he'd reached over and dropped the Bible into Jason's slightly torn shirt pocket. "We want you to have it. There's nothing of greater value we could give you. . . . You know we love you, son." Ricky's voice quavered with emotion. "You've been a good son."

The two men embraced, unable to say any more.

Even now, Jason's heart swelled at the thought of the little treasure in his sock. Just in case he wouldn't be allowed to go back to his tent and retrieve his possessions, he'd kept the Bible with him. He imagined he'd rather eat the pages than let the soldiers take it away from him.

He looked around at the crowd, then at Amanda. "God will take care of us. We won't let them scare us. We won't give in."

"No. We won't."

They clasped hands and prayed quietly.

Fifteen minutes passed. Jason, Amanda, and the rest of the crowd standing outside figured that Ricky and the first group of people taken into the building should be coming out. Where were they? Soldiers came out and escorted the next group into the building. A buzz went through the crowd.

Surely, Ricky and the others hadn't agreed! Where could they have been taken?

Now Jason could see Rosa being taken up the steps with baby Daniel in a sling. Daisy, and the rest of the small children who weren't with Ricky, followed her.

Meanwhile, Ricky and the first group to enter the processing center had been taken along a path behind the Quonset hut and into another building. Several armed soldiers stood inside the small lobby. One of them looked at Ricky and pointed down a long hallway. "You, room three."

When Ricky and the children entered the designated room, a black woman in uniform looked up at him and, in a French accent, said, "Certificates of health please."

He set Angela down and retrieved the papers out of his pocket.

"These aren't all *your* children, are they?" she said, looking at the group.

"Uh. Well, yes they are. This is my daughter," he said, putting his hand on Angela's head, then he reached into another pocket, produced more papers before handing them to the soldier. "And, as you can see, I have legal custody of the others."

The woman set the health certificates and the other papers in a wire basket. "You know, if you were coded, all this information would be loaded into your permanent file. Anywhere you went, it could be accessed."

Ricky knew the time had come. Would he see his Rosa on this earth again?

The soldier began reaching into the pocket of her nicely starched uniform. "Are you sure you wouldn't like us to help you sign up and get all of these on file?"

"I'm sure," he answered quietly.

She extracted a lighter out of the pocket. "It's a pity these are only paper, isn't it?" she said, moving her hand closer to the basket. "You can stop me, you know."

Ricky picked up Angela as the woman struck the lighter.

"Fire, fire, too hot," his daughter said, pointing to the blaze in the basket.

A soldier at the door took Ricky and the children down the hill to a waiting truck.

DALLAS, TX

Miles away, Zachary Gordon stood and stared at the live billboard. Pedestrians in a hurry squeezed through billboard watchers and pressed on toward their destinations. The screen began scrolling the latest news a second time. The headlines moved up the screen:

"TRANSCONTINENTAL CHURCH COUNCIL ALIGNS WITH THE UNIVERSAL MOVEMENT— FIRST SERVICES FOR NEW "GLOBAL WHOLENESS CHURCH" IN U.S. TO BE HELD IN ATLANTA ON FRIDAY >>>> Universal Information Group—your global news solution...."

Michael told Zac the night before, but he didn't fully believe it until now. How could this have happened? His eyes didn't leave the billboard, even when several people bumped him.

After the headline passed, Edith Todd appeared on the screen with a radiant smile. "Hello there. This is Edith Todd once again and I wanted to share some exciting news with you." She shifted around slightly in a bright red chair. "Many of us in America have wondered how we will incorporate our spiritual lives with the new order. Some have thought there would be a conflict between old denominations and the universal movement, but have I got good news! Just this week, the Transcontinental Church Council, comprised of many of the world's largest denominations, has signed a unification agreement with leaders in the new order. I'm happy to announce the Global Wholeness Church is here."

The camera moved closer to her face. "But what is that? Where would it meet? That's the best part! It will be everywhere! People of faith, joining together—isn't that what it's all about anyway?"

Zac turned around and wove his way out of the crowd before resuming his walk down the street. He was there when the Transcontinental Church Council participated in the World Conference on Spirituality. He hadn't given much thought to their motives. It hadn't seemed important at the time, but now he was getting a terrible feeling in the pit of his stomach. *They've sold out! This will be just one more way to slide converts into the new order. How many people from those old denominations will go along with this? How many will dare push against the flow? And what will happen to people like Michael and Linda and me?*

While he wanted to think they could still live without coding, it no longer seemed a certainty.

CHAPTER 55

EASTERN OKLAHOMA REFUGEE CAMP

After a soldier burned all their papers, Rosa and the children had been taken to a truck and loaded with other refugees. Instead of going west—where those riding the train south would be taken—they were heading east. For Rosa, not knowing what had happened to Ricky or the other children was the worst part.

She knew they wouldn't be getting on a train. Would they even live out the day? Where was her Angela now? Panicking wouldn't help. Rosa reached for each of the children near her and thanked God for the opportunity to have loved them.

Thank you Lord, she prayed inwardly as her eyes drank in the silky golden hair and the brown eyes looking back into hers, *for this little girl, Jade. She's so bright and precious. . . . Thank You for our Daisy. Rosa thought, kissing the top of the little girl's head. I'm so glad you gave us the chance to comfort her and love her. . . . Thank You for Alex, she prayed, looking at the boy's sturdy little frame and the clear, blue eyes. He's only nine, but he's a great little man of God already. And thank You for our Daniel, what a gift he's been to me. He looks so much like his father, it always fills my heart to look at him. . . . I'm still not sorry I had him, Lord. Thank You.*

After a thirty-minute ride, the truck stopped on the road and they were given a "last chance" to change their minds. Although some of the passengers cried, no one took the offer. The truck began moving again.

A young man in uniform stood up just behind the cab of the truck and placed his hand on the butt of his gun in his holster. "Take off all your jewelry," he commanded. "Rings, necklaces, earrings, watches. All of it."

Two other soldiers stood up to collect it.

Like most of the people on the truck, Rosa had gotten so thin her wedding ring wouldn't stay on her finger. It hung on the same small chain as the little cross Ricky had given to her so long ago. Ricky wore his ring on a piece of string around his neck.

"Please," an elderly man in the front begged. "It's all I have left. It's my wedding ring. Please."

They took it from him, then worked their way through the passengers, making them empty out pockets if they produced no jewelry. Daisy drew closer to Rosa.

"It's okay," Rosa said to Daisy and the other children. "They want Mama's jewelry. What do we care anyway? We have treasure in Heaven, don't we? No one can take that treasure, because Father God is keeping it safe for us till we get there."

A woman sobbed as she gave them a man's pocket watch.

Knowing they might threaten the children to get cooperation, Rosa had pulled the chain out of her blouse and tried to find the clasp with trembling fingers. Baby Daniel, sitting in the sling she wore, reached out to grasp the pretty golden objects.

The waiting soldier became impatient and quickly snatched the chain, yanking so hard he broke it, startling baby Daniel in the process.

Her eyes welled up as the young man greedily stuffed it in a pocket. *They will have taken Ricky's ring, too, she thought. No! I will not cry over this. I DO have treasure in heaven!* She quickly wiped her face then pulled the children closer and smiled at each one. "Who remembers a good prayer?" she asked. "Let's say one together. . . ."

Fifteen minutes later, the truck pulled through a large gate and stopped.

"Out! Get out!" soldiers with heavy accents shouted when the tailgate dropped. They trained rifles on the refugees until the gates closed.

The air reeked of petroleum products. Once Rosa disembarked, she could see why. They'd parked in a large fuel depot. A very tall double fence surrounded the area. The tops of both fences as well as the space between them had row upon row of razor wire. Inside the compound stood a large number of huge, plastic tanks. Some of them were white, some were pink, others were green.

"Go over there!" a male soldier said.

When Rosa looked where the soldier indicated, she could see another group of refugees. There, head and shoulders above nearly everyone else, stood Ricky. A loud cry escaped her lips and she started moving toward him. Ricky picked up the two smallest children with him and let the other two trot alongside as he moved toward Rosa. When they reached one another, the two adults dropped to their knees amidst an avalanche of small hugs and kisses.

"Papa, Papa," a small, unfamiliar voice said. They turned as Daisy wrapped her arms around Ricky's arm. "Papa, Papa." she said again, "See? God kept us safe."

They cried and kissed her.

# # #

Back at the camp, Col. Ortiz lightly pounded her fist on her desk. She'd just returned from the Quonset hut. How she hated being so close to the refugees. How she loathed looking into their faces . . . looking into their children's faces. They reminded her of the horrible nightmares she'd been having.

So far, only seventy-three people had actually signed the Notice today. With their children, that came to almost two hundred. The Bible verses had worked on some, fear on others. Hopefully a few more would make a good decision before the day ended.

Several hundred yards from her office, Jason McAllister sat in a small room with no windows. A red-haired man, had burned his papers, then looked up at him and shook his head. "You seem like such a fine lad," he said with a Scottish accent. "It's a real pity you've been so brainwashed that you don't know your Scripture."

"What?"

"I said, it's unfortunate you don't know Scripture very well." The officer retrieved a paper from his desk drawer and read from it. "Romans 13 says—and I quote: 'Everyone must submit himself to the governing authorities, for there is no authority except that which God has established. The authorities that exist have been established by God. Consequently, he who rebels against the authority is rebelling against what God has instituted, and those who do so will bring judgment on themselves.'" He looked up from the page, and tried to reason with the boy. "Don't you see Jason? God wants you to obey those in authority."

Jason thought for a moment before speaking. "Then answer me this, why did God reward and protect Daniel when praying was against the law and he did it anyway? What about Daniel's friends who refused to worship the gold statue? And how is it the Apostles were able to keep preaching with signs and wonders, even though using the name of Jesus was forbidden? When you tell me to disobey God, I must disobey you."

An armed soldier opened the door, but the red-haired man held up a hand. "Just another few moments, please."

The door closed again.

The time for the final offer had come. The man leaned forward and motioned for Jason to move closer to the desk. He appeared worried.

"I can see you're a very sincere young man, and I admire your courage. My conscience just won't let me watch that soldier take you out of here without trying to help you. You don't want the others to go on without you, do you?" the man pleaded.

Surprised, Jason blurted out. "Are you saying the others signed it?"

"They've already left the camp."

"I don't believe you. And, even if they had, I know this is wrong, and I have to answer to God for what I do."

# # #

Hours had passed. Rosa, Ricky and all the others stood together, praying. Once again, Rosa briefly looked over the heads of the people across from her, past the double barbed-wire fences to the road. Truck after truck had come and dropped off more refugees, but there'd been no sign of Amanda or Jason.

Thankfully, the hot afternoon sky had become overcast, then produced some rain for them to catch in their hands or soak up in cloth and drink. In the past few minutes, some of the clouds had parted, and the setting sun hung between the layers like an angry, orange eye surveying the landscape.

Something moved in the distance. Was it a truck? She nudged Ricky and when he looked at her, she motioned to the road. She watched him squint at what now appeared to be three trucks moving in their direction.

Within another minute, the transports entered the gates, and the passengers disembarked. More tearful reunions took place, among them ones between the Ruiz family, Amanda, and Jason.

The last truck only had fifteen passengers. This had to be everyone. Ricky estimated close to five hundred men, women, and children now stood inside the fuel depot.

Armed soldiers, talking loudly among themselves, herded the refugees toward the center of the enclosure as the trucks fueled up and pulled out of the compound.

"What do you think, José?" one asked another. "Why are these people here instead of traveling south?"

"I don't know," José replied. "Looks to me like they're being *left . . . again!*"

The soldiers laughed, then returned to the gates at the edge of the compound and, as the refugees watched, locked them.

Little Tyler pulled on Ricky's pant leg. "Papa, I'm hungry."

"Me too," echoed the other children.

Ricky bent down and huddled with them. "Listen. I know you're hungry. We are too. But, we'll be out of here very soon and everything will be all right. Okay?"

The trucks pulled away. Ricky stood up and looked at his wife, "Turn around, Rosa. Don't look."

Knowing the same thing he knew, she turned her back to the gates.

All of the adults began huddling closer and closer together, putting their children in front of them, pressing tighter and tighter together, until they'd formed a tight clump, with no children on the outer edge.

"Father!" one of the men said loudly, "You've said in your word that we will have perfect peace when our minds are stayed upon you!"

"Yes!" a woman said. "We look to You, oh Lord. You are our glory and the lifter of our heads."

"That's true!" a man declared. " The Lord is our light and our salvation; whom shall we fear? the Lord is the strength of our life; of whom shall we be afraid? When the wicked, even our enemies and our foes, come upon us, they will stumble and fall. Though an host should encamp against us, our hearts shall not fear: though war should rise against us, in this will we be confident. One thing have we desired of the Lord, that will we seek after; that we may dwell in the house of the Lord all the days of our lives, to behold the beauty of the Lord, and to inquire in His temple. For in the time of trouble He shall hide us in His pavilion: in the secret of His tabernacle shall He hide us; He shall set us upon a rock. And now shall our heads be lifted up above our enemies round about us: therefore will we offer in His tabernacle sacrifices of joy; We will sing, yea, we will sing praises unto the Lord."

# # #

In the distance, a man with a high-powered rifle sat on the nearby hilltop, paying little attention to the people inside the compound. He only needed to wait until the trucks were at a safe distance, then shoot the two guards at the gate before firing into the tanks to ignite them.

He noted the increase in wind and realized he'd have to adjust his shots accordingly. He looked around for the trucks one last time and noted a dark, fast-moving storm sweeping eastward. He lowered his head for the shot. A sound started blowing all around him. Did he hear singing?

# # #

Traveling away from the fuel depot, several soldiers sat in the back of the last transport truck bragging about what they'd do the next time they got some leave. Two of them used the last moments of daylight to play cards. As far as they all knew, they were going back to camp to search then burn the refugee tents. Before dawn tomorrow, they'd been told, trucks would go back and pick up the people at the fuel depot.

One soldier threw down his card and exclaimed, "Aha!" before a bright light ignited on the road behind them.

They all looked, mouths agape as the flames and smoke billowed into the air. Had those crazy people set the depot on fire? One of the soldiers finally had the presence of mind to beat on the truck cabin and get the truck to stop.

They were distracted by the fire, but within moments, black clouds sent swirling winds around the trucks. Dirt, leaves, and small branches began to blow everywhere. The men closest to the tailgate shielded their eyes from the debris which began pelting them at an alarming velocity. They all heard a roaring noise. One of the soldiers in the cab of the truck opened the small window between the cab and the back.

"Tornadoes! Tornadoes!" he yelled. "Get down!"

They held onto their helmets and ducked down as the trucks sped away.

# # #

The refugees had all begun singing before the fire started. None of them looked. They kept their eyes closed and sang as loudly as they could, knowing it would be over soon. Hopefully, the smoke would get them before the flames did.

Flashes of light and immediate, continuous booms reported all around them as they continued to sing. Each thought they heard tanks exploding . . . but there was no heat. The wind shrieked round and round them, blowing their hair straight up at times, but there was no smell of smoke. Thunders melded into a deafening roar all around them. Popping and twanging noises went off. Blackness engulfed them.

# # #

Captain Kenneth Smith and the other freedom fighters crouched down in a small cave until the danger of the tornadoes had passed. The final light of sunset returned almost as quickly as it had disappeared, and the small troop of men came out of their hiding place.

Smith crawled up on an outcropping of rock and focused his binoculars toward the fuel depot. A swirl of black smoke obscured his view. After a few moments, he moved a bit so he could focus on another hill nearby. He turned on the infrared and turned up the gain. He couldn't see the body of the sniper he'd shot just a few minutes ago. Perhaps it had blown off the hill. He quickly scanned the hillside and eventually saw what looked like a leg sticking up at an odd angle behind a rock.

"There," he said quietly. "Look over there. About two thirds of the way down the hill at your three o'clock. "I'm just sorry I didn't get him before he set all those refugees on fire. I couldn't see him until he'd shot off a number of rounds."

The soldier next to him peered through his own glasses. "Yeah. That's probably him. You want to send someone to verify?"

"Send Rawley and Poncho. Tell 'em to meet us over by the depot. With storms around, no choppers will be up for a while. We have a good window to check it out."

# # #

"Papa, I'm still hungry. Can we eat now?"

Ricky opened his eyes. Tyler had wiggled around to face him and was now peering directly into his eyes.

A few minutes ago, he'd crouched down and leaned forward to cover as many of the children as he could. Now, he straightened, stood, and looked around. To his left, a small tendril of smoke wafted up, visible in the last microns of daylight.

All of the adults stood up, staring wide-eyed, at the same thing. The fire had been blown out.

Ricky felt a tug on his pant leg. "Can we leave now and get dinner?"

"Yes!" Ricky shouted, "Yes! Hallelujah! We're going to leave right now!"

"What will we eat, Papa?"

Ricky laughed. "I can't *wait* to see what Father God has prepared for us!"

People embraced, then they started clapping, whistling loudly, or singing as they led their children or carried them toward the gates. When they got to the entrance, not only were the gates gone, but the fences, and the men guarding them had disappeared as well.

CHAPTER 56

Friday, June 27th

Across America, live billboards flashed the latest headlines:

"REGENERATION APPROVED BY PRESIDENT MOFFIT >>>> RELIGIOUS FANATICS DIE IN BUNGLED ATTEMPT >>>> TO STEAL FUEL FROM OKLAHOMA DEPOT >>>> UNIVERSAL INFORMATION GROUP—Your global news solution. . . . "

A man appeared on the center of the billboard screen. "This is Antonio Ulan with the latest news. . . . Today, at a special ceremony in his new Atlanta office, President Moffit signed into law the Regeneration Rights Bill, allowing all seniors sixty-five and older to undergo the procedure known as regeneration.

"In his remarks after the signing, the president said the landmark legislation would prove to be a tremendous benefit to many seniors in America. In addition, he said, the procedure would ease the huge financial burden formerly placed on families and the country for senior care."

Antonio turned his head to look into another camera before continuing. "In other news, the investigation is continuing in the deaths of a large number of religious fanatics in Eastern Oklahoma. Just hours ago, in an exclusive interview, General Li Chang of UN forces in western vectors told UIG reporter, Leslie Trayson . . ."

SOMEWHERE IN OKLAHOMA

Noon, Sunday, June 29th
Rosa rolled over and opened her eyes. It took a moment for her to focus, then to remember where she was. They'd been on the move for a week.

Yes! I'm in a tent, far away from the camp! Oh Hallelujah! She sat up and looked around, *It's so quiet. Where IS everybody?*

The tent flap slowly opened and the face of her husband appeared.

"Well, hi there!" he said, entering the tent.

She scratched her head. "It must be the middle of the day!"

"Oh yeah."

"Is everything okay?"

He couldn't help chuckling. "Oh yeah."

She quickly looked around. "Where's Daniel? Where's Daisy?"

Ricky gently pushed her back down onto the sleeping bag, then snuggled up next to her. "They're perfectly fine, dear. Amanda and Jason are watching them. And what's more," he said touching the tip of her nose with his index finger, "Daisy's not even clinging onto that nasty piece of one of your old skirts anymore!"

"No."

"Yes."

"And I missed all this?"

"Oh, but there's more, dear. The people here can eavesdrop on communications—wanna know what's going on down South?"

She studied her husband's face a moment. "Do I *want* to know?"

"Since there's so much news about us, it might be appropriate."

"About us?"

He reached over and closed her eyelids. "I suppose you don't know you've been dead for a whole week."

Her eyes popped back open.

"What?"

"We're all dead. Sorry dear. It's official on UIG."

"They're saying we're dead?"

"It was a nice package. . . . They could explain our disappearance to anyone looking for us. They said we were 'fanatics' who, in a foiled attempt to steal fuel, died."

She sat up. "That's terrible!"

"Well, yes and no. It's bad they're blaming us and saying Christians are fanatics, but, on the flip side—we're all dead."

She looked confused. "Perhaps I'm still just tired. Explain how there's an 'up' side to our being dead."

He smiled. "We don't exist anymore. We're 'new' people."

"Gosh. A lot has happened while I slept. Why didn't you wake me?" She smiled. "A woman has a right to know she's dead, you know."

He rolled over on his back and put his hands behind his head. "You were so exhausted you were out of it, so we decided to let you sleep some more before you died again. . . . Besides, it's Sunday. Today is our first official day of rest—as dead people."

A scent came to her. Her eyes opened wide and she turned to grab his shirt. "Meat! . . . is that meat? . . . and coffee? Tell me I smell meat and coffee."

Ricky laughed. "Oh yeah," he said, then tried to look sober. "But don't get used to it."

Later in the day, all the former refugees gathered together. They'd been split up into four groups for the journey, but now, as planned, they'd reunited. They'd need to split up again in a day or two, but today they'd hang out together, discuss their options, and rest.

When his turn came, Ricky stood in front of them all and read the following passage.

"And Jesus came and spake unto them, saying, 'All power is given unto me in heaven and in earth. Go ye therefore, and teach all nations, baptizing them in the name of the Father, and of the Son, and of the Holy Ghost: Teaching them to observe all things whatsoever I have commanded you: and, lo, I am with you always, even unto the end of the world. Amen.'"

He handed the small book to Jason then spoke to the gathering of people. "Just a year ago, how many of us standing here today could have imagined the things we would go through? In fact, if we'd known what we would have to endure, we might have faltered long before now and given up, eh? But, by God's great power and His incomparable grace . . . here we are.

"On this day a week ago, He could have taken us home to His glorious kingdom."

"I have treasure there and nobody else gets it!" Alex, their nine-year-old said loudly. Everyone laughed before Ricky continued.

"That's right, Alex. Each of us has treasure there. And the Lord *could* have let us come to collect it all. But He didn't. I know some of you are a bit sad about it. Your race would have been finished, you could have entered into His presence. . . . But we're all still here.

"And so we must ask ourselves," he said, shrugging, "why? Why are we still here? Is it so we can just hide out in the woods by ourselves until He comes?"

Many responded, "No."

"Your're right. We're still here because we have things to do. Many of you have been sharing ideas this past week, and all of us have been praying. While the Lord will have to continue to shape our plans, I believe He has given us the beginnings of what we are to do, and will continue to lead us in the days to come. None of us can afford to miss God's plan.

"We've been told that, up North, there are still clusters of people—some of whom need the Gospel. We've also been told about Christians in the South. While their level of persecution has not yet reached what we've experienced, they are in the process of forming many underground cell groups. They should hear from us.

"This morning, part of the news I received—aside from the fact that we're all dead," he paused as a ripple of laughter went through the group, "is that there is rioting going on in some places down South. That's probably why no one will come out to chase us. They've got much bigger problems to solve elsewhere.

"While they'd *like* to have everyone coded and accounted for, it's just not possible at this point. They are just a couple of steps above chaos and they're doing everything possible just to maintain a semblance of order. Millions of people are still unaccounted for and millions more remain uncoded.

"While we have this window of opportunity, let's make use of it. We're non-existent people with clean slates. Right now, we can go anywhere and do anything. We still have the command of the Lord to go out and make disciples. The people we've met say we can still find ways to get in down South, or they can show us how to get anywhere else we want to go.

"So let's consider it well. How will we fulfill our commission? Some of us will move further north with this purpose. Some of us will go south and contact underground churches, or help to organize new ones. Just *think* of the great harvest waiting there!

"Lastly, some of us will fan out and establish actual places of refuge, here in the wilderness—like this place—where people can come to rest awhile, and take the time to find or confirm their purpose.

"We know that we were *born* for this time and these circumstances. After what we have witnessed and touched, how can we stay silent? We must go to the north, the south, the east, and the west, and we must do it as messengers of Life."

Within days, they would become sojourners once again.

THE END of Book 2

Thanks for reading my book! If you enjoyed it, would you take a moment to write a review for your favorite retailer?

Thanks again!

Terry L. Craig

This story is continued in SWORDSMAN, *Under the Blood Moon*—Book 3 of the *Fellowship of the Mystery* trilogy,

SWORDSMAN was originally written in the early 1980's and first published in 1987, the novel was a startling, prophetic look at many aspects of society in the future and made its way into the hearts of Christians, college students, and sci-fi readers. In the late 1990's Terry began writing *GATEKEEPER* and *SOJOURNER* (Books 1 & 2) as "prequels" that would fill in the history of events and characters which fascinated readers.

Nearly thirty years after it was first published, much of the futuristic fiction of *SWORDSMAN* has become reality, or can be seen in the not-too-distant future. The storyline remains true to the original book—with an expanded story and added characters.

Many in the world today are looking for the return of Christ, and have heard or read popular predictions on the timing of this event. Are they being informed, or set up for a great fall?

SWORDSMAN is a controversial novel dealing with the issues and emotions of the inevitable conflict between life and death.

While each novel in this trilogy can be enjoyed as a single book, there is a continuing thread throughout the trilogy that readers will savor. If you have enjoyed this book *(SOJOURNER)* but haven't read the other two books in this series, we invite you to explore the rest of the story and your favorite characters in *GATEKEEPER* and *SWORDSMAN*.

About the Author

Terry L. Craig

Born in the Southwest, Terry has lived all over the US and spent many years living in the Caribbean. She's a people-watcher and a comparative thinker who is fascinated with words, art, and ideas. She has a passion to share spiritual life in a way that allows the reader to weigh the values of different ideologies from a non-threatening perspective.

Terry is a follower of Jesus, a wife, mom, and grandma who currently resides in North Carolina with her professional pilot husband (her lifetime love) Bill. The development of true friendships and healthy community life are high on her list of life's essentials.

Paperback copies of all of Terry's books are available at the publisher's website at (www.wildflowerpress.*biz*), or at CreateSpace.com, Amazon.com, and most fine book retailers.

Ebook versions are also available through Amazon.com, Smashwords.com, in the Apple iTunes bookstore and most fine ebook retailers.

To learn more about Terry or connect with her:
Visit her author page on the Wild Flower Press, Inc. website at **www.wildflowerpress.*biz***

Terry L. Craig's newest series:

Scions of the Aegean C

Scions of the Aegean C, Descent into the Wilds **is Book 1 of the series.** More than a century after an entire colony of people crashed in an unknown world, both the written knowledge of the survivors and fragments of the ship they dismantled in their efforts to stay alive are decaying. As eyewitness accounts of the "Firstlanders" pass from living memory, alternate versions of the colony's history are taking shape.

Members of the fifth generation, Shaye, Jariel, and Ty prepare to take their places as young adults in a growing civilization where each person's quality of life is determined by proof of bloodline, valuable skills . . . or possession of strategic secrets. For someone without one of these, an obscure existence of menial labor is certain, and love is an unattainable luxury. Will the wisdom, liberty, and faith that the Firstlanders brought to this world pass into legend, or will they find a foothold in the fifth generation?

For readers 16 and up.

The *Scions of the Aegean C* series illustrates how love, kinship, and personal testimony shape culture. These novels will be enjoyed by readers who relish complex characters in richly-textured cultural settings.

The first book of the series, *Scions of the Aegean C, Descent into the Wilds* is now available in print and ebook formats worldwide.

Through the Land of Cloud and Leaf, Book 2 in the *Scions of the Aegean C* series, will be available in print and ebook formats in the summer of 2017.

For updates on the *Scions of the Aegean C* series, check out Terry's author page at Wild Flower Press, Inc.

www.wildflowerpress.biz

Other Books Published by Wild Flower Press, Inc.

The ***Within the Walls*** trilogy
by Stephanie Bennett

The Within the Walls trilogy chronicles the life of Emilya Hoffman Bowes Brown—technological genius, collaborator in the newest wave of "tek" enhancements to hit the market, and creator of virtual vacations. In Book 1, Emilya finds information that leads her on a journey to a community of dissidents who have chosen to live without technology, exposed to nature and the elements—something that was supposed to be impossible. As the trilogy unfolds, Emilya tries to understand the puzzle of these people in the wild, the way they live, and their use of words like "faith" and "soul." Aren't humans just biology and electricity?

- *Within the Walls*, Book 1
- *Breaking the Silence*, Book 2
- *The Poet's Treasure*, Book 3

The *Within the Walls* trilogy is available in ebook or print through most fine book retailers.

Passport for the Journey, 21 Day Challenge
by Tonya J. Brown

This travel-sized devotional/journal will slip easily into a briefcase, purse, or pocket. Each entry in this book can be read in a couple of minutes, but is enough food to meditate on the entire day—great for a personal devotional, or for use by a group as an opener for meetings. The content is written for Millennial Generation believers who are ready to embark on a new experience with God.

Passport for the Journey, 21 Day Challenge is available in print and ebook formats at many fine retailers.

www.wildflowerpress.biz